OUTLAND

By the Authors

Wasteland

Outland

OUTLAND

by

Kristin Keppler and Allisa Bahney

2022

OUTLAND

ISBN 13: 978-1-63679-154-8

This Trade Paperback Original Is Published By
Bold Strokes Books, Inc.
P.O. Box 249
Valley Falls, NY 12185

First Edition: July 2022

CREDITS
Editor: Barbara Ann Wright
Production Design: Susan Ramundo
Cover Design By Jeanine Henning

Acknowledgments

From us both:

Thank you to the hardworking team at Bold Strokes Books. To Sandy, Ruth, Cindy, and Stacia for always answering our endless questions. Thanks to Jeanine for another amazing cover. And to Barbara Ann Wright for all her hard work and doing her damnedest to turn us into writers. We appreciate you all more than you will ever know! A huge thank you to everyone who's reached out and supported us through our debut novel. We love seeing your pictures and reading your comments and listening to your suggestions and criticism. Your feedback and reviews consistently breathe new inspiration into our creativity, and we thank you from the bottom of our hearts.

Kristin:

Thank you so much to my dad—my biggest cheerleader. Knowing that no matter what, you're in my corner, makes me happier than I could ever tell you. And to my mom for always being my first, and most honest, reader and critic. I value all your advice. To Brad, where would I be without you? I'm so blessed to have you in my life. Thank you for always being there for me, no matter what. I love you. And always, to my sons, who still don't care that I write books. You boys are my heart. I love you all the time.

Allisa:

Courtney, as always, you are my number one support system, and I would be so lost in this life without you. To Theo and Renn, you're too young to know what the heck is going on, but I love you both more than words can ever convey.
Thank you to all of my friends and family (and Kristin's!) for the endless support with this series. Every single text, snap, picture, shout out, purchase, and positive comment has been encouraging and heartwarming.

Dedication

Kristin: For my sister, Laura, you are the strongest woman I know. I love you.

Allisa: For Theo and Renn, you two have given my life more purpose by simply existing in it.

CHAPTER ONE: THE RETRIBUTION

DANI

Laughter and gunfire fill the air. My teeth are clenched so hard I wonder if they'll crack under all the pressure.

"White River is burning," I say into the radio.

"What do you mean it's burning? Are you there? What's going on?" After tossing the radio back on the seat, I reach for my shotgun. "What about reinforcements? Dani? Are you there?"

Ignoring Jack's questions, I slip the shotgun onto my back and make sure my pistols are loaded and holstered against my thighs along with my knife. I pull on fingerless gloves and tie my hair into a ponytail. Jack's voice echoes through the radio, but all I can focus on is the laughter coming from below.

Once I've reached the back perimeter, I secure a maroon scarf around my face. The place reeks of accelerant.

The lightly falling snow does nothing to quell the raging fires that consume the town. A few meters ahead, a tree crashes through the fence. I peer through the newly formed hole and catch a glimpse inside. There are two soldiers with flamethrowers, pyros, slowly making their way through the town, torching everything. Inside, I hear people scream. Why are there still people here? Why didn't they leave? A sick, bitter taste fills my mouth as I watch someone take their final steps before falling to the earth.

I steel my jaw and force down the anguish. The smoke hits my eyes and springs tears, but it does nothing to quell my determination or my rage.

I reach the end of the fence and peering around, find a tank and six buggies parked in a V-shape. Seven soldiers guard the front walls, and there must be a dozen soldiers or more inside.

The tank rumbles to life and creeps forward. I sprint, bringing the shotgun around. The NAF soldiers standing in front are so engrossed with the destruction that they don't see me coming.

The first soldier turns, and I fire two shots straight into his chest. He lands hard on his back. Two more spin to face me, and my pump-action rings out four more times as I press forward. I fire my last two at the next soldier in line and toss the gun to the side before diving behind the closest buggy. Three more soldiers close in.

Pulling both pistols, I take a deep breath and stand right as two soldiers round the side of the buggy. I aim for the chest and unload until they both stagger and fall. The last soldier fires at me from behind, and I feel a sting near my upper arm. It does nothing but fuel me further.

Spinning, I aim for his head. He takes one well-placed round between the eyes before his body drops, lifeless. I glance at my arm and carefully finger the wound, hissing at the contact. It's not serious, but blood is starting to seep through my favorite jacket.

The sound of steel meeting cement fills the air as the tank unleashes its payload on another row of buildings. I race toward it and clamber onto the back. I climb up and open the hatch, wishing I had a grenade.

Instead, I aim inside and take out the commander and gunner. The driver opens another hatch to escape, but I get in before he can crawl out and empty what's left of my magazine into him and the control panel. The tank slows to a stop.

Holstering my empty pistol, I jump out and see two more soldiers rush in my direction. Their shots ping against the side of the tank, and I spend the rest of my spare ammunition on them. Squinting through all the smoke, I can just make out one of the pyros. Rubbing at my eyes to clear the itchiness, I adjust the scarf over my nose and grab my knife.

I close in on the pyro and wrap my arm around his chest from behind. I shove the knife up the neck of his protective headwear and drag the blade across his neck. The stream of fire stops. As the body slowly drops, my eyes connect with a soldier several meters away.

Simon.

Staring back, I tighten my grip on my knife. His uniform is pristine, not one speck of blood or dirt, and his blond hair is perfectly combed. Of course he's not doing any of the dirty work.

He snarls and reaches for his gun.

Shots come from my right. I swipe the pyro's sidearm and dive back toward the tank, firing in Simon's direction, but none of them connect.

He walks toward me, returning fire and screaming, "It's Danielle Clark! Focus all weapons on Danielle Clark. That is an order."

A handful of soldiers turn to me. I toss the gun and climb back up the tank. I lunge at the first soldier to reach me and wrestle him to the ground, feeling something on his belt. Finally, a fucking grenade. I snag it and take a punch to the face. My vision goes black as I try to shake off the blow. He pushes me to the ground, and I pull him closer just as his comrades open fire. He tries to roll away, but I hold him tight, using his body as a shield. He jerks from multiple impacts, and when he goes limp, I take the rifle from his hands. Through a break in the gunfire, I sprint for cover.

Leaning against the side of a half-torched building, I drag my hand across my forehead to wipe away the sweat. The smoke burns my lungs, and I take small, shallow breaths. I check the rounds in the rifle. Sixteen. I peek around the side of a building and spot six more soldiers rushing toward Simon as he continues to bark orders. He gestures in my direction. I need to be behind them.

I try not to think about the people who once occupied the burning structures as I map them in my head. I refuse to look at my home, focusing on the fight. My eyes burn with each blink, and the cracks and pops from the flames snap against my ears. The haunting realization crashes over me that I can no longer hear screaming from the people who stayed behind. I'm alone. But I can't think about that either.

Instead, I zero in on the second pyro scorching the back of the town. I dart from one cover to the next until I'm behind him. He turns at the last second, and the nozzle of fire nearly lights me up. The heat of the flames is so close, my eyebrows get singed.

Panicked, I roll on instinct and bring the rifle up to take him out. He lands on his back, and I cover my head, expecting the tank on his back to explode. Relieved when it doesn't, I look up and hear Simon and the others.

They're coming from the next row of houses. I need to move. The flamethrower's gas canister is leaking. It must be my lucky day. Thinking quickly, I flip and grab the pyro by his ankles, then drag him to one of the few houses that remains upright.

Rushing to the second floor, I hear Simon order his soldiers to spread out. If this doesn't work, I'll be trapped. I'll have to worry about that later. I poke my head out the window. Simon stands a safe distance away, pistol in hand.

"I will find you," he yells in no particular direction. "And when I do, I will relish taking you apart. Bit by bit. Just like your precious little town!"

"I'd like to see you try, you murdering piece of shit," I yell back. Everyone turns and fires at the window. I drop to the floor and wince as I land on my injured arm.

"Hold your fire," Simon shouts. "You're wasting ammo. Go inside and get her!"

I wait until the bulk of them are right at the entrance before chucking the grenade at the leaking gas tank below. The canister explodes; the blast of heat and pressure shakes the house, breaking the glass windows, and launching me off my feet. I land hard, my head bouncing off the hardwood with a heavy *thwack*.

Everything spins. My ears ring. Wincing, I blink slowly and try to focus on the door, trying to lift the rifle, waiting for someone to burst through. When no one does, I stand, bracing against the bedpost until the room stops spinning. Slightly off balance, I go to the window and look.

There are no soldiers, no Simon barking orders. Scanning the street below, I hope to see his body, but I'm not *that* lucky.

I keep my rifle ready and slip out the back, rounding the building to the front. The debris from the explosion covers a handful of bodies, but it's clear none of them is Simon. On high alert, I take careful steps toward the gate.

Slowly, I pass the tank at the exact same place where I strapped bombs to Kate and the others only a few days prior. It feels like a lifetime ago.

One of the buggies is speeding away. I pull the scarf down and suck in a large breath. Fucking coward.

My house is gone. Lucas's, Jack's, Mike's, the clinic, all gone. I search, hoping there are survivors safely hidden and waiting for the all clear. So far, no signs of life. We should've installed bunkers. Maybe then, they would've had a fighting chance.

I stop at every lifeless body. Fifteen. Sixteen. Seventeen. When can I stop counting? I crouch by each one, remembering them, offering a silent apology. They didn't deserve this. Finally, I stop in front of what's left of Rhiannon's tavern, still ablaze. The roof collapses in a puff of smoke and embers, and I drop to my knees, praying to every god I know that Rhiannon made it out and that she's safe.

Around me, I hear other structures fall; the sound feels like blades across my skin. Everything inside me rushes out violently, my stomach emptying as I lean forward. I heave until I have no more breath, and tears stream steadily from my eyes. Sweat drips down the sides of my face, and I cast my gaze upward. Every part of my body aches. My arm. My lungs. My heart. The snow falls, melting before it reaches the ground.

I don't know how long I stay on my knees, staring at the swirling white flakes mingling within the smoke from the dwindling fires. It feels as though the smoke is carrying away my soul as it floats up, up, up and disappears high into the heavens. Everything dissolves out of me, rage, hate, sadness, until I'm numb. Empty. I did this. This is my fault. I'm the reason the town is gone, and these people are dead.

I hear a buggy in the distance, but I don't move. If the NAF has returned to finish me off, so be it. The smell of charred flesh and death has me defeated, all the fight gone.

"Dani?" But it's not the NAF. It's Jack. "Dani? Dani, are you here? Where are you?"

"Dani!" Mike is with him. They run through the streets, calling for me, but all I can do is breathe. In and out. "Jack, she's here. She's over here."

Jack's large muscular frame crouches before me. "Dani?" My eyes slowly meet his. He grabs my shoulders. "Are you hurt?" I wince as he squeezes my wound. "Mike, go get the first aid kit from the buggy." I shrug his hands off. He takes my face in his palms. "Dani, look at me." His dark eyes are deep with worry. "Is there anybody left?"

I have no idea if he's asking about our people or the NAF. Not that it matters. The answer is the same. "They're all dead."

He stares at me and nods. "Okay. Let's get you to your feet." Without waiting, he yanks me into a standing position.

"Where were you?" It sounds like an accusation, I know it does, but I can't help it.

Jack flinches. "We dropped off another group at the coordinates you gave us. I was going to try one more time to convince the others to leave when your message came through."

"How many?" I choke out. "How many stayed?"

Jack runs a hand through his mohawk. "About thirty. Maybe thirty-five."

I close my eyes. Thirty-five dead. Were they kids? Parents? How many of the town's livestock burned because of me?

"I tried to get everyone out." His voice shakes. "Not everybody wanted to leave."

"It's not your fault. I should've been here. I should've protected them."

We stand in silence. Hindsight is a master head game and dwelling on should'ves doesn't change a damn thing.

"Rhiannon's safe." My eyes squeeze tighter with his words. "She was in the first group to leave. She's alive, and she's safe."

Rhiannon is alive. She's safe. My stomach clenches, and I thank the gods. A strangled sound bursts from deep in my throat.

"Elise and Roscoe are with her. About a dozen came with us. The rest went south like you suggested." I can feel his stare. "How did you know they were here? How did you know to come back when you did? Where's William?"

I open my eyes. Kate. She tried to warn me about this. About Simon. I didn't get here in time, but Kate tried. I saved her convoy, and she tried to save my home. I wonder if she considers us even. Is this what we are to each other? Not enemies but not quite friends? Just two people who look out for each other?

Jack looks at me expectantly. I shake my head, not able to give him anything more than that.

"I got the kit," Mike says as he appears beside us, out of breath. "And some water." I take the canteen and chug. "Hey, slow down."

"Where's William?" Jack asks again.

I catch my breath and head to the front gate. "He's not coming. It'll be morning soon. We have work to do before the raiders see the smoke and come to pillage."

"Not that it matters at this point," Mike says. He motions around us.

"What do you mean, he's not coming?" Jack asks.

"He's not coming." My voice comes out scratchy and harsh. I try again. "He's in Sioux Falls. He's not coming."

"Okay." Mike and Jack share a look.

"It was Simon. He did this," I say. Jack's expression tightens, and his fists clench. "He got away."

Mike takes a deep breath. "What do you want to do?"

"I'm going to kill him." My body tenses, and the rage creeps back in.

"We should've already killed him. We should've killed all of them," Jack says.

I don't tell him that killing them would've meant killing Kate. Something I absolutely will not allow.

"Let's burn the bodies while the fires are still going. There's no time to build pyres. Then we'll strip the buggies for tech." I hand the canteen back to Mike and ignore Jack's comment, pushing my emotions back down. I've wallowed long enough; I can grieve when the war is over. Until then, I've got work to do.

"Should we salvage what's left of the town?" Jack asks, looking around as though noticing the destruction for the first time.

"There's nothing left." I say, devoid of any emotion.

"You want to leave it all for the raiders?"

"Look around you, Jack. There's nothing left." He meets my gaze, challenging me. "If you want to poke through charred furniture and debris, fine. But I don't have the energy to fight off raiders. I just want to get what we can use and leave. There's nothing left."

He hangs his head. "I hate the idea of raiders—"

I put my hand on his shoulder, and his body deflates. "Me too." He doesn't have to finish his thought. I'm feeling it, too. The idea of anyone, especially raiders, going through our town like fucking vultures... "But we can't lose anyone else. We have to move."

He takes slow breaths, and I wait. Finally, he nods. "Yeah."

Giving his shoulder one last squeeze, we shift gears and begin to circle the town. I stop at the first of several dead NAF soldiers, taking their weapons and tossing them aside.

"What about your arm?" Mike wonders as he holds up the first aid kit.

"It's fine." I pull my scarf back up over my face, my determination outweighing my pain and search them for anything else. "Let's get to work."

❖

It feels like hours until all the bodies have been cremated, each receiving a moment of silence. We don't speak as we mourn. I don't think any of us knows what to say. At least, I don't. They were our friends. Our neighbors. Instead, I apologize and pray their souls find peace. But even that doesn't feel good enough.

Some are unspeakably harder than others to lay to rest. A council member. A teenager. A mother. My jaw tightens so hard that I'm not sure if I'll ever be able to unlatch it again. I wish I was better at grieving.

Afterward, we get cleaned up by the freezing lake while the fires dwindle behind us. Once the ash and blood have been washed away, we load the buggy that Jack and Mike arrived in with weapons and everything else we managed to salvage. The sun rises, casting a pink glow over the charred shell of our town.

Jack stares at the tank. "Think they'll come back for this?"

I grab my discarded jacket, anxious to leave. "Doubt it. Strip it and take what you can from the remaining buggies. Take one with you back to Pine Ridge. They could use it."

They share a look. "We're not going back to Pine Ridge," Mike says slowly, as if I should've known this all along.

Jack is more direct. "We're going with you."

I head for my Jeep. "You don't want to go with me."

"It's not your call," Jack says.

"Actually, it is," I snap, spinning around and forcing the words through gritted teeth. "I'm going back to Rapid City. You are not. You don't belong in this war."

Jack motions to the remains of White River. "The war is here, Dani. We're in it whether we want to be or not. You're not the only one who lost something today. You're not the only one itching to get in the fight and push these assholes out of our territory. So get over yourself. It's not all about you and what you want."

I stare back at him. Mike is silent as he stands between us. I can see the rage and the pain in Jack's eyes as he remains in a standoff with me. I know him well enough to know that the only way to quell that rage inside is to unleash it. We're too much alike.

"Fine," I say after a moment. "Strip the vehicles, blow the inside of the tank, and then we're heading out. We've already wasted enough time here."

Jack nods once and climbs up the side of the tank, grenade in hand. Part of me is pissed that he and Mike are chasing trouble, but another part of me is relieved to have the best hand-to-hand fighter and the most accurate marksman I've ever known watching my back. Despite everything, despite losing my home, I'm beyond grateful to still have my family.

We pass some raiders on the outskirts of town, and though I left all my fight at White River, I'm glad we aren't still there to see them pick the place apart. The image makes me sick. Gripping the steering wheel tighter, I push on the accelerator.

By the time we get to Rapid City, the sun is high, and my adrenaline has long since dissipated. We park the cars and haul what we can to our rooms at the old Alex Johnson. I've barely made it to the hallway of my floor when a door flies open, and Lucas and Darby come barreling out.

"Holy shit, are you guys okay?" Darby asks, throwing her arms around Mike and then Jack, relief flooding her features.

I barely have time to steady myself before Lucas does the same, pulling me into a tight embrace. I drop my bags and pull him in. When Lucas has had enough, he steps back and checks me over. I know I must look terrible.

"What happened?" Darby asks breathlessly.

"Simon," Jack spits out.

Darby's eyes meet mine. "White River?" I can tell by the rough way she swallows that she already knows the answer. "Survivors?" No one says a word. I shake my head.

Jack drops two bags containing the salvaged tech and looks at me. "I'm going to radio Rhiannon. Let her know what's going on. Do you wanna come?"

"I can't. Not yet." I wouldn't even know what to say to her or to any of them. Jack takes pity on me and leaves without arguing.

"William checked in while you were gone," Darby says quietly. I turn to her, having a feeling where this is going. "He's pissed about the convoy never departing Grand Forks and he's hell-bent on finding out what went wrong."

Her eyes flick from me to Lucas, and I suspect my brother has told her I'm the reason.

"He also wanted to tell you that he was pulling people together at your request to send to White River. He's waiting to hear from you."

KRISTIN KEPPLER AND ALLISA BAHNEY

"Okay." I rub my face, my body tired. "Radio him back and tell him he's too late. White River is gone. Have him send his people to Pierre with supplies before the NAF can get to them. Though it might be too late for that, too."

"Why don't you get yourself cleaned up, kid. You reek and look like death," Lucas says softly.

"Maybe get some sleep," Mike suggests from behind me. I had almost forgotten he was there. "I'll help Jack get the rest of the stuff from the buggies."

I pick up my bag, too tired to argue. "I'll come find you later."

Back in my room, the curtains are drawn open just enough for the sun to shine through. I close and lock the door behind me and toss the bag aside. Stripping off my clothes, I toss them into a pile. They reek of smoke and death. I'll be burning those later.

I wince the second the freezing water hits my skin. But I'm unable to stand the grime that covers my body so I stand under the steady flow and wipe myself clean. Once it finally warms, I sigh and grab what's left of my lavender soap and lather a washcloth.

I scrub until I'm red, and even then, I'm not sure I'll ever be able to wash away the death that has seeped into my bones. Tossing the soap and the cloth to the side of the tub, I press my palms flat against the aging tile. Bowing my head, I let the hot water wash over me and close my eyes, desperately hoping it will ease the tension from my body.

Images of White River engulfed in raging fires flicker behind my eyelids, and the faces of the dead haunt me. I soak in the pictures, the sounds, smells, and tastes, committing every single detail to memory, burying it deep within my psyche. I go over their faces again and again, only hoping that their souls are now at peace, their pain and suffering left behind.

But I refuse to forget. I want the pain to stay with me. Even if the weight of it is crushing.

I shut the water off when it begins to run cold. Taking my time drying off, I examine the wound on my arm, grimacing at the sight. Elise would have my hide if she knew how long it took me to tend to it. A rush of relief courses through me knowing she's safe.

My first aid kit is rather pathetic, but there's some disinfectant and a large bandage so I patch myself up as best I can and hope it won't get infected. I examine my arms, one with stitches and the other a fresh bandage. There will be bruises soon, some are already starting to form along my ribs. I'm a mess.

It takes some effort to pull on a new shirt, but it feels good to be in clean clothes. I dry my hair as best I can and toss the damp towel to the side, my limbs feeling heavy.

The room is cold. I debate starting a fire and warming the air. Most places don't have a woodstove; even here, only the large rooms and suites are equipped, but I'm not sure I have the energy despite the luxury.

Ignoring the low grumble of my stomach, I pull the covers back on the bed and crawl in. I think of Kate and wonder how she's doing in Grand Forks. How was she able to stop the convoy? Is she safe? How did she know where to find me? I turn to face the streak of light streaming through my window and shiver. I think of her face, her hazel eyes sparkling in the firelight after I kissed her. It's the last thing I see before I fall into a thick, dreamless slumber.

By the time I wake, my room is dark. It must be well into night. It takes a moment to light a lantern, then I realize someone slipped a note under my door. It asks me to join the discussion in William's room. I wonder when he got in. With a heavy sigh, I rub my eyes, trying to wake more fully. I still feel groggy, like I could sleep for a solid week, and it may not be enough.

After stretching, I step into a clean pair of pants and pull on my boots. I run my fingers through my still damp hair and loosen the tangles, pulling it into a messy bun.

The door to William's room is surprisingly unlocked. He looks up from a large map, his glasses slipping down his nose. "Dani." He sighs and crosses the distance. He places his hands on my shoulders, and I try not to shrug off his touch. "Your friends told me what happened."

Jack and Mike stand near the window, both looking exhausted. Darby sits at a desk fiddling with some new tech and looking extremely engrossed, while Lucas, Ericson, and Hugo stand at the table with William, elbow-deep in a pile of maps and papers.

"I'm so sorry about White River." William's voice is soft and sincere as he tries to catch my gaze. His mood must've softened at the tragic news of my home. If Jack and Mike told him about my killing spree, he doesn't seem bothered. I guess he wouldn't be. He's seen me do worse. The thought makes me cringe.

Stepping out of his grasp, I make no effort to hide how pissed off I am. "I don't need your pity. I needed your people."

He has the decency to look scolded. "I had to make the hard choice—"

"I don't give a shit about your choices." The room goes still at my outburst, all eyes on me. "I needed you. *They* needed you. Pierre needed you. And you left them all hanging. You're ignoring people who need you."

"It's not that simple," William says. To his credit, his voice is steady. Unwavering. It does nothing to calm me down.

"It *is* that simple." I take a step toward him. No one makes a move to stop me. "Pierre asked for your help. *I* asked for your help. You never came. The NAF saw the opportunity and swooped in."

"What are you talking about?" Jack asks. "What's going on?"

I look at William, giving him the opportunity to explain. He doesn't.

"Pierre asked the Resistance for help. They were hurting and needed supplies. William brushed them off. They had no other choice but to turn to the NAF. Kate and the others were on their way with supplies when they were caught in a sandstorm. Then they were attacked by raiders, and that's what pushed them in our direction. They weren't part of a convoy south. They were on their way to help Pierre because the Resistance chose not to."

All eyes shift from me to William, but he stays focused on me.

"Is that true?" Mike asks.

"You haven't been part of this war for years. You chose to hide and to leave us all behind," Ericson says to me. He steps closer, adding himself to our argument. "You don't get to judge us or our decisions."

"Like hell we don't," Jack says. He steps up to my side, staring Ericson down.

Lucas holds out his hands, preventing anyone from saying another word or moving. "My comrades, the past is the past, and that's where it needs to stay."

William and I stare at each other. We are nowhere near finished with this argument, but Lucas is right. We have a situation on our hands that needs dealing with right now, and fighting about what already happened won't change a thing.

"Fine." I head toward the table to look at the map and papers. "So the convoy never departed." Right down to business.

"It was almost as if the NAF were tipped off," Ericson says, staring right at me.

"Or your intel was bad," I offer, and I look at the maps. There's a giant X over Denver and large circles around Helena and Omaha, both cities near military bases.

"The intel wasn't bad. They just pulled out at the last moment," William explains, glancing at Hugo, who shrugs his confirmation. "Unfortunately, it happens from time to time. Not usually on an operation of this magnitude, however."

"Maybe your guy on the inside is bad," Jack says with his arms crossed.

Hugo bites into an apple. "Our guy is good. Something spooked them. We think there might be a loyalist spy in Fargo."

"If that's the case, wouldn't they have known about the ambush long enough to tell the NAF once the plan was implemented?" I continue to theorize as if I wasn't the one to tip off the NAF regarding the ambush. Something I'm not at all sorry for. "It would've given the NAF enough time to come up with a counterattack."

"That's why we think something else may have happened. Perhaps scouts went ahead and saw that our numbers were greater than they had anticipated and pulled back." William sighs. "This is why we need to be more careful next time."

"Next time?" Jack asks with a snort. "You don't think they'll be expecting you to try again?"

"Not if we lead them to believe we aren't ready to regroup after our failure," William points out.

I wince at the word and share a look with Lucas. It doesn't appear that they have any leads on who tipped off the NAF, and William certainly seems to want to move on from it and rebound as quickly as possible. "Then what's the latest intel?"

William takes a deep breath and points toward the map. "Denver's first personnel convoy was a success. They're planning to run their first supplies soon. Malmstrom, a couple hours north of Helena, is also on the agenda. Both expected to move out in two days. Offutt, just south of Omaha, is also still moving, they just put it on hold. No confirmation on when."

"No word on Omaha, supply run to Denver to coincide with a convoy to Malmstrom in two days, and most of our people and supplies now en route to Pierre. That's all we have?" Ericson scoffs. "Well, that's it, then. We're screwed."

"They're running two convoys at the same time?" Jack asks.

"It keeps the Resistance from funneling too many resources into one area. Either we go after them all and are spread too thin to do much damage or we take one out allowing the other convoys to succeed," William explains. "The convoy that was supposed to travel to Omaha a few days ago was a singular movement. It would've been a huge success."

His statement strikes me as odd, considering the NAF always spreads out. It makes me wonder if the Resistance were actually the ones getting played.

"And now that everyone is going to Pierre, we really are spread thin." Ericson says. "We should've left our people where they were and handled the convoy when it relaunched to Omaha. That was the plan. It should've stayed the plan."

"Ericson, not now," William says.

"You're moving too many people," Ericson shouts. "It's what they want."

"Not running any other convoys when Omaha was supposed to depart should've been a huge red flag. You're lucky the NAF stopped their convoy. You were probably being set up. You should've known better, William." I sound like a mother scolding her children.

Ericson stares at me, shocked. And William sighs, as if he knew it was too good to be true but had decided to try anyway. He's getting desperate and it's starting to show.

Ignoring William and Ericson exchanging a few heated words, I stare at the map, a new sense of purpose coursing through me, fueled by what happened at White River. I'm itching for a fight. "Get me the latest map of the north and Midwest. Specifically old highway maps from North Dakota and Montana. Including all current supply locations and major towns."

Ericson steps out of the way as William and Hugo dig through the piles of maps tucked away in a locked chest beside the fireplace. "You want to try to stop the convoy to Malmstrom? With such short notice? Are you crazy?"

"You're right. We're moving too many people." My agreement startles him into silence. I push papers aside for the maps I requested. "We have more than we need in this room."

"You want to mount an attack with eight men?" Jack asks as he inches closer to the table for a better look.

"And women," Darby adds without looking up.

Ericson leaves his place at the table and falls into the plush cushions on the sofa across the room. "You're dumber than I thought."

"What are you thinking?" William asks as I study the maps.

My mother and her family taught me about the Great Plains, showing me the land in the Dakotas and old Montana. As children, Lucas and I explored much of the territory and learned how to survive off the land. When I was older, my father and I ventured through the Rocky Mountains, establishing Resistance posts in places like Bozeman and the Big Belt mountains.

We drew maps everywhere we went. I loved to know what I'd seen and where I'd been. I would memorize all I could and learn from the land around me. We would find unbeaten paths and stay clear of the main roads, where raiders liked to lurk, and wandered parallel to them, searching for people willing to help the Resistance in old forgotten towns.

I'd been to Helena a few times growing up. It was a large but highly influential town, surrounded by mountains and…

I look to Lucas. "Can you get me Dad's journals and the maps we used to draw? Find the ones that include Helena and Malmstrom."

Absently rubbing the back of my neck, I study the possible routes.

"What's Malmstrom?" Darby asks, her curiosity now slightly more piqued.

"It was an old Air Force base that was abandoned after the third world war," I say. Lucas places the journals and maps in front of me.

"Last I heard, a lot of the structures are still standing," William explains. "No one out here really had any interest in the place after the devastation, and raiders like to camp in the area, so we kind of stayed clear. It'd be a great foothold for the north if the NAF were to claim it as theirs. Back east, there were reports of specialists being sent west, farther out than Grand Forks."

"Knowing what's there, you should've investigated," I mumble.

Jack crosses his arms. "Care to elaborate for us simple folk?"

William takes a deep breath, preparing, no doubt, for a long-winded history lesson. "During the Cold War, Malmstrom was the epicenter for nuclear warhead silos—"

"They stockpiled nukes," I interrupt.

The room once again stills. Darby looks up from her tinkering, and Jack and Mike stand in stunned silence.

Shifting from foot to foot, Mike clears his throat. "Are they still there?"

With a shrug, I study the maps on the table. "A lot of them were fired in the last war before the place went dead, but I'm sure there's still plenty of dangerous shit floating around."

"Why the hell isn't the Resistance there? Why is this place even an open option for the gray coats?" Jack is turning red with anger. "You're all running around like chickens without your heads. Not helping towns in need, not taking over bases with fucking nukes, just blowing up cars and fighting about numbers." He's catching on to why I had my fill of the Resistance and tried to move away from it. The whole movement became way too political.

"Watch yourself," Ericson warns as he begins to advance.

I'm in no mood for such an ardent display of machismo, but thankfully, William steps in and holds his hands out toward both men, stopping them.

"I can appreciate the passion, but now is not the time to get into specifics. In short"—he turns toward Jack—"we don't have enough fighters to maintain, control, and inhabit all the old bases spread around this country or help every single town who requests it. Not when efforts are better spent in the field. As for the threats?" William turns toward Ericson. "Leave them at the door. We need to work together now more than ever. That includes explaining history and practices when warranted to our newest guests. Understood?"

Ericson does nothing but grunt and turns to fall back on the sofa. I give Jack a look of impatience, and he finally relaxes a bit with his posturing.

My attention is back on the maps as I try to figure out the NAF's play. "Whatever they're secretly working on won't be a secret much longer. It's about to become a problem if they're sending an entire convoy."

"You suggest we point our attention there?" William asks.

"I do," I answer. "Hugo, is this a supply run or personnel?"

"As far as I am aware it's personnel."

"Then they're going to want to get there quickly to establish control. We make sure they know we've pulled our fighters out of Sioux Falls and sent them to Pierre. Direct attention there."

William gives me a look. "And the convoy to Malmstrom?"

"With the main roads washed out, they're going to have to go through the mountains where we'll be waiting."

"Going through the mountains would be suicide," Ericson says from his spot on the sofa.

"That's the idea," William says, understanding immediately. He turns to Hugo. "Can you get ahold of your contacts and confirm it's a personnel convoy and find out what path they'll take?"

A drawn-out sigh comes from Jack. "You're forgetting that there's still only eight of us."

"We can station another point person here," I say, pointing at the map and ignoring Jack, "and then we'll know their route for sure. That should leave us enough time to set up here, here, and here."

Ericson scoffs, not even bothering to get up and read the routes. "Just like that? One look at an old map, and suddenly, you know everything?"

"Maps will be what wins this war," I mumble without taking my eyes off the suspected route.

"You'll never get lost when looking at the stars for guidance," Lucas says proudly.

"Issue two," Darby says confidently and incorrectly. She's read the comics that Lucas quotes over and over; how has she never gotten one single issue correct?

Ericson grows impatient and stands, motioning wildly in what I assume to be a mix of anger and irritation. "You still have no idea if any of this is actually going to happen. You don't even know that these maps are accurate."

"They're accurate," William confirms. "The terrain has changed a lot since the war. We spent a lot of time accounting for those changes."

Ericson focuses on him. "I say we wait for intel on the convoy to Omaha and then try again. Some of our people are still in position and ready to attack. Besides, you said they were tipped off. How do you know whoever tipped them off about Omaha won't tip them off about Malmstrom? Don't you think they'll send more scouts this time?

Checking to make sure a possible ambush doesn't happen along every route? Especially through the mountains?"

"Because we keep it limited." I can hear the excitement in William's voice. He's already on board. "Only the eight of us will know our exact location. All other intel will suggest that we've given up on the convoy to Omaha and turned our attention instead to the people of Pierre."

"And the eight of us can scatter and hide in the mountains quickly and easily without drawing attention," Mike says.

"Can you tell me what vehicles the convoy will consist of?" I ask Hugo, finally looking up from the maps. "Tanks, busses, buggies?"

He shrugs. "Give me a few hours and I can give you a rough estimate."

"Do you think you can assemble everything you need in under two days?" William asks me.

"You're damn right I can." I'm confident I can make this happen. I *need* to make this happen. Someone has to pay for this.

"We had over a hundred people ready to take out the convoy to Omaha, and you're telling me you think we can take out the convoy to Malmstrom with just the eight of us?" Ericson laughs. "There is no way."

"You haven't seen what I'm capable of." I say, confident if not arrogant.

"You can assemble enough explosives to take out tanks and trucks in a *day*?" Ericson's tone is laced with doubt.

"I'm a remarkable scavenger." I easily slip back into the role of Daughter of the Resistance. Overconfident and reckless. Feels like home.

Despite the skeptical looks from around the room, William smiles. "I think this could work."

Chapter Two: The Promotion

Kate

I was too late. My warning to Dani didn't arrive on time. And when I got to my mother's office to plead that she spare White River, there was no use. Simon was already gone. I was invited to wait for news on his assignment but declined and took the opportunity to send an anonymous tip to our base about stopping the convoy to Sioux Falls. Without Dani's warning, about two hundred soldiers and I would've driven straight into an ambush. At least I was able to stop that.

Instead, I used the time to anxiously pace a hole in the floor of my quarters. When news finally came, it was early morning. The sunrise cast a golden hue across the monotone and stark Air Force base as a private delivered me a single note written by my mother's assistant:

Your presence is requested. White River has fallen.

My mother is pacing angrily inside her office. No, I correct myself. *The general* is pacing angrily. I have to keep them separate. Especially right now. My hands shake in my lap after hearing the gruesome details of the attack on White River. Whether it's in rage or sadness, I'm not sure. Probably both.

Simon stands off to the side looking mighty pristine for having just come from a mass slaughter. The sight of him burns my insides with a deep fury that I'm having a hard time controlling.

"Twenty-two men, five vehicles, one tank, and two of our best pyros. All destroyed. One survivor," the general recounts. She doesn't spare a glance for Simon.

"But the entire town was taken down," he says as if trying to justify his actions. "Over thirty locals and livestock with it."

The general's eyes snap to him, sharp and with heavy warning. "Were the Clarks among them?"

Simon shifts from one foot to the other and stands a little straighter. "We knew the likelihood of them being there was slim to none."

"You said Danielle came back."

Simon would typically argue but instead clenches his jaw and looks straight ahead. A town was destroyed, and people were murdered, all for what? For show? For the chance that maybe she'd get lucky and kill one or both Clarks if they returned? My stomach contorts. The whole thing is so…vile.

The general takes two calculated steps in Simon's direction. "And you left her there."

"I had to," he argues. Hearing him confirm that Dani is alive causes a rush of relief. "She clearly had reinforcements coming, and she took out all my men."

The silence that follows is suffocating. It's common for Simon to speak out of turn, but to the general? I watch carefully as she closes the distance between them. He swallows roughly and waits. "Where is she hiding? Where are the rest of her people hiding?" she asks slowly.

The fact that Simon can speak so freely without consequence unsettles me. They clearly have a common goal, and she seems to be using that to her advantage. It makes me wonder why I'm even privy to this conversation. I focus on a spot on the floor in front of me to hide my discomfort.

Simon doesn't answer. It takes me a moment to wonder why, and I glance up. The general is looking at me. The question wasn't meant for him.

"I have no idea," I say honestly. And as desperate as I am to know where Dani went, at this moment, I'm truly grateful for not having a clue.

The general stares, her eyes piercing and dangerous. She hums and sits in her oversized chair, folding her hands atop the desk. "Corporal Alexander tells me that you and Clark shared many private conversations during your time as her prisoner."

It seems Simon and the general have, in fact, spoken more than I thought. "We had discussions, yes," I say carefully, "but she didn't disclose her plans or her hideouts. I have no idea where she went."

"Why don't you share what you did talk about?" It isn't a suggestion. The general has clearly given me enough time and space, and now she's looking for information.

My stomach flips as I think back to my conversations with Dani. While she didn't tell me strategies or locations, she did tell me some very personal things. Details that I plan to keep safely tucked away. "Not a lot. As I said, she wasn't very forthcoming with pertinent information."

"Don't be so modest," she says through a twisted smile. "Surely, you must've discussed something of value. Or did you merely exchange observations about the weather?"

Simon looks at me expectantly, with a hint of smugness. I'm not sure I've ever hated him more. "It wasn't until a couple days in that I even realized who she was. She seemed like a regular townsperson."

"Who strapped us to bombs," Simon mumbles.

"That was *after* we realized she was Danielle Clark," I point out. "Up until then, I was trying to figure out who she was and what she was planning on doing with us. I assumed we were being held for ransom."

"And what else?" The general asks with a tilt of her head.

"She appeared done with the war and claimed she wanted nothing to do with it. She said she didn't have any plans of jumping back in," I answer simply. It's the truth, so I decide that's enough. There's no need to get into the journals or how she found herself close to death until the little town by the river saved her and allowed her to stay. Somehow, saying anything more feels like it would be betraying her. I can't pinpoint why that bothers me as much as it does.

"It appears that she lied." She stares at us both, and neither Simon or I dare to move under her intense scrutiny. "Corporal." He straightens and lifts his chin in the general's direction. "You're due for a title change. You've shown tremendous initiative of late."

"Thank you, ma'am."

She looks at me. "I need Danielle Clark. I need someone I trust to do the job." I open my mouth to respond, but before I can, her attention is back on Simon. "Which is why I'm promoting you to second lieutenant."

"Lieutenant?" I'm in utter disbelief. To offer someone a promotion carelessly and without the proper channels? From corporal to lieutenant? He hasn't even been through the proper training. "You can't be serious."

Immediately, she gives me a look that lets me know I've crossed a line. "You would do best to mind your tongue."

I stand a little straighter. "Yes, ma'am."

To his credit, Simon doesn't look smug. Not yet. He's seems as shocked as I am.

"You will assemble a team. You will have access to all the equipment and resources of the NAF. Your sole job is to track down Danielle Clark, Lucas Clark, and William Russell and bring them to me. Preferably alive. I have unfinished business with them."

I stare in shock. The Resistance has been a thorn in her side since before I was born. That aversion has grown over time, simmering into something beyond simple animosity. Outwardly, she maintains professionalism and has preached about becoming a unified country. But for as long as I can remember, she has made it her mission to climb the ranks, her hatred and loathing for the Resistance and for the Clarks and William being her main motivator. It's always been behind every single command she's given and action she's taken. And now that Dani is back in the fight, the general has turned into someone I barely recognize. And it frightens me.

"I won't disappoint you," Simon promises.

She dismisses Simon, and he leaves without another word. Simon has his orders, and my mind is reeling with all that just unfolded. I need to talk to Dani.

The general clears her throat, her expression softening now that we're alone. "I'm worried about you." She turns back into my mother so fast, my head spins. "You haven't seemed like yourself. I'm concerned."

"About me or about my assignment?" I snap. She gives me a disapproving look. I sigh and rub my eyes. "I'm sorry. I'm just tired."

"If I didn't know any better, I would say that this entire ordeal has unnerved you."

"I'm not unnerved, I just…" I close my mouth, not quite knowing what to say. I *am* unnerved. But the last thing I want to do is show any kind of weakness. She may not be speaking to me as the general, but she's always observing. Always analyzing. "I lost so many soldiers. I lost the supplies to Pierre."

My words seem to placate her curiosity. She shows me the briefest bit of sympathy. "Losing soldiers is always difficult. Unfortunately, that comes with the territory of a ranking officer. Their deaths may not always be preventable, but it's a burden you have to carry."

"I know." My shoulders sag. I'm not sure I'll ever escape the weight of it.

"As for Pierre, we'll attempt to carry on with the assignment to assimilate them for now. Listen." She stands and approaches me with a sympathetic look. "I didn't promote you to major because you're my daughter. I promoted you because I know you have what it takes to lead. You understand and value our mission. I trust you to always get the job done. No matter what." She gently runs her fingers through my hair.

It takes everything in me not to flinch at her touch. Her attempt at comfort feels forced, and it saddens as well as repulses me.

"This was a minor setback. It's okay to be a bit shell-shocked. Facing off against the Resistance, against the Clarks, seems to have that effect." There's a bite to her tone as she spits out their name. "I'll take care of them soon enough. I want you to take a few days to rest. Get yourself together so you can complete your assignment. In the meantime, I've pushed up convoys to two other locations. One to Denver and another to Malmstrom. They'll be moving out in two days, and I'm taking personnel from your reinforcement convoy."

In a matter of seconds, she not only insulted my mission but took soldiers away from my command. I absorb it like a punch to the gut. The look on my face must give away my hurt and confusion. "Malmstrom? Isn't that place vacant? Are we setting up a new command there?"

"I've requested a transfer to fill the vacancies for your unit. Don't worry, Major, you will have your troops." She assures me while completely avoiding my question and sitting at her desk.

"Can we afford more soldiers for the transfer?" The situation back east must be a lot better than I previously thought if she's able to pull this off so quickly and without fear of a power vacuum.

"We can't afford not to," she says as if a transfer of that size isn't a big deal. "We have troops arriving in the next few days from the east. They'll be ready to join you in Omaha. I expect you to be ready as well. I'm sending scouts and my best intel chiefs to Sioux Falls to see what the hell happened. If that anonymous transmission didn't come through, we would've lost a lot of people."

"Thank goodness for that," I say, playing dumb.

"I do find it interesting they didn't give any sort of call sign." She stares at me like she knows something. I stand tall, despite my nervousness, refusing to give myself away. Sending a radio warning to the base seemed like the fastest way to stop the convoy at the time, but once things settle, I know she'll want to know who it was and where it came from. If she finds out it came from me…

"I'll check in with the communications specialist to see if there's any update."

"Yes, please do. Keep me updated." I'm relieved, for now, that she appears to drop the issue. "Finish anything you're working on and take a few days. Try to get some sleep. You look awful."

I ignore the insult. "Yes, ma'am."

She doesn't say anything else, and I take that as my cue to leave. I reach the door when her voice stops me. "Oh, and Katelyn? I expect you to make it to your post with your next convoy." The ice in her tone has me bristling. "Dismissed."

I move with purpose through the base, ignoring everything around me and stride up the ramp to Archie's. When I arrive, I glance over my shoulder to make sure no one has followed me. Not that it would matter. Meeting with the cartographer isn't unheard of.

The sun has gotten higher, well into morning. There's a crisp chill to the air, and it feels like snow. Pulling my collar higher, I knock and wait for Archie to answer. When the door opens, he looks both surprised and nervous to see me.

"I hope I'm not interrupting anything," I say pleasantly. "I have some questions about the convoy. Perhaps we can talk?"

Archie leans forward and peeks around the door frame. "Of course, Major."

The door barely clicks closed behind us. "I need to talk to her," I hiss in a low tone, getting straight to the point. "I need to talk to Dani."

"Kate." He sighs and wheels toward the dining area. His breakfast is spread across the table. I feel only slightly guilty for interrupting. "Please, don't do this again. It's too risky."

"Archie, I need to see her." I pull out the chair beside him. "Please. I need her to know it isn't a trap. Maybe somewhere in her territory."

"That's suicide." He reaches for his fork and begins to eat. "We got lucky the first time, Kate. But if you keep doing this, it's only a matter of time before someone catches on, and then we're *both* dead."

"She's back in it, Archie. She took out Simon's team by herself. I just came from the general. She promoted Simon to second lieutenant." His chewing slows, and he looks at me in surprise. "He's been given a team with the sole purpose of hunting down Dani, Lucas, and William. I know you've told the Resistance about the convoys the general is deploying. I need to know Dani's not planning on doing something stupid."

"You don't know that she's planning anything," he says carefully.

I give him a knowing look. "After what Simon just did to White River? Of course she is."

He shakes his head. "She'll never tell you."

"She might if I give her pertinent information. Quid pro quo."

Archie appears to think it over. "I can get her the message about Simon."

"No." He looks at me, startled. "I want you to get her a message about meeting *me*."

"How do I know this *isn't* a trap, Kate? I'm supposed to be helping the Resistance, not setting them up." He tilts his head condescendingly.

"Then help me save her!" I'm quickly losing my cool, and if I'm not composed, I'm not getting anywhere. I need to swallow any and all emotions in order to speak rationally and get what I need. And what I need is to see Dani. She has to know I wouldn't betray her. That I'm not my mother or Simon. I wouldn't do that. Pulling in a long breath, I soften my tone. "Look, what happened to White River...I need her to know I didn't sell her out. That I wasn't lying when I said I would try to protect them. I need her to know about Simon. I can't explain it to you. I just need to see her."

He puts down his fork and doesn't bother to hide his annoyance. "How do you know she wants to see *you*?" His rebuttal startles me into silence.

"Because I would go if she asked me to." My answer seems inadequate, desperate, and probably just a tad too hopeful.

Luckily, Archie doesn't press any further. "There's an outpost about four hours southwest of here. It could be taken over by raiders or collapsed due to the storms, for all I know." He wheels to a desk and reaches under the top drawer for another stash of maps. He rummages through the pile and jots the coordinates on the side of one, marking a path along the old state highway.

"Thank you," I breathe.

"When did you want to meet?" He reaches for a scrap piece of paper and a pencil.

"As soon as possible." I bounce in place. My entire body buzzes in anticipation of seeing Dani again. My heart hammers so loudly in my chest that I can feel it reverberate in my ears.

Archie appears to consider my words. "I can probably sneak the message out early tomorrow morning, but security is tight. It's going to take a day or two to get there."

I try not to think of where "there" could be. He scribbles a few notes on the sheet. I lean forward to try to see what he's written, but he pulls the paper from my view and quickly folds it. "How are you sneaking these messages out?"

He pauses for a moment, tensing. "I can't answer that."

We stare at each other. He lifts his chin a little higher, proud and unwavering in his decision. There are so many things I could threaten him with, but in the end, I need him to get to Dani. And if that means he gets to keep his secrets a little longer, so be it. I'll have to deal with our security breach later.

"So where are you sending me?" I ask, changing the subject. For now.

Visibly relieved, he returns to his meal. "There's a town about halfway to the outpost. You should stop there first, get food and some rest. The outpost is hidden, it'll be hard to find at night, so leave early enough that you'll still have daylight. Most of the main roads are washed out, and it might take some time to get there. Get a truck. And for the sake of everything, don't get caught. Maybe wear something other than your uniform."

I practically bow. "Thank you, Archie."

"Yeah, yeah." He slices into his stack of pancakes as I turn toward the door. "Oh, and Kate? Pack spare linens to sleep on."

My feet come to a dead stop. Is he insinuating something? "I...I don't," I stammer as my face grows warmer.

"Like I said, it's probably been abandoned for a while," he elaborates. "A foldaway mattress might not hurt either. Who knows what kind of condition the bed is in?"

"Right. Of course. For sleeping. Yes. Thank you." I dash out and let the door slam quickly behind me.

I spend the rest of the day with the supply specialists, making sure all my supplies and troops are all set to be sent to new locations, doing my best to ignore the sideways glances and pitying looks from my unit. It's fine, I tell myself, I have more troops coming, nothing's being taken away from me in the long run. Besides, that's not what's bothering me. What I'm really concerned about is Dani.

Is Archie right? Will she even want to see me? Does she blame me for what happened?

I guess I'll find out soon enough.

By the time the morning arrives, I can't sit still any longer. I start throwing a change of clothes and linens into a duffel, still unable to focus on anything but the prospect of seeing Dani.

I'm frantically spinning in circles, looking for soap and trying to calm my second thoughts when a voice startles me.

"Packing already?"

Ryan. My shoulders settle, but my stomach tightens.

"I tried knocking but…" His voice trails off. "I didn't think we were leaving until the end of the week after the reinforcements get here." Ah. So he heard about that. Of course he did.

He stands in my doorway, his hat in his hands and his uniform pressed. His blond hair is shorter than when I last saw him. He looks every part the soldier and equally handsome.

Still, I don't have the energy for the argument I know is coming.

I finally find my soap and avoid eye contact as I carefully tuck it inside the bag. "I'm scouting out a few things before we move out." It sounds like a lie, even to me.

"We literally have scouts for that." His voice is hollow and dry. His suspicion is clearly growing, but I need to keep him at bay. If anyone knew where I was really going…well, they don't take kindly to traitors around here.

"I need some R and R." It's not much of an explanation, but it's the truth, and it'll have to do.

"I see." He eyes my bag as I add my brush and pull the zipper tight. "Does the general know about this?"

"You mean, did I ask my mom?"

"That's not what I meant."

"Ryan." I pinch the bridge of my nose. Addressing him by his first name and not his title has officially dropped the chain of command. Not that there ever was one with him showing up in my bedroom unannounced. Old habits and all that.

"What's going on with you, Kate?" A hint of desperation laces his tone. "You've been skittish ever since we've been back. Does this have anything to do with Simon?"

"Fuck Simon," I snap. "What he did was horrible. What he did to that town, to those people…"

"Was in the bounds of the law," he finishes carefully.

"The *law*? Burning an innocent town to the ground for no reason? That's not our *law*," I remind him none too gently.

"They weren't innocent, and there was a reason."

"Are you listening to yourself?" I find it difficult to believe he would dismiss what Simon did as acceptable. I've known Ryan for just about my entire life. We were once so intimate that we knew each other inside and out. But now? I'm not so sure.

"Are you?" He fires back. When I don't respond, he takes a deep breath and softens. "Katie…" The nickname that once made my heart skip now prickles my skin.

"He slaughtered them," I whisper. "In the middle of the night like a coward. He destroyed everything. How can you be okay with that?"

He shakes his head. "I never said I was okay with it. I just said he was following orders."

"That doesn't make it right!"

"It doesn't matter. That's what we do. Follow orders. It's not our place to question them."

"Then whose job is it?" I am absolutely astonished. He shakes his head again, seemingly unable to answer. "Is this what being a loyalist means? No regard for human life? We don't slaughter innocent people, Ryan. The NAF is supposed to unite and rebuild. Not murder and destroy."

"They were a Resistance-led town—"

"I can't do this." I hold up a hand and turn away. It wasn't just some Resistance-led town. It was Dani and Lucas and Rhiannon and Elise, people we got to know. This time, it just feels different.

I hear Ryan sigh. "What's really going on?" I don't respond. I'm entirely too angry and way too exhausted to get anywhere near personal or honest with him. "Where are you really going?" He reaches for my hand, but I recoil before he can get there.

"I need to clear my head for a few days," I state, matter-of-factly. I straighten my shoulders and transform back into his superior, sending a clear message that what I say goes. Even in the privacy of my bedroom. "The general ordered a few days of R and R. She said after everything, it might be good to clear my head before regrouping and moving out. So that's what I'm going to do. After all, I'm just following orders."

He's quiet as I recheck my bag. I can tell the dig at his previous argument stings. "I care about you, Katie." His voice is soft, quiet. Sad. "If there's something going on, you can talk to me. You can trust me."

"After that little outburst? Hardly." I scoff.

His expression is so dejected, so unsure. It deflates me, even though I'm still reeling. I know most of what I'm feeling isn't because of him. He's just caught in the crossfire.

"Simon was promoted to second lieutenant," I confide quietly.

Ryan looks startled and stares at me for a moment, perhaps waiting for me to tell him I'm joking. The punchline never comes. "Well, that's... unsettling."

That's an understatement. "There's going to be a lot more destruction now that he's been given his own task force. It doesn't sit well with me, and I'm just..." I sigh.

Ryan waits, his expression full of sympathy and understanding.

I pull my hair back into a neat bun at the base of my neck. "I'm going to go visit Private Miller. Would you like to come?"

He straightens, showing no sign of surprise at the change of topic. "Of course."

I slip on my jacket and button it to the top and run my hands down my uniform. When I'm satisfied that I look presentable, Ryan gestures to the door and follows me out.

❖

Private Miller has his own room. The military treatment facility, which is more like a one-story field hospital, isn't exactly brimming with activity. The majority of the soldiers stationed here haven't engaged in much fighting outside of combat training and the occasional raider outside the gates.

We're shown in by a field medic, and she gives us our privacy as Ryan and I step inside. Miller is lying in the single bed, looking out the window, Private Silva sitting beside him. Miller nudges Silva, who stands, both of them saluting when we enter.

"At ease, Privates," I say.

Miguel remains standing. "Major Turner, Chief Matthews."

I motion for Miguel to sit and turn to Miller. "How are you feeling?"

"Good," he says. "Better. They said I can return to my quarters tomorrow, but they're not sure if I'm 'of the right mind' to handle explosives just yet."

Ryan and I share a look. We know what that means.

Miguel excuses himself to find more chairs. Miller looks younger than his nineteen years. It upsets me to think of him being so young and dealing with so much trauma. "It's okay to not rush into anything right now. You were very badly hurt and then taken prisoner. There is absolutely no rush to jump right back in the thick of it."

Miller nods and looks back toward the window. "That's what Miguel said."

I glance at the pill bottle and the plate of untouched food on the bedside table and frown. "Have you been eating?" I ask.

"Sometimes."

Miguel walks in with another chair and excuses himself again to give us privacy, promising to be back soon. Once he's out of the room, Miller turns to me. "Can I speak openly?" he asks.

"Yes. Please."

"I'm confused. Everything's a blur. We were on our way to help people. Then the sandstorm. Then the raiders." He pauses and swallows roughly. "That town, they kept us alive and took care of my injuries. But they're Resistance. They're the enemy."

I don't correct him and tell him that the town actually *wasn't* Resistance; like with Ryan, I know it would fall of deaf ears. The most important thing now is for Miller to speak honestly and know that we're listening. "What's confusing you?" I gently prompt when he hesitates.

His dark eyes meet mine. "Why would they do that? It's in their nature to kill us, right? That's what we were taught. So why didn't they? Why didn't they let us die?"

"Maybe not all supporters of the Resistance are evil," I offer.

Ryan shifts awkwardly but doesn't disagree. I can feel his eyes on me, but I avoid looking at him.

"But that doesn't make any sense," Miller continues. "They're murderers. They're trying to stop the unification. They're…lawless and reckless."

"They aren't lawless."

"They just don't believe in the law of our country." Ryan gives me a pointed look that I continue to ignore.

I make sure Miller is focused on me. "They just believe in different ideals and the path that leads them to those beliefs. They are no less human than you or me."

Miller thinks for a moment, his brow furrowed, seemingly determined to understand. "But we killed them. They let us go, and we turned around and killed them."

"*Lieutenant Alexander* killed them," I correct. I absolutely loathe addressing him by his new and unearned rank.

Ryan clears his throat. "Major…" It's a warning I probably should heed.

Miller doesn't seem deterred. He looks from me to Ryan almost desperately. "They released us and saved my life. And we killed them. Doesn't that make *us* the murderers? Aren't we the ones who are supposed to be helping people?"

I finally meet Ryan's eyes. He places a hand on Miller's. Not even Ryan has a rebuttal for that question. I try and offer a reassuring smile when Miller looks at me, but the entire exchange just makes me feel sad.

"Excuse me, Major?"

Miguel stands in the doorway. I excuse myself and join him in the hallway. "Is something wrong?" He hesitates. "You can talk to me."

He shifts nervously. "Anthony and I are supposed to report to duty soon, and I was wondering, if it's okay, to maybe take a few days off before we do."

I place my hand on his arm. "I'll make sure you get a couple days to regroup. In fact, I'm doing the same thing." He looks so relieved that I can't help but think there's something else going on. "Listen, if you need to talk, about what we went through or anything really, I'm here to listen. It's not every day we're held by the Resistance and strapped to live bombs." I offer a small smile. "And whatever you have to say stays between us. Okay? Purely confidential. That goes for Miller, too."

"Thank you, ma'am."

"Come on. Let's go sit with Miller a little longer." I follow Miguel back into the room and make a mental note to check on my soldiers more routinely.

❖

Leaving the MTF, I feel drained. We were only there for thirty minutes or so before we were asked to leave so Miller could rest, but it felt so much longer. It's clear he's dealing with mental trauma over his experience, and I can't blame him for that. I'm not sure anything Ryan and I could've said to him would've fixed anything.

Before leaving, I scheduled a follow-up with his doctor to discuss his progress, or lack thereof, in depth. Maybe by then, I can think of something better to say to reassure him we aren't the bad guys.

I rub my forehead, the ache behind my eyes intensifying. I just want to get back to my quarters, make sure I'm packed, and try to get some rest before I leave.

Ryan insists on walking me back, and I have a feeling he has more to say. We get about halfway to my quarters before he breaks the silence. "He's not eating."

"I noticed. I have a follow-up with his doctor when I get back. Maybe we can figure out if there's anything more we can do for him."

"I'll check in while you're gone." Our steps are slow, measured, and I know he's drawing out the walk. He shoves his hands in his pockets and sighs. "I'm sorry about earlier. I didn't mean to pick a fight. I'm just worried about you."

"Why are you worried?"

"What happened when we were in White River, Kate?" I stop walking. He does too and turns to face me. "Something happened." He leans in closer, as if he's about to share classified information. "What did she say to you that you aren't telling us?"

"She?" He gives me a look, as though we both know exactly who he's referring to. But I don't budge. "You sound just like my mother.

We've had this conversation before. I'm tired of talking in circles." I start walking again with Ryan hot on my heels.

"Maybe people keep asking because you never actually give any answers."

"*Maybe* that's because there are no answers to give," I call over my shoulder and pick up the pace.

"Hey, wait a minute." He grabs my wrist, stopping me. "I'm here for you, Kate. I'm on your side. You can talk to me."

"Can I?" I yank my arm out of his grip.

He recoils as if I just slapped him. "You know you can."

Once upon a time, I would've told him everything, held nothing back and voiced all my concerns and confusion so we could've worked it out together, knowing that my private thoughts were safe with him. Looking at him now, there's a part of me that still wants to believe he'll keep me safe.

I take a step closer. "What if I told you she saved your life."

"What?"

I lower my voice. "That convoy to Omaha? The one that was going to be ambushed near Sioux Falls?"

"The comm specialist intercepted an anonymous tip to hold and pull back," he says, reciting the reason the general gave.

I shake my head. "It wasn't anonymous."

"What are you talking about?"

"*She* told me."

"Danielle Clark…told you?" He stares. I flinch when he says her name.

"She told me to stop the convoy. She's the one who told me about the trap and saved our lives in the process. I'm the anonymous tip." He's clearly speechless as he clearly tries to comprehend. "You want to know why I'm questioning things and why I'm having a hard time with the war, *that's* why. Because everything we've been taught isn't how it actually is. There's a bigger picture here, Ryan, and I just want to know what the hell it is."

If he knew the whole truth, what I've done, what I'm going to go, I doubt very seriously he would be on my side. I've already said way too much. And there's no way I'm telling him she snuck on base and divulged vital information in between kisses.

I take a step back. "Things aren't exactly as they seem, and I'm trying to figure it out. And in order to do that, I need you to back off and let me think." We're silent as a small group of officers walk by. I wait until they're out of earshot. "I trust you won't speak about this to anyone else."

He looks pale, as if I just sucker punched him in the gut. But as promised, he slowly nods. "I won't say anything for your sake. But Kate," he adds, "when you get back, we need to have a serious talk."

That's only fair considering what I just dumped on him. "Then I'll see you when I get back," I say, then continue to my quarters alone.

Chapter Three: The Convoy

Dani

"This isn't going to work."

"It's going to work," I say without looking up. Twisting the last set of wires around the transmitter Darby assembled, I nod a little to the beat of the music thumping through one of my earbuds.

Ericson shakes his head, his arms crossed as he looks out across the mountains. "The range is too far."

"It'll reach." Carefully, using both hands, I close the casing and pull on the wire sticking out of the small hole in the gap of the road. I gauge the distance of the next explosive. Satisfied, I motion toward my open bag. "Give me that pin."

"We should've used a satchel charge on the base of the mountain," Ericson says for the thousandth time. He flexes his biceps under his extra tight shirt.

Unimpressed, I wrap the wire around the top of the pin and pull slightly at the additional wire lying on the ground that's attached to the bomb buried several feet away. With both sets of wire wrapped around the pin, I fill the hole with nearby rocks and activate the trigger.

"So you've said," I mumble. Wiping my hands on my pants and shoving the other earbud in my pocket, I stand and stare down the stretch of road, the sun causing me to squint through my sunglasses. It's getting late.

"Gas lines are set." Jack approaches from behind. He looks at the rocks covering the hole and then at Ericson waiting impatiently. "You good?"

"I'm good. You worry about you," Ericson bites back.

Jack takes a threatening step, and I hold out my arm against his chest. "Are we on schedule?" I ask into the radio.

"Approximately ten minutes until you have a visual." Hugo's static-filled voice comes through after he's checked in with our lookout several miles away.

I glance at Ericson, who takes the hint and grabs the bag of remaining explosives off the side of the road. "You hear from Mike?" I ask Jack. He shakes his head. "Eagle Eye armed and ready?" I ask into the radio.

His reply is immediate. "Eagle Eye in place."

Jack scans the mountain ridge a couple hundred meters away, no doubt trying to find Mike in his sniper's position. After hitting his shoulder with the back of my hand, I nod toward my Jeep. "All set. Let's move out."

Ericson places the explosives in the bed of the Rubicon Gladiator and slips in the back. I get in the driver's seat and toss the radio in his direction. I peel out so fast, Jack barely has time to get in and close the passenger door.

He turns to me and lays his rifle across his thighs. "You should've checked in with Rhiannon."

I wince, knowing I've been an absolute shitty friend for not doing so already. But every time I go to call her, I think of the front of her tavern caving in, and I can't bring myself to do it. The guilt is too overpowering. "I will when this is over."

"If you don't die today, she'll kill you herself." I can't help but smile at the sentiment. That sounds about right. He nods toward my injured arm. "You gonna be able to fight?"

I scoff. "Please. This is nothing."

He smiles while I pull the Jeep out of sight high on one of the cliffs overlooking the road.

Lucas is waiting with Darby, the only pair of thermal goggles we could access resting atop his head. Both of them are snacking on apples like they're on a freaking picnic.

Darby looks up expectantly. "Is it time?"

"All set." I grab my old load-bearing chest rig, preloaded with eight grenades and extra ammunition, complete with Kevlar plate inserts for a nice layer of protection. I haven't worn this in years. Being a scavenger didn't call for the extra protection, but I never could get rid of it. For so long, it was part of me, something I wore frequently and proudly. It was custom-made, and parting with it would've felt like parting with a large piece of myself. I wonder if I somehow knew that one day, I'd be wearing it again.

As I snap the rig around my waist, it feels like coming home. The familiar adrenaline weaves its way through my veins, and my entire body thumps with anticipation. "Remember the plan," I say. "Jack and Hugo will distract with the explosives. Lucas and Mike will snipe from either side."

"Are you sure you don't want Hugo behind the scope? He's a deadeye," Ericson says.

There is no way I'm giving up my cover to someone I barely know. "I need Hugo with the rockets. Lucas and Mike will snipe on either side." Hugo nods but appears disappointed. "Ericson, William will meet you at the front of the convoy, and I'll take the back for when they try to retreat. Darby, when they get to the start of the bottleneck, blow the secondary device to block their path forward. Standby for my signal, and when I tell you, come and get me from the entry point. Once I set the mines to blow the tank, I'll need a fast exit."

"How do you know they'll try to retreat?" Darby asks.

"They always retreat," I say and take her binoculars.

"And keep moving positions." Ericson adds. "You don't want them to spot where the fire is coming from."

"He's right. Take a shot and run like hell. These tanks don't need pinpoint precision to launch an attack in your general area. They'll be firing right back at you." I don't miss their nervous expressions. "And they'll have no problem creating smoke screens to make it hard to see. Focus fire in the middle, Ericson and I will remain on the edges."

Looking down the road through the binoculars, I see the first of the vehicles. We're cutting it mighty close. The convoy creeps down the road, right on time and straight for the trap we placed for them. I hand the binoculars back to Darby.

Lucas tosses his apple core to the side and picks up his rifle. "I can smell it in the air. War's a'brewin'."

Darby lifts the binoculars to get a better look. "Issue fifty-six."

"Jesus Christ, Darby," I say. I swear her guesses get worse and worse. It only agitates my adrenaline-filled state.

"Here they come." Jack's statement brings our attention back to the fight. Reaching for the detonator in my pocket, I flip the arm switch and flick open the safety cap. My finger hovers over the detonation button.

Two tanks, four buggies, one officer's vehicle, and two busses. Maybe eighty to a hundred NAF soldiers involved. Hugo's estimate was pretty spot-on. More will come, along with supplies, once they're established, but for now, it's the standard personnel to get the base up and running. This will land a devastating blow if we can take them out and prevent the base from being fully operational. At the very least, it'll send a message that the Resistance won't sit idly by and watch the NAF expand.

"Stand by for detonation," Ericson says in the radio, alerting everyone else scattered along the mountain ridge.

The convoy creeps by so slowly that it's as if time has virtually stopped. We are silent as we wait for the front of the caravan to hit the farthest explosion point. I hold my breath. They are in a predictable formation: tank, bus, two buggies, the officer's vehicle, two buggies, bus, and tank.

My eyes linger on the officer vehicle while my finger hovers over the button. I think of Kate in a convoy like this, picturing her inside that lone armored buggy. Intel confirms she's due to run the base in Omaha, but I still hesitate to detonate. What if they changed it up at the last minute, and Kate is now in charge of Malmstrom? What if she tried to tell me, but I never got word?

I run my thumb across the button as the officer's vehicle approaches the center mark. Kate got word to me once before. I'm sure she would've been able to do it again. She's not in the vehicle. Kate is somewhere far away from here.

"Steady men," Lucas says from behind his scope.

Kate is far away. She's far away. Kate isn't here.

"It's now or never, men," Lucas yells. I hesitate. "Atomic Anomaly, now!"

His use of my code name sets a chain of events in motion, and I slam my thumb down on the button.

For a split second, the world stops. The birds overhead are silent, and the wind stills. No one breathes. It's as if all sound was sucked in a black hole and deposited someplace else entirely. And then the sound pushes back out, and the officer's jeep flies into the air with a deafening boom, engulfed by a plume of fire.

I say a silent prayer that Kate is far away.

The chain of explosions trickles out from there, launching buggies into the air and knocking the busses on their sides. The tanks rock, but as expected, their armor prevents them from taking too much damage. They were designed to take a beating.

Jack brings the grenade launcher to his chest and lifts the sight. "They like to play with fire, let's give them something to play with." He launches the first grenade at the tank leading the convoy.

William launches a grenade at the tank bringing up the rear from the opposite mountain ridge. As the surviving soldiers scramble out of the fire-ridden busses, Mike and Lucas begin picking them off.

Pulling my scarf over my face, I look at Ericson. "Get ready to move," I tell him. I grab my rifle and a bag of secondary explosives. "Stay low and if something happens and they find you, get in the Jeep and get the hell out of Dodge," I tell Lucas and Darby. "Jack, hit the buggies with the launcher. Anyone scrambling will try to retreat if they can. Make sure they don't."

Judging by his grin, I doubt at this point that I'll ever be able to pry the launcher away from him. "We got your back." He runs in the opposite direction and fires another grenade.

Crouching low, Ericson follows me down the ridge. We stay behind rocks and anything else we can use for cover. Once we're most of the way down, we duck behind a large boulder. "I don't think grenades are going to cut it," Ericson says as Jack fires again.

"They're meant to provide a distraction. We'll eliminate as many gray coats as we can and worry about the tanks last." Ericson nods, seeming to understand. "Wait for another blast and then get into position."

"The smoke screen is gonna be a real bitch," he reminds me.

"Could be worse," I say with a smile. "They could've been in an Abrams."

Ericson grins. "That's the truth." He hands me the radio. "Let's hope your plan works."

"Too late for hope. Going radio silent. Fire at will." I shut off the radio—not wanting to give up our position—and slip it into the satchel across my chest.

Fires blaze, and shots ring out as dozens of soldiers scream and scramble with nowhere to go. With Mike and Lucas, it doesn't take long for the NAF vehicles attempt to retreat.

That's our cue. We separate, and I spring to the back of the convoy as Jack and Hugo launch explosives at the vehicles. I fire as fast as I can hold down the trigger. It's chaos. The soldiers seem to have no idea where the firing is coming from. They shoot wildly all over the ridge. The blasts from the tank shake the ground, and a smoke screen appears just like we knew it would.

I race toward the end of the convoy and fire blindly within the smoke, wishing I had Darby's stupid goggles. I pull the pins of a few grenades and lob them into the center of the smoke and hurry forward. I hear calls for retreat and orders to fire at will. Maybe they'll all shoot each other, and we can go home early. Knowing I'm not that lucky, I empty the magazine straight ahead.

The tank in the back continues to fire high into the ridge. Pieces of earth crumble down as it shoots off as many rounds as it can. The smoke parts in a gust of wind, revealing a small group of soldiers. Using their confusion to my advantage, I take them all out.

I aim at a few who are trying to dive into a nearby vehicle, but I'm knocked backward as a grenade hits the buggy, flipping it and taking out the soldiers. I hit the ground hard, barely avoiding landing on the satchel of mines draped across my body.

I can't tell if that blast came from Jack or Hugo, but that was way too close for comfort.

Trying to regain my bearings, I see a soldier near the blast slowly get to his feet. He notices me noticing him. Dramatically, he pulls a knife from his belt. Well, shit. I try to stand, my legs only slightly wobbly, and bring up my rifle. He stares as if he's waiting for me to shoot. Happy to oblige, I pull the trigger, but nothing happens. My gun is jammed. I smack it a few times, but it's no use. Letting out a string of curses, I glance at the soldier now smiling at me.

Even through the blood on his face, it's easy to see the hatred in his eyes. He lets out a yell and races toward me. I barely have time to toss the rifle aside and slip the bag from my shoulder, dropping it to the ground before he slams into me.

All the air is knocked from my lungs when I hit the ground. Pain shoots through my chest as the real-life Hulk sits on my waist, pinning me to the pavement. He lifts his blade with both hands and jams it downward. I raise my arms and cross them at the wrists to block the move. He shifts angles, the blade now hovering right below my armpit. He leans into it, using his weight. For the first time in this fight, true fear consumes me. I grab his forearms and try desperately to push him off, but I'm no match for his oversized muscles. The tip of the blade closes in despite my best efforts. I clench my teeth as the knife presses through my shirt. Shit, this is gonna hurt.

I cry out as the blade pierces through my skin, sinking slightly between my ribs. Digging my heels into the dirt, I focus all my strength into getting him off me. The knife slips in farther. I forgot how much it fucking *sucks* getting sliced open. Just as my arms start to give out, the pressure lifts, and I'm able to shove him off. I scramble away as his body drops, lifeless, a hole through the side of his head.

I rip the scarf down and gasp for breath, pulling in as much oxygen as I can. Pressing a hand over the wound, I hiss and wince. Feeling more wetness than I anticipated, I curse. Definitely not my best performance.

I look left to where the shot came from. Lucas. "Thanks, Maelstrom," I mutter. Not the first time my brother has had to bail me out of a sticky situation and the exact reason I wanted him through the scope. I take a quick peek at the wound. It doesn't appear to be as bad as I feared, though it stings like hell. "I'm getting too old for this." I groan.

Scooping up my pistol, I pull the scarf back over my face. I wipe the blood on the leg of my pants and push down the pain. Slipping my bag over my shoulder, I pull out the radio, bringing it to my lips, while trying to catch my breath. It hurts to breathe.

"Lucas, get the Jeep to me. Arming the mines." I shove the radio into the bag and glance at the battle that's still raging. While pressing my hand to my ribs, I sprint to the side of the road.

The tank is reversing, focusing on the retreat. I lie flat in the shallow ditch between the base of the ridge, and muscle memory takes over, and I set the mines as quickly as possible.

Popping my head up, I see the tank and one of the busses. Soldiers are clinging to the sides, wanting anything to get them out of this death trap more quickly. Another grenade hits, and I use the explosion to race toward the path of the reversing tank. I pull the mines, lining them up across the road. As I lay each one, I turn the indicator to "armed," then sprint out of there, zigzagging as best I can to avoid enemy fire.

The Jeep shows up out of the smoke. Lucas leans over and opens the passenger side door. I dive in, oh so gracefully, pressing my hand to my side, and he's peeling away before I can even pull the door shut. He races back up the side of the mountain and away from the fight below. "This is no time for getting hurt." His voice is filled with worry.

I grit my teeth and pull the scarf down. "Would've been much worse if you'd missed that shot. You're my guardian angel." I pat his leg. We're barely away when an explosion rocks the entire cliff and rattles the Jeep. The tank must've hit the mines. Lucas glances in my direction, and I roll my head on the back of the seat to look at him with a smile. "Nailed it."

I unhook my rig and take a deep breath. Pressing on the wound, I groan and shut my eyes. I hope William and the others can put an end to the fight quickly and without me in the trenches. I'm about tapped out.

Lucas takes us high up and out of sight, the sound of explosions continuing to echo from the valley below. "How do we look?" I ask when we stop.

"If we stay on target and don't be stupid, we'll come out of this alive," he says.

I slip off the rig and place it on the ground just outside of the passenger side door. "Does that mean we're winning?"

He nods. It's rather reluctant, but he nods all the same. I stumble out of the Jeep and carefully lift my shirt to inspect my side. Oh, I'm going to have some lovely bruises and a brand-new scar. At least the bleeding has slowed. I turn up the radio, waiting to hear if William or the others have an update. Lucas stares at me with a concerned expression, one I wave off. "I'm good. Go back and help. I'll be fine."

I kick the passenger door closed, and Lucas takes off to the cliff edge, rifle in hand. I sit on the ground and wipe the sweat from my face, collapsing backward on the grass and closing my eyes. This was a really stupid plan, and one of these days, my arrogance is going to get me killed. Or the people around me killed. Again. The weight of that realization hurts more than the stab wound. I listen to the gunfire and explosions for a moment while I try to regroup. My entire body hurts.

"Are you dead?"

Opening my eyes just a crack, I see Darby standing over me. She looks more annoyed than worried. "Not yet."

She sighs. "Jack wants the Jeep so he and the others can take a final sweep. You mind not dying while we're gone?"

Instead of answering, I close my eyes and wave her off. It's only then that I notice the sound of gunfire has dwindled, and there are no more explosions.

"Don't fall asleep," Darby singsongs. "There are still raiders lurking around."

I manage a grunt and listen as she takes my Jeep. I wish I had the energy to yell out a warning not to crash my car. Does she even know how to drive? In the silence, I think of Kate and wonder if I'll ever see her again. I wonder if after today, she'll even *want* to see me again. I hesitated today when I thought Kate might be out there. I don't know how I'm going to fight in this war if keep hesitating because I may hurt Kate. What if I'm unable to pull the trigger when it really counts?

Looking at the orange sky, I shiver at the sudden drop in temperature. Can I separate personal feelings from what needs to be done? Do I even know the difference anymore? Focusing on the breeze and the faint sounds of the others down the cliff, I take slow breaths and try to clear my mind.

Slowly, I open my eyes when I hear the Jeep return. The sky is darker, and the sun has all but set. Lucas, Jack, and Darby file out. Lucas rushes to my side with a canteen, and I wave away his concern and gulp down the water.

I wipe my mouth with the back of my hand. "Took you long enough," I say, trying to make light of the situation.

Jack pushes the sunglasses on top of his head and stares at me with his arms crossed. "Would've taken less time if you hadn't tapped out early."

I can't help but laugh. A groan quickly follows, my hand finding my injury once again. Ugh, it hurts to laugh. "I'm so out of shape."

Jack reaches out and hauls me, none too gently, to my feet. He gives me a once over. "Stabbed again?"

"Unfortunately." He snorts, and I narrow my eyes. "You know, you didn't have to blast that car right in front of me. You almost blew me to bits."

He looks incredibly confused. "I didn't blast anything near you."

Must've been Hugo. "Some deadeye," I mutter bitterly.

Mike drives up in the buggy he used on the opposite side of the ridge and jogs over.

"You okay?" I ask.

He spits out his gum and wipes his brow with the back of his hand. "Yeah, yeah, I'm good. You?"

"Never better."

Lucas hands out more water, and we all take a moment to collect ourselves. Once I've had my fill, I lower the tailgate of my Jeep and wait for William, Ericson, and Hugo to join the rest of us.

"Here." Jack tosses me the small first aid kit.

I wince again when I reach to catch it. I carefully remove my shirt and reinspect the wound. It's hard to tell the damage with the dried blood caked around it.

Mike places his rifle beside me and removes his shooting gloves, exchanging them for the medical gloves in the kit. "Let me help." Gently, he rinses and cleans the area, and I get my first real look at what we're dealing with. It's not as bad as I feared, but it's still deep enough to give me trouble if I don't tend to it.

Mike carefully probes the skin. "You might need stitches."

"We don't have time for that." I take a deep breath and nod toward the bandages. "Just patch me up. I'll take care of it when we get back to town."

Mike looks at me as if he knows I will *not* be doing that.

The others finally show. "I still think we should've stayed in Sioux Falls and gone after Omaha," Ericson mumbles.

Mike applies a stack of gauze pads and holds them to my side. I groan. "Attempting another ambush at Sioux Falls would've been reckless."

Jack laughs from his position against the side of the Jeep. "Yeah, like what we did today wasn't." His posture is relaxed, negating the disapproval in his tone. It's clear he loved the fight and a chance for some revenge.

"They went through the mountains," I say. "We'll always have the advantage through the mountain ranges. Ow!" I look down as Mike wraps tape around my ribs a little too tightly.

He looks at me sheepishly. "Sorry. Elise is much better at this."

"She's definitely gentler." I swat his hand away. "Omaha is gone. The whole area around it is under NAF rule."

"Dani's right," William says, Hugo at his side. "The best we can do is stop them from pushing any farther west. Today was a huge success. We prevented them from establishing a foothold in Malmstrom with no Resistance fatalities. You all right?" he asks me, and I nod.

Mike finishes wrapping me up like a mummy. "That should be good until we get back."

"Thanks," I say. And I mean it. I take a moment to look at them all, beyond grateful that none of us were seriously injured or worse. I really need to start keeping my people at the forefront of my brain before my impulses cause irreparable damage. Like White River.

"We better head out," William says. "Raiders will be coming to check out the area, and I'm not looking for another fight today."

"What about all the stuff down there?" Ericson asks.

William tosses his vest and guns in the back seat of one of the buggies. "I'll give the Resistance stationed at Bozeman the coordinates when we get there, but I'm not sure there's much to salvage."

"They're going to love being on cleanup crew." Ericson chuckles.

As much as I'd like first dibs in the wreckage, I'm not going to argue about a fast departure. It'll be a miracle if I can make it back without falling asleep. Slipping off the tailgate, I grab my things and load them into the Jeep. That's when I notice Darby staring at the horizon.

"You okay?" I ask her.

"What? Yeah. I'm fine." She dismisses the question, but the waver in her voice says otherwise.

Lucas puts his hand on her shoulder and takes her shaking hands to steady them. "Casualties of war is something you never get used to."

Darby nods and rests her head on his shoulder. "Issue four."

I don't have it in me to correct her.

"She'll be okay," Jack says, sounding as if he's trying to be reassuring. "I'm sure it's just all the explosions and shit that has her rattled."

"Maybe," I halfheartedly agree. Being thrust into war is different than defending your home from the occasional raider attack. I've been in it so long that when I'm fighting, I feel separated from reality, desensitized. I forget sometimes that this kind of thing isn't normal for most of humanity.

Frowning, I watch Darby settle into the back of the Jeep. A gust of cold air whips through, stinging my skin and bringing with it the smell of smoke and gasoline. My entire body itches, and I'm desperate to get clean.

"You good to drive?" Jack asks from beside the Jeep, snapping my attention back to the mission.

"Yeah," I tell him. "Yeah, I'm good."

He holds out his arm to keep me from sliding in the driver's seat. "I meant Mike. No way I'm getting in this thing with you behind the wheel."

I'm offended until Lucas pats the seat beside him in the back, looking content to sit between me and Darby. Sighing, I get in and pull the door shut while Jack gets in the passenger side and Mike in the driver's seat.

The ride to Bozeman isn't terribly far, but I fall asleep well before we arrive. When Lucas wakes me, the Jeep is parked, and the others are already unpacking. My side hurts. My arm hurts. My body hurts. But no one was majorly injured, and we all lived to tell the tale of taking out an NAF convoy singlehandedly.

Lucas helps me carry the last of our supplies to our rooms for the night. Darby excuses herself. She looks rough. "Is she going to be okay?" I ask. No one knows her better than my brother.

"The sun will rise again," he says and sighs.

"Too tired to think of something that might make a little more sense?" I ask lightheartedly. He laughs a little and shrugs. I put my hand on his shoulder. "Thanks for today. For saving my life. Again."

He smiles. "The sun will rise again."

Rolling my eyes, I give him a playful shove. "Go get some sleep. You're delirious."

I wait until he's in his room and go into mine, lighting a single lantern and making a beeline for the shower, not minding at all that the water isn't connected to a generator and never gets close to warm.

Once I'm clean and my wound has been reassessed and dressed, I throw on a sweatshirt and sweatpants and crawl into bed. My last thoughts are of Kate and what she'll think of me after hearing about the convoy. Will she realize I'm the monster she was warned about? Or will she still think of me as the girl she got to know back in White River?

It doesn't take long before my questions fade, and images of White River burning and tanks exploding take over once again, thrusting me into a restless slumber.

We roll into Rapid City after lunch, still weary and exhausted. Avoiding William, who's escorted to the debriefing, the rest of us manage to drag ourselves to our rooms. Jack wants food, and Mike offers to go with him, promising to bring something back if we take up all the bags. Not sure it's an even trade, I sling his duffel over my shoulder and make him promise to bring extra whiskey with my lunch.

Lucas drags his feet behind me, shouldering his bag and Jack's. Darby whines from behind him, and I glance at them as I open the door to my room. "How can you two still be tired? You slept the entire way back."

"It wasn't real sleep," Darby protests and drops her bag within the doorway of my room before dramatically falling on my bed. Lucas mimics her.

"You two have your own room, you know." They both ignore me, and I head to the bathroom to wash my hands. "At least come clean your hands before you touch all my stuff."

The only response is someone banging on my door.

"That was fast," I say, assuming it's Jack and Mike with lunch. But it isn't lunch. "Jess? Are you okay?"

Her long, red hair is pulled back, and she clutches her walking stick tightly in her hand. Her oversized sweatshirt makes her look younger than sixteen. "Are you alone?"

"Lucas and Darby are with me. What happened?"

She takes a step closer, and I lead her in the room. Her brow is creased, and I'm worried that something awful has happened. "You have a message. A courier hand delivered it to me this morning, bypassing proper channels. He said it was urgent." She pulls out a sealed piece of paper from her jeans pocket.

"Does anyone else know about this?"

"Wyatt. He led me here and is waiting down the hall." She uses her walking stick to find the bed. Lucas guides her to the edge, and he and Darby scoot over to make room.

"What does it say?" Darby asks.

"It's a set of coordinates with a date," I say. "Marked urgent priority from Kate." My stomach drops. I don't know if she's warning me about something or wants to confront me about the convoy. I hand the piece of paper to Lucas, who rushes over to the maps.

Jess is quiet for a moment before asking, "Who's Kate?"

Lucas glances at me, the same worried look on his face that I must have on mine. "She's the general's daughter," I tell Jess.

Her face reads a million things, a million questions. "Katelyn Turner? One of the prisoners you held at White River?" I can see the gears working overtime as she tries to piece together the puzzle. "Dani, are you working with the NAF?"

The accusation hits like a slap across the face. "How can you even ask me that?"

"I don't know, you like to keep secrets," Jess fires back. I ignore the hum of agreement from Darby.

"She's the one who tipped me off about White River being under attack. She's more of a…contact?" No, no that doesn't seem right. She's more than that. Much more than that.

"A contact you want to get naked with," Darby supplies.

I turn to her with a glare. "Not helping." I take one of Jess's hands. "I promise that I'll tell you later. I'll tell you everything. But do not mention this message to anyone. Not even George. Please."

Jess nods slowly, though I know she isn't happy. I don't ask her to keep things from her grandfather lightly, but this isn't something I want anyone to know about. Not yet, at least.

Lucas points to a spot on the map. "There weren't many places Major Maelstrom felt safe, but this place was one of them." I rush over to see.

A million thoughts go through my mind. Kate wants to meet at an old Resistance outpost. Immediately. Either something big must be happening or it's a trap.

"I have to go." I frantically start throwing things into a bag. If I take the Jeep, I can stop and refuel, get some food, and get there by sundown. But I have to hurry.

"How do you know this isn't a trap?" Jess asks.

I shake my head, knowing in my gut that Kate wouldn't do that. "It's not."

"Retaliation?" Darby supplies.

"A warning," Lucas says and hands me a radio.

"Must be big if someone you held prisoner who wants to see you naked is willing to meet with you face-to-face," Jess says.

I shoot another look at Darby for making that a thing. She shrugs innocently. "Whatever it is, I'm going to find out." I grab my bag and take the jacket Lucas hands me. "I'll be back in a day or so. I'll check in so you know I made it." I turn the radio to a specific frequency and show Lucas.

He nods. "Major Maelstrom standing by."

I pat his arm awkwardly, trying to provide a little comfort and turn to Jess. "Lucas has the frequency. Remember, don't tell anyone."

"I don't like this," she says. She wrings her hands nervously in her lap.

She has a point. Why does Kate want to see me? My gut tells me it's not a trap, and it also tells me it's not retaliation. Lucas is probably right.

It's gotta be a warning of some sort. But face-to-face? It's something big. It has to be. And I need to find out what.

It has nothing at all to do with the fact that I'm buzzing just to see her again.

I lean in and kiss Jess's cheek. "I promise, I'll be fine."

"Bring protection!" Darby calls.

Giving her the finger, I fling the door open and run straight into William. So much for a swift exit.

"I was just coming to see you." He looks at me curiously. "What's going on? Where are you going?"

I say the first thing that comes to mind. "I have to run an errand."

"Is everything okay?" He looks at the radio in my hand.

Hastily, I shove it into the duffel. "Yup."

Whether he believes me or not, he presses on with the reason for his sudden appearance. "Your errand is going to have to wait. The mayor wants a meeting. Now."

I push past him and roll my eyes. "Yeah, well, I requested to meet with her days ago, and she ignored me. Now I'm busy."

William's voice stops me. "Dani, this is serious. She says it's urgent."

"Yeah, well, so is my errand."

"Dani."

I grip the strap of the duffel and take a deep breath. I turn, and William looks at me with a serious, yet pleading, expression. I can tell that this is important, but after him ignoring my request for aid and the mayor ignoring my request for an audience, I'm over people telling me no and then making demands when they need my help.

"It was urgent when I requested to see her. It was urgent when I asked you for help. It was *urgent* that you both listened to *me*. You chose not to. Lucas can fill in for me if it's that important. He's more diplomatic and forgiving than I am, anyway." I turn back toward the staircase. "Now if you'll excuse me, I have an *urgent* errand to run."

CHAPTER FOUR: THE OUTPOST

KATE

With my bag slung over my shoulder, I stare at the old pickup. It's more pink than red, and there's half a logo, worn and peeling, across the driver's side door. It's not much to look at, but it's been sanctioned for my leave, and it'll off-road, so I'm not going to complain.

I wait for the supply specialist to finish gathering trade items and the rest of my requested gear and wonder if this was such a good idea. Should I have let Archie send the warning to Dani instead of requesting a meet? Is this an unnecessary risk I'm taking for purely selfish reasons?

"Nice civvies."

I bristle at the unwelcome voice that strikes through my panic. If we weren't on base with other personnel around, I'd gladly take that smug tone down a peg or two.

Simon focuses on my duffel and casual clothes. "Sneaking off somewhere? Or finally deserting?"

"I am still your commanding officer, *Lieutenant*," I remind him. "It would be in your best interest to remember that."

"Oh yes, forgive me." He turns and gives a casual salute. "Ma'am."

I clench my teeth and control my tone. "I could write you up for insubordination."

"You could." He leans closer, his warm breath on the side of my face making me flinch. "But I'm on a personal and critical mission from the general herself, so I doubt any charges made against me would be pressed. You see, the general outranks you, and that makes me virtually untouchable."

I flex, itching to deck him. What he just did to White River and the people there deserves a whole hell of a lot more than a swift backhand. It enrages me that he walks around, proud of what he did, boasting to anyone and everyone who will listen.

"You burned down a defenseless town, Simon," I say, disgusted and unimpressed. "Hardly something to brag about."

He scoffs. "They weren't defenseless. Danielle Clark was there."

"Except she wasn't when you set fire to everything. And when she showed, you couldn't even stop her from murdering your entire unit. Instead, you ran like a coward. Nothing about your assignment was impressive, least of all you." His smug expression is replaced with one of anger, and he takes a step toward me.

"Here are the keys, ma'am." The supply specialist reappears before Simon can respond. "And a long-range radio. Your requested items are currently being loaded into the bed of the truck." She stands at attention and salutes when she sees Simon. "Sir."

"At ease, soldier," he says, turning back into arrogant-asshole mode. He points to an officer's vehicle. "I need one of those for me and my men." He leads the specialist away, and I glare, my body still buzzing with adrenaline.

Gripping the keys tightly, I slip on my officer's headset, connect it to the radio, and toss them both, along with my bag, on the passenger's seat. Once the rest of my items are secure in the truck bed, I give Simon one last glance and slide into the cabin.

Any doubts I had about warning Dani in person are gone as I start the truck and get the hell out of Dodge.

The first hour of the trip is smooth sailing, considering the state of the roads and landscape, but I can't stop checking my rearview mirror. Nothing important has come through the sporadic chatter on my headset, although I don't put it past my mother to secretly have me followed. I can't remember the last time I was off base alone even with the occasional shore leave. Having the general's permission to leave seems too good to be true.

The second half of the trip is less than desirable. Archie wasn't kidding about needing a truck. Too focused on the road, I don't have time to be paranoid about being followed. Overgrown grass splits the old pavement so widely, I'm constantly having to detour.

The quick two-hour trip slowly turns into four, and I'm looking forward to getting out of this truck and stretching. Rubbing my lower back after hitting another bump and flying off my seat, I make a mental note that I should have someone look at the suspension on this piece of junk as soon as I get back.

By the time I arrive, the sun is almost set. Double-checking my map, I pull up outside a quaint little town about a hundred or so miles southwest of the base. There doesn't appear to be much here, just several houses and few buildings bordering a large lake. I scan the perimeter again. This is the place Archie directed me to?

I shove the headset and the radio into my bag.

The town's defenses aren't anything to brag about: homemade fencing; no guards on rotation, minus the one standing at the entrance; no mounted guns. They don't seem at all hostile. Interestingly enough, I'm not sure this town considers itself a part of anything, let alone the Resistance. Although it's hard to tell by just one look. It's not as if Resistance-supporting towns hoist a banner with their upside-down triangle along the gates as a welcoming sign.

Either way, this place appears to be devoid of alliances at first glance. And by the look of it, I doubt they are harboring any ex-Resistance fighters. They're probably fishermen and farmers, not yet touched by the war. It makes me sad to think of them having to choose a side sooner rather than later. With the war on their doorstep, I doubt the town will stay quiet for much longer.

I stop as the single guard holds up a hand. He appears middle-aged, with shaggy brown hair graying on the sides. He has an old rifle slung across his chest, his finger nowhere near the trigger. He doesn't look as though he's expecting to use it. That's his first mistake.

I roll down my window.

"Good evening, ma'am. Care to state your business?"

"Just passing through," I say. "Only need to stay the night and make a few trades if you're willing. Then I'll be on my way."

He glances in the bed of the truck and carefully pulls the tarp back. Nothing but a rolled-up mattress and sleeping bag. He peers inside the cab next, his gaze on my duffel. "Any weapons in that bag?" Second mistake. Check, don't ask.

"Of course," I tell him honestly.

He stares for a moment, seemingly surprised by my answer. "Intend to use 'em?"

"Not unless I have to." It's a strange question and his third mistake—not assuming someone intends to fire their guns—but I gather he's sizing me up more than anything. I'm alone and outnumbered. It would be stupid to take on a single town on my own.

Then I think about Dani defending White River against Simon, and my stomach flips. I picture her rage and anguish at seeing her home burning, and it makes me sick to think I had any part of that. If only I was successful in preventing it.

"Well, all right, then." The guard's voice snaps me out of my thoughts before I can venture down that rabbit hole. "You can leave your truck over there." He points to a clearing beyond the gates. "There's a building about fifty meters beyond that with a sign on the door. They'll take you in for the night. Don't go causing any trouble, you hear?"

"Yes, sir. I won't be any trouble." Mistake four, taking me at my word. He hums in acknowledgement, and I slowly pull my truck to the clearing. There are a few people wandering around, some with fish strung on a line, others with tools. No one seems that interested in my arrival beyond the occasional curious glance. Mistake number five. At this point, I need to just stop counting.

A cold breeze floats past. I shiver and zip my coat a little higher. Who knew the wasteland would get this cold this fast?

I pull the tarp back over the items in the back and with my duffel in tow, hurry to the lodgings to get warm.

A bell rings when I step inside and take in my surroundings. There's a counter with a handful of old stools and a few tables scattered around the side. Behind the counter are some items for trade, and I wonder how much I can get with the modest amount of tech I was allocated. The place looks to be a cross between a general store and an eatery.

I clean my hands thoroughly in the water bowl by the door and wipe them on a provided towel. Eventually, an elderly woman shuffles in from the back. She looks surprised to see me. "Good evening," I say. "I was directed here to inquire about a room for the evening."

"Oh, my goodness," the woman says with a kind smile. She examines me closely. My navy-blue jacket and dark pants are plain and give nothing away about who I am, but somehow, they still manage to stand out. "We don't get many visitors out this way. Nonetheless, I'm Marium, and this is my establishment."

"It's lovely." I look around with a smile. "I have some items for trade if you're interested."

"Of course, dear. I'm always up for a good trade. What are you in need of besides the room?" She takes a step closer, a sign of trust. Her eyes are a deep blue that seems to sparkle in the light of the lanterns and stand out in contrast to her light complexion.

"A warm shirt, maybe a new pair of pants. A hot meal would be nice." I place my bag on one of the stools and open it to reveal several batteries and an old countertop fan that surprisingly still works.

Marium hums. "We don't use much tech out this way," she says. I wait while she looks it over. "The fan might be useful during the warm season. What we really need are parts for our generators. Voltage regulators and a new battery charger. You got any of those?"

"I'm sorry, no."

She stares at me for a moment and smiles. "I'll go ahead and take it all."

Watching as she goes through the items, I'm impressed with how carefully she runs her calloused fingers over everything. Her bright eyes finally lift to mine. There's a kindness there that not even her age has extinguished, and I'm guessing she's seen a lot.

When she's finished, she shows me her spare clothes, and I pick out a thick red sweatshirt and a worn pair of denim jeans. She tosses in a navy-blue wool hat with a large white pom-pom on top. "My son's wife made this. It'll match your jacket," she says with a wink.

"Thank you." I take the clothes, glad to have a spare outfit.

"I'll put you in the best room and bring up some warm water for you to wash. How does some bread and a plate of our catch of the day sound?" At this point, anything other than prepackaged snacks sounds wonderful, and I tell her so. "Grab your bag, I'll show you to your room."

I follow her up the loud wooden stairs, holding the clothes against my chest. We wind around two landings and finally arrive at the top. Marium pulls a long key from her pocket and guides it into the lock until it pops open with a loud click. She steps to the side to allow me to slide past her into the small space.

She places a lantern on the table beside the bed. I fight a yawn as I take in the double bed with a thick red quilt. There's a single chair in the corner by the lone window and a table with a basin by the door with two towels. It isn't much, but it feels cozy, and it'll be all I need tonight.

"This is perfect, Marium. Thank you."

"I'll be back with hot water and food in a bit, dear. I think I have a heater around here somewhere, too. It'll be getting cold tonight."

"I appreciate your generosity," I tell her honestly.

She pats my arm and leaves me with the single lantern.

For a brief moment, I wonder if she would be so kind if she knew who I was: Major Katelyn Turner of the NAF. Swallowing a groan, I rub my eyes. It's going to be a struggle to stay awake long enough to eat, despite the early hour. I think about turning on the radio from base to listen to the chatter.

Deciding I don't want Marium to ask questions if she hears it, I leave it off and in my bag. I'll check in in the morning. I doubt very seriously anything significant has happened in the few hours I've been away. Instead, I collapse face-first into the mattress and await Marium's return. My stomach rumbles just thinking about it.

Unsurprisingly, my thoughts wander to Dani while I wait. Is this what it feels like to be a scavenger? Hungry and paranoid? I'm not accustomed to fending for myself. I lived a privileged life from one military base to the next where necessities were always provided. I think I could do it, though. Scavenge through the wastelands with Dani by my side.

Immediately, I laugh at myself. From NAF officer to rebel scavenger? I'm clearly more tired and delirious than I realized.

I wake right after sunrise. The room is nice and warm, thanks to the small heater, and it takes me a few minutes to get out of bed. The thought of seeing Dani motivates me to push off the blankets and get dressed in the new clothes, noting that the pants are a little snug but not uncomfortably so. I clean up and grab my jacket, nervous that Dani either never got my note or will choose not to meet me. I don't know which scenario is worse.

Not wanting to dwell on that, I decide to get something to eat and then check in with what's going on back on base. I still have a drive ahead of me, and I really don't want to overstay my welcome here.

When I get to the main level, Marium is awake and sorting through the items on display behind the counter, including what I've given her. She turns and smiles. "Why, hello there." She beckons me to the counter. "Sleep all right?"

"Yes, ma'am," I say. "The room was great. Thank you."

An older gentleman sits off to the side, head tilted toward a battered radio that doesn't appear to be on. He picks through a plate of food, and like most of the town, doesn't seem interested in my arrival.

I leave a stool between us and take a seat.

Marium motions at my shirt. "The clothes seem to fit. Do you like them?"

I look at myself. Despite the small hole in the knee, the entire outfit is just what I was looking for. "They're perfect."

She looks very pleased at my response. "We didn't get to speak much last night. Where are you from?"

"East." It's an honest answer and one I hope doesn't give away too much. I'm not in my territory. And I still have no idea how these people feel about the war or the NAF. I chance a glance at the older gentleman. He's wearing an old hunting vest on top of a long-sleeve flannel shirt, rolled up on his forearms, revealing his deeply tanned skin. His hair is carefully styled and combed to one side, and the backs of his hands are scarred and worn.

She pours me a glass of water. "What brings you this far west?"

I take the water gratefully. "I'm relocating."

"By yourself?" She tsks. "That's mighty bold. Any place in particular?"

"Eventually farther south, nowhere permanent as of yet." The radio clicks, and the man leans in closer, but nothing appears to come through.

"Well, if it's the simple life you're after, southwest is the way to go," Marium continues. "There are plenty of folks who would gladly take you in if you're willing to work. Looks like the NAF is moving north, if that's who you're trying to avoid."

"Not if the Resistance has any say about it," the man says, finally showing interest in something other than the radio. "I'm glad they're finally doing something about those gray coats around here. They've been messing around back east for too long, if you ask me."

Marium shakes her head. "Nobody *did* ask, you old coot."

I focus on him, my heart rate picking up. "What do you mean?"

"Oh, there was an attack up north last night," Marium says waving a hand as if she's trying to dismiss the incident as no big deal.

I freeze. "An attack?"

"An entire NAF convoy was destroyed," the man says simply.

All the air deflates from my lungs. My head spins. This can't be happening. An attack? Was Dani involved?

Marium sighs. "Not sure how they wrangled enough fighters to pull that off."

"They didn't need many. Not with Danielle Clark leading the charge. William's been too focused on politics. All that talking and not enough doing. Good to see Danielle back in the saddle. Things can finally get done." The man glances my way with a toothless smile.

"Oh hush, you don't know anything of the sort," she scolds.

"I do, too."

Dani led the charge? How could she do that without telling me? Are any of my colleagues alive? Is *Dani* alive? I imagine what must be happening back on base and how my mother is handling this development. Why the hell did I turn off my radio?

I should get back. I need to get back to base. They're probably pulling together enough units for a counterattack. No, I can't get back to base, I have to warn Dani. If she's alive. I hope she's alive.

"Are you okay, dear?"

Marium regards me with a strange expression. Ignoring her, I turn to the old man. "Were you there? At the attack? Did you see it?"

He laughs and shakes his head. "Me? No. The radio said—"

"You and that damn radio!" Marium throws her hands up, clearly annoyed. "Can't you see you're upsetting our guest?"

Their arguing seems muted as I try to figure out what I should do. Two convoys departed yesterday. One to Denver and the other to Malmstrom. "You said the convoy was up north?"

"Resistance took the whole thing out," he confirms.

Marium waves, trying to prevent the man from talking any further. "You're as pale as a ghost. Stop with all this nonsense, Earl." She turns to me with a smile. "Never you mind all this gossip. What would you like to eat, hun?"

"Anything is fine. Really." After hearing the news, I'm not really that hungry anyway. "Do you know if Dani survived?"

The man gives me a quizzical look. "It's Danielle Clark. Of course she survived." My stomach flips, and I breathe a sigh of relief. "I heard she took out a hundred and fifty soldiers, too."

Ninety-five, I think solemnly.

Ninety-five people who had families and friends. Who had hopes and dreams. All gone.

I swallow the nausea down, grateful at least that Dani appears to be fine. That's all I wanted, wasn't it? For Dani to be safe? Then why am I equal parts relieved and pissed?

My face must give away a range of emotions because Marium continues to stare like she knows I'm not quite being honest. Instead of pressing, she slowly nods, almost like she hears my internal conflict. "I'll go ahead and get breakfast started for you. Then we can see about packing you some food so you can be on your way."

If she suspects me of anything, she doesn't voice it. When I turn back to the old man, he's returned his attention to his food, his head tilted toward the radio as it clicks once more. It's only then that I see a Resistance tattoo on his forearm half-hidden under his sleeve.

The drive to the outpost is stressful. The headset is turned up to full volume, and I listen intently to the Grand Forks frequency. All the frantic chatter coming through has confirmed my suspicion that the base is in a complete and total frenzy. I was so stupid to have left it turned off for so long.

From the sound of it, the general has ordered a unit to the scene to recover what they can and reinforce the base at Malmstrom before that too, falls to the Resistance. She also requested even more troops to start pushing this way from the east.

Surprisingly, my unit is still moving to Omaha later in the week. Knowing the general, she's already deployed scouts to make sure the road is secure, something she should've done with the convoy that Dani destroyed near Malmstrom. Hindsight is a funny thing.

Still, I know she won't make that mistake again.

I wonder if my mother regrets giving me a few days off. There's no doubt she'd be grilling me about this attack. Did Dani tell me about it? Did I know she was going to do this? Am I certain she didn't hint at where she's hiding?

"I was her prisoner not her goddamn guest," I yell into the empty truck.

Prisoner. The word seems so inadequate. But that's all it was, right? I was merely her prisoner, and she was my captor. I can't even convince myself of the lie. No wonder my mother doesn't believe me.

It was so much more than that. Deeper somehow.

I worry for the hundredth time if she got my message. Or is she still up north after her assault? Surely, Archie didn't send my message all the way to Malmstrom. Wait, did he know about the attack? Is that why the message was going to take so long to get to her? Archie and I need to have a serious discussion when I get back.

I listen anxiously for mention of my name. But it never comes. Another name strangely absent is Simon's. My gut tells me he's either off the grid or receiving orders through a highly classified and encrypted channel. Both are unsettling.

After two hours of overanalyzing and dissecting every move made by both Dani and my mother, and lack of news regarding Simon, I reach the coordinates and slow to a stop. Is this right? I get out and climb on the hood and then up the windshield to stand on the roof for a better advantage. The midmorning sun is harsh, and even with my sunglasses, I have to use my hand to block some of the light. There's nothing but high grass and a scattering of trees.

I scan the area again when I see a structure tucked between overgrown bushes. Climbing back in the truck, I make my way over slowly with my pistol balanced on my thigh. I haven't seen any raiders or that there's any indication that Archie set me up for an ambush, but after yesterday, who knows what could be out there in this overgrown landscape?

The closer I get, the more uneasy I become. I see no vehicles. I know Archie said Dani wouldn't even get my message until this morning, and there was no way she'd beat me here, especially not with her adventures last night, but I still can't help but wonder if I'm in the right spot.

Pulling the truck to the side of the building, I kill the engine. I roll down the windows, waiting and listening for any signs of people or an attack. All I hear are birds and bugs chirping and buzzing in the tall grass.

The wind whistles through the open windows. But other than the sounds of nature, I hear nothing.

Slowly, I step out of the truck and hold the pistol tightly. There's nothing but a few caved-in houses scattered around. Turning back toward the only building still standing, I prepare myself to enter and find who knows what waiting inside.

The structure itself is pretty sound, if extremely old. The windows are cracked but sturdy, and at least the door is still on its hinges. Turning the knob, I ready my pistol and lift my glasses, steading myself. The door creaks open and lets in a flood of light.

Inside is still and silent. I half expect a bomb or some other trap to go off the second I step past the threshold.

Just in case, I take a careful step within. The floorboard creaks, and I flinch and stop. Nothing happens. Taking another cautious step forward, I look around. There's an old sofa covered with a plastic sheet facing a fireplace to my right. Straight ahead is a small kitchen with a square table in the center and two chairs. The appliances are worn and definitely not usable, but the table and chairs appear to be in good shape.

To my left is a wall with an open door. Stepping closer, I peer inside. The tattered curtains are pulled closed, casting the room in darkness. In the middle of the room is a decent-size bed with a dresser and a closet. A solid wood chest is at the foot of the bed, with a lantern on the single nightstand.

I walk inside and press on the mattress. The dust that fills the air makes me cough. Archie was right about that, at least. Definitely won't be sleeping there.

A washroom is attached to the other wall, and I know for certain that running water will not work out here. Not that I'd trust it anyway. I close the door and open the curtain to let in more light, relieved to find the place void of raiders, animals, and so far, bombs.

Once I tie back the curtains, something on the window frame catches my eye. A symbol carved into the wood: an inverted triangle with a horizontal line splitting it in half and two more diagonal lines along the right-hand side.

The sign of the Resistance. At least I'm in the right place.

❖

After wiping down the surfaces and uncovering the sofa, I pull the nightstand from the bedroom to the front door and place a bowl of clean water and a towel atop the surface. I find plenty of wood stacked off to the side of the fireplace for a fire.

Not bothering with my headset, I set my radio on the table and listen to the chatter on a low volume after checking in. The only reply was a "Roger that," and there wasn't a request to come back. Relieved to be able to stay, a part of me is curious that I wasn't demanded to return.

Trying to stay away from conspiracy theories as to why, I focus on getting set up when, *if*, Dani arrives. Something else I don't want to dwell on.

First, I open the windows. The smell of the house is musty, and there's dust on the floor, but the fresh air should help. Despite the chill that enters through the window, I want to be able to hear anyone approaching.

Adding oil to the two lanterns I brought, I take the third from the bedroom and set them aside. Next, I push the sofa back as far as I can and set up the air mattress. It takes a while to inflate with the hand pump, but I'm grateful for the distraction. Once filled, I cover it with my sleeping bag and fresh linens, placing the top of the mattress against the front of the sofa, which will act as a makeshift headboard, while keeping the bed close to the fireplace. I wonder briefly if I should move the sofa in front of the door come nightfall to act as another barrier. The thought makes me wonder where Dani will choose to sleep should she show up. My stomach shifts uneasily, and I wonder if I'm too presumptuous in thinking she'll want to share a bed.

Not going to worry about that, either. I glance at the two pillows on the bed in the other room and decide against them, not wanting to encounter what could be living inside. The thought makes me shudder. Quickly, I lock them in the closet. With nothing left to do, I settle at the table near the kitchen to eat a late lunch and wait. I try not to think of the convoy or of Dani not showing and instead listen to the chatter. Not much has changed. Things are still relatively frantic, but the barking of commands seems to be slowing while they try to regain some sort of control.

Still, I wonder if I made things worse by leaving.

A huge part of me is relieved I left when I did. If I had waited until this morning, I would've known about the attack. And I know with absolute certainty that I never would've been able to slip out, and Dani would've come to an empty rendezvous point. That thought is somehow more upsetting to me than if she doesn't show.

I tap my foot anxiously. I hope like hell Archie was able to relay my message.

The sun begins to set, and the sky is colored with vibrant pinks and oranges. I start a fire and light two lanterns, placing one by the sofa and the other on the kitchen table. The fire crackles, as does my radio. Things are quiet back on base, but my nerves are still fried.

I don't think Dani is coming.

I try not to be disappointed, but I fail miserably. Archie warned me this was a possibility. I should've taken him more seriously.

Resigning myself to the fact that she isn't coming, I close and latch one of the windows and move to the second when the distant sound of a car engine stops me in my tracks.

Rushing to turn off the radio, I grab my pistol and carefully slip back to the window and peer out. I hold my breath. Relieved, I register Dani's Jeep. But the relief is short-lived, and my heart speeds up with panic. Is she angry with me? Did she bring anyone with her? Is she okay? Was this a bad idea?

She steps out of the car, and I retreat into the house. When the front door opens, my heart feels as though it stops beating altogether. She stands in the doorway, the orange light behind her casting her in shadow, and my breath catches. She's still wearing her red sunglasses, but her scarf is pulled down around her neck. Her hair is partially pulled back, down but out of her face, and the brown waves seem to cascade behind her.

My eyes trail slowly downward from her tight, black, long-sleeve top and fitted pants, her fingerless gloves shoved carelessly in her front pocket, down to her clunky boots, strapped tight high above her ankles. There isn't a trace of any kind of weapon, but she still looks deadly.

And absolutely stunning.

She glances at the gun still held tightly in my fist, and I quickly place it on the kitchen table. Every word I have ever known gets caught in my throat. I watch her shoulders rise and fall until she tilts her head to the side ever so slightly, almost curiously, staring at me.

I want her to say something. Anything. I'm desperate to hear her voice. But the simplest movement, the slightest tick of her eyebrow rising ignites something inside me. "I'm surprised you came. You must be exhausted after taking out an entire convoy." I'm angry at what she did to my soldiers, and I'm pissed at her reckless behavior.

To her credit, Dani doesn't flinch. She lifts her hand and removes her sunglasses, hanging them from the front of her shirt. Her eyes don't leave mine. All I can do is stare back and try to control my breathing.

Finally, she turns and cleans her hands at the bowl by the door, taking her time.

"Did you leave *any* of them alive?" My voice cracks ever so slightly, and I hate myself for it.

Dani slowly dries her hands and looks at me. I can't read her expression, and her silence is absolutely unnerving. The way she stares cracks something inside. Now is not the time for anger. It doesn't matter how casual she appears; I know this is how she grieves. We saw it after her father died and now with White River…

"Dani," I whisper, knowing how she must be hurting and regretting my outburst. "I tried to warn you about Simon. I swear I didn't know. I didn't know my mother—"

She swiftly strides across the room, and my sentence is swallowed by her kiss. She glides her fingers through my hair and holds my head tightly. It's desperate and hard and conveys everything I know she wants to say but either can't or won't. It takes one eager swipe of her tongue against mine, and my body melts.

I grab the front of her shirt and fist the fabric tightly, urging us closer together. Our lips remain touching as I pull back just enough to breathe another apology. "I'm so sorry." I'm desperate for her to understand just how sorry I am.

She kisses me again.

"Dani, I'm—"

Dani pulls back and cups my cheeks. "I know."

I search her stormy gray eyes for any sign of betrayal. I see only sadness and loss. It breaks my heart. "He's coming after you, Dani. Simon. He won't stop. He—"

Her hands fall to my waist, and she pulls me against her. When her lips meet mine again, it's absolutely clear that she's not in the mood to talk. There are so many things I need to tell her, to warn her about, but it all seems to fade away into the back of my consciousness when she pulls off my shirt.

Succumbing to the moment, I eagerly kiss her back and reach to undo her pants.

I'll tell her everything in the morning.

The sun has long set, and the fire and lanterns are the only light in the small house in the middle of nowhere. With my head propped up on my hand, I look at her, fast asleep on her side facing me, one arm tucked under her head, the other loosely draped across my hip. I take note of the bandage that adorns her ribs, and my hand hovers over the second bandage on her shoulder. Gently, I run my fingers down her arm, stopping at the black ink on her forearm.

I loop my finger in circles against the sharp edges of the inverted triangle. The Resistance. Something I'm reminded of again and again as I continue to trace along the lines of her tattoo.

I can't help but notice how peaceful she looks when she sleeps. She doesn't look like the country's most ruthless killer. She doesn't look like a dangerous vigilante or the heartless renegade I'm constantly led to believe she is.

She looks like a woman. A beautiful, haunted woman.

I thread my fingers through hers and rest our joined hands on my hip, thinking of all the explosives she's built and all the harm they have brought. Of the convoy she just destroyed and the way she easily pulls the triggers of her guns and recklessly throws punches. My fingers slide against hers, and I also think about her rebuilding her home and burying my comrades. The same hands that fished and scavenged for her people and helped plant crops. I think about the gentle way these same calloused hands mapped out my body and easily pulled pleasure and release from me.

I lower my head and tuck my hand underneath so I'm level with the sleeping woman beside me. My body still thrums with aftershocks, and my mind continues to replay the way Dani shuddered as she murmured my name against my throat.

How is it that the one person I'm supposed to hate more than anyone else stirs these beautiful feelings inside me? How can that same woman awaken a part of me that I forgot existed? How can she make me feel beautiful and cared for when she's supposed to hate me?

I gently stroke the side of her face, pushing her hair behind her ear. She sighs and leans into the touch but doesn't wake. It makes me smile.

There is so much I want to ask her and even more that I want to tell her. I want to wake her and kiss her again and confess everything I'm feeling. But I know the burden she carries is heavy. And the weight of it has left her exhausted. So instead, I let her rest.

As I finally drift into slumber, I can't help but imagine what life would be like if we weren't on opposite sides of the war. Would we be able to find peace together? Would we even want to try? Or is the division the reason for the heightened tension between us? I know we can't keep this up, this fighting and risking everything for a few stolen moments. But here, right now, in *this* stolen moment, I am going to allow myself to dream of a life unburdened by war and the happiness I could find living in moments like this every single day.

Tonight, I'm going to forget about the bloodshed and the constant battles that rage around us. I'm going to forget that we are supposed to hate each other. I'm going to forget about the convoy and my mother and Simon. I'm going to try to just exist right here, right now. Tonight, I'm just going to forget.

Chapter Five: The Morning

Dani

I wake up slowly, pulling in a deep breath and inflating my lungs before slowly releasing a long, drawn-out sigh. My back arches, and I try to stretch only to find that my entire body aches with the motion. A sharp pain pulls at my side, and I press my hand against the bandage still taped below my armpit. Groaning, I open my eyes and try to regain my bearings. I blink several times and squint at the light pouring in through the window. It's well past sunrise. Crackling sounds of a fire and soft chatter from a radio off to the side only add to my initial confusion.

There's another soft sound beside me, and I turn to see Kate lowering a steaming cup of what I can only guess is tea, on the table where she's seated. She turns off the radio, silencing the sporadic voices coming through. The previous night comes rushing back at the sight of her.

A slight smile tugs at the sides of her mouth. "I wasn't sure you were going to wake up anytime soon. You sleep like the dead."

Taking in her dressed appearance, I frown. "How long have you been awake?"

"Long enough to restart the fire, wash up, and make some oatmeal and tea. Would you like some?"

How could I not have heard any of that? I rub the sleep from my eyes. "Why didn't you wake me?"

"It seemed like you needed the rest." She motions again to the bowls and kettle on the table in front of her. She wasn't kidding about the oatmeal and tea and lifts an extra cup, her eyebrows lifted in question.

"Yes, please." I yawn into the back of my hand and sit up, leaning against the front of the sofa. Reaching again to my side, I wince.

Kate watches me, worried. "You should change that bandage. It'll get infected."

Despite her worry being utterly adorable, I dismiss her concern with a wave and drop the sheet to get a good look at it. "It's fine. I've had worse. It's really not that deep." She squints at me skeptically for a brief moment. Whatever argument she was going to give dies, and her eyes drift to my exposed chest. I arch an eyebrow. "Why don't you come here, and I'll prove it to you?"

She shakes her head and gives me a scolding look. "You need food." She walks over and hands me a steaming cup of tea and oatmeal. "And wrap up, it's still cold in here."

Tucking the sheets back under my arms, I let the witty quip about her warming me up go unsaid. I ignore the pain in my side and sip the offered beverage and manage to suppress the whine at the sudden shift. Now that the adrenaline from the night before has passed, my side actually hurts like hell. Not that I'll never admit that to Kate.

Stirring the oatmeal, I try to muster the courage to actually eat the bland-looking food. If this is the type of gruel they serve in the NAF, it's a wonder Kate hasn't starved to death. I send a silent thank you into the universe for Rhiannon and her cooking. The thought stabs at my heart as the memory of her tavern burning resurfaces.

I shove a spoonful into my mouth and do my best to bypass all of my tastebuds. Eating for the sake of survival and not flavor is something I haven't had to do in a long time.

Kate is back in the kitchen, cleaning out her bowl using a jug of water. We sit in silence for a few minutes, avoiding each other's eyes. The silence is awkward and thick with tension. I'm sure she has a lot to say. It's not like I gave her the opportunity last night.

After forcing a few more bites of oatmeal down, I place it to the side. If we don't clear some of this air, we'll suffocate. No more procrastinating. I suck in a loud breath so she knows I'm about to plunge right in. "When are you going to Omaha?" I know her convoy will be leaving soon. I'm curious why Kate is here with me instead of preparing with her soldiers.

"Planning on putting people in position?" Her tone isn't aggressive, but the blow still lands.

"That's fair," I mumble, letting her have this one.

With a sigh of resignation, Kate makes her way over and slides down the front of the sofa, sitting on my left. She brings her knees up to her chest and rests her forearms on top of them. She drags her bare feet across the rumpled blanket. "My mom has more units coming in from the east. I leave at the end of this week once they get in." She turns to look at me. "Will you be attacking my convoy, too?"

And for a second time, it stings. Especially since I saved the last convoy she was on. "Second time's a low blow, Kate."

"Is it?" She shakes her head, her expression once again softening, hopefully realizing the bite of aggression is uncalled for. "Honesty hour?" she asks instead.

I'm not sure I want to change the subject, but until I've had my tea, I don't want to throw down just yet. I pick up the cup and take a hesitant sip of the hot liquid before settling in for her familiar game. "You first."

I barely have time to take another sip before she dives right in. "Why did you really tell me about the ambush on the Omaha convoy?"

"I needed the Resistance fighters in Sioux Falls relocated to White River, and William wouldn't do it until after the ambush," I tell her honestly.

Something shifts in her gaze. "So you used me to stop the convoy." Slowly, I nod. It sounds really, really shitty when she puts it like that. She has to know there's more to it than just that. She must know I couldn't stand to see something happen to her. "That's it? That's the only reason?" Okay, maybe she doesn't know.

"No. That's not the only reason." She stares at me and motions for me to continue. I redirect instead. "Why did you ask me to come here?"

She shifts a bit. Not uncomfortably but nervously. "I told you. Simon—"

"Is that the only reason?" I flip her question back to her.

Her tone matches mine when she answers. "No. That's not the only reason."

She looks at me for a long stretch, either debating whether she wants to continue or waiting for me to ask another question. I remain silent. This game was her idea, and I know by suggesting it she must have something else she wants to say.

"I think my mom is up to something," she blurts. "Something big. But I don't know what. After your latest attack, the base is buzzing, and

I don't just think it's because she lost another convoy. She took my unit from me and sent half of them to Malmstrom. A base that I didn't even know was operational. Something's going on that I don't know about. By destroying the convoy, you put a dent in her plans."

I can't help feeling smug, and it must show on my face. Putting a dent in General Judy's plans makes me feel all warm inside. But knowing she's up to something that Kate doesn't even know about is rather unsettling. And Kate's disapproving look makes me clear my throat, the smugness vanishing. "What do you think she's planning?"

"I don't know," she confesses. "Are *you* planning something?"

I take a slow sip of tea. "Not personally, but I can't speak for the rest of the Resistance."

We sit in silence, processing all the new information. I wonder what else she wants from me. From the short time I've known her, I've learned she isn't satisfied after just one or two questions. She's smart, cunning, and picks my mind like she's playing a game of chess, with a few simple moves before she makes her big play. She challenges me, and for some reason, I'm completely drawn to it.

"What was your other reason for coming to see me on base?" she finally asks.

Ah, there it is. The en passant. I wonder if she wants to hear that I came for her. To see her. To kiss her. If she wants me to admit that I care for her.

I take a moment and let the silence surround us while I study her as she moves her thumb over each fingernail on her hand, something she does when anxious. A small tell that one would only notice if they had spent as much time studying her as I have.

I do care for her, but I'm not sure I can admit it yet. Not out loud. It would make me more vulnerable than I'm ready for. "Because we didn't get a chance to say good-bye."

"You risked your life because you didn't get to tell me good-bye?" She sounds skeptical if not a little annoyed.

"I prefer hellos." I give her my most charming smile and take her hand. "Don't you?"

Kate rolls her eyes exaggeratedly and snorts out a laugh. "Yes, I risked both our lives to get you here so we could be naked together and say hello." The amusement, however, is short-lived, her expression shifting to worry. She slides her fingers against mine. "My mother *is* up to something, and Simon *is* coming after you."

That's not really news. "Yeah, you said as much last night."

"So you *were* listening," she says. This time, I'm the one rolling my eyes. "No, Dani, I mean it. He's really coming after you. He received a ridiculous promotion and a team of his choosing, and his sole focus is to hunt you down."

"Then let him come," I say. "I have unfinished business—"

"And Lucas." She effectively stops my rant. "And William. He's coming after all of you." She motions to my side. "And you can barely move without wincing."

"I can move just fine," I say, taking my hand away. "As evident from last night."

"Please be serious." She pulls my hand back and holds it tight.

"I *am* being serious. If that asshole wants to fight, I'll give him a fight. Next time, he won't be able to run away like a coward. I'll kill him before he can even look at Lucas or William." I refuse to think of anyone hurting my brother. My love for Lucas is a weak spot for me, and while, yes, he can hold his own, I will fuck Simon up until he's unrecognizable if he dares to even breathe in my brother's direction.

"Dani..." She seems to struggle to find what she wants to say. "About what happened to White River—"

"Don't." I don't want to hear it. I didn't want to hear it last night, and I don't want to hear it now. I turn away, clenching my teeth in anger.

"I'm sorry." It comes out as a whisper that barely registers.

"Yeah, you keep saying that." I shake my head. It's not her fault, I know it's not, but it still hurts. Pulling away, I reach for my cup of tea, giving my hands something to do and try to steady my breathing. It doesn't work. Her apology nags at me. "But what are you sorry for, exactly?"

"I should've known my mother would initiate retribution. I should've gone to her and asked for control of the situation. Instead, I waited and..." She trails off.

"We knew she'd respond. *I* knew she would. Nothing you could've done would've stopped it." This is on me. It's my fault. I'm angry because *I* didn't do nearly enough to stop it.

"Are you back in the war?" she asks softly, pulling me from my guilt. "Was the convoy a one-off retaliation, or was that just the first of many?"

"Does it change anything?" I hate how defensive I sound.

Her expression is sad and knowing. "It changes everything."

Everything. With me back with the Resistance and Kate in the NAF…What we're doing here isn't going to work. My weakness for her is what got my home destroyed. I suddenly feel very stupid for my silly infatuation. What the hell am I doing?

I put the tea down and push off the covers. Grabbing my shirt, I hastily pull it over my head, no longer caring about the pain in my side. No longer wanting to suffocate in this room over repercussions from decisions I made and decisions I have yet to make.

"Dani."

"I need to go." I can't be here, like this, with her. "You told me what you came here to tell me. Consider the message received."

She places a hand on my shoulder, her touch gentle and hesitant. I tense for a moment, then deflate. "I didn't mean it like that." Her voice is quiet. "I just meant, if I were to come across you in battle, I won't be able to… I couldn't…"

I think about how she had the chance to take me out once already in the middle of a fight. And she chose not to. I also think about how I hesitated when it came to attacking the convoy near Malmstrom. Taking her out isn't an option for me, either. "Yeah."

Her eyes meet mine. "I care about you, about what happens to you. I just needed to see you, to be near you. And I think you feel the same."

Just like that, Kate has spoken this thing between us into existence. The room feels thick with her confession. "But what's happening out there is bigger than you and me. It's bigger than this." She motions between us.

I take her hand. This thing between us isn't just a silly infatuation. "I don't know, Kate. This feels pretty big to me." I confess softly, scared that if I admit it any louder, it may be ripped away from us. I know that being with her is a terrible idea, but being without her feels…wrong. How is it possible to feel both things so deeply?

Her smile doesn't quite reach her eyes. "Do you ever think about what it would be like outside of the war? To just walk away from it all?"

Gently, I cup her face. "I did that, remember? I walked away for seven years."

"What was it like?"

"Quiet." She nods like she was expecting such an answer. I shift closer, grab her by the back of the neck, and pull her close, pressing our foreheads together. "I'm sorry," I whisper. "I'm just angry. And sad. My home…"

"I know." She leans in, and our noses touch. "I promise, from now on, I'll do what I can to keep you safe."

Emotions bloom in my chest at her promise. I have people who care for me deeply, but I never expected one of them to be Katelyn Turner, NAF, major, and daughter of my enemy. My throat tightens at the sentiment, and for a moment, I'm scared I may show too much emotion. I may feel too deeply, and then the universe will try to take her away from me.

I shake my head and clear my throat. "I don't need you to do that. I need you to keep yourself safe." I pull back and hold her face. I wait until she's looking at me, so she knows I'm serious. "I don't want you sending messages through Archie anymore." She seems about to protest, but I silence her with a kiss. "Whatever is happening here, with us, it puts everyone in danger. Including you."

She nods and looks away. "I know. Just the thought of not seeing you again, of only seeing you out there on opposite sides of a fight—"

"Hang on, I never said we wouldn't see each other again." She looks at me, confused. "We just have to be careful. And smart." I tilt her face upward. "I need you to trust me."

"But what if—"

"Do you trust me?"

It takes her a long moment to answer. And when she nods, I sigh, relieved. Her trust isn't something I take lightly. Leaning in, I kiss her again, then pull back just enough to speak against her lips. "And for the record, I would never let you defeat me on the battlefield."

She smiles and puffs out a small laugh. It sounds and feels like pure happiness.

❖

I pull the laces of my boot tighter. "You aren't going to ask where I'm staying?" I don't know why it bothers me that Kate hasn't asked. She didn't want to know when I snuck on base to see her in Grand Forks, and she doesn't seem to want to know now. I'm starting to wonder if it's out of protection for me, or she really doesn't mind not knowing. Either way, it feels weird wanting her to ask.

She pulls a red sweatshirt over her T-shirt and smiles when she catches me looking. "No. The less I know, the better. Trust each other, right?"

So it is the whole, I'm protecting you, thing. Sighing, I know she's probably right. It's better that she doesn't know. "Soon you'll be back in Omaha."

"Ever been?" She pulls the hair out from her shirt and rakes her fingers through, detangling it as best she can. I'm struck with how absolutely beautiful she is like this: disheveled and relaxed. I can't stop staring.

"No," I say, ignoring the fact that I already calculated the distance from Rapid City to Offutt Air Force Base and that it'll take eight hours on a good day. I don't mention that I know it's size and that more than half of it was destroyed prior to the third war or that I've already called in favors to get the base layout. Instead, I shrug. "But I'm sure I can find my way around. How different can all your bases be?"

She gives me a look. She's not amused. She begins folding the linens, and I roll up her sleeping bag for her. "It's different now, Dani. Security is tighter than when you snuck into Grand Forks. You won't be able to pull that off again. You're being hunted, remember? We're already on high alert."

"I'm always hunted." Again, she's not amused. I give her my best smile. "Oh, ye of little faith." I love a good challenge. Especially when my reward is a few stolen moments with Kate.

"*Ye* doesn't want to see you killed." She tosses the linens on top of her duffel and puts her hands on her hips.

Placing the sleeping bag on the sofa, I step around the inflatable mattress and pull her toward me by her belt loops. "Who would've thought? The Daughter of the Resistance and the general's daughter, tangled in a romantic web."

She slips her arms around my waist with a bemused look. "I'd hardly call this romantic." She looks around the old outpost for emphasis.

I tug her closer. "Oh, come on, I charmed the pants off you."

"More like ripped them off," she mumbles. "Without so much as one of those hellos you were going on about." She smiles and tightens her grip around me.

"Hello." I lean in to kiss her, unable to keep from smiling. "I didn't hear you complaining."

Her hands slip up the back of my shirt. "You *were* rather distracting."

"A most excellent strategy, I agree." And with that, I silence her once more. Her hands roam beneath my shirt, careful and delicate, and I wonder why we have to stop and why I was so desperate to escape just hours before.

A buzzing sound comes through her radio. Oh yeah. Duty and all that. She drops her forehead to my shoulder and sighs. "Why did I turn that back on?"

"Guess we better deflate this mattress," I say. "I'm kind of going to miss it. All the— "

"No! Whatever you were going to say, just stop right there." Her embarrassed groan makes me laugh. "How do you have the badass reputation that you do? Ruthless, merciless, destructive…When you're mostly horny, handsy, and immature?"

I can't stop the laugh that erupts from deep within my chest. "Badass, huh?"

She pushes me away. "Incorrigible."

I help her deflate the mattress and tie it together and look around the room. There really isn't much else to pack. Kate makes sure the last of her supplies are in her duffel, and when everything seems to be in its place, we make our way to the door.

Kate stops in the doorway and looks around. "This place kinda grew on me."

"Yeah, I've never been. It's kinda nice." I empty the pitcher of water by the door and take the empty bowl and towel.

She shrugs. "Who knows, maybe we'll be back one day." The words come out casually, but the avoidance of eye contact speaks volumes.

"Like a summer cottage?" I ask.

"Like a reprieve from the war," she corrects. She takes the towel and shoves it in her bag. "Leave them," she says, motioning toward the pitcher and the bowl. "Just in case."

I flip them over so they don't collect dust and place them back on the table by the door. The thought of her being serious about coming back sends a warm feeling through my chest. I follow her to her truck, and she pulls on a knit cap. "Nice hat," I tell her, flicking the large white pom-pom atop her head.

She swats my hand away. "Don't make fun. It keeps me warm."

"Who's making fun? I think you look cute." She makes a humming sound, as if she doesn't believe me. "Is it standard issue or…"

Kate pushes me, and I laugh. It feels so good to be carefree like this. Weightless. I haven't felt like this in a long time.

"The weather here is weird," she says and squints toward the sky. "Just weeks ago, I was sweating. Now I can't get warm."

"You seemed pretty sweaty and warm last night." I wink for extra effect.

She responds by rolling her eyes. "Do you ever stop?"

The radio comes to life from within Kate's bag, and she tosses it in the front cabin. And just like that, reality comes crashing back down.

"A lot of classified information coming through that radio," I say. She makes no move to reach for it. I throw her sleeping supplies in the back and pull the tarp over them. "Pretty far range. You're what, two hundred miles away?"

"Two-forty," she corrects. "My dad actually designed it. Short-range walkie to a ham, minus the repeater stations. It was a gamechanger. It can reach up to three hundred miles."

"That's impressive." I don't take her mentioning her father for granted. She keeps her memories close, and I know sharing them doesn't come lightly. Knowing that William was the one who killed him makes me sick to my stomach. I feel like I should say something, but I don't know what. Apologize? No, it would feel hollow no matter how much I meant it.

With her small smile as motivation, I push aside the thought and retrieve a handheld radio from my Jeep. "Then he would've loved these. Darby modified it. Rhiannon used to make me take it when I was out scavenging, even though it was kind of overkill. More than double the range. Should reach Omaha."

Kate looks at me, surprised.

"Go on," I tell her with a smile. She takes the radio and examines it. When she turns it on, it's already preset to a specified frequency and channel. "Just in case you need me."

Her eyes meet mine. "Dani."

"Don't get caught with it. Obviously. It's preset to a Resistance-encrypted frequency. I won't always be on the other end, so don't use it unless it's an absolute emergency. I really don't need Jack hearing about how much you miss being underneath me." The look on her face is worth the immature statement. "Seriously. I can't always have it on and with me. Jess is stationed on comms and will be listening for messages from you, too, so just be careful what you say."

"Jess?" she asks. I can tell by the look that she wants to press that issue a little more, probably remembering my vague description of her the last time we played Honesty Hour. Instead, she examines the radio. "This is…" She shakes her head, not finishing her thought. "Do I get a code name?"

"Not one that Lucas picks, that's for sure." I laugh, but I can tell she isn't quite in on the joke. I look at her for a moment, contemplating telling her that it's her choice. She can call herself whatever she wants. But my mouth bypasses my brain and chooses for her. "Songbird," I whisper as a familiar tune fills my mind. A song from the old jukebox that reminds me very much of Kate for reasons I'm not willing to elaborate on.

She tilts her head, her lips curved up in a slight, bewildered smile. I can tell she's thinking it over, wondering if I'm serious. Finally, she nods slowly.

"It'll put a bullseye on your back. So if you don't want to take it—"

"I want to take it." Her response is immediate and final. She turns it on and then off and looks at me. Her eyes search my face, and I can tell she's still not sure what to say. "Songbird," she whispers. "What's yours?"

I hesitate. I've had so many over the years. Different places call me different things. Different missions call for different names. But there's one that's special and sticks no matter where I am or what I'm doing. "Atomic Anomaly."

Kate chuckles. "That's slightly cooler sounding."

"Yeah, she's a character from Major Maelstrom. But yours comes with a beautiful melody." Maybe if we ever get another stolen moment like this, I can play it for her.

Kate stares at the radio again. She reaches for her headset and holds it up. "Think it'll pair with these?"

"Headphones?" I ask, confused.

"Officers are required to keep a radio on them at all times in case we're needed. The headset keeps me hands-free. Just a habit of wearing it I guess." She blushes and tosses the headset back in the truck.

Instead of teasing her, I step closer for a kiss, finding her embarrassment endearing. "I'm glad you sent for me," I whisper against her lips. "Even if you are kind of weird."

"I'm glad you came." She sighs and pulls away. "Please don't," she warns when I smirk at her poor choice of words. "You know what I mean."

"Yes, I do." I laugh, and we stand looking at each other.

Separating from her feels impossible. The word good-bye tastes awkward in my mouth and sticks in my throat. It feels inadequate and too heavy for this moment. I'm not quite sure how to do this, how we're supposed to part. I wasn't sure back in White River, and I'm not sure now.

It's a dangerous game we're playing, and it's putting people's lives at risk. For a brief moment, I wonder again if we're being too selfish. But then Kate grabs the front of my shirt and pulls me in for a deep kiss. With my hands on her hips, I press her against the side of her truck with every intention of dragging out our good-bye just a little bit longer.

By the time the gates of Rapid City come into view, I am utterly spent. All I can think about is a hot bath, a hot meal, and twelve hours of sleep. I'll consider myself lucky if I get any one of the three. William will probably want to grill me about where I was and why I left, and Lucas will want to know what's going on with Kate. My radio needs charging, and I need to tell Jess to keep Kate's new radio frequency on her rotation. I have yet to have a serious chat with the mayor since my arrival, so that's probably also on the agenda. Plus, I really, *really* need to check in on Rhiannon and the others. No more procrastinating.

The guards wave me through, and I head directly to where I'm staying, hoping I can at least change my clothes and get a quick shower before tackling the rest of my to-do list.

After parking, I swing the duffel over my shoulder and wince, the wound on my side pulling painfully. Groaning, I mentally add tending my side to my ever-growing list. The air outside bites at my face, and I'm vaguely jealous of Kate's ridiculous hat.

I slip on my sunglasses and shove the car keys into my front pocket. A clipped bark pulls my attention. I glance to my left and see a black and white herding dog sprinting in my direction. His tongue dangles from his mouth as if he's smiling.

"Roscoe?" I bend to scratch behind his ears just as he reaches me. My heart soars at the sight of him, but I am deeply confused about how he got here. "What are you doing here, boy?" He makes happy noises and grunts as he shifts so I can scratch his butt, his tail wagging incessantly. "I missed you, too. Are you enjoying the colder weather with this thick coat?" He flips to his back and lets me scratch his belly. I'm about to lie flat on the ground with him so I can kiss his face when a voice pulls my attention.

"About time you showed up."

My gaze lifts to see a familiar face, and my stomach flips as she approaches with her arms crossed but a smile on her face. I freeze in complete shock. "Rhi?"

Her dark hair is pulled back, and she wears dark pants, ankle boots and a dark green jacket zipped all the way up. Mirrored sunglasses cover her eyes, and I can see the smile tugging at the corner of her lips. She casually strolls over as if she wasn't over a hundred miles away from Rapid City when I left yesterday.

She's not supposed to be here. She's supposed to be somewhere far from here and away from the war. Somewhere safe. Regardless, seeing her makes me feel positively elated. And in that moment, I can't even fathom being upset.

I race toward her and lift her into a bone-crushing hug, burying my face against her neck and making no effort to hide how happy I am to see her. The pain in my side is almost unbearable, but I don't care. I squeeze her tighter.

"Whoa, there, easy on the squeezing," she says but makes no effort to pull away. "I need to breathe."

"What are you doing here?" I hold her shoulders and lean back so I can examine her, finally releasing her. "Are you okay? Did something happen?"

"I'm fine. Nothing happened. I just couldn't take being away from my people." She shoves her hands in her pockets. "It's getting cold. Can you believe it snowed already? Means a harsh winter is on its way."

"How did you get here?" I ask, ignoring her rambling about the weather.

She shrugs. "Jack." I try to hug her again, but she stops me. "He told me you all weren't planning on coming back soon, and you hadn't radioed in days, so I made him come get me." Her look is accusatory.

"We needed you to be safe, Rhiannon. I needed you to be safe."

"I know. And as lovely as it was to see Pine Ridge, I needed to be with my own family." She's being sincere, but I still catch a hint of annoyance at being left behind. I can't even argue with her. We both know I would've done the same thing.

I smile. "I'm glad you're here."

"I'm still mad at you for not checking in." Her smile is gone.

"I'm sorry. Truly. I just...didn't know what to say to you."

"You didn't know what to say to your best friend? You could've started with hello." She stares at me for so long, I have to look away. She's right. "Jack told me about White River," she says quietly. "He said they destroyed everything." I nod because what else is there to say? I should've called. I should've checked in. I should've stopped them from burning our home. So many "should haves" that I failed to do. "He also said you went on a rampage."

I'm not ready for this conversation.

Rhiannon sighs. "It was dumb to go charging in like you did. In the town and with the convoy. You all could've been seriously hurt. Or worse."

"It's war, Rhiannon," I say bluntly.

"It's stupid," she counters. She examines me for a long time, and I can tell by the way her teeth clench that she wants to say more, but just like Rhiannon, she knows when to push and when to stop. Instead, she takes a deep breath, brushing aside the inquisition for what I can only assume will be another time.

"Speaking of hurt." She smacks my side with the back of her hand. I hunch over in pain. "Heard you got stabbed. Again."

"What the hell?" I wheeze. "I take it back. Not glad to see you."

"Not healing?" she asks innocently.

"Not when people go around hitting me." I wince and hold my hand against my side. I don't dare ask if she knows about the injury on my arm.

She shows no sympathy for my pain. "Where have you been? I got in yesterday. Jack said you took off and didn't tell anyone where you were going. Poor Lucas had to meet with the mayor and introduce me to William. He's a little overwhelmed, and William is pissed."

I do my best to stand up straight, keeping one hand securely over my bandage. "I had an errand to run."

"An errand." Her voice is deadpan, and she crosses her arms. I don't have to look at her to know she doesn't buy it for one second. I offer a shrug and can practically feel her narrowing her eyes. She hums and starts to walk away but not before calling over her shoulder, "By the way, you smell like Kate."

Wait. What?

Roscoe leaves me to walk alongside Rhiannon, his excitement over our reunion gone. I chase them both. "How the hell do you know what Kate smells like?"

"Lucas told me where you went," Rhiannon admits as I catch up to her.

I huff. Of course he did. "Traitor." We take several steps in silence, and I glance at her from the corner of my eye. "Are you going to lecture me on that, too?"

"That you're sleeping with the enemy in the middle of a war?" My step falters at her comment. It makes her smile. "Maybe later. Right now, we have more important things to do." She motions down the street. "Come on."

"Where are we going?" I glance longingly at the Alex Johnson as we pass it. Any hopes of taking that languid bath, eating food, or sleeping are disappearing with every step I take.

"To see Elise. I'm sure you were too busy with Kate to have changed that bandage."

"Elise is here, too?" I smile at the news and pick up my pace. A bath, food, and sleep can wait. I have my family back.

Chapter Six: The Assignment

Kate

By bypassing the town where I stopped on my way to the outpost, the ride back to base is a little easier. I look at the radio Dani gave me every few minutes, wondering if I should turn it on just in case. It's a ridiculous thought. Realistically, I know she's not going to contact me on her own drive back. We aren't love-stricken teenagers, but a small part of me still wants to check in to make sure the radio works. Nothing more.

I already miss her.

Unable to concentrate on anything but the silent radio beside me, I opt to slip on the headset over my hat and turn up the volume on my NAF one instead.

Things go from relatively quiet to frantic in a matter of minutes through the static. It seems as though half the troops from the east have arrived early, and the general is pushing up the convoy to get us all to Omaha. Is this something I should tell Dani?

And just like that, my thoughts are back to Dani. I can't stop thinking about her or the smile that won't leave my face. The mere thought of her pulls a giddiness from me that I forgot I was capable of experiencing.

My smile grows at the memory of her pressed against me and gently stroking my face. I'll have to wear the mask of major soon enough, but for now, I just want to be Kate. No title. No rank. Just a girl thinking about her crush and pretending that we both live normal lives.

The blissful daydream is short-lived, however, when the base finally comes into view. Seeing the large sign at the gate brings me back to a steady unease. Warriors of the North. I clench my jaw and sit a little straighter, slipping back into my role.

Even from a distance I can tell that security has tightened since my departure. I hide the radio from Dani deep within my bag and make a beeline to Ryan's. Everything feels...off.

Ryan's door flies open before my knuckles can touch the wood. He practically pulls me into his quarters. I briefly wonder if he was waiting for me or just happened to be on his way out. He breathes a sigh of relief, even though his body language says anything but relaxed. "It's a good thing you're back. They moved up the convoy."

"I heard as much, half of us now, the other half when the rest of the troops arrive. Guess the general assumed I wasn't going to take her up on that mandatory R and R despite signing off on it."

He looks nervous. "The general is in a frenzy. She's calling for troops from all over to push farther west. She's pissed that William and the Clarks made it out of the convoy attack alive. Heads are rolling. She also had the lieutenant general from Griffiss come this way to oversee the transfer in her absence and moved Colonel Treague from Malmstrom to Warren right around the time convoy was hit."

I freeze. There's so much to unpack in that one sentence alone. "Around the time the convoy was hit? Does that mean before or after?"

He shakes his head. "I don't know. Directly after, I think?"

Even if it was directly after, something doesn't seem right. And then there's the sudden movement regarding command. The lieutenant general all the way from New York to Grand Forks and pulling the colonel from Malmstrom to Warren? I didn't even know Colonel Treague was heading operations at Malmstrom. I thought he was in Pennsylvania. None of this makes any sense. Then something else nags at me: "What do you mean, 'in her absence'?"

He frowns. "Where did you get that hat?"

I pull the knit cap from my head and shove it in my jacket pocket. Why is everyone so concerned about my damn hat? He takes in my civvies for the first time. I don't have time for this. "Ryan, focus."

He eyes my duffel but doesn't press the issue. "She's going to Ellsworth. The lieutenant general will be taking over here at Grand Forks."

Dread overwhelms me. Ryan stares as if awaiting a response, but I can't seem to piece together a rational explanation. She's changing command all over the place. What exactly is my mother up to?

The plan was always to oversee the progression of the land acquisition from a distance while the NAF reestablished Midwest control. Once it was settled, Denver would be up and running, and my mother would move there while the push for uniting the rest of the country was established. She's leaving the north and the east totally exposed. All for what? To control the wasteland? Why?

"Kate—"

I hold up a hand, needing a moment to process and pace. Changing the plan abruptly seems irrational. And going to Ellsworth? Again, why? I think back and try to picture the base. I'm certain it's in former South Dakota, close to Rapid City, but it's never been on the transfers list.

I place my bag on the floor and cross my arms. "What aren't you telling me?"

He runs his hands over his perfectly trimmed hair. "The general wants to take the wasteland by the end of the year."

The news is a slap in the face. "By the end of the year? But the season is already turning." That doesn't give her much time, especially as the harsh weather approaches. She wants to take the wasteland in three months, when the original plan was to have it under NAF control in twelve? And even *that* is generous. "What happened to the prospect of peaceful transfer of power throughout the year? Those were our orders: acquire as many townships for ownership under a peaceful transition of power in *twelve* months."

"Those were General Trent's orders. New leadership, new agenda. Your mother wants the wasteland, Kate. She wants it enough to pull officers from their post and transfer them out west." He looks me in the eyes. "Bad enough to transfer locations herself with no real notice."

My head is spinning. All the work I've put into trying to unify towns into our law. All the towns that still need our help. Everyone agreed: peaceful transfer of power at every opportunity we were afforded and control of the majority of the Midwest in twelve months.

There's obviously a big piece of this puzzle I'm missing. I think back to my mother going to Ellsworth. "Ellsworth isn't even there, is it? Wasn't it destroyed in the third war? Why would she go there?"

"I don't know. To see the damage? To see if it can be reinstated? To try to negotiate with command at Rapid City herself?" Ryan takes a few steps toward the window. He looks out as if expecting someone. His nervousness is infectious.

I can't remember a time when my mother ever tried to spearhead taking a city peacefully. Why would she start now? Is Dani close to Rapid City? I should've asked. "I take two days away from base, and everything goes to shit."

"I don't think the general has any other choice. The Resistance is fighting back and expanding. She needs to move swiftly and forcefully just to keep ahead of them." He turns back toward me with a pointed look as if to say, *I told you they were bad news.*

Against my better judgement, I take the bait. "Of course they're fighting back." I practically scoff at him. "We're in the middle of a war for their territory. The movement started in the Midwest. This is their home. Their foothold."

Ryan takes a forceful step in my direction. His voice is low and angry. "Blowing up an entire convoy—"

"I know." I don't need to hear him explain it. I know what we lost. And worse, I know that I could've also lost Dani. No. I can't let thoughts of Dani cloud my better judgment while I try to figure out what's going on here within the NAF.

"Where did you go? Where were you these past two days?" Ryan asks quietly, looking at my clothes once again. His expression is pained, like he already knows the answer.

I refuse to let him make me feel even guiltier for leaving than I already do. I straighten my shoulders. He is no longer entitled to know what I do in my personal time, friend or not. "Ryan." I close my eyes and put a palm to my forehead. I can't even begin to explain what's going on with Dani when even I'm having a hard time understanding it.

He takes a step closer. It's not threatening, but it causes me to tense. "Who were you with, Kate? Who did you go see?"

"I went to a nice little fishing village and met a lovely older woman named Marium who gave me these clothes and my new hat in exchange for some low-grade tech." It's not a lie.

There's a knock at the door, and Ryan gives no indication that he intends to answer it.

I, on the other hand, am more than happy for a distraction from this standoff.

As I open the door, a soldier salutes. "Major. I apologize for the interruption, but the general requests your presence in her office."

"Thank you. I'll be right there." I dismiss her and look at Ryan. "I need to get into uniform."

He nods, but I know that another conversation is coming, one that I promised him before I left and one I'm not looking forward to.

Straightening my jacket, I await entry into the general's office. I pull my hair into a tight bun, knowing how much my mother hates it when I look disorderly. My shoulders straighten when I'm given a quick nod by the soldier stationed outside.

The first thing I notice when I step inside is the papers scattered about the large oak desk and the maps pinned to the wall to my right. I let out a long shaky breath. The room echoes the chaos felt within the base, and if I wasn't unsettled before, I'm definitely there now. It's unusual for her to be so disheveled.

She gives me a quick glance, then goes back to reading. "Did you enjoy your R and R?" Her voice is steady, and she doesn't bother to look up again.

My mind goes to Dani and the way she looked when smiling at me with the sheets tangled around her waist. Her unruly and tousled hair curtained her face in the glow of the morning sun. My fingers twitch at the thought of my hands entwined with hers. The memory sends a sharp pang through my chest. Instead of answering, I pivot. "I heard about the attack."

The answer seems to satisfy my mother, who never did enjoy small talk. "Yes, well, it's a shame they weren't able to stop William Russell and the Clarks. You'd think with all that firepower..." She trails off and sighs deeply, finally looking at me. "You are leading the convoy to Omaha tomorrow morning. Be ready to depart at sunrise."

I don't question the change in orders. Instead, I focus on the assignment and push away all personal feelings and thoughts of Dani. "Yes, ma'am."

"I've already deployed scouts to ensure safe travel. We're dispatching decoys and leaked false information of how well-equipped these empty convoys are in order to"—she pauses and smiles through the next word—"*misdirect* any possible attackers. Tracking devices are being installed in all officer vehicles. What happened with you, wandering lost in the wasteland, will never happen again. From now on, we will know exactly where our officers are at all times. I'm doing everything in my power to keep you safe."

Her smile is pinched, like she's more annoyed than anything else. I suppose I should feel grateful, but instead I'm angry. Why weren't these security measures put into place before?

She sighs and motions to the chair opposite her desk. "Katelyn, sit." The lack of rank indicates she's about to get personal. I'm not sure I'm ready for that type of intimacy with her. It feels safer to have our ranks as a barrier.

Like I feared, once I'm seated, she continues as my mother, not the general. "My plan was to brief you on your new assignment once you arrived in Omaha. I intended to travel with you and show you around and check on the progress at Offutt Air Force Base. But with the Resistance attack disrupting our plans, my attention is needed elsewhere. I'll be heading farther west."

I say nothing and wait for her to continue because I'm still having a hard time following anything that's happening.

"My adjutant general will be riding with you and will debrief you on your new command. In the meantime, I've had to push up your promotion." She reaches for a small box on the corner of her desk and hands it to me unceremoniously, but it still manages to catch my breath. "Effective immediately, you are now Lieutenant Colonel Turner."

Slowly, not believing this is happening, I open the box, revealing the silver oak leaf within. I let out a long breath. Lieutenant Colonel. Elated, I carefully run my fingers over the pin. After everything that's happened since I arrived in the Midwest, I didn't think this day would ever come. I didn't think myself worthy of this. Pride and a newfound sense of determination consumes me and then is instantly replaced with worry when I consider what Dani would think of this situation.

I sense my mother's satisfaction even through her neutral expression. The only time she's ever proud of me is when I'm promoted. I hate that I crave it.

"Once you have been debriefed and things in Omaha are under control, you will move south to take command of Joint Base San Antonio."

My eyes snap to meet hers. "Texas?" It's one of the few states that managed to expand its borders after the fall of democracy. This is huge.

Her eyebrow arches in a way that lets me know there is absolutely no room for negotiation about my orders. "Is there a problem?"

I straighten in my chair. "No, ma'am, just surprised."

"This country will be united, and in order to do that, I need people I trust leading by my side. Loyalty has been severely lacking as of late. I'm dealing with several internal failures." Her eyes land on the new pin I still hold delicately in my hands.

The message is clear: be loyal or pay the price. This isn't just a promotion because I've done something well; it's one of convenience. The realization steals some of my pride and replaces it with disappointment.

I stand when my mother does. She removes the gold oak leaf from my jacket replaces it with the silver.

"You're not getting the official ceremony you've earned, but I am so very proud of you, Katelyn. Your father would be, too." She dusts imaginary lint from my jacket and puts her hands on my shoulders. We stand at the same height as we stare at each other. "We're going to accomplish great things together. I'm sorry he's not here to see it."

I try to smile despite the sadness that sinks to the bottom of my stomach. When I was young, after every promotion, Dad would pull me into a crushing hug, smile with tears in his eyes, and kiss my temple. *"I'm so incredibly proud of you, Katie. You're going to be a great general one day."*

He only saw me promoted twice.

I try to thank my mother, to tell her I appreciate her confidence and that I won't let her down, but the words are caught in my throat. I'm not sure if it's because of the sudden grief I feel for my father not being here or the fact that I'm not sure I'm ready to lead the entire southern army. Perhaps a bit of both.

I have a feeling that things just got a hell of a lot more complicated, and my first thought, is wondering what it means for me and Dani.

I drag my feet all the way to the medical building to check on Private Miller. The pride that originally consumed me at the promotion has quickly dissipated, replaced by a rock of dread in my stomach.

Something feels off with my mother's abrupt plans, and I can't quite place what it is. My mind goes to the radio from Dani. I wish I could dig it out of the bottom of my bag and talk to her about it all.

"Good evening, Major." A figure to my right straightens and startles me as I reach the entrance of the building.

I turn quickly as Miguel steps into the light. His nose and cheeks are rosy from the chilly air, and I wonder how long he's been standing out here.

"Private Silva," I return with a nod. "Good evening."

Ever observant, his eyes fall to the leaf pinned on my uniform. His shoulders push back even farther. "Lieutenant Colonel," he corrects. "I apologize."

"At ease, Private," I smile. "I'm sure the memo will be released eventually."

He nods quickly, no doubt missing my attempt at a joke. The worry etched all over his face gives way to a deep frown. Being held at White River seemed to do a number on him.

None of us had ever been held captive before, but what we experienced there seems a far cry from actual imprisonment. Yet he and Miller haven't been the same since.

We were taught that the Resistance is full of inhumane and vile human beings who would dance on the graves of fallen NAF. Then we met the people of White River. Aside from the bombs around our ankles, our treatment was relatively decent. We even built relationships with them and on some level, trust.

Between the sandstorm, raider attacks, and being held captive, we lost a lot of soldiers on a routine humanitarian mission. Privates Silva and Miller signed up to bring about peaceful change in the Midwest and then had to watch those around them suffer and die. Private Miller, though wounded, made it out alive. Survivor guilt can be a hard thing to live with, especially when the enemy ends up saving your life.

I drop the formalities. "Miguel, talk to me." As soon as the words pass my lips, Miguel's shoulders drop, and his posture turns small. He still looks hesitant. I cover my rank. "Think of me as a friend, not an officer. Remember, there are no repercussions here, and it'll stay between the two of us."

He thinks for another moment and then nods. "I can't stop thinking about the people we left in White River. They just—"

"I know." And I do. Burned. Murdered. By the hands of our own. It's one thing to hear intel on towns burned or numbers of fatalities. It's an entirely different thing to have looked into the eyes of those people, some of them children, and know you had a role in their later violent demise. Especially when we're the ones who are supposed to be bringing peace. It's utterly crushing, and my ability to compartmentalize it is waning.

Clearly, so is Miguel's.

Unshed tears glisten in his eyes. "It's Private Miller, too. Physically, he's improving, and I know he'll be put right back into combat when he's discharged, but he doesn't think he can do it. Be a part of something like that."

"He doesn't think he can attack the Resistance since some of them saved his life in White River?" My assumption is confirmed when Miguel nods. "Listen. I know you're listed to depart for Omaha in the morning. I can make sure Private Miller is cleared, and he can join us as well. No combat for either of you for the time being. We can keep an eye on him together."

"Yes, ma'am." He releases a soft breath of relief, and it puffs into the cold air. "Thank you," he whispers.

"Why don't you give Private Miller the news while I speak to his doctor and initiate the transfer? I'll be in to see him once I get it sorted out." I open the door and allow Miguel to lead me into the warm building as I prepare to start on an exorbitant amount of paperwork.

At least my new promotion gives me more leeway to keep my soldiers safe and under my command. And that's a start.

❖

I stare at the radio from Dani. My finger hovers over the push-to-talk button while I debate if this is a good idea. *Emergencies only*, she said. Is this a true emergency, or am I just unjustifiably panicking?

Maybe I'm just worried that she won't know about my convoy tomorrow. That's stupid; she's known about every other convoy. Why wouldn't she know about this one? On the other hand, my mother *did* say she was spreading false information.

Sighing, I toss the radio on my bed. What am I doing? Why would I tell her any of this? Besides the threat of Simon poking around, which she now knows, there's nothing else to warn her about. There is absolutely no need to risk getting caught just to tell her I'm on my way to Omaha and to beware of wild-goose chases.

Still, I don't want her doing anything reckless. Grabbing the radio, I press the button and bring it to my mouth. What if Dani's not on the receiving end? And I have to justify to Jess, or worse, Mohawk, why I'm reaching out? I'll just seem like a lovestruck fool. Again, I toss the radio on my bed and stare at it.

I scratch lightly at my scalp and try to get control over myself. Is this about protecting Dani or something else? Is her safety more important than my own people? Is this big enough to warrant a call that may get us both caught? What the hell am I doing?

My own indecisiveness is giving me whiplash. I shove the radio back into the bottom of my duffel and begin to throw every single one of my belongings on top of it. Out of sight, out of mind. Dani is fine. She's perfectly capable of taking care of herself. And I am an officer in the National Armed Forces. A lieutenant colonel. My loyalty is here. My duty is here. My focus needs to be *here*.

I zip my bag and decide that "emergencies only" isn't today.

Standing with my feet shoulder-width apart and my hands clasped behind my back, I watch as the remainder of the convoy is loaded.

Ryan inspects every single aspect of the convoy. Once he's satisfied, he comes to stand beside me. After a quick salute, he says, "We're on schedule."

"Great." The tension between us feels palpable and slightly uncomfortable. Last night's conversation remains unfinished, but I know he's too professional to continue it in public.

He finally breaks the silence. "Congratulations on your promotion, Lieutenant Colonel."

I motion to the papers in his hand. "Was it officially announced?"

"You made the front page. Looks good on you." He gestures to my new chest candy and the newly polished silver pin.

"With the way the general is going after officers, I'm sure you'll be upgrading in no time."

He smiles. "I like being your advisor just fine. Do you mind if I put my notebooks in your duffel? Mine's already been loaded."

I open my bag at my feet and allow him to drop his notebooks inside. The exchange is short-lived as the adjutant approaches, a serious expression on her face. "Come on. You're our driver."

The adjutant general is slender, with blond hair and shiny blue eyes. She's taller than me, and her skin much lighter, as if she has never been out in the sun. She's in her early forties and rarely smiles, but her stern demeanor only adds to her effectiveness. She's arrogant, cunning, loyal, and smart as hell. It's no wonder she climbed the ranks to major general quickly and became my mother's most trusted advisor.

Ryan and I salute, a gesture she returns before motioning toward the officer's Jeep. I pick up my duffel and fall into step alongside her. "General Foley, nice to see you again."

"Same to you, Colonel Turner. Chief Matthews." She looks at Ryan, who holds the door for her.

Ryan and I share a look. We may have our disagreements, but I know I can always trust him, and anything General Foley has to say, I want him to hear.

I hand him my headset. "I hope your multitasking skills are still decent. I'm going to need you to take mental notes," I say. It's said under my breath, and Ryan offers a quick nod to indicate he heard. He slips on my headset, and I take a steadying breath before sliding in and placing my personal duffel at my feet.

The convoy is barely out of the gates before the adjutant is rummaging in an overstuffed tote and pulling out folders. She hands two of them to me. "We have a lot to go over and not a lot of time so it's best if we just jump right in."

I catch Ryan's eyes in the rearview mirror. If she thinks almost eight hours isn't a lot of time, then whatever she's about to drop on me can't be anything good. Uneasiness floods my body. What was I just promoted into?

She points to the top file. "We evacuated personnel from Malmstrom and relocated them to different bases. Some will be joining you and your command at Offutt."

"Evacuating?"

"As a precaution," she says dismissively.

"How many are being relocated to Omaha?" I ask, flipping through the pages of personnel records.

"Fifty."

"Where are the rest of the soldiers going?"

"That's classified."

The dates and times are covered. I try another angle. "Did you evacuate Malmstrom before the convoy was destroyed?"

"Also classified."

Okay, then. Clearly, this conversation doesn't include receiving answers to my burning questions. Not having all the pieces to the puzzle, I continue to shuffle through the papers, looking for any kind of clue as to what's going on. A lot of the info is blacked out. My expression must show confusion because General Foley looks at me almost sympathetically.

"I know you have questions. Let's push through this, and then you can ask them." She gestures to the thick file still on my lap. "In addition to personnel, you will also be receiving supplies. A checklist of all materials and items are included in the convoy from Malmstrom to Offutt."

I scan the first page. Then the next. And the next. My stomach drops, and my heart rate picks up, and the puzzle slowly starts to come together. "These are drones?" It comes out more of a question than a statement.

"That is correct," General Foley answers. It's casual and dismissed with a shrug, but she waits as I process. Something I seem to be having a hard time doing.

My father used to study all technology, which included working on drones, but the research was confined to Scott Air Force Base. When did we expand his operation out west? On top of that, there's been a no-fly order and flight blockers in place since the third world war. In order to get anything in the sky, they would need a general to…

Oh my God.

Five minutes into the journey and my head is spinning. The order to remove flight blockers had to have come from my mother. This information feels like the ultimate betrayal. How in the world could I not have known about *any* of this?

"Malmstrom was working on top secret, sensitive experiments. Experiments that your father made tremendous progress on before he died."

My throat tightens at the mention of him. Ryan watches me in the mirror, but I can't bring myself to meet his eyes. I hadn't yet earned the clearance for this information, but I'm still embarrassed that I didn't know. Especially since both of my parents were involved.

General Foley pushes on as if she didn't just stir up gut-wrenching emotions with the mention of my father's involvement in secret experiments. "The engineers at Malmstrom have made extreme advancements with drones and have done low-level and short-distance flying within the compound. Unfortunately, we have been unable to test outside with the sandstorms and now with the Resistance attack, but Offutt Air Force Base has been authorized to take temporary control of the flight tests until we are established enough in Texas."

"Joint Base San Antonio," I say. More of the plan is slowly starting to click into place.

"Correct."

"The blockers…" I start, unable to finish my question.

General Foley seems to understand. "Once General Turner took full control, she had access to all of the preventative measures that were put in place after the third world war. Her first command was to assemble all locations and begin removal of them. There was quite a bit of pushback in the east. The other generals were highly skeptical of their removal. A compromise was reached that a selected number of blockers here would be removed and flight demonstrations would begin in the wasteland, and if successful, operations would continue out of Texas."

"Why here?" I ask, my throat dry.

"Less population," she answers casually and hands me what looks like a photo album. I barely have time to close the other two files on my lap before she thrusts it in my direction. "The current plan is to have several drones up and running and able to assist before the first major snowfall."

I open the book to see various states of progress and photographic evidence of proof of flight. It takes my breath away. "Assist with what?"

General Foley smiles. "Whatever we need."

Her tone makes me still. I look up from the papers and photos and glance first at Ryan, who is looking straight ahead, and then to General Foley smirking beside me. Food, medicine, supplies…that's what I was expecting her to say. To aid with necessary supplies. When she doesn't, I wonder if we're on the same page at all.

"Before we go through all the tests and results, I think it's time you understood your new assignment." She reaches into her bag for yet another folder. And like everything else she's tossed my way, this too, is marked as top secret and highly classified. "You will now oversee that the drones take flight. Under *your* leadership, the wasteland will fall."

Air feels trapped in my lungs, and it takes my brain giving a gentle reminder to breathe and release it. My stomach twists painfully at what is now expected of me. Ryan was right about the speed with which the wasteland needs to be taken, but what we both failed to realize was *who* was going to be the one overseeing it.

"Don't you mean the wasteland will be *acquired*?" I keep my voice steady, but I am overwhelmed with surprise.

General Foley doesn't seem deterred. "Once that happens," she continues, "you, along with the aerial team and equipment, will move to Joint Base San Antonio where you will receive another promotion and get the drones in the air. You will take control of the entire Southern Armed Forces to reclaim the southern territory, and the country will finally be untied and enforced under one law."

This plan is bold, even for my mother. I'm not convinced. There is absolutely no way we can oversee that kind of control in such a short time *and* convince the rest of the generals and nation that this is the way to go.

This plan explains, however, why my mother was so exasperated that the Resistance put a damper on her plans for expansion in Malmstrom. She was secretly building an aerial army. And with my dad's help? She's been playing the long game. Like a queen sitting at the back of the board, directing her pawns.

And now my mother has access to drones. With this move, she will dominate the entire country. This is her checkmate. I thought I excelled in strategy but this? This has left me completely blindsided.

❖

By the time we arrive in Omaha, my head is pounding, and I am mentally drained. I feel betrayed. All of the files and photos are shoved back in a leatherbound tote, and they weigh heavy on my shoulder.

I adjust my personal duffel on my other shoulder and think about Dani. I want to tell her everything, I want to warn her. But what do I say? My mother is testing drones, and I'm going to be in charge of utilizing them to claim the wasteland? We should be using them to help. But I'm not sure that's how these drones are meant to be used. I need to figure this out. How do I convince Dani I want to use them to help people? How do I convince my mother?

General Foley motions for me to walk with her. "I know you're anxious to get settled and process your orders, but I've been asked to bring you in for one more meeting."

It takes every ounce of willpower not to groan. After eight hours, there really isn't much more I can take. The guard at the door has me curious, and he salutes before opening it at General Foley's nod. What is he guarding?

As I step into the side office, a woman turns to greet me.

My mother.

It catches me so off guard that I hesitate to salute. She's supposed to be in Ellsworth.

She smiles and dismisses General Foley, who slips out of the room with a knowing grin.

"Don't look so surprised to see me, Katelyn." The general casually takes a sip of her drink. "Remember, it's all about misdirection."

Chapter Seven: The Unease

Dani

R hiannon grabs the front of my shirt and pulls me inside Jess's lodgings. "I couldn't find Jack or Mike, but I did find this one wandering around," she announces as we pass through the small lobby. Glancing in the small sitting area in the next room, I see a few people already gathered near the fireplace.

"It's about damn time." Elise stands, smiling as wide as I've ever seen. She takes two long strides and throws her arms around my neck in a tight embrace.

I hold her tight, unable to stop grinning. I'm so happy to see her that I feel like I could burst.

Over her shoulder, I spot a not-so-scrawny boy with black shaggy hair who is leaning close to Jess and announcing my arrival to her. Wyatt Richardson. A far cry from the chubby little jerk who used to tease Jess and pull her hair when they were kids. I still don't like him.

"I'm so glad to see you," Elise says.

I squeeze her just a little tighter. "Me too."

She puts her hands on my forearms and looks me over in the clinical way that I'm used to. "I heard you got pretty banged up."

"Nah, I'm all right," I say, dismissing her concern. "Mike patched me up."

Elise frowns. "Now I'm really worried." She turns to Jess, who is now sitting in the blue settee in the corner. "Jess, do you have a medical kit I can use?"

Wyatt stands. "I'll go get it." My eyes don't leave him until he exits the room.

There's a steady, high-pitched whistle from the kitchen, indication that tea is going to be served. Rhiannon perks at the sound. "And I'll go get *that*. You just sit down so Elise can look at you."

"This is my punishment for not checking in, isn't it?" I ask dramatically. Elise glares and motions for me to sit. There's no use in arguing, so I do what she says. Besides, she may be small in stature, but she's a lot stronger than she looks.

"Hey, kiddo." I reach out to put my hand on Jess's shoulder and lean in to kiss the top of her head as I settle in the chair closest to her. "Anything exciting happen while I was away?" Surrounded by friends, I can almost feel the tension leaving my body.

"No more messages, if that's what you're asking," Jess quips. Her tone is light, but we have a lot to discuss, and much like Rhiannon, Jess won't let me forget.

"About that," I start and shift uncomfortably, "if you receive any messages from codename—"

"Here's the kit." Wyatt comes back and hands the box to Elise, who opens the lid to rummage inside.

"Wyatt Richardson," I say. I used to intimidate all the kids who teased Jess growing up. This time, however, Wyatt stands straighter and lifts his chin in challenge.

"Dani." He's tall. Almost as tall as Lucas. His baby fat has disappeared, replaced with lean muscle. He can't be more than seventeen, but it's clear from the spots he missed on his neck that he's shaving and has the build of a man, not a teenager.

As we stare at each other, I wonder how seven years could change and age these kids so much. Little Wyatt Richardson isn't so little anymore. Instead of running away playfully in the streets after getting caught swiping fruit, he stands tall and proud, an air of seriousness about him. It makes me wonder if this is how people viewed me after my dad died. Forced to grow up too quickly.

"If you two are done sizing each other up," Elise says as she turns to me, "I need you to take your shirt off."

"Wyatt." Jess reaches out. Wyatt turns, takes her hand, and kneels in front of her. Jess smiles. "Girls only."

He laughs lightly and kisses her knuckles before placing her palm on his cheek. "I'll check on the guests and be prepping for supper if you need me."

I guess he's not the same brat that I remember from all those years ago; otherwise, Jess wouldn't put up with him, but I still don't like the idea of Jess dating. In her case, sixteen is still too young.

He's barely out of the sitting room when Rhiannon returns with a tray of several mugs and a steaming pot of water. "Who wants tea?"

"Rhiannon, you don't have to do all this," Jess says. "You are my guest."

"I know." She sets the tray on the side table and goes about pouring the water and steeping the tea in the first glass. "But it feels very strange not to be doing something. To give back. To cook."

My heart sinks at the waver in her voice. She avoids looking at me as she continues to pour the water. I have yet to digest the true repercussions of Rhi losing her tavern. Bile rises in the back of my throat at the thought of her never owning another, and for a brief moment, I honestly think I may get sick in front of everyone.

"I'll take some tea," I say, trying to break the suffocating silence.

"It's the mint kind I keep trying to get you to drink instead of all that whiskey." Jess clicks her tongue disapprovingly.

"I like the taste of whiskey."

Rhiannon groans. "No one likes the taste of whiskey."

"Jack does," I try to argue.

"Just drink the tea, Dani." Jess laughs. "It's good for you and will help clear your thoughts."

Sighing, I take the offered mug, resisting the urge to mutter that whiskey clears my thoughts just fine. It's not that I don't like tea. I do and drink it often. I'd just rather have a glass of whiskey to swirl around. My dad used to drink it. Sometimes, just holding it in my hand, I feel like he's here's with me. There have been many times that I'll drift so far off into my own mind that I won't even take a sip. I just swirl it, over and over.

"Dani."

Elise holds cleaning ointment and gauze in her now gloved hands. She nods in my direction. "Your shirt."

Once it's over my head and I've sat up to give Elise better access to my side, I clear my throat and try to change the subject to something a little happier. "So, Rhiannon, Elise, I see you've met Jess."

The smile on Rhiannon's face lets me know I was successful in shifting the conversation. For now, anyway. "Oh yes. George brought me straight here. She's even more lovely than I anticipated." Rhiannon reaches out and takes Jess's hand. "And Wyatt! He's fantastic. Did you know he's an excellent cook? We've been swapping recipes."

I carefully balance my tea in the hand opposite of where Elise is checking, ignoring the statement about Wyatt. I lightly blow on the top and after braving a hesitant sip, I sit back with a sigh, thinking of the cup I shared this morning with Kate. I wish she was here.

"You know, we were having a good time gossiping about you before you showed up and crashed the party." Elise's voice is teasing, but I can't help but think there's some truth to it. She carefully removes the bandage on my ribs, and I wince when it pulls at my skin. She lets out a low whistle. "Mike either did a shit job patching you up or you haven't tended to this like you should've."

"I vote for the latter." Rhiannon gives me a look, but I don't give her the satisfaction of telling her she's right, per usual.

Elise shifts her attention away from my ribs. "I see you've removed the stitches from your arm. It doesn't look too bad." She looks around to my other side. "When did you hurt your shoulder? How many injuries do you have?"

I wince. "It's fine. It doesn't need stitches, it's just a graze."

Elise takes my tea and places it on the table next to her.

"Hey," I protest.

She holds up a solitary finger. "I need access to both sides of you without you spilling scalding tea on both of us."

"Fine." I pout. Jess laughs from behind me, the sound soothing.

"A graze from what?" Rhiannon asks, her ice-cold tone pulling me from my reverie. She knows damn well from what, and I refuse to answer her.

Elise *tsks*, and I know she's going to tend to the wound regardless. "You should've stitched up your side. You're lucky it hasn't gotten infected. You know better."

"I did my best," I protest. "Not like I had access to proper medical supplies."

"Whose fault is that?" Elise counters. I sink down in my seat, chastised.

"So tell me about this codename. Who am I listening for?" Jess asks and thankfully directs attention away from my lack of preparation.

I glance at Rhiannon, who sits beside Jess and arches a brow in my direction. Blowing the steam off my tea, I attempt to procrastinate for just another moment. "Uh, codename Songbird."

After another sip, Elise grabs the cup again and puts it back down. As I give Jess the frequency and channel, Elise presses something to my side that is both freezing and stinging, making me hiss and almost knock over the side table.

"Songbird?" Rhiannon asks. "Like the song on the music box? The one about being in love?"

I can feel the blush start at my neck and creep up my face. "What? It's not...I mean, it isn't..."

Elise snorts, and Rhiannon smiles knowingly. I'm about to fire off a retort when the door flies open, and Lucas bursts inside, looking around frantically.

We all turn to him, concerned. "Lucas?" I call.

Out of breath, he hurries to the sitting room. His hair is pulled into a bun atop his head, with pieces of it falling out of the tie. "Hold the line," he says. He pauses to suck in a deep breath. "The enemy approaches."

"The NAF is here?" Rhiannon asks and sits up, panic in her voice. She reaches to twist the little star that dangles on the end of her necklace. Lucas shakes his head, and we all deflate just a little bit. "Raiders?"

Lucas shakes his head again.

"Maybe don't use that line, Lucas," I scold half-heartedly. He blushes, and I realize that if there was any type of serious threat, the town alarm would've sounded.

Jess grips her walking cane, pulling it close. "Who's coming, Lucas?"

Someone enters before he can respond, and I slump, disappointed. It's just William. He gives Lucas an annoyed look and then averts his eyes when he sees me shirtless in the middle of the room. "Very mature, Lucas, running away like that."

Lucas flashes me a sly grin, which I return. Just like when we were kids.

"Dani, I'm glad you're back. The mayor requests your presence immediately." He acknowledges the others in the room without looking at me. "Ladies."

Ignoring his "immediate request," I look to Rhiannon. "Have you met William?"

"Briefly." Rhiannon smiles. "It's nice to see you again."

"Hello, Rhiannon." He bows his head in her direction.

"Wow, I seemed to have missed all the introductions." Can't say I'm sad about it since I was with Kate, but it would've been nice to at least introduce Rhiannon and Elise to Jess. "Can I bathe first?"

"Your presence is requested *now*, Dani." His tone means it's nonnegotiable.

"You should really let her bathe," Elise says, her nose wrinkling slightly. I'd be offended if I wasn't so desperate to wash.

Lucas shakes his head rapidly when I look to him for help. "This is no longer my fight."

I wonder how many meetings he's had to sit in with the mayor and William while I was tucked away with Kate.

Elise applies the new bandage and hands me my shirt. "Godspeed, Atomic Anomaly."

I glare at her and pick up my mug off the table, pulling it close to my chest. "Fine. But I'm taking my tea."

I lean against the wall outside the mayor's office, finishing the remainder of my tea while I glower at William, who stands with his hands clasped behind him. I'm still angry, and he knows it. That's why he's not pressing me to talk about feelings and all that other shit I tend to repress. The convoy we took out was a stress reliever, a direct retaliation against the NAF for what they did to White River. But that doesn't mean I've forgiven William for ignoring me and my requests for protection.

A pipsqueak of a human comes rushing out of the room and motions for us to go in. I knock back the last of my tea, pretending it's something stronger, and hand the man my empty cup.

Mayor Thatcher Price is elbow deep in correspondences and ushers us in with a wave without looking up. A broad woman in both weight and stature, she towers over most men, and when she really ramps up, has most everyone cowering in fear. She's lived in Rapid City for as long as I've known her, a true hometown girl.

I first met Thatcher when I was about nine, when my dad and William came for a meeting. I remember watching her dark skin marked with darker ink as she touched up the Resistance tattoo on her bicep, flexing at us with a wink. She was kind to me then and has been kind to me since. Thatcher advocated for me and Lucas to become residents when I arrived here at twenty years old, looking for a more permanent place to settle. She wasn't mayor then, just a member of the advisory committee, but she's always had our backs.

It's been almost seven years since I've seen her, and looking at her slumped over her desk, I notice a few changes. She's a little thinner, her hair is a little grayer, and there are a few wrinkles around her eyes. The price of politics, I guess.

She looks up, and her dark eyes shine when they land on mine, her lips tugging into the barest hint of a smile.

"Danielle Clark. Daughter of the Resistance. Glad you could find some time to meet with me." There's no malice in her voice. It's even, deadpan.

I hold my hands up and shrug. "Hey, I asked to see you days ago."

She stares for a moment, and William shifts uncomfortably next to me but remains quiet. I flash my most innocent smile.

It only takes a moment before she grins and stands. She may have lost some weight, but she's still intimidating as hell as she crosses the room and pulls me into a tight embrace. My face squishes against her chest, and she pats my back a little rougher than I'd like.

She pulls away to close the door and give me a once-over. "You look older."

"Speak for yourself." I motion toward the gray in her cropped black hair, which causes her to laugh.

"I'll blame that on stunts like blowing up an entire convoy without full Resistance support." She gives William and I both pointed looks and motions toward the two chairs opposite her desk. "I wish we had time to catch up, but I'm afraid this is a matter of utmost importance."

"This can't be good," I mumble.

"We received some interesting intel last night." She holds up a letter and hands it to William first. "My informants have caught wind of the convoy to Omaha being pushed up. It leaves first thing in the morning, along with a clean-up crew to Malmstrom. They're also gathering more supplies to reestablish their connection with Pierre, but we aren't sure when they will be deployed."

My stomach twists at the mention of Omaha. That means Kate will be on her way sooner than I expected. "Do you know who's running the base in Omaha?" I ask casually.

"As far as we can tell, Major Katelyn Turner is still in charge of that area. But with her mother being the general, things are changing so rapidly that we can hardly keep up." Thatcher leans back in her chair and watches me closely. I do my best not to show any kind of reaction at the mention of Kate's name. "It wasn't your best decision to let her go."

Instead of getting defensive about my decisions in White River, I roll my eyes. "Save it, Thatch. I did what I thought was best for my town. Considering I had no help defending it, I'd say my home burning to the ground is punishment enough."

Her expression changes to sympathy, and honestly, that's worse than a lecture.

William scans the letter, still silent, then hands it to me. "Interesting intel. From the looks of it, they're moving quickly so we can't regroup."

"Speaking of informants, you might want to get Archie out as soon as possible." Thatcher and William look at me curiously. "If the NAF find any more towns not listed on their official maps, they're gonna put two and two together since Archie is their map guy. He's compromised."

William and Thatcher share a look. "If you're sure, I'll have him removed from his post immediately."

"They've beefed up security," I warn. The room is silent, and it takes me a moment to realize it's because both William and Thatcher are still staring at me. "What?" I ask. "You think you're the only one with informants?"

"Do you want to fill us in on who you're speaking with?" William asks.

"Do you want to fill me in on who *you're* speaking with?" I fire back. He says nothing. Returning Thatcher's report, I cross one of my legs, my ankle resting on my knee. "What else?" There has to be something. Thatcher wouldn't be this stressed over rearranged convoys and supply runs.

"The most interesting piece of intel was a few hours ago." Thatcher hands William another slip of paper with a hurried message written on it.

His head snaps up to meet her eyes. "Is this legitimate?"

"It appears to be."

Leaning over, I snatch the paper out of William's hands.

It's an updated report on the general. She's planning a quick and indiscreet venture to Ellsworth. If this came through Jess, why didn't she say anything?

"This can't be right," I say. My heart pounds in my chest. "It says she's due to leave at midnight. You didn't know about this?"

William shakes his head. "Hugo would've come to me right away about something this big. My people didn't know."

"This came directly to me. It didn't come through any other channels," Thatcher says as if reading my thoughts. She folds her hands on top of her desk and leans forward. "If we are going to take these reports at face value, then we must move quickly."

I'm pretty sure I know where this is going. "Then let's not take them at face value. I say we wait until there's a sighting. There is no way I am going to plan an attack on an officer's movement if there is no verification of departure. Even if that officer is General Judy herself."

"I agree." Thatcher nods. "That's why I've sent out three scouts. One near Grand Forks, another at Bismarck, and the third near Sioux Falls. If confirmed, you will still have enough time to gather your team and move." She turns to William. "You will still have the people you've requested to scout Malmstrom. Word of more NAF soldiers being deployed there has been confirmed, so if you want to move, you better move."

I look at William. "You're going to Malmstrom? Why?" It seems risky to go toward a base with so much movement. Especially when we don't know their operational status.

"For information. To see if we can find out anything to give us an advantage."

"We have scouts for that."

"And if it's vulnerable," he continues impatiently, "blow it from the inside. It's best we take them out now amidst the confusion." His tone is clear. I would've known and had a say in this if I was here the past two days while arrangements were being made. But still, something seems off about his reasoning, and it makes my skin prickle.

Thatcher sighs. "I can spare another five alongside the fifteen I already promised, but I'm afraid that's it. With the Resistance holding fort at Pierre and now Lincoln, we're stretched pretty thin."

"Lincoln? What's going on in Lincoln?" I ask. Obviously, I missed a hell of a lot during my two-day rendezvous. Not that I regret it.

William looks almost dejected. "They want to acquiesce. We tried to get there first, but unfortunately, the NAF are moving fast into major cities. We can't keep up."

"But I thought Lincoln was doing fine." I don't understand what's going on. I know I've been out of the war for a while, but there's no way things could've gotten that bad without someone letting me know, could they? "Why would they submit to the NAF?"

"That doesn't seem to matter," Thatcher says. "Townships and cities are choosing sides by who they think will have the better outcome. They're looking to be protected, and the NAF is the one with the tech and the weapons. Rapid City is also doing well, but with the general moving closer, people are getting nervous. I can only keep them calm for so long without something to show for it. We need a big win for the Resistance if we want to hold their favor."

"Like taking down the general," I supply.

"Or taking out a base." William looks at me expectantly. "It's your call, but you have to choose right now."

"I guess we attempt both, right?" I ask, sarcastically.

"Okay. I'll take Ericson and Hugo with me, along with the people Thatcher is providing, and we'll continue to the base. See what we can dig up." William faces me in his chair. "We could use all the tech experts we can get. Do you think Darby would be willing to join us?"

His question makes me slightly uncomfortable since I've never even seen her fire a gun. I doubt she knows how to protect herself under extreme pressure. Plus, blowing up an entire convoy and leaving no survivors probably wasn't the best introduction to the Resistance. Instinct tells me she'll go, but she won't be happy about it. "Maybe. If the building is empty. If it's not, you're going to be dealing with a very upset tech expert, one that will refuse to help. And she'll probably only go if Lucas goes, too."

"Lucas is with me, then." He says it matter-of-factly, and it grates on my nerves.

"If he wants to be." My tone is hard, leaving no room for negotiating. No one, including William, gets to make my brother do something he doesn't want to do. If the general really is on the move, it's only right that Lucas is there to get some closure.

"I won't force him to go," William promises. "But we could use him."

"Fine," I relent. "Jack, Mike, and the newly spared five are with me, but I'm going to need some extra firepower. Don't send me in blind. How many explosives can you spare?"

"I'll make sure you both have what you need." Thatcher jots down something on a scrap of paper and seals it. She hands me what I can only assume is an order to release supplies into my care. "Now that that's settled, we have one more issue to discuss. The traitor."

My eyebrows lift to my hairline. "Now there's a traitor? I was only gone two days!"

"We're sealing the gates," Thatcher says, ignoring my comment. "No one in or out unless they have the proper codewords. My chief of security, Isaac, knows the codes and will remain at the gates. Communication will only come from our top Resistance coders, and all other messages, including through courier, will be confiscated. No one is to be trusted."

"That's…a lot." I say, trying to remember a time Rapid City ever all but shut down.

Thatcher looks downright despondent. "The traitor could be a regular who seeks trade or even a current resident. We just don't know."

"I hate to be the one to ask the obvious," I comment dryly, "but if you think they might be living here, then what good is locking the gates?"

"They won't be allowed to leave, send outgoing messages, or receive messages or parcels without our approval, so that should buy us a little bit of time to investigate."

"Unless they're slipping their messages through obvious cracks in your fence," I mutter.

"There are no cracks in my fence," she argues.

"There are always cracks in a fence," I counter. William sighs from beside me.

Thatcher glares but doesn't argue further. "It doesn't look good that the NAF are expanding so quickly. People are getting scared and desperate, and that leads to unsavory alliances. Be very cautious with whom you speak to. Loyalties are being tested."

"And you're sure there's a traitor?" I press again. "What the hell happened?"

"Nothing obvious," Thatcher says. She takes a deep breath. "But there are murmurings of secrets being sold to the NAF. Rumors all over the place, and no one seems to know where they began. If it's not one person, it's several."

"That isn't comforting." I look from Thatcher to William. "Is this about the convoy to Omaha?" I ask hesitantly.

"Partially," he says but doesn't elaborate.

"Okay, well, that could've come from someone in Fargo or Sioux City." I reach for the piece of paper with the instructions to give me whatever kind of firepower I need from Thatcher's desk. I do my best to play innocent and not give away any sort of tell that *I* was the one who tipped off the NAF to help Kate and to have access to Resistance fighters to help me protect White River. Not that I was successful with the latter.

"Fargo and Sioux City are doing the same lockdown. Along with Deadwood and Cedar Rapids. Bismarck and Aberdeen need some convincing. I'll be working with them while you two tend to the issues with Malmstrom and Ellsworth." Thatcher rubs at her temples. It's clear that everything is taking its toll on her.

Glancing from Thatcher to William, I sense there's something else at play that they aren't telling me. When neither of them says anything else, I rub my hands on my pants and break the silence. "If you'll excuse me, I need to prepare to face the general. Not that I think she's actually going to show." I stand and turn to the door.

"Prepare as if she will," Thatcher says. "Be careful. Don't tell your team what you're doing until you're on your way to limit the spread of more rumors. Retreat the second you believe it's a trap."

"So we agree," I say, turning back to face her. "That it's a trap."

"It could always be a trap." She looks at me, her expression serious and commanding. "Danielle." I cringe. The full use of my name is never good among friends. "If it's not a trap, bring her in alive."

I curl my fingers into fists. "Why the hell would I do that?"

"To put her on trial. To make an example of her through justice." Thatcher is serious, and it almost makes me laugh.

"Justice?" I step back toward the desk. "Put her on trial where? On what grounds? Under whose rule? With the new government that has yet to be written or implemented?" This time, I do laugh. "You just want to parade her around town in a blatant display of power."

Thatcher stands and clasps her hands behind her back. "She will stand trial here in Rapid City, and the people will decide. After all, Ellsworth is still within my perimeter." Her message is clear: her jurisdiction, her rules, her call.

"That won't sit well with anyone," I say and shove the paper with her orders in my back pocket. I offer my best smile, putting little effort into making it appear less condescending. "But fine. I'll bring her in, and when her jurors decide she needs to die, I'm going to be the one to take the kill shot."

Thatcher and William exchange another look. Their secrecy is starting to piss me off. "Dani," William starts, but I don't want to hear it.

I turn to leave again and ignore William calling after me until I'm out of Thatcher's office. They're getting under my skin. I don't like being left out.

William quickly follows, and once the door is closed and we are out of earshot, I round on William. "A traitor? You told her there was a traitor?"

"I didn't tell her anything." He turns to look around and then pulls me into the nearest stairwell. "Dani, Thatcher was right about the unease here in town. It's growing with every passing day. The NAF is making people nervous, and the Resistance is stretched so thin—"

"Call everyone back east. Get them here," I say. He releases my arm, and his face falls. He looks old and defeated, but I continue anyway. "Plan more attacks. Hunker down in more cities. Protect who we have left." I shake my head, frustrated. "You and Dad used to be three steps ahead. Now, you're barely keeping up."

"There were a lot more of us then. People are tired of fighting. And after what happened in Hot Springs and White River…" He rubs his hands over his face.

Mention of White River is a punch to the gut, and it only fuels my anger. I'm not going to stand for this sad, broken, old man version of William. "And what's this bullshit about bringing in prisoners? Haven't your orders always been to shoot on sight?"

He straightens his shoulders and holds my glare with one of his own. I've touched a nerve. "I'm not in charge anymore, Dani. It's turning political. The Resistance has chosen to play politics rather than playing soldier. And I agree. We need visionaries if we're going to take back this country and get better leadership into place. We need a fair system."

"So Thatcher is in charge?" I ask. "Of the political side and of the troops?"

"In this part of the land, yes. She's one of several who will help put this country back on course. She's heavily involved in writing the new constitution. They know what they're doing. *She* knows what she's doing. We have to follow their lead."

His confidence in Thatcher and in a fair system almost has me convinced. Almost. "So much so that she can't even figure out if there's a traitor inside her gates? Or keep one city, *her city*, from getting so restless they turn their backs on her?" I throw my hands in the air and shout into the empty stairwell. "What an amazing visionary!"

William gestures for me to keep my voice down. "We are lucky she offers us a safe place to convene."

I roll my eyes. "Oh, we are so blessed."

"It's different now, Dani. A lot has happened in the seven years you were gone." His tone is clipped.

"Clearly." I snap.

He sighs and closes his eyes, trying to regain some of his sanity, no doubt. "I'm leaving at midnight. Will you come with me to talk to Lucas and Darby?" His voice is soft. The change of subject is a truce on this conversation, one I'll gladly take because I'm sick of talking about it.

The last thing I want to do is go tell my brother and his sidekick that they have to do recon work in enemy territory and be part of a mission to blow up a military base with unknown personnel. There is nothing that sounds less appealing. "Fine. But I'm taking a shower and eating first."

He pushes past me. "Meet me in Lucas's room at half past the hour."

I throw my head back and groan.

Convincing Darby to go with William was easier than I thought. I just had to dangle the prospect of new tech in front of her, and she perked right up. The whole thing makes me feel unsettled. Maybe it's because I had nothing to do with the planning. Deep down, I know it's because I just lost my home and some of the people I've spent the last seven years of my life with. I'm not ready to lose any more. Especially my brother.

But after asking him a million times if he was sure, he finally pushed me out of his room and threw a few quotes at me from the sixty-four-page double issue crossover event. I've never figured out a good comeback to the arc where Major Maelstrom fights alongside Atomic Anomaly as they wax poetic about being together while being apart.

Damn Lucas and his perfectly timed quotes.

I spend the rest of the day gathering my supplies and meeting with my team and coming up with my own plan. I take a quick nap and then meet William, Darby, Lucas, and the others loading their vehicles near the garage.

A cold breeze pulls my attention to the sky. The clouds are gone, and the moon shines bright, lighting the darkness. I close my eyes and take a deep breath. There's a distinct chill in the air that adds to my own unease.

Darby attempts to toss a small bag into one of the buggies and misses. The clang of whatever's inside brings my attention back to her. She scrambles to pick it up and catches me watching her. She flashes me a double thumbs-up, a gesture I refuse to return.

Instead, I sidle up next to Lucas. "Smells like winter." I bump his shoulder with my own.

"A proper night is that of summer heat and cold drinks, my friend," he grumbles. Lucas has never liked the cold.

"Issue one hundred forty-three," Darby calls out.

"Darby…" I sigh. "The issues never went past one-oh-five, how can you seriously—"

Lucas pulls me close by my shoulder. "Patience, Private. Patience will bring you victory and earn you prestige."

"Issue thirty-two." I smile at him and pull his knit cap farther down on his head. I take a quick glance around and see everyone is ready to head out. "Listen, Lucas, if things aren't right at Malmstrom…" William and Darby are within earshot, but I don't care. This is really for all of them anyway. "If anything feels off at all, get out of there, okay? I mean it. Nothing about any of this seems right, and it's not worth getting hurt or worse."

"You ready?" William presses Lucas to join him in the front vehicle.

"That means you, too, William." Regardless of our disagreements, I don't want anything bad to happen to him. He's still my family.

He nods. "I know."

"And you, Darby. If you have a bad feeling, you don't have to do anything you're not comfortable with." I shoot a look at William, making sure he knows not to force her into anything.

Darby gives a wave and tries a smile. It looks more pained than anything else. She's nervous, that much is certain. "Compartmentalized and ready to go."

I frown. "Darby."

"I'm good. You guys said you needed me, and so here I am. I can do this." Her expression softens a little. "I just want to help."

"She's in good hands." William pats Darby's shoulder. It's probably supposed to be comforting, but Darby tenses.

Lucas places his hand on my shoulder and smiles.

"Don't do anything stupid." I can tell he wants to say something witty, but I beat him to it. "Just nod and agree, okay? No more double-issue quotes."

"Affirmative." He pushes away a moment later and leans into the buggy, pulling out my Kevlar vest and handing it over. It's patched up and restocked with grenades and ammunition after the attack on the convoy.

Smiling, I look it over, happy to have it in better condition than I left it a couple days ago.

"Survival is about patience, critical thought, and taking care of your gear," he says.

My eyes meet his. I can count the number of times we've been separated in a fight on one hand. He's always had my back, and I've always had his. I know this is his way of trying to watch out for me, too. "You take it." He shakes his head and motions to the back seat to his own vest. That makes me feel a little better. "Darby, then."

"I do not want grenades strapped to my chest, thank you. That's your thing." Darby slides in the back seat, and I sigh. It's hard to let the people I care about go off and do something stupid without me. But Lucas gives me another reassuring smile.

"Be safe," I say one last time. He nods.

William starts the buggy, and Lucas climbs in the back with Darby. "Maelstrom never liked good-byes."

"Issue one twenty," Darby shouts.

"I'm gonna hurt her."

"This seems dumber than blowing up the last convoy." Jack stands beside me with his hands on his hips while I hide a row of spikes stretched along the road. The morning sun is bright, but the air is bitterly cold, cutting through every piece of clothing I'm wearing. I just want to get this done so I can warm my hands.

Wendy, the only female of the borrowed five from Thatcher, speaks up. "I didn't think we were blowing them up." She's staring at the grenade launcher near Jack, something he refuses to part with after using it against the convoy.

"We're not. The grenade launcher is our contingency plan. We've been ordered to bring the general in alive, so let's try and avoid all the booms, okay?" I see several heads nod in understanding, and I look up at Jack. "That means you, Mohawk." I can't see his eyes through his sunglasses, but I'd bet my life that he's glaring at me. The nickname reminds me of Kate, and I feel a slight bit of dread at the prospect of bringing her mother in. The feeling of having any kind of regret over capturing the general is foreign, and I don't know what to do with it. I push it down and focus on the game plan. "Mind helping me out here?"

Begrudgingly, Jack gets down and helps me push dirt over the second row of spikes a little farther down the road.

"Any word on the convoy?" Mike asks.

"Just that all sightings have been confirmed, and they are on their way and on time. The intel seems legitimate," Dobson, the smallest of the five, explains.

"How do we know we aren't right smack-dab in the middle of an ambush or getting played?" Jack asks.

"We don't," I tell him. "And my gut tells me we are." The rest of the team starts to look around nervously.

Jack asks the obvious question, "Then why are we here?"

"Because we were ordered to be," I answer honestly.

No one says anything else while Jack and I finish covering the spikes. The quiet makes me think of Lucas and wonder how he's faring. I'm anxious to radio him. It's been hours since they checked in, and the silence is making me uneasy. *All of this* is making me uneasy.

Jack and I make quick work of camouflaging our trap, and I wipe my hands on my pants. "You know the plan. We blow their tires, and when they come to a stop, we pull our cars in front and behind and trap them in place. We make them get out of the vehicles, and we bring them in. Expect them to resist and expect them to open fire, so stay near cover. If they try to make a run for it, then, and only then, take them out. But try to keep the general alive."

"And if it *is* a trap?" Dobson asks. Clearly, they're still nervous. Not that I blame them.

"Get the jump on them and fight like hell." I shrug. Pep talks were never my thing.

Jack gives me a look and gestures for me to continue.

"What?" I frown at him.

"That's it? That's your speech?"

I throw my hands up, not knowing what else he wants. "What? You want me to recite the St. Crispin's Day Speech?"

"I was thinking maybe a little Patton, circa second world war."

I stare at him for a moment, and he stares back, his expression serious. "You only know about that speech because he talks about the enemy's balls."

His serious expression never falters. "So?"

I motion for people to move. "Just get into position." Everyone nods, except Jack, who mutters something about twisting balls. I slip on my vest, strapping it tightly around my midsection. It's as good as new thanks to Lucas.

Sliding in the driver's seat of my Jeep, I keep my eyes on the dirt road ahead. This isn't my best plan, but it's all we've got, and I need to make sure it works. Mike sits beside me in the passenger's seat, and Jack is in the truck behind us. Four of Thatcher's people occupy two of their own vehicles down the road and out of sight, ready to box the convoy in on my mark.

Our remaining man, Zach, is on the ridge and radios in that a four-buggy convoy has been spotted. They'll be here in a matter of minutes. It's not unusual for an officer to travel without a lot of firepower when it's meant to be kept under wraps. But when you're trying to keep the movement secret, it doesn't normally come with a high-profile sendoff.

I toss Mike a piece of gum. "Keep your eyes on everyone. Watch for weird movements. Especially if it looks like someone is going for a weapon or anything else that might seem threatening. If a hand disappears into a pocket or behind their backs, take 'em out." I'm not risking my people for William and Thatcher to hold a trial.

Mike unwraps the gum and pops it into his mouth. "Understood."

I give one last order through the radio. "Remember, they're probably expecting us, so we need to flip the script and make sure no one gets in from behind us. Keep your eyes peeled, and we'll be just fine."

At the sounds of vehicles approaching, I pull the scarf over my face. Putting my foot on the break, I shift to drive and get ready to peel out in front of the convoy. I glance in my rearview mirror and see Jack straightening in his seat.

There's no visual yet on the cars, but a quick update from Zach says to get ready. I wait for the sound of tires popping before accelerating onto the road.

We hit three of the four buggies with our spikes. With their tires blown and with Jack and I blocking their path forward and the other two cars blocking them from behind, the convoy has no choice but to sit still between us, the one good car trapped with nowhere to go.

I race out of my Jeep with both pistols drawn and pointed at the windshields of the first buggy. I can't see inside; the glare of the sun and the tinted windows make it impossible. My guns won't do much damage to the bulletproof glass, but it's a threatening sight just the same.

Jack holds up his grenade launcher and stands in front of both me and Mike, and I can see the other four flanking from the rear. Their buggies are stuck, with two sets of launchers pointed at them and a bunch of flat tires. There's really no other option other than to exit the vehicles firing or just flat-out surrender.

I hold my breath while they choose.

My chest flutters at the possibility of coming face-to-face with the general. Every fiber in my body is humming for revenge, and I grip my pistols tighter. If there is even the slightest chance that she's inside, I want to be ready. The thought of seeing her, of being face-to-face with the one woman I've wanted dead for most of my life makes my trigger fingers itch.

Another moment stretches on. By now, it seems clear that they have no intention of getting out. At least not without a little incentive.

"Kill the engine. You've got nowhere to go. Turn 'em off," Jack yells, clearly thinking the same.

"We've got you surrounded," Wendy yells from the rear.

"Get the fuck out of the buggy. Now," Jack's voice booms, and he adjusts the launcher to let them know he means business.

Mike holds perfectly still beside me, his large rifle resting on the hood of the Jeep to steady it as he stares through the scope.

"Do you see her?" I ask him.

"She's not in either of the front two buggies from what I can tell," he says. "I can't see in the other two. Do you think they're waiting for reinforcements?"

"I don't know," I say honestly.

Slowly, a door opens from the vehicle closest to the front. After that, it's a trickle effect, and all the driver's doors follow suit. "Nice and easy. Let me see your hands," I shout. A young man in a private's uniform steps carefully out of the first buggy. A woman with a rank of what appears to be a specialist emerges from the second. Another two from the third and fourth, both privates.

This is all wrong. The general would be riding with more experienced personnel. These are just children, no more than eighteen or nineteen years old.

"She's not here," I say. "We've been played."

"What?" Jack glances at me and then back at the four gray coats with their hands in the air.

Despite the immense disappointment, I stare at the specialist, who looks straight ahead, her arms shifting slightly. Three privates and a specialist. My mind races. A specialist of…what?

"Going to bring us in?" the specialist asks, drawing our attention to where she stands in the front. Her question throws me. The privates that surround her look nervous. Too nervous. "We have intel in the back. It's yours if you let us go."

"What kind of intel?" Wendy yells from behind.

"I'll round them up," Jack says and takes a step forward.

I extend my arm, stopping him. "Don't." My mind races. Officer's convoy with no officer. Elaborate sendoff. Promise of intel… "Don't go near them," I shout to the others. It's a diversion. My eyes lock on the slight movements of the specialist's hands as she goes to reach within the sleeve of her jacket. "Shit. Mike—"

I don't even have time to finish my warning before a loud crack slices through the air, and the woman's head snaps back, her body crumpling to the ground.

The three privates all fall to the ground at the sound and cover their heads.

"What the hell is happening?" Jack asks from a crouch.

"Nobody move, or you'll all get a bullet in the head," I call out. I step forward and glance at the woman and the detonator poking out from her left jacket sleeve. "Check them," I say to Jack. "Make sure no one else tries anything and tie them up. Mike, help me check these buggies." I holster one of my pistols and talk to our point guy on the ridge. "Radio base and tell them it was a trap. No general here. Keep your eyes peeled for any other movement from your vantage point."

I go straight to the second buggy while Mike checks the first. Quickly, I open the door and stand out of the way in case anything or anyone is inside, and when nothing appears, I step around the door to have a look.

I let out a low whistle at all the gasoline and propane tanks in the back seat and trunk. There's enough firepower in here to put a hole in the earth. I get low to the ground. Attached under the seat are two small receivers connected to a large box nestled on the floor.

Already knowing what I'll find inside, a tangled mess of wires and other explosive devices, I choose not to even bother looking. It's a pretty rudimentary setup, one that was quickly done but would've been effective all the same.

"Wow. Okay," Mike says. He slowly backs up a few steps. I don't tell him backing up is pointless with this amount of firepower. It's a wonder they didn't blow us from inside their cars. There was no need to try to lure us any closer. "What are we going to do about that?"

"Check the other cars." I close the door and walk away, bringing the radio to my lips. "Maelstrom, come in." I wait but receive no answer. "Maelstrom, it's Atomic Anomaly, repeat, come in." Still no answer. I try for William. "Skull Splicer, come in, it's Atomic Anomaly."

Finally, after a long, agonizing minute, the radio crackles to life. "Major Maelstrom reporting for duty."

Relief washes over me at the sound of Lucas's voice. I glance at Jack and the others pushing the handful of NAF soldiers into our vehicles for the ride back. "Engagement has been made. It was a trap. We're heading back to base."

"The mission was a failure?"

"Unfortunately. How's it going on your end?" There's a slight rustling on the other end before a new voice comes through.

"It's Darby."

I close my eyes and pinch the bridge of my nose in utter exasperation. "You aren't supposed to say your name. That's why you have a codename, so no one knows who you are. We talked about all of this last night."

"Well, excuse me, I don't remember my codename, and I don't understand all of your stupid rules."

"Jesus Christ." Even from over five hundred and fifty miles away, the girl still manages to grate on my every nerve. "Just tell me what's going on."

"For starters, there's, like, no one here. Thankfully."

As happy as I am to hear there wasn't a firefight, the information doesn't sit right with me. I have the same nagging feeling as before. An empty base? They couldn't have *all* evacuated. "What do you mean there's no one there?"

"Exactly what I said. There's no one here. A few guards out front that William took care of, something I don't want to think about, but no one inside that we've seen. And, Dani, you're not going to believe this, but there are planes here. Like, two big planes, real scary-looking, too. No motors or anything, those are gone. Just two big plane shells. And drones. Pieces of drones and tech that looks like it was left behind when everyone up and left. Kind of like, they were too rushed to pack everything? I mean, we passed a kitchen where there were still meals on the table. Anyway, they're putting a lot of resources in getting around the blockers to get these things flying. We're looking for the fuel source now."

I ignore the use of my real name. I even ignore the information dump about the planes and drones and food. I'm still hung up on the "alone" and "fuel" part. "Are you still inside?"

"Yeah, we're trying to salvage as much as we can and pull any kind of data while—"

I look at the dead specialist on the ground with the bomb detonator beside her and then to all the fuel inside the back seat. "Get out of there. Now."

"We aren't finished—"

"It's a trap," I say, the words coming out in a rush. "Get everyone out of there right now!" Panicked, I rush to Jack as he shoves the last of the prisoners into one of the cars.

He looks at me, startled, and I stare back, motioning toward the radio.

"She says we have to get out," I hear Darby tell the others.

"Now, Darby!" I yell. I need her to hear and understand the urgency in my voice. The soldiers inside the buggy watch me. I'm not sure if they know what's going on or if they were only given their own marching orders and nothing else. But they still observe the exchange between me and the radio with curiosity.

"What the hell is going on?" Jack asks.

I don't answer him. I look at Wendy. "Keep your guns on them. If they so much as blink, shoot them."

She nods, and the rest of Thatcher's people tighten their grips on their pistols pointed on the gray coats. I pull both Jack and Mike away from enemy ears.

"You think we were all set up?" Jack asks.

"Yeah, I do." I look back to the small convoy stopped in the middle of the road and rub the back of my neck as I try to settle my nerves. I never should have let them go to Malmstrom.

"Would the mayor give us bad information?" Mike asks. It's a good question, and I'm glad he's thinking the way he is, especially since there's been a lot of misinformation floating around. "Do you think she's…"

I shake my head. "I doubt it. Thatcher's been Resistance since before I was born. She's always been loyal and true." I glance at the four still holding their positions, guns on the prisoners. "But if there's a chance that Thatcher is compromised…"

"I'll babysit." Jack pulls his shotgun from his back and stares at Thatcher's crew.

"Come on," I mumble and start to pace. "Come on, Darby."

A voice finally through the radio cuts through. "Hello?" It's Darby.

"We're here." Mike watches me anxiously as I answer. "What's going on? Are you with Lucas? Where's William?"

"Calm down, Atomic Whatever. We're on our way out. Well, most of us. I'm not sure where—"

Whatever else Darby was going to say is cut off. The sound of a loud explosion crackles through the speaker before the radio falls deathly silent.

"Darby? Darby?" My heart races, and all the air forces its way out of my lungs. "Darby! Are you there?" I look at Mike, who stares back with wide eyes. When there's no reply, my stomach twists, and I double over, thinking I'm about to be sick.

CHAPTER EIGHT: THE VISION

KATE

Why would my mother would pretend to go to Ellsworth? I doubt very seriously that all the grandeur around leaking her nonexistent trip to Ellsworth was just about keeping me safe. As disappointing as it is not to be my mother's main priority, it's something to which I have become quite accustomed.

"I trust that General Foley gave you a full debrief?" She takes a step closer to me.

"Yes, ma'am." I do my best to hide the fatigue from the ride here and listen closely to her choice of words, which are apparently loaded with intel.

"Excellent." She eyes me carefully, and her expression changes into a motherly one. It's subtle, but it's there, the way her posture deflates just slightly, and her features soften. "You look exhausted."

I shake my head, dismissing her worry. "It was just a long drive. And a lot to take in."

"You still have questions." She states this more than asks and then sighs. Her tone is laced with annoyance.

Pushing my hesitancy aside, I ask, "Permission to speak freely?"

"Granted." Her shoulders square, and in a blink of an eye, she is back to being the general.

I gesture to the tote filled with files by my feet. "Are we ready for all this? Do we have enough soldiers? Supplies? Time? General Trent—"

"General Trent was a damn fool and had no intention of unifying anything, let alone the nation." Her face hardens, and she sneers as her tirade continues. "He twiddled his thumbs and was happy with controlling the east and letting these…heathens out west do whatever they pleased. He had no vision of progress. No concept of unity. He was a buffoon, and his death was the best thing for our future."

My eyebrows rise at her outburst. It's not often I see my mother lose her cool and rattle off so passionately. I'm about to respond when she continues.

"There is no chance of unification until the Resistance is destroyed. Until every single insurgent is taken out. This lawlessness has gone on long enough." She huffs out a last, harsh breath through her nose, like a bull who was prodded one too many times.

I need time to digest everything she's said so far. She can't possibly be suggesting that the best option for *peace* is *murder*. Unfortunately, I don't have time to analyze it at this moment. Doing my best to redirect, I bring up the files again. "Yes, well, using drones to provide supplies to those in need will be crucial to our cause of *unification*."

My mother's expression shifts again from anger to amusement. "You are so much like your father. He always looked for the positive side of problems, ignoring the difficult choices."

"I don't understand what that means."

She motions for me to sit at the small desk behind her. Once we are seated opposite each other, she folds her hands atop the surface. "Your father had a vast desire to help people. No matter where we were, he'd always see someone who needed help, and he would do everything in his power to do so. He'd give you the shirt off his back or the food from his table if you said you needed it."

I look at my lap and swallow hard. She doesn't have to remind me how generous he was. My father was the kindest man I knew, and thinking of him in past tense always hurts.

"But Theodore also ignored the difficult decisions regarding the big picture. Just like you are now. The people need to fall in line, or our goal of a unified country will never be accomplished." Her tone is angry, not inspiring. Her leadership skills have always seemed to be lacking in some way to me, and now I can see why. The general incites fear, not encouragement. It may work on some, but it leaves a bad taste in my mouth.

Straightening my posture, I push back. "Fall in line? What if the people in the wastelands are happy living this way?" My mind is with the people of White River. The happy chatter and music coming from Rhiannon's tavern that I heard on a nightly basis could never be considered as people suffering or hating their circumstances.

"Happy?" she bites back quickly. "These people wouldn't know joy if it struck them on the head. More and more of them are absorbing the Resistance way of thinking with each passing day. Then they reach out to us because they are in need of food and other necessities, something the Resistance isn't giving them. They want our handouts but don't want to live by our laws, and I will not allow it."

To some degree, she's correct. But despite our best efforts to help, we don't have a great reputation among the people here. They can't like what they don't understand, and the Resistance has taught them that our laws are harsh and unjust, something we desperately need to rectify. "If we could just open a line of communication and offer to help, to show them—"

She slaps the desk, causing me to jump. "Do you really think people like William Russell or Danielle Clark are capable of civilized conversation? They are Neanderthals, and they only speak one language: violence. And if that's what they want, then that's what they'll get."

She's being completely unreasonable and clearly doesn't want to listen to anything I have to say. But it doesn't stop me from trying. "You're talking about using drones to threaten people."

"I'm talking about giving people a choice. Join us under one nation, or pay the price for insubordination." She sits back in her chair and casually reaches for her drink.

My stomach lurches when I consider what price that may be. Especially for Dani. "I just think there's a better way to bring about unity than to kill everyone who disagrees."

"Katelyn." She sucks in a long breath before starting again, softer this time. "Katelyn, don't you think I would do it that way if I honestly believed that was for the best? For centuries, the generals of the great National Armed Forces have tried to pacify everyone. They have extended olive branches and attempted peaceful transitions. It just doesn't work. The Resistance lives on in this country like a cancer. They are poisoning us from the inside. It's time we remove them once and for all. It's the only way we will begin to really thrive."

I bite my tongue. There is no point in telling her that peaceful transitions *have* been working, albeit slowly. I want to ask her why this has to happen now, why she can't let us progress as we have. What's the urgency? I don't ask because I fear her answer. "With your permission, I would still like to try to take the surrounding area peacefully without excessive force. At least until the aerial unit is operational. I think we're making a decent impact on the people here and have already shown success."

It's a gamble, but it's the best card I can play right now in the shitty hand I've been dealt. She seems to think about it, which is more than I expected, but she still seems unsure. Though without her drones ready to take flight, I doubt she has any other choice. It's either my way or do nothing, and my mother has never been known to stand by and do nothing. "I will allow negotiations of peaceful transitions to continue so long as progress on your new assignment remains at the forefront of your command." She sits straighter and gives me a pointed look. Her terms are nonnegotiable.

"Understood." We stare at each other a second too long for my liking; her gaze is piercing, intimidating, like she's studying me and knows more than she's letting on. It makes me uncomfortable. "Permission to be excused, General. I have a lot of paperwork to go through, and I'd like to get started immediately."

This seems to appease her ever so slightly. She nods and stands, and I follow suit, anxious to get away from her.

"Lieutenant Colonel." Her voice is hard, and it stops me in my tracks. "I have placed much faith in you with this particular assignment. It would be unwise to fail."

Her meaning is clear, and it fills my chest with dread. I don't even want to think of the consequences if I don't deliver. I'm running out of time to stop my mother from needless attacks, and I'm beginning to doubt myself. My new rank is heavy, and I'm not convinced that I'm equipped to carry it.

I was expecting Ryan to be waiting for me, but I'm surprised to see a woman I don't recognize. She stands at attention and salutes as I pass. "Lieutenant Colonel." I offer a quick salute of my own and press forward.

The first order of business is to ensure the supply specialists are ready for the incoming stockpile of equipment. Then I need to drop off my personal items and start going over these plans again. Speaking with Ryan is also high on my priorities and of course, overseeing the arrival of the convoy. Somewhere in there, I'll probably need to eat and sleep. And honestly, if I could drop everything and talk to Dani, I would do that first. But until I can excuse myself from my obligations here, that too, is going to have to wait.

"I'm sorry, ma'am, I beg your pardon," the woman says as she falls in line with me. "I'm Command Sergeant Major Rodrigues. I've been assigned to assist you."

My steps don't slow, but I do glance over to get a better look at the short young girl keeping pace with me. She's dressed in fatigues, and her dark hair is pulled back into a low bun nestled under her cap. "Assist me with what?" I ask.

"Anything. Everything, ma'am."

"Who assigned you?" I frown.

"General Foley under the orders from General Turner herself, ma'am."

My next step falters. I straighten and act like her words didn't just trip me up. The thought of my mother personally assigning someone as my assistant doesn't sit well with me. Is this her way of spying on me, or does she honestly think I'll need help with the new workload? I briefly wonder when I became so damn paranoid. Then I remember the radio from Dani stuffed at the bottom of my bag. Yeah, I can probably pinpoint that being the pinnacle of my paranoia.

Ignoring the anxiety in the pit of my stomach, I decide to stay on track before putting any more attention on my suspicious new assistant. I look around for Supply Specialist Talib and find him already giving commands and pointing people in different directions around the warehouse. He stops to salute when I approach with my new assistant hot on my heels.

"At ease," I tell him. "Are you set for the incoming supplies?" In my peripheral vision, I notice Rodrigues settle slightly behind me to my right.

"Yes, ma'am." His smile seems excited. He always did like coordinating and maintaining. It's why he's the best supply specialist I've ever worked alongside. "And may I say, it's good to have you back, ma'am."

A forced smile pulls at the corners of my mouth. "It's good to be back." I notice a large box not far from where we stand with all sorts of odd-looking items inside. Normally, I wouldn't give it any kind of thought, but there's a strange old shirt draped over the edge with the same logo I saw Lucas wearing back in White River. "What is that?"

Talib turns to look. "Our reconnaissance team recovered some old Resistance propaganda on their last sweep of the nearby towns."

"Have you been through it?"

"No, ma'am, I just haven't had the time. The news of the acquisition of supplies from Malmstrom has kept me busy today. I will comb through it immediately."

I wave him off. "That won't be necessary. You have enough on your plate. Sergeant Major Rodrigues," I say, turning to my new assistant. "Have you ever gone through Resistance propaganda?"

"No, ma'am."

I make a disapproving sound. Back east, it was required to sort through propaganda, looking for clues and learning our enemies. "Today's your lucky day. Grab that box, and let's go."

It takes us much longer to get to my office than expected. Officers and soldiers stop to welcome me home and ask how I am. I should feel grateful and appreciated, but I'm only irritated and tired. Where this place once felt like home, now it feels foreign and cold.

The door to my office is open when we finally arrive, and Rodrigues places the box on the floor and wipes her brow.

I scan the room. I don't know why, but it feels weird to see stacks of papers off to the side right where I left them. My chair is still tucked under the wooden desk with the chipped left corner. It's like I was never gone. But somehow, I still feel displaced.

Light shines from the large window on the opposite side of the room, illuminating the thin layer of dust on the virtually empty bookshelf on the adjacent wall. I stare at the old country's flag, folded in a perfect triangle in a pristine case in the middle of the top shelf right next to the NAF flag, red and white vertical stripes with a blue circle in the center with a singular white star within. Looking at it used to bring me a sense of pride. Now it makes me confused.

Next to the flags are a few stacks of binders and a pile of maps. Other than that, the shelves are empty. If this is home, why are they empty?

"Are you okay, ma'am?"

Rodrigues's voice startles me. "Just thinking how weird it is that my office looks exactly how I left it." She tilts her head curiously. I drop the duffels beside my desk and motion to the guest chair. "Please, sit. And thank you for carrying that."

Rodrigues removes her cap and places it in her lap and glances at the box she lugged all the way across base.

"While we have a few quiet moments, why don't you tell me about yourself and how you became unfortunate enough to be assigned as my assistant." I offer a smile, one that hopefully says she can be candid with me.

She remains stiff in posture. "That's easy, ma'am. I asked to be."

Now that has me curious. "Oh?" I lean back and unbutton the top buttons of my uniform but leave my jacket on. It's chilly in here. Fuel for my heater, that's what I need to get.

She nods almost bashfully. "My last commanding officer was approached by General Foley. They were looking for people who know flight procedures, with a high-level security clearance. My name, along with a few others, was brought up, and we were asked if assisting the new commanding officer of the aerial unit here in Omaha would be of interest."

"And clearly, it interested you enough to say yes. Did you know it was going to be me?" I take a moment to really look at her, gauging her intentions by the way her eyes dance when I make such assumptions.

Her smile grows. "There were rumors it was going to be."

"Ah," I say, reaching for a bottle of water within my desk. "Easy access to my mother?"

"Actually, ma'am," she says and hesitantly takes the bottle I offer. "I was hoping it would be you because of your father." She must notice my confused expression because she rushes to explain. "I've studied flight and your father's work my entire life. It's always been of interest to me. Working on drones at Malmstrom was a dream come true."

She's younger than me, which may contribute to her bright-eyed passion. I don't let on that I had no idea about what was really happening in Malmstrom. Or respond to her comment about my father.

So far, Rodrigues reminds me of myself ten years ago. I would smile at the prospect if I wasn't so conflicted on whether that's actually a good thing anymore. I lost soldiers, I was taken prisoner, and I slept with the enemy. I try to focus on the issue at hand, briefly wondering why my mind keeps slipping back to the people of White River at any given chance. "And what do you think being my assistant means? What do you think it grants you?"

"An opportunity to remain with my life's work and advance in my field." Her answer is swift. "That is, if you let me continue, ma'am." I catch a hint of nervousness in her voice for the first time. "Working on top secret assignments proves I am trustworthy with confidential information, and I'm hardworking, so multitasking won't be a problem."

"You think it's a faster way to a promotion," I guess.

She blushes wildly. Can't say the woman isn't driven. "I was hoping it would be a faster path to actually get to fly one day," she says candidly.

I appreciate her honesty even if I don't understand why someone would ever willingly get in an aircraft and hover high above the ground. "I'll tell you what," I offer, "you help me with the projects I'm working on, and I will allow you to oversee the progress and research of your current work. We'll see how well you can multitask and if that promotion is in range."

She straightens in her seat. "Yes, ma'am, thank you."

I sit forward to match her posture. "Let's jump right in and see what you've got. The first thing I need you to do is go find Chief Warrant Officer Matthews and have him meet me here. Do you know who he is?"

"I will find out, ma'am."

That's a good answer. "Then, I need you to get me an updated list of cities and townships in the area. We need to commence providing aid to those in need. We'll go through the propaganda after that."

"Yes, ma'am." Her eyes remain locked with mine.

"And please for the love of all that is holy, find me some propane for this heater. It's freezing in here."

Rodrigues puts her hat on and swiftly exits, leaving the door wide open after her departure. I swivel and look out the window at the activity on base. Not many people are out and about, and I have a feeling it has nothing to do with the chill in the air but more because they know the general is around. Not that I blame them; if I could hide from my mother, I'd be doing the same.

My entire body shivers, and I blow hot air into my hands and rub them together. How was it so much warmer only a couple weeks ago? Just another thing I don't understand about the wasteland. The more I come to realize about this place, the less I understand it.

Glancing at the large bags by my feet, I take a deep breath and decide now is as good a time as any to unpack the endless amounts of files. It doesn't take long before the contents of the duffels are deposited atop my desk, the chaos now visibly present.

Staring at the mounds of papers, I lean back and press my palms against my eyes, attempting to keep the impending headache at bay. Knowing it'll be fruitless, I unfasten the rest of the buttons on my jacket and slip it off my shoulders. I toss the stiff garment aside, roll up my sleeves, and get to work, cold be damned.

I go through the personnel stack first, thankful that they are meticulously labeled, until I get to the R's. Shuffling through the papers, I come across the one I am looking for: Jenisis Rodrigues; Command Sergeant Major. Twenty-six years old, born at Scott Air Force Base.

I scan it quickly. Both parents are current members of the NAF, both in specialty positions, noncombative, moved to Joint Base Andrews when she was a kid, enlisted at sixteen, completed combat training by eighteen, and then remained at Joint Base Andrews until she was twenty, when she was transferred to Malmstrom where she has been for the past six years.

Six years. Malmstrom has been operational for six years, and not once did I ever know what the hell they were working on. I keep reading.

There is absolutely nothing in her file that indicates her opinions about using drones one way or another except that she loves flight and has been working hard to remain in that field. She's seen combat, mostly clearing outposts and pushing back raiders, from the looks of it, but she received high marks in marksmanship and has other accreditations in weapons' combat and leadership. Though she's moderately decorated with achievements, she's chosen to pursue research and development with the intent to lead an aerial division.

I close the file and toss it atop the tall stack on my desk. These personnel files contain the absolute bare minimum in regard to anything that may help me get to know them as actual people.

I release my hair from the bun and comb my fingers through it, scratching at my scalp. Where should I even begin now that my quick review of Rodrigues is finished? So much has been thrust at me in such a short time, and all I can think about is how nice it was to get away from all my responsibility and spend a relatively normal day with Dani.

For a moment, I let myself picture the impossible. Living with Dani in our own place, maybe a small cottage that overlooks a body of water. We could garden and learn to cook together. Or read books by the fireplace at night. No war. No military. Just us…existing in the same space, happy and without obligation.

My shoulders deflate quickly as the impossible daydream evaporates from my mind. Maybe now is the time to try to reach her, tell her about the drones before anyone comes back into my office. Would that be too risky? Waiting until I get back to my house may be better. There are eyes and ears everywhere.

I swivel and stretch my legs. My foot bumps the box that Rodrigues carried over for me. Crouching next to it, I sift through the Resistance propaganda. I look at the shirt first, gray and torn with two overlapping M's in the center. Lucas was wearing something similar when I was being held in White River.

Pushing it aside, I grab one of the three issues of *Major Maelstrom* comics. It amuses me that this comic superhero held such a pivotal role in the anti-military Resistance movement during the third war. I keep rummaging.

There's a stack of old recruitment flyers that appear never to have been posted, some old newspaper clippings, decaying and stained with headlines about bombs and the closing of the country's borders.

So far, there's really nothing worth keeping. Something shiny catches my eye at the bottom of the box. It's a pin. I brush my thumb across the circular shape and then across the Major Maelstrom logo in the middle. It's in great condition, no rust or grime. Smiling, I muse over how excited Lucas would be to have this.

"You wanted to see me?" Ryan's deep voice startles me, and I stand quickly, almost as if I was caught doing something I shouldn't have been, and shove the pin in my pants pocket. I motion for him to enter. "Close the door."

"What's all that?" He peers into the box.

"Resistance propaganda. Nothing new, it's all old war stuff. The newspaper clippings are interesting, though." I push the box away and sit in my chair.

"Why are you going through it?" he asks, lifting one of the yellow-tinted papers.

"Procrastinating," I say and smile. "It's been a while since I've been through a stash of Resistance memorabilia."

"You always loved those lessons. 'Propaganda and Ideology: The Downfall of the Nation.'" He tosses the paper back in the box and holds up a new canister of propane.

"Wow, she really does seem to know how to multitask," I say while Ryan replaces my empty can and starts up the heater. "Thank you."

He sits across from me and eyes the folders and binders. He lets out a low whistle at my mess. "Now I can see why you have an assistant."

I sigh. "What do you think of her?"

"Command Sergeant Major Rodrigues?" He shrugs. "I only met her long enough for her to tell me you wanted to see me and for her to shove some propane into my hands. What do *you* think about her?"

"I don't really know yet," I tell him honestly. "I don't know whether to be insulted that my mom assigned me a babysitter or thankful that I can pass some of this workload off on someone else." I pat the piles in front of me for emphasis. At this point, I'm not sure what is stressing me out the most: my mother, Dani, Rodrigues, or this pile of paperwork.

Ryan nods and chuckles. "I'd say the latter." He looks at the mess on my desk but doesn't make a move to touch or examine them any closer. "Drones, huh?"

My stomach sinks, and I mentally add "drones" to the top of my stressor list. Maybe I should've tried to talk to Dani in my few minutes alone. "Looks like." I rummage through the pile and hand Ryan the folder containing the photographs documenting flight progress. "My mother wants to drop bombs. She told me explicitly." My voice is steady, but my insides are jittery. Every moment that passes since I spoke with the general is another moment that the weight of the fallout from this development crushes me a little more.

"Guess she didn't go to Ellsworth," Ryan says warily.

"Misdirection," I say robotically, repeating her earlier sentiment.

"Or a trap," he supplies.

"Or a trap," I repeat and swallow hard, knowing that Dani is her target. "Do you know her motives?"

"I haven't had time to dig." He stretches his arms high in the air and rests them on top of his head as he relaxes in the seat.

I slouch back and shrug. "Maybe I'll have Rodrigues look into it."

"See? Having an assistant is already coming in handy." He smiles.

I groan and bury my face in my hands. I'm trying to wrap my head around everything, but I can't seem to grasp at a single thing at a time. Too much is circling in my mind.

"Did you know what was going on in Malmstrom?" I doubt very seriously he knew. There have never been secrets between us, and if he heard something, I know he would've come to me first. It makes me feel guilty when I think of the radio shoved in my bag.

"No. I thought they were manned enough to keep a presence but had no idea they were using the base as a research facility. Honestly, I just thought they were scoping out the landscape and maybe setting up outposts."

"Yeah, me too." I tell him, defeated and embarrassed.

He stares. The only sound is the soft hum from the heater that is finally putting out enough heat to begin to warm the room. "Are you okay?"

For a long time, I don't answer. I'm not sure how to voice all my uncertainty. "Ryan, I don't think I can be in charge of a unit that drops bombs. And I'm not talking about on just the Resistance. I'm talking about regular people. Disagreeing with us shouldn't be a death sentence." Even saying the words pulls at my chest.

"Maybe it won't come to that." He's trying to help, I know he is. But it's not working. I'm not a murderer. It *can't* come to that.

"The general wants the wasteland and everything surrounding it taken by the end of winter. How can we get all the major cities and towns to peacefully relinquish their homes to the NAF? How can we convince them it's in the country's best interest?" I have serious doubts, and I need to hear his assurances. Ryan has been a steady source of support for me for as long as I can remember and right now, I could really use it.

He frowns as if what I've just asked is idiotic. "If it appears to be that or death, the choice should be easy." He lowers his arms to his lap and sits up a bit straighter. He's not wrong; on paper, the choice would seem simple. Either submit or die. But he's forgetting the human side to every decision. Assumption tells us that nobody would choose death. Reality is that people have been dying for their rights, freedom, and land since the beginning of civilization. No one wants to just hand over their home to someone else.

"So now we're giving them ultimatums?" I shake my head, frustrated. "Using the drones and bombs as leverage? This isn't what I signed up for." I quickly shift from worried to angry.

"How many cities and townships are we talking about?" He's all business, trying to rationalize things with the data. That's how Ryan works. That's how the NAF works. It's a numbers game, and those with the highest numbers win.

"Rodrigues is pulling that information for me now," I say flatly.

He leans forward and calmly replies, "We have some time. Not a lot, but there's still time. I think you should keep doing what you're doing. Full steam ahead on peaceful transfers and hope that we can flip the area before the last snowfall. Don't give up hope."

He always manages to find a positive spin to reel me in. "It seems impossible," I say pathetically.

"So did surviving an encounter with Danielle Clark, yet here we are." He snorts.

I steel myself at the mention of her name. Dani. Surviving an encounter with Dani was never an issue for me. It's surviving without her that feels so damn hard. I do my best to not let Ryan see how much I'm affected by his comment and change the subject. "I don't even know if we'll have enough people to take the wastelands. This is a lot of territory, and our soldiers aren't used to this kind of terrain."

"I can check in with the recruiter. See if he's made much progress with some of the people out this way."

I nod along with his line of thinking. "That would be good. I'll get a total count on personnel in the area and reach out to whoever I can about sending additional troops. We're going to need all the help we can get." I'm torn between what *I* want and what the job *needs* me to do. I'm loyal to the NAF, and I will complete my assignment. But I'm going to try like hell to do it my way. And that means no bombs for as long as I can hold out.

"That, I agree with." Ryan slaps his knees as he moves to stand.

"See? Who needs Rodrigues when I have you helping me?"

He chuckles, and the sound makes me happy. It's been too long since we were like this. It feels…nice.

A knock on the door interrupts us, and the lightheartedness disappears with the sound. "Enter," I say loudly.

"Excuse me, ma'am?" A soldier opens the door and stands at attention. "The general requests your presence for an unscheduled intelligence debrief."

I share a look with Ryan and glance at the silent radio on my desk. It must be fairly confidential if the request wasn't transmitted. "We'll have to continue this later." He stands as I do and dismisses himself with a nod. I look to the soldier waiting to escort me, still standing in the doorway, and I slip on my jacket and pull my hair back. "Lead the way." Turning off my heater, I sigh, disappointed. The room had just gotten warm, too.

There aren't many people in the conference room when I arrive. It does appear, however, that I am the last to join my mother, General Foley, and Captain Daniels.

The general waits until I've taken the remaining seat before diving right in. "Now that we are all here, let's begin. General Foley."

General Foley squares her shoulders and robotically says, "At approximately 0930, under the command of Second Lieutenant Alexander, Malmstrom Base was successfully destroyed. Essential supplies, information, and equipment were extracted before the blast. As predicted, Resistance personnel were in the vicinity when the detonation was executed. We are still awaiting word as to casualties."

Whatever I was expecting to come out of her mouth, that isn't it. I sit perfectly still, stunned and confused. *Simon* blew up Malmstrom. Captain Daniels shares a worried look with me. It helps to know that I'm not alone in my surprise.

I want to ask what the hell happened, and why we blew up our own base, but General Foley presses on as if she's bored with the entire debrief.

"General Turner's decoy was a partial success." She looks down as if checking her notes when it's clear that she's actually attempting to keep herself stoic at the bad news. "We received word from our specialist with a visual sighting on Danielle Clark and a handful of other Resistance fighters attempting to intercept as expected. Lack of communication with the deployment team seems to suggest all NAF personnel were either captured or KIA." The annoyance in her voice is palpable. My stomach bottoms out, but I keep my face as neutral as possible.

My mother nods, as if expecting such news. "Please get in touch with Lieutenant Alexander and commend him for his success regarding Malmstrom. Then order his team to confirm if our soldiers near Ellsworth are dead or alive. I would also like to speak with him about commandeering the local gas supplies."

I close my eyes and take a deep breath. Taking possession of their gas is not the way to gain favor. This is quickly spiraling out of control.

"Yes, ma'am," General Foley says and jots down a few notes.

"Are the supplies from Malmstrom still secure?"

"Yes ma'am, secure and on time," General Foley confirms.

"Excellent. Does anyone have any questions?" My mother glances around the table.

"I do." I have so many that I'm not sure where to begin. "Why did we take out Malmstrom? I thought that base was essential to the success of our flight research and development?" I want to add why didn't *I* know about it beforehand but keep that part to myself.

Without so much as blinking, my mother robotically spouts an answer she no doubt has given before. "The Resistance has gotten too bold in the area, and it was compromised. We wanted to secure the base, but after a tip that our convoy was in jeopardy, we had to take drastic and unfortunate measures. We could not risk the Resistance taking over. With no time to arm or defend the base, we moved locations and proceeded to destroy all remaining evidence of our work before the Resistance could take it for themselves. In the meantime, we will hold a strong presence in Helena so we don't lose our foothold in the north. When the rest of the troops arrive from the east, we will use them to move in on neighboring towns, and the north will once again be ours."

"Did you know Danielle Clark would go after your decoy in Ellsworth?" I ask, unable to keep quiet about Dani.

"Intel suggested she and William were in the area, and we expected at least one of them would take the bait. It was too tempting. My only regret is not sending in a more competent team."

So that's her play. Setting traps and hoping one of them will ensnare Dani or William. I have to tell her not to fall for anything else or trust information from any other informants. From now on, it's not just Simon she has to worry about.

There are a thousand more things I want to ask, but my mother places both hands on the table and pushes her chair back. "That is all for now. Dismissed."

I immediately head to our comms specialist and ask for an update on exactly what happened in Ellsworth. He has no additional news but promises to contact me when he is cleared to do so.

Frustrated with the lack of information, I head back to my office.

I'm so sick to my stomach that I barely notice the two privates waiting for me outside the building that houses my office. They salute the moment they see me. "At ease." They relax as I step closer. "Private Silva, Private Miller. What can I do for you?"

"May we come in and speak with you, ma'am?" Miguel asks.

"Of course." I nod at the guard at the door, and he salutes as we pass.

They follow me closely up the set of stairs to the third floor. Ushering them in first, I close the door behind us and turn the lantern key. The office illuminates with a soft glow. The heater is next, humming as it springs to life. When I turn, both men are standing, unmoving, barely inside.

After an awkward and silent moment, I offer them a chance to come in farther. "Why don't you two relax a bit? It'll be warm in here soon." I motion for them to sit in the chairs pulled up to my desk and push some of the mess to the side.

They still don't speak. I lean back in my chair, relax my shoulders, and drop the formalities. "Miguel. Anthony. You're being weird. What's going on?"

Miguel sucks in a slow breath. "We wanted to discuss the possibility of—"

"I don't want to do this anymore," Miller says abruptly and loudly. I sit back in my seat, surprised by his outburst.

"Stop," Miguel snaps. "I told you we need to do this the right way."

"There is no easy way or right way," Miller shoots back at him. He turns to me. "I want out. I don't want to be a part of something that does what Simon did to those people in White River. Not after what they did to save me." His voice is deep and pleading. "There were good people there. People like Elise."

Miguel appears nervous. "Anthony, we—"

I hold up a hand, silencing their argument, and take a moment to look at both of them. They're exposed and vulnerable because there is no taking back what Anthony just said. The hurt in his voice and on his face is a predictable response to everything we've endured, but what's alarming is the fear illuminating their eyes. Are they scared of Simon? The NAF? Of me? Fear has always been the leading factor in all the political propaganda on both sides, but when did we start scaring our own to this extent? They're desperate, and as much as I don't want to admit it, I'm having a similar internal battle.

"This could be viewed as treason. You both know that, right?"

"We know, Lieutenant Colonel," Miguel whispers. "That's why we came to you."

"I can't do it anymore." Anthony's voice cracks as he repeats himself. "I won't survive here."

Seeing a soldier, a friend, so close to collapse is incredibly disheartening. I believe him. He will die if he stays here, and I hate to think that it may be by his own hand. "I can't promise you anything right now, but I hear you. This will stay between us, and I promise, I'll figure something out." They exchange nervous glances. "I give you my word."

Finally, Anthony breathes a sigh of relief. "Thank you."

"I think it goes without saying that you can't discuss this with anyone. Not even your therapist." It's a dangerous move to ask him to bottle his emotions with his mental state as it is, but I don't have much of a choice. If he truly wants out, he needs to be silent until I can try to put a few pieces into place. "Miguel, stay with him. Do you understand?"

"Understood." He nods once. He knows I'm what I'm asking, and it's a lot. "We appreciate you listening. We won't take up any more of your time."

"Miller?" I call before they can open the door. "Hang in there for a little bit longer, okay? I promise, you won't be ignored."

He squares his shoulders and salutes, but there's a grateful expression on his face. A determined one, no doubt from knowing there's an end in sight. And there has to be. I can't let him down.

They vacate quickly and quietly, and I swivel to look out the window. It will be dark soon, and I have yet to hear anything about Dani or the team my mother sent. Should I try Dani's radio?

The door isn't closed more than a few seconds before a knock breaks through the silence, as if someone was waiting outside my office for their turn.

"Enter." I sigh, not really in the mood for any more issues tonight.

Rodrigues pokes her head in. "Sorry for the interruption, ma'am. I have the news you requested."

Quickly, I motion for her to come in fully, my nerves kicking into overdrive. "Tell me."

"The mission in Ellsworth was unsuccessful. One casualty," she says sadly. I hold my breath. "One of our best explosive specialists. It appears that Danielle Clark remains impossible to bring down." I sink in my seat, relieved about Dani and saddened about losing one of own. I exhale slowly. "We are still waiting on further details."

Rodrigues watches me curiously, and I try to keep my emotions in check. "Have you eaten dinner?"

She appears startled by my question. "No ma'am."

I shut off my lantern and heater as I stand. "Come on."

The mess hall is practically empty as we and only two others make our way through the ration line.

"This looks interesting," Rodrigues says, poking at the mystery meat with her fork.

I can't help the laugh that bubbles to the surface. "You don't have to pretend for my benefit. Some bases are better than others with food selection." The service worker doling out the slop seems to take that as a challenge and uncovers a new selection she was keeping warm off to the side: steamed vegetables, fresh fish, and warm bread. That's more like it. "You've been holding out on me, Edith," I tell her with a smile.

"Never," she says, dryly, despite my knowing I'm her favorite, and adds the food to our plates.

Rodrigues looks from the food to me, eyes wide and questioning. I answer with a wink.

We grab some juice and sit at one of the many empty tables in the large cafeteria, Rodrigues sitting across from me. Someone is mopping the floors, and Edith begins sloshing the leftovers into empty containers. The sight makes me shudder. It's clear they're getting ready to close up for the night.

Rodrigues stares at her plate and folds her napkin neatly in her lap. "How'd you score the good stuff?"

"Perks of running the base," I say.

"I appreciate you sharing your rations, ma'am." Rodrigues smiles and takes a large bite.

We eat for a few moments in silence. I can't stop thinking about Miller and Silva. They were both so loyal to the NAF and had such long careers ahead of them. But after what Simon did, I don't blame them for not wanting to be a part of that anymore. And this was before he blew up one of our own bases.

But how do I get them out? Is it even possible? They're both too young for retirement, and I fear requesting a transfer to someplace with no active combat is just a Band-Aid over a bullet hole. Perhaps I can figure out a way to get them an early discharge. "Can you pull all files on soldiers who asked for reassignment or discharge and early retirement over the past five years?" I ask.

Rodrigues slows her chewing and looks at me curiously. "I'll have it on your desk first thing tomorrow morning."

"Thank you." She stares for another minute, and I sense she wants to ask me something, but I don't push.

Finally, "Is it true? The explosion at Malmstrom?"

I freeze for a beat and then stab at another piece of squash. So the cat's out of the bag. "Yes."

She opens and closes her mouth a few times, looking absolutely devastated. Probably trying to figure out what she wants to say. "How?"

I look at her sympathetically. "It's classified."

She nods, her gaze lowering to her plate. "Right. Of course." She takes several deep breaths. "There's a rumor that the NAF did it." When she meets my eyes again, I say nothing.

I watch her for a moment, the way her posture loses its confidence and how she pushes the remainder of her food around on her plate. "Did you have any idea that something like this might happen when you were stationed there?" I ask.

She shakes her head and wipes her mouth. "None whatsoever. We were told we were all being transferred and that operations would be continued when we arrived. We had a timetable to pack everything up, and that was that. It was very sudden."

"And no one thought to ask why?" I've been transferred a dozen times in my career, but I have never seen an entire base just up and move without a solid reason. I find it highly suspicious that no one asked why.

"No one asks Colonel Treague anything. He tells us to do something, we do it." I know what she means. I've met the man a few times. He's very large, very loud, and very scary. "Why did they do it?" She doesn't look at me as she asks.

Sighing, I put down my fork, debating how I want to answer. "Why do you think someone would blow up their own compound?"

She puts down her fork and sits back. "To cover up something they don't want found," she says. I nod. She really is smart. "But when were we compromised?"

"Very good question." While still not sure I can trust her, I appreciate her intelligence and willingness to ask the hard questions. "When do you think?"

She's been able to figure it out up to this point. I have complete faith she'll manage to put the entire puzzle together without much assistance.

She takes her time analyzing the data provided. "There was a sense of urgency right before the convoy was attacked. We were given a day to pack and leave, with warnings that anything left behind would fall into enemy hands." Taking a deep breath, she continues, "If I had to guess, I think the NAF knew the base was in jeopardy and then used the convoy from Grand Forks to Malmstrom as a distraction so we could sneak out." Her eyes meet mine. "How am I doing?"

I nod, impressed. "Not a bad guess."

"Which would mean we set our own up for an ambush."

"Yes, it would," I tell her sadly.

Rodrigues looks at her plate and appears lost in thought. She picks up her fork and pushes some food around but doesn't take a bite. Her brows furrow again, and I get that feeling that she's wrestling with something else.

"Just ask, Rodrigues."

She straightens as if gathering courage. "This is probably way off base and completely none of my business, and if you don't want to answer, that's obviously fine."

I roll my eyes. "You just asked me about classified information, and *now* you're getting shy?"

She takes a deep breath. "What was she like? Danielle Clark?"

My entire body stiffens at the mention of her name, and I'm wishing I hadn't pressed her to ask.

"It's just, we hear so much about her, but you actually spoke with her and spent time with her, and I guess I just wanted to know if the stories are true. I mean, obviously most of them have to be, since she just about singlehandedly took out that convoy."

Carefully, I wipe my mouth and place the napkin on my lap. I stare at the table as my stomach twists with my memories of being with Dani. All of them seem to flash in front of me, from the moment we met on the battlefield, her pistols aimed at my face, to the soft whispers and gentle kisses.

"I'm sorry. My questions were out of line. I didn't—"

"Yes and no," I tell her softly. "She is absolutely every bit as deadly and intelligent as we were led to believe. But she's also funny, caring, loyal." I shake my head, knowing I've probably said way too much. "She's a person. Just like you and me. The entirety of a person can't be taught in a classroom by those who don't know them."

Rodrigues stares with an expression I can't quite place. I reach for my glass to give me something to do and take a long sip, wishing I hadn't answered. Anything regarding Dani and my time with her is so deeply personal that uttering anything to someone who doesn't truly know her feels like a betrayal. Of what, I'm not quite sure.

Rodrigues opens her mouth as if to say something, but Edith suddenly appears, scowl set firmly in place. "You two about finished? I gotta clean up."

I have never been more relieved to get out of a conversation. "Yeah," I say without so much looking at Rodrigues. "We're finished."

CHAPTER NINE: THE TRAP

DANI

I'm here." The crackling words that come through the speaker deflate the tension from my body.

I let out a long slow breath and bring the radio back to my mouth. "Lucas? William? The others?"

The response is delayed and spotty. "I don't...the building, it..."

Panic sets back in, and I reply louder than I intend. "Darby, where are they?"

I share a look with Mike, and he pushes his sunglasses atop his head. The longer we wait in silence, the more dread I feel.

After what feels like an eternity, William's voice crackles through the radio. "We're here. They were expecting us. It was a trap."

Glancing at the NAF soldiers still guarded by Jack, I walk farther away. "Yeah, so was ours."

"Are you okay?" William asks, his voice coming in more clearly now.

"We're fine. We have three prisoners, a dead soldier, and several cars full of explosives. You sure you're good?"

"A little shook up but uninjured. We're going to take what we have and meet you back home."

"Copy that. See you when you get back." I take a moment while I'm away from everyone to catch my breath. That hit too close. My brother's life being at stake is one of the reasons I left this shit behind. Closing my eyes, I focus on my breathing and the way the sun hits my face. I think about Kate suggesting we revisit the outpost as a reprieve and wonder if it's too soon to take her up on it. After one more slow, steadying breath, I walk back and hand the radio to Mike.

"All good?" he asks quietly.

Nodding, I look at the prisoners. "Split them up and search them again."

I crouch to stare at the detonator poking from the specialist's sleeve. She looks even younger up close. I can't help but wonder if she volunteered or was ordered into this suicide mission. Either way, it's such a waste that it makes me angry. And all for what? A diversion?

"What about their buggies?" Mike asks.

"I'll take care of them." Slowly, I push up the sleeve a little farther and eye the wire going all the way up her arm. It takes a minute to unbutton her jacket and push up the shirt. Sure enough, attached to her chest is the power source.

"So now what?" Jack asks, hovering behind me.

"I'm going to get this transmitter unwrapped and disassemble the explosives." I pull the knife from my belt and carefully begin cutting off her shirt.

"You're not going to blow the cars?" His voice is closer now, and there's no doubt in my mind he's trying to get a glimpse of what I'm doing. Jack is always curious about explosives but never brave enough to handle them. Smart decision on his part.

"Hoping I won't have to." He stays silent as I manage to free the specialist of the power source and detonator. I spin the device in my hand, examining it. "It's not a bad design, if a little rudimentary."

Jack grunts, clearly not impressed. "When you're done ogling the explosives, you mind if we get the fuck out of here?"

Standing, I notice the cars are loaded and ready to head out. "You guys go. I'll meet you at the gates. Have Mike radio Jess and tell her you're bringing in three prisoners alive but no general. Don't say anything else."

"Got it," Jack slings his shotgun over his shoulder and struts to the truck. "Don't blow yourself up, Clark."

Once my team is far enough away, I grip the detonator and get to work. It takes longer than I'd like to disarm the bombs. It isn't difficult, but I take my time, making sure I get it right. There are parts and pieces attached to one of the main buggies that don't look familiar to me, and I shove them, along with the pieces of the disassembled main charge, into a backpack from my Jeep. Maybe Darby could use some of this stuff.

With the gas canisters safely away, I leave the buggies where they are so Thatcher can have someone salvage them.

By the time I get back to Rapid City, the prisoners have already been led away, but a lot of people are milling around the gates, their expressions worried and nervous. I park my Jeep away from the main road and head straight to see Jess.

"What happened out there?" She greets me with a question before I've barely stepped inside her communications room. George is standing just inside the doorway, and I nod hello to him and turn back to Jess, who sits behind a small desk.

"It appears we got played." Stepping closer, I notice her old Perkins Brailler sitting beside large green stacks of military radios. It feels strange to have that old machine used for Resistance purposes. I remember when she wanted to use it to write poetry. "Looks like the general wanted to draw us out and cause a distraction. Anything come through on what she's distracting us from?"

George remains oddly quiet but watches us curiously.

"I believe this might interest you." Jess pulls the paper from the brailler and runs her fingers over her notes. "There's been confirmation of not one, but two convoys *leaving* Malmstrom. Both heading south. They were gone before William and the others even arrived."

"They knew we were coming and cleared out their equipment before blowing up the base to prevent us from getting it. They were probably hoping to take some of us out along with it." I'd be more impressed if my brother wasn't almost caught in the crossfire.

Jess sits back for a moment. "Do you know what they were trying to hide?"

"Darby said there were remnants of drones and two big plane frames." Even before I'm finished, I can feel the emotional shift in the room.

"Drones and planes?" George says. He sounds nervous. Not that I blame him. None of us have ever witnessed anything but birds flying far overhead. There were always rumors that one day, we'd regain access to flight, but no one ever thought it would be in their lifetime. "Have they gotten them in the air?"

"Don't know." I shrug.

George takes a step closer. He's a bit sweaty and shaking. "Dani, if they're able to get things to fly again, who knows what they could do? The Resistance won't stand a chance. *We* won't stand a chance."

I hold out my hands as if physically steadying him. "We don't know anything right now. Let's not panic yet." I eye the beads of sweat on his brow. "Are you all right?"

The fear in his expression is clear as day. "I think it's time we talk to the mayor. Maybe surrendering now would be the best thing."

Jess turns in his direction. "Grandfather!"

I place a hand on his shoulder. "Take a breath, George. We aren't surrendering anything." He doesn't respond, but he's still wringing his hands. I've never seen him so worked up, and it's a bit startling.

Jess tilts her head back in my direction. "When you took out the convoy on the way to Malmstrom, what were they carrying?"

"Just people. No supplies from what I could see. We blew most of it all to pieces. But I sure didn't see any planes. Didn't see much of anything. I was just trying to hit and run."

She hums as if trying to get a full picture based on the information she has. "The timing of it all is a bit odd, don't you agree?"

I think I know what she's implying. That they seem to know our movements, and Thatcher may be right about a traitor. It's a concern I don't vocalize. "Do you know where the convoys that left Malmstrom are now? Or where they're headed?" I ask, trying to remain hopeful for an affirmative.

She sighs and shakes her head. "There aren't many occupied NAF bases along the southbound route. Maybe Wyoming or Colorado? Nebraska? Maybe they're going to Texas. Who knows, they may be going somewhere completely off grid."

"Have you spoken with Thatcher about any of this?"

"No, I was directed not to leave the radio, and she would come to me. I just pass along information. We don't discuss tactics or anything else." She seems disappointed, but I'm relieved to hear that.

"Keep doing what you're doing, and I'm sure you and Thatcher will be talking strategy in no time," I say, trying to cheer her up. It seems to work a little if the uptick of her mouth is any indication. "Anything else?"

"William checked in just to say they're stopping halfway home to rest and will see us tomorrow." She reaches for her notes and runs her fingers along the paper. "And the convoy from Grand Forks to Omaha is on the move. I'm supposed to let Thatcher know when it arrives."

I'm disappointed there isn't a message from Kate, but I know it's because she's nestled in an officer's buggy for a fairly lengthy drive. I wonder if she'll try to get ahold of me once she's settled in. I want to ask her about Malmstrom. It's not at all because I want confirmation that she's all right or to hear her voice.

I give Jess's hand a squeeze. "Even though I hate that you're involved, it's nice to know someone I trust is the one collecting information. You're doing great, kid."

"Can you please refrain from fronting attacks and dodging traps for a few days? It's stressful enough out there without having to worry about you all the damn time." Her voice is hard, and her expression serious.

My gut reaction is to tell her this is normal for war living. But her concern is so palpable that I squeeze her hand again instead and hope that it's at least a little reassuring. "I'll do my best."

"I'm glad you're okay," she whispers.

"Me too." I pat George's shoulder on my way out the door, hoping he'll calm down. "Things have been bad with the NAF before, and we got through it. We'll get through it again."

He nods, but I'm not sure he believes me. I'm not even sure that I believe myself.

❖

Thatcher is at her desk, surrounded by maps and papers, and she barely casts a glance in my direction when I fall into one of the empty chairs. "Nice vest," she says.

"Thanks." Unfastening the clips, I toss it on the empty chair to my left and stretch my side, wincing as the bandage pulls against my ribcage. I press my hand to the spot just under my arm. "Wish it came up a bit higher, though."

"I'll bet. If you keep getting sliced open, you won't be able to walk, let alone fight." Her tone is dry and her volume low. She shuffles some papers from one side of her desk to the other.

"Wouldn't be the first time." I opt not to remind her more specifically that I spent the better half of a decade constantly injured, sometimes gravely, and still managed to pull through.

She ignores my comment anyway. "A decoy, huh? You read that move right, after all."

I sit up straighter. "Good ol' Judy is too smart to let her location slip like that." I may have been out of this fight for the past few years, but some things never change. "But I think you knew that, too. I should be pissed at you for pushing me into that deathtrap."

"We don't get many leads these days. We have to take the crumbs we're offered, and there aren't many good people who could've handled that situation." She sounds a bit defeated. Not that I blame her. Though I do wish she'd use someone else to go after these *crumbs.* "Three prisoners, though. That's something."

"Yeah, I wouldn't get too excited. I doubt they'll talk. Even if they do, they don't know what's going on. Lambs sent to the sacrificial altar. They probably thought they were part of a training exercise." I give her a look. "Don't send me into a trap like that again."

Thatcher nods and at least looks a bit admonished. "Do you think she knew she'd draw you and William out?"

"I think the possibility was intriguing enough." Thatcher hums, seemingly agreeing. "I just saw Jess. She said two convoys left Malmstrom not too long before William got there. She still isn't sure where they're going."

She doesn't seem surprised. "I heard about the explosion. I'm glad they're all safe."

All I can do is nod. I can't bear to consider the alternative.

Thatcher seems to notice my discomfort and clears her throat, pressing on. "Planes and drones and mysterious convoys."

I relax a bit. Focusing on business is something I can do to distract from worrying about what-ifs. "Looks like it."

"We need to know if they've been able to get anything in the air."

This seems to be the number-one priority, and not having that answer is stressing everyone out. "I'd put all I own on yes," I say. "At least to the drones. Those don't take fuel. I wouldn't put it past the NAF to have figured out a way around the blockers." I lift my hands dramatically. "Hell, maybe they lied about the blockers in the first place and have been using drones this whole time."

Thatcher scribbles something on a blank piece of paper. "I'll push my contacts."

I don't know who her resources are, and I wonder if her contacts know more than mine. Kate is a direct line to the general; she has to know something. Though it surprises me that she wouldn't warn me about the traps or tell me about the drones this far west. Maybe I put too much faith in her. That's a thought I really don't want to linger on. She doesn't have to tell me anything, and I stupidly told her more than I should've.

Thatcher sighs. "Dani, holding prisoners is going to make my town even more restless. Seeing NAF soldiers within the walls, even as prisoners, can be rather unsettling."

"Tell me about it." I can easily recall how the people of White River reacted to seeing me haul in our visitors.

"It's only going to stir up more chatter about the NAF closing in. And if General Turner *was* trying to make a play at you..."

I think I know where this is going. "You kicking me out, Thatch?"

She shakes her head, but we both know harboring the Resistance's biggest names will only stir up trouble. Even if Thatcher is also on that list. "No, no. I'm just saying, be careful. Watch what you say and do and...maybe lie low for a little while."

"I'll do my best."

"The people here love you. But they're scared. It's been years of peace, and now trouble is ramping back up. They don't know what to think."

"No, I get it." And I do. It's unsettling and alarming to glimpse a drastic change on the horizon. Especially war and death. Plus, the fact that the last town that welcomed me is now nothing but rubble and ashes, I can see why the people would be uneasy.

I have a feeling our one-to-one is coming to an end as she shuffles some of her papers. A sudden thought nags me. "Hey, George is kind of jittery. Has he talked to you about his concerns?"

"Only every chance he gets." Thatcher sighs. Okay, so his recent behavior is noticeable to more than just me. "I told him not to leave for a while. He isn't happy, but I want to keep an eye on him."

George is a staple around this city. Everyone knows and trusts him. If he wasn't so keen on adventure and meeting new people, they would've roped him into the political scene. Trading around the wasteland is his passion, and the people look to him. They know he sees and hears things the politicians don't. "Do you think he's the reason people are getting antsy?"

"Could be. But they also know he's gotten a little skittish in his old age. Jess will make sure he stays out of it." The answer is short and dismissive. I think she's leaving something out, but she's ready for this conversation to be over, and so am I. "Let me know if you hear from William. He's more likely to go through you than the proper channels."

I let the dig slide. "Will do." I get to the door before I remember something important. "Oh, I disarmed the bombs rigged to explode inside the decoy convoy near Ellsworth. They'll need new tires because I blew them all to hell, but the cars might come in handy." She can stash the cars, but I'm keeping the gas.

Thatcher looks pleased. "Another consolation. Please give the coordinates to Wesley out front."

"The little dude that sits outside your door?"

"Dani," Thatcher scolds.

I make a grand display of giving Wesley the information and use the last of my energy to drag myself to my room. I'm itching to check in with Lucas and make sure they're still good on their way back. I'm also anxious to get a message to Kate. A huge part of me hopes she didn't know about the traps. I want so much to believe she would've told me, even though I know that she owes me nothing. But she promised to keep me safe. I have to believe she didn't know.

Elise smiles and waves. "There she is."

The White River crew is waiting for me in the two large wingback chairs in the lobby. Rhiannon sits on the arm of the seat occupied by Jack, and Elise sits comfortably on Mike's lap in the other. They're disgustingly cute, and it makes me wish I had that with Kate.

"Hurry up, we're hungry," Jack yells.

"You didn't have to wait to eat." I laugh as I join them, delighted that they did, in fact, wait.

"Come on," Rhiannon stands and motions toward the bar area, "before they stop serving lunch."

We must have just missed the rush as most of the tables are unoccupied. The five of us squeeze at a small round table in the back corner. It takes only a moment before Jack disappears to find beer. It feels weird to be here with them and not at Rhiannon's tavern, but at least they're all safe.

"Darby checked in a few minutes ago. They're going to stop and sleep for a few hours at 'some podunk town probably swarming with raiders' and said not to wait up. Her words, not mine," Mike says as he hands back my radio.

I place it, along with the bulletproof vest, under my chair and wince. My entire body hurts.

"Did Jess have any news?" Rhiannon asks.

"Not really. Just that the NAF cleared out of Malmstrom before they blew it."

"Why would they blow their own base?" Elise reaches for my shirt, no doubt trying to check my injury, and I slap her hand away.

"To get rid of whatever they left behind." I scoot away as she pokes at my side where she knows I'm hurt. "Would you quit it?"

Rhiannon looks over her shoulder and leans in closer. "Like the drones?"

"Like the drones," I confirm. "I just hope William and the others managed to get ahold of something they might've left behind before the place blew."

Rhiannon takes a deep breath as if steadying her nerves. "I'm just glad they made it out."

"Everyone's staring at us," Jack says and places a large pitcher of beer in the center of the table. "Gotta get the glasses."

"Get me a tea, please," I say, eyeing the beer, not sure it's supposed to be that color.

"Oh, I'll take a tea as well," Elise says excitedly.

Jacks gives us a look of disapproval. "Two teas for the queens coming up."

I glance around, and sure enough, the handful of people spread out over the room are indeed staring. I give an elderly man a little wave, and he quickly looks away. "Well, it's either hero worship, or they think we're the reason for all the NAF trouble as of late. Can't tell the difference these days."

"It's the latter, right?" Elise says. "I mean, you *are* the reason for all the fighting and the prisoners, Ms. Daughter of the Resistance."

"Thanks," I tell her, deadpan. "And don't call me that. It's weird coming from you."

She shrugs and winks. I regret ever telling her about my nickname.

"What are you going to do?" Rhiannon whispers, rather loudly to be considered discreet.

I run my hands through my hair and pull it out of my face, tying it behind me. "I'm thinking of getting in touch with my contact."

"You mean your military girlfriend?" The four of us shush Jack as he comes back with an assortment of glassware. "What? That's who you're talking about, right?"

"Lower your voice," Rhiannon chastises. "And where's the food?"

Jack mumbles something about needing a drink first.

"What good would contacting her do?" Elise asks.

"She's helped me before. Maybe she can give me something that might help again." I drop one of the tea bags in a mug of hot water and lift it out again.

"Will she really be that forthcoming with information about something of this magnitude?" Rhiannon glances over her shoulder again. I *have* to teach her how to be more subtle. "About the drones?"

I roll my eyes. "I don't know, but it's worth a shot. And can you stop saying the word drones?" I bring the scalding liquid to my lips and blow. "We can talk about this later."

Jack grunts his approval. "Good, more drinking, less gossiping."

"When you talked with the mayor, did you get the impression she set us up?" Mike asks.

Rhiannon balks. "You think the mayor set you up?" She reaches for the star on her necklace, twisting it nervously.

"Rhiannon," I groan. "Please, you are not anywhere near as subtle as you think you are." She blushes and sits back in her seat. "And no. I don't think Thatcher set us up. I think the general was trying to divert attention from the convoy taking the supplies out of Malmstrom so she sent out a decoy as a distraction."

"In the hopes of catching you," Mike adds.

"Maybe," I say and shrug. "She could've been going after William."

Elise eyes me almost suspiciously. "I don't know. The general *really* seems to hate you."

"Why does everyone keep saying that?" I whine. "She hates William just as much, and he's killed more people than I have, including her husband. Why does everyone conveniently forget that?"

"William's not the one sleeping with her daughter." Rhiannon doesn't even *try* to whisper that one.

I choke on the tea, and slowly, everyone around the table looks at me. It's incredibly uncomfortable and awkward, but I do my best to be casual. "There is no way the general knows that."

"That you know of," Jack fires off.

I bring my tea to my lips again, feeling the heat in my cheeks. "Now that my sex life is out in the open"—I shoot Rhiannon a look—"can we *please* talk about something else?"

"Anyone else think it's earlier than usual for snow?" Mike asks, changing the subject.

Rhiannon sighs and, thankfully, also relents. "I'll go see what food is available."

Warmth spreads through my chest at being with my family even if the conversation is embarrassing.

I toss and turn for what feels like hours. Mostly because every time I close my eyes, my mind wanders back to Kate, wondering if she knew about the traps and how much she knows about the drones and planes. As much as I try to push it from my mind, I can't seem to think of much else.

When I'm unable to take it anymore, I reach over to the nightstand and grab the radio. Kate's channel has been silent since I gave it to her. Her convoy had to have arrived at the base hours ago, but she's probably been swept up with orders and assignments. That has to be the reason she didn't reach out to me. And it's the reason I'm telling myself I haven't tried to contact her, either.

But now, deep into the night, when everything's quiet, the temptation to attempt communication is almost unbearable. I wish I had Dad's journals to look at. At least poring over maps and personnel notes would take my mind off Kate. How she messes with her hair when she's nervous. How she fits against me so perfectly and that ticklish spot when I kiss her on her neck just below her ear.

Pulling my pillow tightly over my head, I let out a loud and frustrated groan. I can't get her out of my mind. Her eyes, her lips, her hands. What did I even think about before we met? The weather? New trading posts? Guard rotations?

I toss the pillow aside and look out the window. With the curtains pulled back, I can see the glow of the moon, and I wonder if she's looking at it, too.

Rolling my eyes at myself, I sit up. My infatuation with the general's daughter is becoming a nuisance. I can't lead and protect the people I love if I keep missing sleep over wondering, worrying, and longing for Kate. Or by spending hours driving just to see her. I'm needed here. I need to focus on my own agenda, my own people.

I lie back down, eyes still on the moon, and decide that the only way to stop thinking about Kate is to see her. Just to get it out of my system and confirm whether or not she knew about the explosion and the decoy convoy. Once I know, one way or another, then I can focus on my own stuff.

It's a lie I'm willing to believe if I can just see Kate.

❖

The bell dings when I step into Jess's small inn. I smell something baking and think about heading first to the kitchen. Instead, I go to the back and knock on the door. Walking into the room after Jess grants me permission, I pull out the chair across from her and eye the fresh muffins on her desk. "Morning."

"Good morning, Dani. Did you get anything to eat from Wyatt?"

"No," I tell her, happy I bypassed the kitchen. It's too early for a run-in with Jess's boyfriend.

"Too bad," she says. "He makes the most delicious muffins. He and Rhiannon hit it off immediately. I think they're even meeting up today to swap recipes."

"Sounds fun." I try to keep my tone neutral, but no one could pay me to sit in on that little gathering.

Thankfully, Jess shifts straight into business. "You just missed Thatcher."

That gets my attention. "Did something else happen?"

"There's chatter from several neighboring towns. It appears that they've been getting hit with letters urging them to meet the NAF's notice to rapidly cooperate in a peaceful transition of power."

Peaceful transition is Kate's jurisdiction, but it doesn't sound like her to force anyone's hand. "How many?"

Jess runs her fingers over a piece of paper still in her braille typer. "Half a dozen so far. Including Lincoln and Pierre. It could be really bad if they're met with the Resistance stationed there."

The sudden insistence on transferring power sounds more like the general than Kate, but I guess I can't be completely sure on that, either. She occupies every space of my brain, but we still have a lot to learn about one another. "Has Rapid City been notified?"

"Not yet. But the NAF are moving fast. I wouldn't be surprised if it happens in the next few days. It's almost as if something big is on the horizon. Can you feel it?"

"Yeah," I say reluctantly. "I feel it."

Now I *really* want to talk to Kate. Despite the precautions of our private channel, this is too big to risk talking about over a radio. Again, I decide I have to see her.

Licking my lips, I lean forward, my heart racing at the idea of what the something big may be and whether or not Kate has any part in it. "Jess, I need you to send a recurring message. Don't stop until it's been confirmed." I hesitate slightly. "But please don't tell anyone. Not Thatcher. Not William. Not even Wyatt or George."

Jess appears to think seriously, then lowers her voice. "Is this to Kate?"

"The message is to Songbird."

Jess nods, all business, and reaches for the stacks of radios to her right. "I opened the channel you asked me to, but there's been nothing. Remember, if we're all on the same channel…" She lets the implication linger. "Limit what you say."

"Don't say anything I wouldn't want you to hear. Understood."

Jess readies herself at her typewriter. "What's your message?"

Omaha is just under nine hours away. I'll have to leave at midday and take the extra fuel I commandeered if I want to get there on time. The recurring message to Kate plays over and over on a low volume on my radio. I'm just waiting for Kate to confirm.

When the answer doesn't instantly come, I toss spare batteries, extra ammunition, a clean pair of clothes, and an extra wool cap into a backpack. I'll need to grab some food, but I still have time to do that.

I turn the radio to the channel I use with Lucas just in time to hear Darby on the other end. "There better be a welcoming party with cake."

"What the hell are you talking about?" I ask.

"Oh, there you are, Atomic Something. Been trying to reach you for the last five minutes." I close my eyes and count to ten, taking slow, deep breaths to keep from being an asshole back to her. It's too early for her shit. "Anyway, we're here."

My eyes snap open, and I grab my jacket before racing out of the room.

I see William first. He's greeted by Thatcher and surrounded by guards. Her message clearly got through to everyone but me. The guards search the vehicles while Ericson and Hugo unload the bags from the first buggy. Darby watches from close by, directing them to be careful with the equipment. They both seem to be ignoring her.

Finally, Lucas rounds the second buggy wearing his blue-mirrored sunglasses with his hair pulled out of his face. He rubs his hands together, warming them, and snuggles deeper into his thick coat. I jog over, unable to keep from smiling.

He barely has time to steady himself before I slam my hands on his shoulders, examining him. "Still in one piece?" I ask.

He grins. "That was a dangerous mission." I nod, and he pulls me into an embrace. I take full advantage and squeeze as tight as I can. When he releases his hold, I take a step back, and he gives me a onceover as well. "Have you returned to the injured list, comrade?"

"We're good," I assure him and pat his shoulder again. "Did you get any intel?" I ask, unable to wait a second longer.

"We got some," William answers, stepping into our bubble with Thatcher hot on his heels. "I'm glad you're all right."

"Yeah, you too." I grab his forearm in greeting. He looks as if he hasn't slept in days. It's a relief to see him.

Thatcher places a hand on William's shoulder. "Why don't you take some time to get cleaned up and get something to eat. We can meet later this afternoon, away from curious bystanders, and discuss this further."

Looking past William, more and more people are slowing and staring our direction. I used to love this kind of attention. Not anymore.

"Yeah, you look like crap. A few hours of sleep might do you some good." I bump his shoulder. We haven't been seeing eye to eye lately, but I'm relieved to see him alive and kicking.

"You know me," he chuckles.

"No rest for the wicked?"

"Exactly."

I watch the group head for the hotel and feel a sense of relief. Now that they're back and safe, I can finally focus on my meeting with Kate.

"I can't believe I went to the base that used to stockpile nukes." Darby says, dropping a large duffel on her bed.

"Most of them were launched in the third world war," I say and sit on Lucas's bed. "The odds of any still being there—"

"The place blew up," Darby yells. "So there sure was *something* there."

"But it wasn't a nuke," I point out, equal parts annoyed and amused.

"A bomb is a bomb," she mutters.

Lucas and I exchange smiles. "Not really." Lucas starts a fire in the woodstove, and I scoot closer to the heat. "If it were a nuke, there'd be nothing of you left."

"Not comforting, Danielle," she snaps and begins to sort through the bag, organizing parts and pieces into small piles. I don't even pretend to understand her system.

I try to look into her bag, but her rummaging gets in my way. "Did you get your hands on anything besides tech? Blueprints, maybe?"

She pushes her wild blond hair from her face and nods excitedly. "Oh yeah, a few binders full. I think they were meant to be destroyed, but the NAF ran out of time, or someone must've forgotten to take them."

"Have you gone through them?" I ask when she doesn't elaborate.

"Briefly, before William took them."

"Well?"

"Well, what?"

I take a deep breath, my patience wearing thin. "What did they say?"

She looks at me, confused. Just as I'm about to blow a gasket, Lucas speaks up. "Go on and tell her, tell her the good news," he prompts.

Darby reaches into her back pocket and unfolds three pieces of paper. She holds them up proudly, as if I have any clue what the scribbled notes mean. "They're close to finding a way around the blockers."

I shouldn't be surprised, but it still feels as though the air has been ripped out of my lungs. "How long until they do?"

"Don't know." She shrugs and shoves the papers back into her pocket. "I swiped a bunch of notes about their progress. It looks like they removed the blockers around Malmstrom in order to do tests on them. I haven't had time to fully examine their work."

"You haven't shown those notes to William?" I ask, even though I know the answer. She barely has time to shrug before I chastise her. "Darby."

"What? He took everything else," she justifies. "It's not like Thatcher and William would be able to follow these calculations and blueprints." She holds up a motor and some propellers she's just pulled from the bag. I'm slightly impressed with the amount of crap she has shoved in there.

"They would've wanted to talk about it, and I was anxious to try to start rebuilding."

I give Lucas a look. "Good luck sleeping tonight."

He smiles, seeming proud. "The air is electric. A storm is brewing."

"Issue seventeen," Darby mumbles.

Not even bothering to correct her, I watch as she fiddles with the motor. This is so much more serious than I thought. Everyone knew the NAF was swimming in tech, but this is a development I didn't see coming. And I feel pretty stupid for it. "I'm going to talk to Kate."

Darby groans and tosses the motor into one of her piles. "Here we go again."

"Do you have any connections to the NAF? Because if you do, I'm open to suggestions."

Lucas sits beside me on his bed and watches as Darby takes the last few parts out of the bag. "It's a dangerous path ahead."

He's definitely not wrong. Leaving now isn't a good idea. But it's too risky to have this conversation over the radio. "I'm going to sneak out through the tunnels."

Darby's head snaps up at that. "The what?"

"The tunnels. There's an underground tunnel system that leads in and out of Rapid City."

She stares in disbelief. "Does anyone else know about them?"

"Most of them lead to underground bunkers built before the third world war. All the locals know about those. The one that leads out of town isn't common knowledge. George might know."

"Bunkers for bombs?" she asks, still looking startled.

I shrug. "Yeah. They helped save a lot of lives during the last war."

"Should you really be sneaking in and out right now? Especially to break into a military base?" Darby stands looking at me with her hands on her hips. She easily slips back into annoyance, and I do not need a lecture.

"I'm not sneaking onto a base. I asked her to meet me somewhere else." I stand and grab my jacket, not looking forward to going back into the cold. "But I have to leave now if I want to make it on time."

"We must report our findings to the commander," Lucas reminds me with a frown.

"Yeah, about that. If anyone presses you on where I am, tell them I'm meeting with a contact, and I'll touch base when I'm back. Thatcher knows I've been meeting with an informant." I slip my arms into my winter coat.

"If Thatcher knows, why are you sneaking out?" Darby asks.

"The town is on lockdown. I was politely asked not to leave." Lucas and Darby stare at me knowingly. "Darby, you should meet with them," I say, changing the subject. "Show them what you found. Woo them with your nerd speak."

With the way her expression changes, anyone would think I asked her to clean the shit out of the horse stables. "Why would I want to do that?"

I motion to the piles scattered along her bed. "No one else can make sense of tech like you and this is something they need to know. Like it or not, you're now essential to the Resistance."

"Fantastic." Nothing about her tone screams excited.

"I have my radio, but don't use it unless it's an absolute emergency. I'll be back tomorrow. Jess knows where I'm going, so if you can't reach me for whatever reason, I'm sure she can." I give Lucas a pleading look. "I just, I have to know what Kate knows. I have to know if she knew about the diversions and the drones and everything else that's going on. I have to see if I can get something. Anything."

Lucas thinks for a moment and then sighs. "This is all a convoluted situation, but I'm doing my best to make sense of these orders from the brass."

"Issue number one," Darby calls out.

"Number three." I pull on my hat and look at my brother.

He meets my gaze and nods. "Be safe in your journey, soldier." I do my best to smile.

"Show them the blueprints," I call over my shoulder and pull the door closed behind me, anxious for my meeting and hoping like hell that Kate gets my message and shows.

CHAPTER TEN: THE OFFER

KATE

I have spent the entire day poring over personnel records and trying to figure out a way to help Privates Silva and Miller. It's hard to focus. I'm desperate to know more about the blast on Malmstrom and who, if anyone, was caught in the crossfire. After reading the same line over and over for the fifth or sixth time, I drop the file on my desk and rub my eyes. The only thing that seems to settle my nerves is knowing that Dani wasn't at the base. Instead, she went after my mother near Ellsworth.

How did my mother know Dani might be in the area? She said the radio would reach about five hundred and fifty miles from Offutt Air Force Base. That's a rather large circle for her to be in. Though she did say someone else may be on the other end, which may mean that she's even farther out than that and just has a contact within that parameter.

She could be anywhere. I really should've asked where she was hiding.

I try to focus on the reports, something I *can* control, instead of something I so clearly can't. Scanning the names of all of the soldiers who have requested early retirement, discharge, and transfers, I try to find a pattern. The problem is, there's not much here. It's unsettling to say the least. Over the past five years, fewer and fewer requests for transfer or discharge have been granted. Only two soldiers that I can find and they were officers way above Silva and Miller's rank. Not one private has been given such permission.

Looks like discharge isn't an option. And transferring them somewhere else isn't on the table either. Who knows where they'd be sent and what they would be asked to do? I knew this was a long shot. But it seems the NAF is more short-handed than I previously thought. They can't afford to let anyone go, and my hope of helping them is quickly deflating.

I'm exhausted. My eyes feel dry and tired, and I've unbuttoned the top buttons of my jacket so it doesn't feel as suffocating in the now stifling room. My hair is unwashed and falling out of the pins used to hold it in place at the base of my neck. I must look like a disheveled mess.

Turning down my heater, I switch over to skim the reports Rodrigues has been working on regarding the drones. Her notes are immaculate, using her research from Malmstrom and referencing the supplies that arrived this past afternoon on base, I know the general will be pleased.

With that read, I go over her update about sending out messages to several locations regarding the transfer of leadership to the NAF. There has been no reply regarding any of them but no pushback either.

"That's a start," I mumble to myself. The more cities and townships that willingly relinquish control to the NAF, the better. I wonder if Dani is residing in one of them. Staring at the piles of files spread out across my desk, I groan. The work is never-ending, and it's hard to keep it all straight.

Knowing I should get some rest, I gather my files and head home. The walk back to my house is quiet. I figure most everyone must be in bed or getting ready to head that way. Yawning, I can't help feeling jealous of anyone who gets more than a couple hours of sleep. It's been hard to come by recently. Between the traveling and nightmares, I don't even remember what a peaceful night feels like. The closest I've come was the single night I shared with Dani. Even then, I was up half the night...

I let my thoughts linger there awhile longer, unable to keep from smiling.

I reach my quarters and can physically feel the proximity of my bed. Yawning again, I know the first thing I need to do before I sleep is try to get ahold of Dani. I couldn't reach her last night or this morning. If I can't reach Dani tonight, I'm ignoring her warning about using Archie and will get ahold of him up in Grand Forks in the morning.

My hand hesitates on the knob, a strange feeling coming over me, and I'm not sure why. Cautiously, I push open the door and am met with silence, save for the fire burning strong in the sitting room. A fire I didn't start. For the briefest of seconds, I remember the last time a fire was lit in my place of residence without my knowledge.

I hold my breath, a wave of excitement coming over me as I look farther into the room, only to exhale in disappointment at seeing Ryan waiting for me and not the girl I was hoping for.

"It's late," I tell him and drop the files on the table by the door so I can wash my hands. The look on his face as he refuses to so much as glance in my direction makes me pause. Even the fire does nothing to slice through the chill in the room. "Is everything okay?"

I can see his jaw flex in the firelight, and it's only then I see what is resting on his knee. My stomach drops. He lifts the radio but still refuses to look at me. "What's this?"

I finish cleaning my hands slowly as I try to calm the panic rapidly growing in my belly. I do my best not to appear guilty of anything. Ryan knows me too well for me to play dumb, but I try anyway. "Where did you get that?"

"I was getting my notebooks from your bag and found it at the bottom. It seemed odd that you had a non-NAF issued radio. It took me a minute to realize exactly what it was." He turns to me, his gaze cold and hard. "Are you a spy?"

I take my time drying my hands. It's clear the radio is mine; there's no way of getting around that. I should've hidden it better. But then again, I didn't really think anyone would go through my personal items inside my bedroom. There's a penalty for entering an officer's house without permission. But I doubt I can leverage my situation with that, considering what Ryan found.

I try to figure out how much he's pieced together or whether he's turned it on and scanned the frequencies to see who may be on the other end. I wonder if he's tried to make contact. And for the first time since Dani gave it to me, I hope that no one has tried to reach me.

"Answer me." His voice echoes through the room, making me jump. I'm surprised at the anger behind it. I haven't heard him use that tone with me, well, ever.

Slowly, I put the towel down and take several steps into the sitting room. "No. I'm not a spy."

"Then what is this?" He gives the radio a little shake. My eyes fall to it, hoping again that he didn't turn it on. "Tell me what the hell is going on."

"First of all, you need to lower your voice." My tone is clipped. If we are going to do this, I don't need him yelling for the whole damn street to hear. And I sure don't appreciate his tone. I go to the window and peek through the curtains to make sure no one is out despite not seeing much of anyone out and about on my walk here.

This time, when he speaks, his voice is softer but still dripping with accusation. "It's from her, isn't it? You're still in contact with *her*."

I pull the curtains shut tightly, but I don't loosen my grip on the fabric as I try to steady the pounding of my heart. "It's not what you think," I say without turning.

"No? So you didn't leave base under the guise of an R and R for a secret meetup with an active member of the Resistance?"

Okay, so it's exactly as he thinks. My shoulders slump. I take a deep breath and shake my head, not able to find the words to explain to him my situation with Dani and not even bothering to hide the fact that he's right. "It's complicated." I finally turn and look at him.

"Well, I've got time. Uncomplicate it." He looks betrayed. Hurt.

I sit on the chair beside him and drag my palms over my thighs to steady my nerves. "I told you that she was the one who warned me about the ambush on the convoy to Omaha." I swallow hard. "I tried to warn her about Simon and White River. But I was too late."

His expression shifts to confusion. "You tried to warn her? Why would you do that?"

The question ignites something in me, pushing my nerves into anger. "Because those people didn't deserve what happened to them. They didn't deserve to be massacred. They at least deserved a chance to surrender peacefully or evacuate."

"You gave away confidential information. You gave away our position." He looks absolutely flabbergasted. "Kate, she killed the unit that we sent there."

"And *they* killed innocent people. Destroyed their home. And for what? Revenge?" Now I'm the one who needs to lower my voice, but I'll be damned if I let Ryan believe that Simon was in the right here. "We didn't give them a chance to surrender. There were children. Elderly. Slaughtered, Ryan. In the middle of the night while they were sleeping.

Is that what you want the National Armed Forces to be known for? Murdering people in their sleep? The actions of *Simon*?" All my doubts about the NAF come spilling out like water through a broken dam.

Ryan's jaw clenches, and I doubt we'll find any common ground on the issue tonight. Maybe not ever. It makes me sad to think of our friendship slipping away over this. "What happened to you when we were in White River? What did she do to you?"

"She didn't *do* anything." I can't keep the annoyance from my tone. The way he asks makes it seem like she tied me up and brainwashed me with her elusive magic. "You were there. Nothing happened."

"Something must've happened."

"We talked. That's it," I tell him honestly. "She told me personal things. Things I never knew about her."

My mind goes back to her story about what happened with Jess and how her recklessness caused a child she loved to lose her eyesight. How she so desperately wanted to be a different person than that. How hard she tried to be normal, to start over.

"We painted such a clear picture of her at the academy. And it turns out, she's a lot more complex than that. She's a human being with feelings, just like the rest of us. She's not some emotionless monster. Everything she's been through, what Lucas has been through…My mother ordered the death of their father. Right in front of them." I turn toward the fireplace and stare at the orange and yellow flames. "I would've shot the enemy's daughter in the head on sight if it was me."

I can feel Ryan staring. "Are you defending the terrible things she's done because of how she handled her grief?"

"Of course not," I snap. "I just understand a little bit better why she did them. We had people telling us what she was like, people who hadn't even met her. How does that make any sense?"

He opens his mouth but closes it again as if reconsidering. I turn back toward the fire and wait. Finally, he speaks, and it's so quiet, I almost don't hear it. "Are you sleeping with her?"

Of all the questions I thought he was going to ask, that was not high on the list. And it's not a topic I wish to discuss with him. Or anyone. An image of Dani pulling me into her lap as she kisses me pops into my mind.

I turn away without answering, beyond grateful that he can't read my mind, but my silence appears to be enough.

He exhales deeply, as if I just punched him in the chest and forced all the air from his lungs. We sit in silence for a moment. I have no desire to get into more detail about that part of my relationship with Dani, and I refuse to let him make me feel guilty about it.

He clears his throat. "Do you have feelings for her?"

Despite that very question being always on my mind, I don't allow myself to think about it. I'm scared of what it may mean if I do. Uncertain how to answer, I deflect. "I'm not a spy or a traitor. I'm not." Thankfully, he doesn't push.

Finally, I turn and meet his eyes only to find hurt and sadness. This isn't just about the NAF. I know it goes deeper than that. More personal. "But you told her about Simon."

I stand, unable to stay seated any longer. Not with all these emotions coursing through me. I pace in front of the fireplace, my agitation building at the mention of his name. "Simon is out of control. No one deserves to be executed like that. He's out there blowing up bases, burning towns, and reveling in the destruction. My mother has given him free rein to do whatever it takes to draw Dani out and kill her. Including sacrificing our own. And before you ask, yes, I told Dani that Simon was coming for her."

"Jesus, Kate." He sits back in the chair, slumping into the cushions.

"It's not right, Ryan. There are rules of war. Rules of engagement. And my mother has no problem breaking them. Then we have the audacity to act surprised when the Resistance does? We can't have it both ways. My mother was willing to sacrifice her own soldiers, blowing up our own bases, at a chance of taking down members of the Resistance, and we're supposed to be okay with that? And all for what? Why? What is it about the Clarks and William Russell that my mother hates so much?" My blood is boiling now, and all the exhaustion that previously consumed me has taken a back seat to the anger that has been building inside me since leaving White River.

Ryan slams his hands on his legs. "That's what war is! Sacrifice for the greater good, but you can't bear the thought of those tough calls, can you?"

His words are like a slap in the face. I glare at him. "You sound just like my mother."

He leans forward and motions to the radio he tossed on the small table between the chairs. "How long have you had this? Have you been in constant communication with her since we left White River? What else have you told her?"

"Nothing." I stop pacing and cross my arms. "We haven't spoken since I got here."

"But that's what it's for, right? To give her a heads up regarding our orders?" I don't answer. "Would you have warned her about Malmstrom? About the decoys the general sent?"

Yes. "I don't know."

"Are you going to tell her about the drones?"

I don't say anything. He lets out a noise of disbelief and turns toward the fire. The room is eerily silent except for the crackling and pop of the flames.

"Are you in love with her?"

It's asked so suddenly that I'm not prepared for the way my body rocks. I steady myself; the weight of his question feels heavy. "I'm..." I snap my mouth shut. To say I'm not feels like a lie. This is the reason I've been avoiding thinking about my feelings. Hearing Ryan speak it into existence shocks me to my very core.

"You have to be. Otherwise, why do all this? Why jeopardize your entire career, your life?" He looks at me with an expression I can't place, but it's almost as if he's struggling to keep tears at bay. He blinks rapidly and clenches his jaw. "How do you know she's not using you? Playing you for information? Saying what you want to hear?"

I shake my head adamantly. No. No. Dani wouldn't do that. I know she wouldn't. I know it with every fiber of my being. "She's not."

"How do you know?" His voice is pleading, begging me to reconsider.

"I just do," I say with all the certainty I'm capable of.

His voice wavers. "Did she make you promises after you were intimate? Promises you wanted to believe because you're—"

"That's not fair, and it's certainly none of your fucking business." I give him a look of warning, one that I hope says he's dangerously close to crossing a line he doesn't want to cross with me.

"You're literally sleeping with the enemy and sharing NAF intel." His voice cracks, and I can see now that he was unsuccessful at keeping his tears at bay. "I think it's worth a closer look at her intentions. Especially since you think you're in love with her."

"Just stop," I yell and have to refrain from covering my ears. "You don't know anything about her."

"And you think you do?" He stands and motions toward the window as if actively showing me the damage she has caused. "I know she single-handedly took out a convoy a few days ago. Killed almost a hundred people in the blink of an eye. Not to mention all the other people she killed, families she destroyed, after her father died. But you're too wrapped up in what Simon's doing and the way you *think* you feel about her to care about any of that, aren't you? What else is there to possibly know, right?"

I have absolutely no idea how to respond to the pain in his voice. Especially not when he doesn't want to listen.

He hastily wipes at the tears on his cheeks.

I suck in a slow, steadying breath. "There's more to her than just killing."

"You want to know what I think?" I really don't, but he doesn't give me a chance to voice my thoughts before continuing. "I think, *you* think, you love her as some twisted way to get back at your mother."

I punch him. His face snaps to the side with the force of the blow. I flex my fingers, the adrenaline too strong to feel any pain.

He brings his hand to his face and opens and shuts his mouth, working his jaw from side to side.

I stare at him, my chest heaving as I try to steady myself.

As if realizing the gravity of the insult, he slumps and looks away. "I need to think."

Panic mixes with rage. Despite our history, despite his loyalty to me, he has *always* been unwavering when it comes to his commitment to the NAF and to me. The news of my relationship with Dani has put him in an impossible situation, both personally and with the NAF. For the first time since I've known him, I'm not sure who he'll choose.

He makes his way to the door, and I follow, desperate for him not to do or say anything about the radio and what I've done but still so angry over his outburst. I hate that he's so clearly hurting, but he had no right to say the things he said.

"Ryan."

He stops at the door and turns his head slightly in my direction. I can already see a bruise forming along his jaw. He doesn't look at me. "I won't tell anyone, Kate. Not yet. But you need to reevaluate if this is where your loyalty lies and if you really want to be here. Or if you're devoted to someone else." His gaze finally meets mine. "It's only a matter of time before someone else figures out what you've been doing. And when they do..." He lets his warning linger for a beat and then leaves.

I drag myself back into the sitting area and collapse into a large chair as the door clicks into place. The look of utter betrayal on Ryan's face leaves me unnerved. I have no reason to believe he will turn me in tonight, not while he's still processing everything, and his temper is so hot, but I haven't seen him look at me like that since I ended our own relationship.

Shaking my hand, I look at my knuckles with a frown. The pain is finally seeping in and not just with my hand. His accusation of not being loyal to the NAF stings just as bad.

There are times where I question NAF methods, but I have always remained loyal to the cause. I have always remained loyal to my duty and to my land. To be accused of treason makes me sick with guilt.

I warned Dani about Simon, but I refuse to believe that was a betrayal of the NAF.

And it certainly wasn't because I was in some lovesick haze. I was trying to protect innocent people. White River wasn't harboring Resistance. They didn't deserve to be punished as if they were. Dani had quit; she wasn't part of the Resistance anymore. She was just a normal townsperson living her day-to-day life as a regular person. It was immoral to slaughter those people, plain and simple.

I lean back in the chair and take the pins from my hair, letting it down and running my fingers through the tangles, hissing when I stretch my fingers wide. I really decked him hard.

His words really hurt. I'm a good soldier. I can do a lot of good here. I can make sure people are taken care of, and I can help unite this country into something great. I can alter the course of the war. I owe it to the people of the wasteland to try.

What I'm doing with Dani has nothing to do with getting back at my mother. Getting back at her for what, exactly? Undermining me? Ignoring my proposals and ideas? Neglecting to be an actual mother when I needed her to be?

I close my eyes. No. What I have with Dani isn't a revenge play directed at my mother, and it certainly isn't love. It's...it's attraction.

And fondness and maybe the element of excitement. That's it. It's surely not love.

But it's something.

I'll talk to Ryan again in the morning and make him see that my attraction to Dani has no effect on my long-term plan for bringing this nation together. I'll tell him that our affair was a lapse in judgment, and seeing her won't happen again.

I lean my head back in the chair and groan. I can't even convince myself of that lie.

What the hell am I doing?

Is he right? Is my loyalty shifting? Am I letting my feelings get in the way of common sense?

I reach for the radio. I wonder if the best thing is to just toss it into the fire and be done with it all. Be done with Dani and push aside this growing attachment I have to her.

The thought of ending things with her without even speaking with her first makes me sick to my stomach. Turning the radio on, a voice I've never heard before comes through, repeating the same message over and over. It's not Dani, but the message is still from her. Increasing the volume, I listen carefully. It's a set of coordinates along with a time. I glance at my watch.

"Shit."

All thoughts of loyalty and devotion are gone, along with any trace of skepticism about ever seeing Dani again as I race to get a map. I feel alert and anxious. I wonder how long the message had been playing and if Ryan had heard any of it.

Memorizing the coordinates, I drag my fingers across the latitude and longitude on my old state map. It appears to be a house near the old courthouse, outside of the base parameters.

Once I've gotten the location, I press the PTT button. "Copy that, Songbird affirmative."

The radio falls silent. Reply received. Quickly, I roll up the map and run upstairs to grab a small backpack. I shove the radio from Dani, along with my NAF-issued one, inside the bag and slip on a thicker coat. Snagging a flashlight, I race out the door and pull my blue hat over my headset, knowing that not seeing Dani again was never really an option.

❖

This is stupid. So incredibly stupid.

The words play like a mantra in my head as I put the buggy in park. I'm looking for a residential house, and despite the disarray this building is in, I believe this is the place.

Removing my headset, I shove it into my backpack, grateful to have gotten off base without any issues. Grabbing the pistol from my holster, I slip out of the buggy and face the building. It's quiet. Eerily so. I use my flashlight to check the windows for any sign of movement. I don't see any.

I glance around again. There's no sign of anyone or any sort of vehicle. If Dani's here, she must've parked far away.

Taking a deep breath, I head for the front door, again reminding myself that this is stupid. The front door is closed, and I hesitantly turn the knob. With one last look over my shoulder, I push open the door. Resting one wrist over the other, my pistol on top, I scan the interior. The light barely brightens the decaying wood and paint-peeled walls within.

Taking several, slow steps, I listen for any sound of movement. I venture in farther. The back part of the house has caved in, and the fireplace has collapsed, and I wonder how this place is even still standing. There is no furniture, nothing of value, and no trace of anyone being here in a very long time. How did Dani even know this place existed?

"It's a wonder you didn't get attacked by raiders or attract your guard units with all the noise you made getting here."

Startled, I spin around to the staircase opposite from the front door, my pistol and flashlight aimed at the source. Dani peers around the wall, squinting and holding up a hand to block the light shining directly in her eyes. Sighing in relief, I lower both the flashlight and my gun.

She stares at me for a moment as my heart settles. "You look like shit."

"Well, excuse me," I fire back. "I'm tired, and it hasn't been the best night thus far. I haven't slept much in the past fifty-six hours, and I didn't have time to primp when your urgent and ominous call came through."

Dani smiles, clearly amused at my struggle, and motions for me to follow her up the stairs. I eye them skeptically. They squeak as she goes, and I wonder why they didn't squeak on her way down or if she was there lurking in the stairwell the entire time. I sure hope I don't end up with a broken leg out of this whole adventure.

I take the stairs quickly, hoping that if I move fast enough, I won't fall through, and Dani is waiting for me in the room that overlooks the front of the building. Height advantage to scan the perimeter. Smart move.

Dani lights a lantern in the far corner, keeping it low, and I holster my gun and slip the flashlight into my bag. I drop my backpack to the floor and am immediately pulled into a tight embrace. My arms go around her neck, and our lips crash together as if neither one of us could wait one more second without contact. I didn't realize how badly I needed to see her until this very moment. My body relaxes.

"Are you okay?" I ask between kisses.

"Much better now," she says. I can feel her smiling against my lips. It's easy to forget that being together is a death sentence when Dani sounds almost happy. "Are you?"

"I had a fight with Ryan. I punched him."

She pulls away slightly, and her expression shifts from what appears to be jealousy to surprise. She takes my hand and gently drags her thumb across my bruised knuckles. The gesture stirs up butterflies in my stomach. "Do you want to talk about it?" Her tone makes it seem as though she'd rather not, and with accusations of love being at the forefront of our argument, I'm more than happy not to elaborate.

I shake my head, and after one more kiss to her full lower lip, I rest my forehead against hers. We don't have a lot of time before I need to get back. And once again, I find myself with so much to say to her. "I didn't know the general's escort was a decoy. I didn't know about Malmstrom." Her warm breath caresses my face as she sighs, sounding relieved. I cup her cheeks and meet her eyes. "Dani, I would've told you they were traps if I had known."

"Hey." She adjusts my hat with a fond smile. Moving her head down slightly so that we're level, she searches my eyes. "I don't expect you to tell me everything, Kate." *We're still enemies* goes without saying. "But it's a relief that you weren't part of the setup."

I lean into her touch. "We're rebuilding and expanding the aerial unit. Everything the NAF was secretly working on in Malmstrom has been transferred down here." The confession comes out as a whisper. It isn't lost on me how Dani fails to show surprise or that I so easily gave her more NAF intel.

"I know," she whispers and kisses my forehead. "Lucas and William were at Malmstrom when it blew."

I take a step back. "Lucas?" I can feel the few contents of my stomach rising.

"He's okay," she assures me quickly.

I release a deep, steadying breath knowing that Dani's brother is all right. The Clark siblings have weakened my ability to compartmentalize. It was noticeable before, but now it's glaringly obvious. Maybe it's my lack of sleep, or maybe it's me recognizing that Ryan had every right to be worried about me, but I'm definitely waning on the loyalty I claimed to have only a short time ago. "I didn't know anything she had planned. Simon blew up the base. Everything that's happening lately, I'm learning after the fact. It's like a constant game of catch-up. They were researching drones at Malmstrom for six years, and I had no idea."

"I guess being the general's daughter doesn't make you privy to everything." She motions to the silver oak leaf pinned on my jacket above my name. "Congratulations on the promotion."

I look at the pin peeking out from my jacket and change the subject. "What did you find out at Malmstrom?"

"Not much. Just pieces of drones you weren't able to smuggle out. Two planes cleared of tech." She watches me for a moment, unmoving. "When did you start removing the blockers?"

"As soon as my mother became general," I confess with a frown.

"And how long have you been trying to get around them?" She asks.

I think about my dad and all his studies. How he worked endlessly to get drones and planes and other aircraft back into the air. He studied the effects of the third world war and flight his entire life. Just like his father did before him. As far as I know, we've been trying to reactivate flight since the day it was taken away. I wish he was still alive to help guide me through this. "I'm sure they were working on a solution as soon as the first planes fell."

Dani's jaw tightens and relaxes over and over, as if she's chewing on whatever else it is she wants to ask. I don't give her the chance.

"I'll do what I can to find how close they are to succeeding," I say without thinking. "After my training with the aerial division here, I'll be taking over the southern army and full aerial unit in San Antonio."

Hurt floods her soft features. "What?" Taking a step back, she runs a hand through her wavy hair and turns away, her other hand resting on her hip. "You're going to be in charge of..." She doesn't finish before she launches with another question. "Did you give the order for all cities and townships to acquiesce?"

The subject change throws me, but I answer regardless. "Yes, but it's for everyone's best interest." She looks at me disbelievingly. "Dani, I didn't have any other choice. I'm trying to avoid unnecessary bloodshed."

"Until you take charge of the main aerial unit in San Antonio. Then you get to command all those drones, right?"

I chance a step forward. "We can do a lot of good with the use of aircraft." I take her hand. "They can provide food, supplies, medical necessities to towns faster than we could on land."

She squeezes my hand. "Is that what you think is going to happen?" Her tone is condescending, and I hate it.

"It is if I convince the majority of the wasteland to transfer peacefully." I pull her closer. I need her to hear me in order to fully understand that I'm doing my best to make this a cordial transition.

Her laugh is humorless, and she pulls away, taking a step back. "Or until the general overrules you and straps bombs to the drones the second they are in the air."

A biting insult about strapping bombs to things hangs on the tip of my tongue. I come dangerously close to spitting it out, but I shake my head instead. "I will always push for a peaceful transfer of power."

"It doesn't matter what you want!" Her voice gets louder with each word, her stress and anger pushing through. "You're not the general. As much power as you think you have, she'll always have more. Malmstrom is proof of that. You said it yourself, she's keeping you in the dark. The only thing the general cares about is power."

"She wants unification." Even as my words are spoken, I know it's not the full truth. The lie tastes bitter in my mouth. I wet my lips and try again. "She wants to unite this country."

"Unification by murdering anyone who disagrees with her. It's a false flag operation, Kate!" Dani runs both hands through her hair and turns away from me.

"The general wants everyone under one law," I repeat, ignoring her accusation. "Her methods aren't always ideal, and I don't agree with all of them, but she is focused on making it happen. And with me in place, I can help assure that it happens the *right* way. Peacefully."

"Yeah, because that's working great so far." Dani paces several steps away and then comes closer. "The third world war fractured us. What's left of this country will not survive a full-blown civil war, and I'm getting really goddamn tired of fighting for my own land."

"Then allow me to help *peacefully* so we can stop the fighting." I beg her to understand. I beg her to listen.

"You want us to just stop fighting for what we believe in and join your cause? You want us to surrender to the NAF to stop the war? How about *you* surrender to *us*." She's angry. And we both know no one is planning on surrendering just to stop the bloodshed. Now when both sides are holding strong to their ideals.

"You won't win," I challenge. "Help me to prevent another civil war. Cities like Pierre and Lincoln, God knows who else, they need help. Jesus, Dani, let me help them."

"That's not the point. You shouldn't even be here. This isn't your land to take!" I flinch at her words and the volume. I've never seen her this emotional. It doesn't scare me as much as it confuses me. Dani closes the distance between us and takes my hands. Her expression has softened into something more desperate. "This isn't going to go the way you're hoping it will. The general doesn't share your affection for helping people. That's not how she works. Unification isn't her goal. Dominance is. She is an affliction to my people and this land."

I take a step back and lock eyes with her, ripping my hands from her grasp. I'm tired of people yelling at me and telling me what I should or shouldn't think. "And you know my mother so well that you can say that for certain?" Dani stands up straighter, defiant. It only makes me angry. "Oh, that's right. You have entire journals about her."

I'm met with silence. It's a low blow and does nothing to appease my irritation, but it does muffle my anger into something similar to regret. I sigh and try again without all the fury. "The general plans on taking over the wasteland by the end of winter. And whether we want her to or not, she'll make it happen. It would be better for everyone if you led the Resistance to a peaceful transition instead of a violent one." I look her in the eyes. "Please." My desperate plea is caught in my throat. I cannot bear the idea of leading an attack against Dani, but unless she gives, I fear I'll have no other choice. I can only bend my orders so far.

She shakes her head. "You're not hearing me." Her voice is sad, dejected.

Honestly, I think it's her who's not hearing *me*. "Dani."

"I'm not turning myself in. Or my friends. I'm not surrendering my home. Not for you and certainly not for her." She looks betrayed. Utterly and devastatingly betrayed.

"I'm not asking you to. I'm just asking…" I get lost in my own pleas, knowing full well that that's exactly what I *am* asking. I rub my eyes, weary of fighting and tired of trying to justify my good intentions. "I'm just asking you to stand down and stay out of it."

"I can't do that, either."

I straighten and pull all emotion from my next attempt. "I have to make sure supplies are on their way to Pierre and Lincoln. Please, pull your people back," I request.

She huffs a humorless laugh and steps back, too. The growing space between us doesn't go unnoticed. "It's not my call. Just stand down, Kate." She clips my name sharply. "Our people are stationed there, and they aren't moving. We'll take care of them. Pull back your aid."

"The agreement's been made, Dani," I return her name mockingly. "If they side with the Resistance now, they will be held accountable. Just let the NAF take care of them per our agreement."

"Take care of them? Is that what you think this is? You think you just swoop in and save them?" She throws her arms up dramatically and bellows into the rafters of the abandoned building. "Make way! The NAF are on their way to come save the day with their supplies!"

I step forward. "That's exactly what we do," I say through a clenched jaw.

"No. That's what you *think* you do." She leans forward and points an accusatory finger. "Instead, you give them an ultimatum: join us and our way of thinking and follow our laws or starve to death, and if you change your minds, we'll kill you. This time, we'll do it with bombs. What kind of choice is that?"

"That's pretty hypocritical coming from someone who's built their reputation on blowing things up." I can see the fire in Dani's eyes, but I don't give her a chance to respond. "You want to talk about choice? They *had* a choice," I yell. "They came to *you* first. They came to the Resistance, and no one cared enough to answer them."

"*I* cared," she snaps.

"*You* hid," I stab again.

"I wasn't hiding," she says through clenched teeth. "Don't blame me for the sins of someone else. I did my best. I'm just *one* person. I can't help everyone!" She attempts to step farther away from me, but I quickly follow with a long stride forward.

"Well, *we* can," I press.

"No, you don't want to help. You want to dominate. Just like your mother." Her words are a physical blow and stop me in my tracks. "If you cared about the people here, if you *really* cared, you'd help them survive without conforming to your laws. Without the fear of dying if they refuse. If you even stopped, for just one second, and *listened* to what they want instead of *telling* them."

I shake my head and divert my eyes. Her words sting like a deep betrayal. I only ever wanted to do what was right. "We don't stand a chance if we aren't united."

"But not like this. Not where one person makes all the rules and kills everyone who doesn't agree."

"We can't progress as a singular nation if we aren't united," I repeat as my jaw tightens again.

"And we aren't united unless *everyone* has a say."

"So what are you proposing?" I ask. "If you refuse to help me unify peacefully, and neither of us is willing to surrender, then what are you suggesting?"

She takes a step forward, finally allowing me to be close to her again. "Come with me."

"What?" I stare at her, bewildered.

"Come with me."

I release a shaky breath as a not-so-distant memory comes to the forefront of my thoughts: Dani and I sitting close by the bank of the lake in White River. The way she looked at me, sad but hopeful, as she confessed to wanting more people like me within the NAF ranks. Then she released us.

"You said it yourself, your mom is too narrow-sighted," she continues after my silence drags on. "She's leaving you in the dark. Come with me, Kate."

"That's not what I—"

"You can help me win this war. You can help me unite people the right way." Her voice is laced with a desperation that I'm not accustomed to when it comes to her.

"And then what?" I push. "What's your plan? Do you have a new constitution written? A revised declaration? A list of grievances? Do you even have a plan if you win the war? Who will take charge? How will the transition of power go? How will you spread your message? How will you stop a power vacuum?"

Our eyes lock. She doesn't have the answers, and we both know it. The Resistance has been fighting against the NAF for so long that they've lost sight of what they would do if they were to actually take control. Logically, I can't commit to a side without a plan of action to take care of its people. More so, I can't just walk away and abandon everything I've ever known.

Anger deflates me, and once again, I just feel utterly exhausted. "I can't leave. This is who I am. This is my life. I know our methods right now aren't perfect, but I can still do good here. I have to try."

Her eyes search mine for a long, quiet moment. "There might be some truth in that." Her shoulders slump. "But who are you trying to convince? Me or yourself?"

Her question catches me off guard and makes me uneasy. I open my mouth to respond, but nothing comes out.

She takes another hesitant step forward, a sad smile touching the sides of her lips. "I know you'd be remiss if you didn't ask your biggest Resistance contact to surrender."

"It's not like that. I would be absolutely devastated if anything happened to you. I would never turn you in. Ever. You mean more to me than..." I shut my mouth before I can say something I may regret. There's already been too much talk and thoughts of love. "I'm not using you for information. I'm not using you to climb the ranks or to betray you when you least expect it. I'm just being honest about this fight. You can't win, Dani. You're outnumbered and outgunned. I'm doing what I think is right in the long run."

She takes my hands again. "Maybe that's a bit too broad. You're looking at the big picture without seeing the steps it'll take to get there. Or what harm it will do to the other side. You're trying to avoid making the hard choices."

I laugh humorlessly. "You're the third person to tell me that."

She takes another step closer and squeezes my hands. It takes all my willpower not to pull her against me. I just need to be near her.

She ducks her head and lowers her voice even more. "Maybe you should really think about what it is you're doing here. Think about what the general wants and if her way is really the best way to unite the country. And if you want to be a part of that."

It's the way she's looking at me that keeps me from saying anything else. Her eyes shine ever so slightly in the moonlight that seeps in the windows and the soft glow from the lantern. Her eyes search my face, slowly and carefully.

It's under that tender gaze that my resolve crumbles, and I squeeze her hands. I try to respond, but all I can do is nod to let her know that I'll think about it all, the bigger picture and what's happening here and now, including the tough choices.

She brings my hands to her mouth and places several soft kisses across my bruised knuckles. "I'm in Rapid City. But I don't know for how much longer. If you change your mind, tell the guards at the gate, 'Songbird Delta Six.' It should at least get you in."

I'm relieved to finally know where she is but startled that she would give me access within the city walls.

My expression must show enough because she smiles softly. "Don't look so surprised. I was serious when I asked you to come with me."

Wrapping my arms around her, I bury my face against the side of her neck. Dani rests her chin on the top of my head and gently rubs my back. It calms me just a little.

Inhaling deeply, I take in her scent and grab fistfuls of her jacket, holding on to her as if my life depends on it for these last few moments together.

Chapter Eleven: The Warning

Dani

Nothing has ever looked as glorious than the large bed in the center of my room. After dropping my bag on the floor, I fall face-first into the mattress and groan into the soft blankets. I could sleep for a week. It's early afternoon, and my nap outside Omaha has done nothing to help the exhaustion that has consumed my entire body.

Shifting, I try to stretch out the tightness in my legs and butt. Over eighteen hours in my Jeep has left me sore and spent, but leaving Kate behind again just about wrecked me.

The entire drive back, I wondered if I crossed a line asking her to come back with me. To try to convince her that everything she ever believed in was wrong, and she needed to be here instead. Was I doing it for the right reasons, or was I being selfish because I just want her around all the time? I probably should've kept my mouth shut.

Either way, it's out there. And just because it may have been inappropriate doesn't make it any less true. I do want her here. What Kate does next is up to her.

My stomach grumbles, angry and empty, and I wonder if sleep is eluding me because I'm hungry or because of the immense guilt I feel in dumping all my anger about the NAF solely on her.

Just as I'm considering trying to reach out to her and apologizing, the radio in my bag crackles to life, and I sit up, hoping that Kate has the same idea and has beaten me to it.

Jess's muffled voice comes through instead. I flop back into the pillows, frustrated, and wait until her message plays two more times before dragging myself over to the bag.

"I'm here. Can you repeat that?" I yawn loudly, not even attempting to swallow it.

"Better go see Thatcher. She knows you're back, and she knows you snuck out of the tunnels. And put your radio on our channel. I've been trying to get ahold of you all damn day."

I wince, properly scolded. "Sorry."

"You're lucky she didn't have guards set up to greet you when you got back. She's pretty pissed."

I'm honestly surprised she didn't have me escorted in either. Something tells me that she's going to chastise me about this being the last straw, and I want nothing more than to avoid it. "Think I can squeeze in a nap first?"

Jess's response is quick and clipped. "Um, no. I'm surprised she's not actively banging on your door."

The tone in her voice leaves no room for argument. "Fair enough. Thanks, Jess."

Tossing the radio on top of my bag, I fall back on the bed. There is no way I have the energy for Thatcher's interrogation.

Just as my eyes close and I relax, for just a minute, there's a firm knock on my door. Damn, Jess wasn't kidding.

"It's unlocked," I say, unwilling to move. If I'm going to be chewed out, at least I can be comfortable.

The door opens and closes, and whoever enters is silent for a moment before a low whistle fills the space. "Now there's a sight."

Rhiannon. My entire body deflates, relieved. "I'm napping," I say as I turn and bury my face in a pillow.

"I brought food."

I risk a peek. She holds up a plate. "What is it?"

"An omelet. Eggs were fresh this morning." She places it on the table next to the bed and sits beside me as I finally sit up. "Wyatt has chickens." She almost sounds giddy. I love her excitement but ignore the fact that it's over Wyatt's chickens. "I heard you snuck out again."

"Clearly, my stealth is waning." I cut into the omelet and take a large bite. It's so good I can barely suppress a moan. "What else did you hear?"

"That when you lived here, you were in a relationship with an older woman named Rebecca, and you were apparently so in love that—"

I throw a pillow at her face and glare. "Not what I meant."

She laughs but thankfully doesn't continue. Who did she hear that from? I shudder to think. Either way, I do *not* need to dwell on my first heartbreak. "I was cooking with Wyatt when Thatcher came bursting in to see Jess, looking for you. You really shouldn't put Jess in the middle like that. You know she's loyal to you first. She got a pretty good tongue-lashing."

I hang my head. "I know, you're right. Putting Jess in the middle really was crappy and selfish. I shouldn't have done it. I'll talk to Thatcher and take full responsibility. I just, I've never been good with trusting other people. With everything going on, it's hard to know who to turn to."

Rhiannon sighs, and I'm grateful that she doesn't push the topic or continue to lecture. "How are you?" Her tone is serious. "Don't bullshit me, either. Be honest."

So much has happened in such a short time, I haven't really allowed myself to stop and really *think* about anything except what needs to happen next. I fear that if I slow down to process it all, the emotional damage may be too much.

"I should be asking you that," I say. My voice is quiet. Strained. I stare at the plate in my lap, unable to look her in the eyes. Everything that happened with White River hangs heavy between us. The air feels thick, but I'm not even sure where to begin to alleviate it.

"We can get to me later. Right now, I want to know about you."

It's not often that people check on me, I mean *really* check about my well-being, but I can always count on Rhiannon. Even when I don't want to face the truth. "I'm hurting," I answer honestly. Everything hurts. My wounds, my body, my mind, my heart. It's like I'm being sliced apart in different directions.

Rhiannon hums as if she understands. "I have a Grandma story." She changes the subject, and I silently thank her for it. Rhiannon recalls her grandmother's stories often, captivating anyone who's willing to listen just as easily as her grandma did years ago. Or so I'm told. The stories have been passed down over three generations.

I sit a little straighter. "I'm ready."

"Well, you know she helped raise me," Rhiannon continues as I eat. "And for bedtime stories, she would talk about life before all this." She stops, and I look over to see her staring at the wall across from us. "She used to say there were two sides of this war beyond the color of the coats. There's the hopeful and the hateful, and that no matter how many winters she survived, she was at peace, knowing she was on the side of hope." She turns to face me, revealing a rare side of herself. Vulnerable. "People live, fight, and die for their beliefs. The ones who fight for hope know that no matter the outcome, they were on the right side."

I don't say anything. Honestly, I'm not even sure what to say. That's one story she never told me, and it feels like a privilege to hear it now. Knowing how my father fought with hope for a better future creates a wave of calm that rushes over me. Maybe it brought him a sense of peace in death. Rhiannon always seems to know what people need to hear when they need to hear it.

Rhiannon clears her throat and pulls me from my reverie. "Dani, if we hadn't left White River, if *I* hadn't left—"

"Don't," I beg. Not now. I don't want to think about the ifs. I don't want to think about Rhiannon being one of the people left behind. I don't want to think about how she could've been...I shake my head.

"Not just me. Any of us. Jack, Elise, Mike, Darby, all of us. We would have been at peace being on your side. That's what you do for people. You ignite hope. I wouldn't have...I *don't* blame you for what happened." She takes my hand. "We need people like you. To remind us what we're fighting for."

"That's not—"

She squeezes my hands to shut me up. "Keep your head." Her voice tightens. She's done being gentle, and the Rhiannon I'm used to is back. "You wanna bring democracy and finish what your dad gave his life for? Be that spark. Ignite that hope and be a leader. What happened to White River was fucking terrible, and I'll mourn it and the people who died until my very last breath, but don't let it be without purpose. People will die for hope. It's as unavoidable now as it ever was. You can't blame yourself for every bad thing that happens."

Pulling her into me, I hug her as tightly as I can muster. "We lost our home." I barely choke out the words.

She squeezes me tighter. "We didn't lose our home. Home is where your family is, and our family is right here. *Home* is right here."

"All those people," I manage to squeak out before my throat feels tight. Turning my face into her neck, I start to cry. I can't hold it back. All the emotions over the past week have drained every ounce of energy I have left, bringing down the walls I so carefully built around allowing myself to feel anything. Suddenly, I feel the weight of them all at once. It's absolutely crushing.

Rhiannon holds me tightly as I finally let go and allow myself to just *feel*. She rubs my back, comforting me and letting me know I'm not alone in my grief.

When I'm finally finished crying, it's as though a huge weight has been lifted off me. Pulling away, I wipe the tears from my face and use my sleeve to wipe my nose, knowing I must be the definition of "messy." I barely have time to take a few deep breaths before Rhiannon decides that's enough of getting myself together and shifts her focus once again.

"Now. Let's talk about Kate." Groaning, I flop back on the bed, spread-eagled, and stare at the ceiling, still sniffling. "I'm assuming that's who you snuck out to see? What does she have to say about all of this?"

I rub my eyes. "You talk about hope. Well, she's hanging on to some *misplaced* hope that she can run things peacefully on the NAF side. She still believes she can help people."

Rhiannon flops on the bed beside me. "And you don't think she can?"

"I think she's in over her head and doesn't know it yet. Sometimes, hope only gets you so far." I take a deep breath. "She didn't know about the drones in Malmstrom."

"How is that possible? Isn't she an officer?" Rhiannon asks, surprised.

I sigh. "It gets worse. She's going to lead the new aerial unit in the south."

Her expression is the picture of confusion. "Wait, she didn't know anything about the drones in the north, and now she's supposed to be in charge of them in the south? What kind of sense does that make?"

"I think the general has trust issues and is playing her cards close to the chest."

"Yesterday at lunch, you said William killed her father. How? When?" Rhiannon asks after a beat of silence.

I stare at the ceiling. "A long time ago. I was, like, nineteen. He set an explosive and just..." I shrug, not able to finish. I feel guilty whenever I think about it, like I was part of it somehow. But Rhiannon's right. William killing her father is very much a big deal.

"She's never talked to you about it?" Rhiannon asks softly.

"No, and I haven't brought it up."

"Maybe it's too painful to talk about." She says it gently, hesitantly, as if she might trigger sadness regarding my own father.

Refusing to look at her, I take a deep breath. "When William did it, I was happy. My dad died two years before that, and I thought it was great getting back at the general like that. What kind of horrible person thinks that?"

"You were a kid who was grieving," she says, her voice soft, almost understanding. But it's the look of pity I know she's giving me that stirs the anger in the pit of my stomach.

"It doesn't make it right, and someone else lost their father because of it," I say, sitting up. "I think he was a good man. And now, knowing Kate…" I trail off, struggling to find the right words. "I feel like an asshole for ever being happy about it."

"Again, you were a different person then." Rhiannon says gently.

"Was I?" I ask. She looks at me and waits. I think about when I was nineteen, where my head was, what I was feeling. Then something dawns on me that I never considered. "You know what's weird? William never really talked about it. Killing her dad. You'd think he would've been gloating, but he never really mentioned it. He never gave specifics in the journals either. I'm the one who added that he was deceased."

"Why so secretive?"

I try to come up with a reasonable answer, but nothing comes to me. "I don't actually know."

"Maybe William knew he was a good man, and he didn't like what he did." That's an interesting thought. Rhiannon shakes her head and sighs almost dramatically. "I will never understand the politics of war."

I snort. "You and me both."

"Are you going to ask him about it?"

"Maybe." It might be worth bringing it up with him. I close my eyes and groan, thinking of William and Kate ever coming face-to-face. Something they'd surely do if Kate were to come back with me. "I asked her to leave. To come with me here. I didn't even think about the position that would put her in."

"That…that's something." Rhiannon regards me with a curious expression. I can almost hear her unspoken question before she asks.

"She said no." I look at my hands in my lap, anything other than Rhiannon's knowing gaze. "Of course she said no. How selfish and stupid can I be?"

"You have a lot on your mind. And if she hasn't brought it up, then maybe it's not a big deal." Rhiannon reaches out to pat my leg.

"To be face-to-face with the man who killed her father? Of course it's a big deal. That's like Kate inviting me back to her base and putting me in direct contact with her mother."

"Why do you want her here so bad?"

"What?" I ask, massaging my temples.

"Why do you want her here?" Rhiannon asks again. "Does she have some kind of superpower that will magically help the Resistance win, or is it something else?"

"I told you," I start, the question catching me off guard. "She's different. She can't do any good there no matter how badly she believes she can. I don't want to see her get hurt."

"Is that all?" Rhiannon presses.

"Isn't that enough?"

"You're being very shortsighted about all of this." She regards me carefully.

"I'm not following your abrupt line of questions," I say, annoyed and confused.

The way she's staring at me is rather unsettling. "Do you love her?"

"What? No!" I stand and turn away. Of all her questions, that's the most absurd of them all. "No, I don't..." I stop and cross my arms. This thing I feel for Kate can't be love. "I haven't known her long enough for it to be love."

Rhiannon laughs. It's not mocking, just a light sound of disbelief. "Dani, do you think there's a set time frame for knowing someone before you're allowed to love them?" I don't answer. Mainly because I don't know. Isn't there? "Sometimes it takes an instant, and sometimes it takes a lifetime. It doesn't matter if it makes sense or not."

"That's stupid."

"You gave her the codename Songbird," she teases.

"It was just the first song that popped into my head," I mumble and hope I'm not blushing.

"And you don't think that holds some kind of significance? That a song about love pops into your head when you think of Kate?" I don't bother answering. "How long did you know Rebecca before you knew you were in love with her?"

I groan. "Rebecca and Kate are totally different," I say, refusing to look at her.

She pushes on my lower back. "It's okay to be in love, you know."

"Do you love Jack?" I ask, spinning around.

She laughs again. "Of course I do."

"Wait. What?"

Her laugh only grows louder. I wasn't expecting her to answer that, most of all with a confession. "Stop deflecting. If you love her, tell her. If you want her *here* with you because you're in love with her, then tell her that. Stop making up lame excuses."

"They aren't lame."

Rhiannon gives me a look that says otherwise. I chew on the inside of my cheek. This is an incredibly uncomfortable conversation.

"What if she doesn't love me back?" It passes my lips so quietly that I'm not sure she can even hear it.

Rhiannon smiles, but it's not mocking or pitying. It's one of understanding. "You have to figure out if she's worth the risk and be patient. You unloaded a lot on her. Asked her to give up her entire world and join the man who killed her father. I'm betting that was fairly overwhelming."

She's right. She's always right. Kate is dealing with so much. I can't expect her to just walk away. I can't be selfish. Not with this. No matter how desperately I want Kate to be here with me.

Rhiannon takes a deep breath and stands.

"You're leaving?" I ask, sadly. She's pushing my emotional limits today, but I love having time to talk when it's just the two of us. We haven't had a heart-to-heart in quite a while. It's nice.

"Yeah, because you need to go see Thatcher before she comes storming over here. I definitely don't want to be here for that. And you should probably tell her who you've been sneaking out to see. There are murmurings of a traitor within the Resistance, and with you sneaking out for days at a time, well, I'm sure you can figure out the rest."

"What? I'm not a traitor," I say as Rhiannon opens the door to leave. "I've never betrayed anyone."

"Except Rebecca."

"She cheated on me first," I yell, exasperated.

She glances over her shoulder with a knowing smirk. "Go talk to Thatcher."

"I'm the Daughter of the Resistance," I call out just as the door closes.

❖

Staring at the outside of Thatcher's office, I feel like a kid about to be called in for discipline by an elder. There's a clock on the wall that no longer works. The hands are frozen just a few ticks apart, making time literally stand still. I wonder what was happening when the clock stopped ticking at 1:17. Was it in the afternoon or deep into the night? Was someone else waiting for a scolding?

I rest my head against the wall and turn it ever so slightly to look at Wesley. He seems completely unbothered behind his desk, reading a book. Is he Thatcher's errand boy, or is he supposed to be some type of security? I hope not the latter because a large gust of wind could probably knock him off his feet. I shudder to think what would happen if he was the last line of defense for Thatcher.

The door finally opens, and Thatcher motions me in without a word. I'm definitely in trouble.

I flop in the chair across from her desk and hear the door softly close behind me. She decides to be extra dramatic and pour herself a scotch from her fancy refreshment cart before sitting in her large chair. She brings the entire bottle but doesn't offer me a drink. Instead, she stares at me and takes an unnecessarily large sip. I wait. There's no way I'm starting this conversation.

After another moment of silence, Thatcher rubs her temples as if I'm already giving her a headache. "I thought I told you to lie low."

"I did," I say in protest. "It's not like the whole town saw me leave and come back." That was probably not the best thing to say.

"Dani," she scolds, her eyes hard and not in the least amused. "Using the tunnel without permission is not permitted."

"I didn't know there was a rule about that," I say innocently. "Besides, no one tried to stop me." Again. The wrong thing.

"The tunnel is for emergency use only. Do you know what it could do to us, to this town, if you were to be seen by the wrong people?" She looks tired and stressed. I feel guilty adding to it. "Where did you go?"

"Omaha," I say truthfully. "I have a contact down there." My answer seems to pique her curiosity. Rhiannon's suggestion to tell her the truth crawls to the forefront of my thoughts, and I sigh. "Inside the NAF."

"They must be important for you to drive all the way to Omaha and back, burning all that excess gas you kept for yourself from the decoy convoy." She regards me carefully.

I picture Kate and consider just how important she is, for several reasons. Knowing I need to give Thatcher something without giving up Kate's identity, I nod. "Very important. Didn't want to risk relaying classified information over the radio."

Her eyes narrow, clearly invested. "And what did this very important contact have to say?"

"They didn't know about the ambush near Ellsworth or that they were going to blow Malmstrom. And that tells me the general is being extra secretive."

"It wouldn't be the first time," Thatcher points out. "A lot of high-ranking officials don't let information trickle down. The NAF is prone to leaks, as evidenced of this contact of yours."

She's not wrong. The only way the Resistance has been able to stay afloat in this fight against the NAF is because of people who were planted and the few key informants who flipped. If the general's daughter doesn't even know the grand plan, then the general not trusting anyone isn't that absurd of an idea. "They're going to strap bombs to the drones and take the wasteland by the end of winter."

Thatcher curses under her breath. She knocks back a large sip. "That's what I'm hearing, too. Doesn't give us long to mount a defense. But the good news is, it puts us in a great position for control in the east. The bad news is—"

"We get nuked in the Midwest," I finish for her.

Thatcher sighs and meets my gaze. "Look, Dani, I respect that you have confidential informants. We all do, but we're playing on borrowed time. Soon, we're going to be outnumbered and outgunned. We need to make sure we're all on the same page while we figure out how to handle this. That means no sneaking out of the city, including through the tunnels, without clearing it with me first. And no more involving Jess in private matters." She gives me a pointed look, and I nod, knowing she's right. If she's going to respect not asking for more information on who I'm meeting, then the least I can do is stop abusing her hospitality. "Now," she continues, seemingly satisfied with my nonverbal response, "I've been working with William on the matter of the NAF attempting to cut off our gas supply. I've also been given information about additional NAF troops along—"

The door flies open, and Wesley bursts through with a panicked expression, making Thatcher and I both jump in surprise. "We have a situation." He holds up a radio. "It's Deadwood. Your presence has been requested. Both of you."

❖

The ride to Deadwood is silent. Aside from Thatcher grabbing two vests and a rifle on the way out, she hasn't spoken or acknowledged me in any way. My stomach clenches at the possibility that whatever we're about to drive into is somehow my fault.

The whirling sound of the buggy is the only thing that fills the silence, and the radio balanced on Thatcher's thigh in the passenger's seat is quiet. Bruce, her large and longtime security guard, drives, and I wonder if *he* knows what's going on.

"Care to fill me in?" I chance a question from the back seat.

No one answers for so long, I sigh and give up pressing any further.

After another stretch of silence, Thatcher finally speaks up. "Deadwood received a message from the NAF about the transference of leadership. The people were getting anxious so I sent my best man, Hawthorne, to try to calm them down. He was supposed to check in over twelve hours ago. When he didn't, we reached out to them. Haven't been able to get ahold of anyone."

"So you sent William went to investigate?" I ask, my nerves starring to ramp up.

"Let's just get there," she says abruptly. Her response sends my worry into overdrive.

I see the plumes of smoke long before we actually arrive.

When Deadwood finally comes into view, the first thing I notice is the blown cement barrier, and the buildings near the perimeter are charred and fallen, some of them still burning.

"Holy shit," I whisper. Flashes of White River stir up a familiar feeling of dread and anger. The NAF was here.

As we get a little closer, I see William pacing in front of his buggy. Relief courses through me at seeing him okay. Ericson leans casually against the side of the car with his arms crossed, and Hugo sits patiently on the hood. William stands with his hands on his hips as we slow to a stop. With their causal appearance, it's unlikely there are any NAF still around. I wonder why they aren't inside trying to help.

"What happened?" Thatcher asks as she gets out, rifle in hand. I strap on a vest and approach William as well.

"The NAF. They got here before we did. We found this." William reaches in his buggy and pulls out an EMP the size of a large ball. It's clear the thing is spent, but the sight of it is still unnerving. "It must've been detonated before the attack, which is why no one reached out for help."

"Or why we couldn't get ahold of anyone here." Thatcher eyes it suspiciously. "Where did you find it?"

"We went in looking for survivors but got rushed by raiders. We found the device in the center of town." He looks defeated.

"Think it was someone on the inside?" Thatcher asks, her tone indicating that she already knows the answer. William doesn't respond.

My hand falls to the grip of one of the guns on my thigh. "Did you find any survivors?"

"We didn't see any." Ericson brings a cigarette up to his lips and takes a long drag. "They scorched half the town."

"That's not all," William says reluctantly. "We found something else before we were jumped. And fair warning, it's not pretty."

Ericson takes a final drag and flicks his cigarette away and pulls up the gaiter from around his neck to cover his nose and mouth. Hugo slips off the buggy easily and does the same, a large rifle casually resting across his soldier.

Thatcher and I exchange a glance and reluctantly follow them within the hole in the perimeter. I pull my scarf up over my nose and pull a pistol. Scanning my surroundings, I step carefully just in case there are more raiders.

We walk slowly through the city, half of it completely in ruins. It's bizarre and disturbing and so similar to White River that it takes all my mental strength to differentiate the two. It's Deadwood, it's Deadwood, it's Deadwood, not White River. I repeat it over and over in my head so I don't completely lose control.

The town is eerily silent. No crying. No screams. No sounds of children playing or dogs barking. No sounds of looting or ransacking. Just the sounds of fire and the occasional fall breeze that carries the smoke in our direction. It's the silence that gets to me the most. It's abnormal and unsettling.

We weave through the charred front half of the city, stepping over the occasional raider, until we reach the center of town. William stops and motions straight ahead. "It's this way." The look he shares with Ericson makes me swallow hard and wonder exactly what I'm about to see.

Something akin to a snarl breaks through the silence. A large blur drops from a building in front of us, and William fires off a shot faster than I can aim my gun. A raider. He staggers forward, and William puts a bullet between his eyes, dropping him flat.

Two more flank us, and Thatcher takes out one and Ericson the other before they get too close. We all wait, listening and expecting more. I scan the buildings, checking the windows and the roofs, but see no further movement.

After a moment, we all take a collective breath, and William motions us forward. I step over the raider that William took out and grip my pistol a little tighter.

We slowly pass through a row of buildings. I'm not quite convinced that's the last of the raiders, but we press on until William stops at the entrance to a warehouse on the far edge of town. There's a padlock that dangles open, a bullet hole through the center. William and Ericson exchange a glance that does nothing to settle the anxiety.

After William nods, Ericson grabs the sliding door with both hands and pulls. The smell hits me first. I bring my hand up, pressing my wrist into the scarf covering my nose to try to block it out.

The setting sun illuminates the interior, casting a soft orange glow on bodies dangling in rows from the rafters. There are more than I can count, and I quickly look away.

"Lord have mercy," Thatcher whispers behind me, her voice full of disbelief and sorrow. "How many?"

"All of them," William says. "All the Resistance fighters stationed here and most of the guards."

"There has to be at least thirty," Thatcher says, finally looking away. "Hawthorne?"

William bows his head.

Bruce, a man of solid muscle and strength, rushes past us after getting a look and empties the contents of his stomach. I can't say I blame him.

"I don't get it," Thatcher says, anguish all over her features. "First, they send a letter urging to peacefully transition and now this? Without waiting for a reply? Why bother sending the letter in the first place?"

"Maybe it was a fake," Ericson supplies.

I think about Kate sending the letters, trying desperately to do things peacefully. This wasn't her. It wasn't part of her plan. This was a rogue operative, someone authorized to do this under command of the general herself. Someone with a totally different agenda.

William motions for Ericson to pull the door closed. "There was a note pinned to one of their bodies."

He hands it to me. I keep my back to the warehouse and skim the messy scrawl, my eyes starting to water from the stench.

Hi, Danielle.
Your brother is next.

Crumpling the paper, I hold it tightly in my fist. "Simon." I say it through clenched teeth, wishing he was still here, lurking, so I could finish him off.

"Have you checked the tunnels?" I ask. "I bet civilians are hiding down there."

William shakes his head. "Not yet." He motions for the others to follow him. I stay put and try to steady myself.

This attack was personal. They are trying to draw us out. Draw *me* out. Kate was right. Simon is on a deadly rampage, hunting me like a fucking sadist and taking pleasure in destroying everyone and everything around me. There is absolutely no doubt in my mind that Hot Springs, White River, and now Deadwood are the first of many that will burn.

Chapter Twelve: The Choice

Kate

With my hands shaking, I fasten the last button on my uniform jacket. My hair is still damp from my ice-cold shower, and there's a chill in the room, all causing me to shiver. I couldn't sleep at all last night after my fight with Dani. Fight. Was it a fight? That doesn't sound right. My *disagreement* with Dani plays over in my mind. The weight of her words feels heavy in my chest. Am I really wasting my time here? Am I really unable to make a difference?

I sit on the edge of the bed and look at the radio on the nightstand. The silence feels suffocating in the quiet room. I don't want to believe what Dani said about the NAF, about but the more I uncover, the more I'm starting to see that maybe I don't really know the NAF at all. I'm desperate to call her and tell her that maybe she was right.

Maybe we don't belong here. That this isn't our land to just swoop in and claim. There should be negotiations and conversations about what both sides want and need. I thought that I could help with that, that I could be the bridge that brings us all together. But now, it doesn't seem possible. Ever since meeting Dani, I'm unsure where I belong.

The path my mother wants me to take is not something I want to be part of. And if I can't change her mind, then there isn't a place for me within the NAF.

I close my eyes and take a deep breath.

"Come with me." Her plea echoes in my mind. Staying may not be an option, but I doubt I'm capable of leaving either. This is all I've ever known.

Standing, I smooth out my uniform jacket and will my hands to stop shaking. I need to get myself together.

After several deep breaths, I pull my damp hair back into a bun and shove the radio under the mattress. Hopefully, no one, including Ryan, will let themselves in while I'm gone.

Ryan. Just another thing to worry about. I stare at my reflection in the mirror. On the outside, I'm a picture-perfect soldier. On the inside, I feel like a traitor.

Rodrigues is waiting for me at the door to my office with two cups of coffee and some folders stuck under her arm.

"Talib has finished the inventory of the supplies we received from Malmstrom. We may have a problem," she says before I can even tell her good morning.

Taking the folders, I notice her pursed lips and intense gaze. She opens the door, and I take that as a sign that this isn't something she wants to discuss in the hallway. Once we're both inside and I've started the heater, I take a sip of the lukewarm coffee and skim the papers in the first folder. "What am I looking at?"

"Everything highlighted is a part or piece missing from the inventory."

Our eyes meet. "Missing?"

"As in, they weren't on the trucks that came in, but they were listed on the bill of lading. There are also four people who never arrived who were supposed to be traveling here, to Omaha, with the supplies."

I shuffle through the rest of the papers until I find the personnel files of the four missing soldiers. "Are you sure they weren't supposed to be on the other convoy, and this isn't a simple mix-up?"

"I'm sure. I think someone pulled the missing soldiers and the missing pieces at the last minute."

"Does Captain Daniels know about this?" I ask, remembering that the general put him in charge of inventory.

Rodrigues nods. "He was given his own inventory. When Talib mentioned that the bill of lading didn't match, he didn't seem concerned and told us there had been an update of records and to destroy our copy."

"Instead, you're bringing it my attention." I watch Rodrigues closely. She shifts in her seat, but I can't tell if it's because she's anxious about what she's just admitted to me. Even if it's not, I'm grateful for her. "Tell me about the missing parts."

She swallows roughly and clears her throat. "Propellers, motors, battery packs, and other parts and pieces. It looks like two full drone's worth of parts."

The air is sucked from my lungs, but I have to make sure I heard her correctly. "Two large drones are missing?"

"They're disassembled, but yes." Her eyes meet mine, concerned. "The last order we were given was from General Foley. She wanted a camera in the large drones and longer airtime. We pulled them apart to rebuild."

This entire project is much bigger than I thought. How in the world was this going on without anyone knowing? No gossip, no rumors, no information leaks...How? "Where else are they building and testing drones?"

"They moved operation from Scott to Lackland about ten years ago. Then they expanded to Malmstrom a few years after that, and Warren has recently jumped into the game." She motions to the files still in my hand. "The missing personnel are the controlmen for the drones."

"How did I not know any of this?" I ask. Rodrigues doesn't answer. I take a deep breath and try to shift my focus. We have more important things to worry about than my wounded pride at being left out. "Let's assume the missing supplies were offloaded on purpose. Where is the second convoy?"

"Talib says they went to Warren."

I can't help but laugh. "I'm supposed to be running this base, and I haven't a goddamn clue what's going on. Radio Warren and see if they have my parts and my missing soldiers. If they do, what are they planning on doing with them?"

Rodrigues nods. "Yes, ma'am."

I take the lists and put them back into the folder and shove it in my desk drawer. "I'm the future commanding officer of the southern aerial unit, and I don't even know where all my supplies are," I repeat, still in disbelief. "I need you to also get the reports from General Foley regarding troop placement along the trade routes and all Resistance gas supply locations."

"Yes, ma'am." She stands the second that I rise. "What are you going to do?" she asks.

"I'm going to do what I should've done this morning, go ask the general what the hell is going on." I practically rip the door from its hinges, irritated that I didn't have the courage to confront her sooner.

General Turner and General Foley are meeting in a conference room with a man I've never met before. He's talking to them about airflow as I burst through the doors, ignoring the guard's protest.

General Foley stands, expression irritated at the interruption. "Excuse you, Lieutenant Colonel, we are in the middle of a private meeting. You can't just burst—"

My mother sighs deeply, almost as if she expected this. She must see something in my expression. "We can take a five-minute break."

My eyes don't leave my mother's, but I can feel the glare Foley is giving me. The unknown man waits until General Foley motions for him to follow her out of the room, leaving me alone with my mother. I know I'm only granted this because I'm the general's daughter, something I have refused to take advantage of since the day I took my oath to the NAF, but I'm too pissed to care about protocol and the proper chain of command.

The guard stationed outside apologizes profusely, but my mother just waves him off. Presumably to deal with him later. "I suppose this unannounced visit is about the recent changes that were made regarding your orders." She leans back casually in her chair.

Her statement catches me off guard. "What changes?"

"You sent out a message to several towns regarding surrendering peacefully. Rapid City wasn't among them. It's the main hub for Resistance trade in the wasteland, so I would've expected them to be at the top of your list. By taking their main city, the others will surely fall," she says as if this is common knowledge. "I had your message sent to them this morning."

My entire body tenses at the mention of Rapid City, and my heart pounds so hard, I can feel it in my ears. I have to talk to Dani.

"I've also ordered the drones in the air within a month."

The panic I feel ramps quickly into anger. "Why put me in charge if I have nothing to do with any of the decisions being made?"

"Katelyn, you're behaving like a child."

"Am I?"

"Things change. Orders change. The situation has *changed*."

I think about taking my hair out of the bun at the base of my neck. Or maybe unbuttoning my jacket, anything to get a rise out of her. "Where are my drones?" I blurt instead.

Slowly, she lowers her mug, her brow furrowed. "Your drones?"

I cross my arms and stare at her. "I'm missing four soldiers and parts and pieces of at least two drones. Where are they?"

With a *tsking* sound, she stands to be eye level with me. "Your first mistake was thinking they were *yours*."

"I'm supposed to be running this base, and I don't even know where all my supplies are." I know I'm yelling, but I'm angry, and I can't stop myself from being so disrespectful. I've reached my max patience. "I'm clearly no longer in charge here since I don't know what the hell is going on!"

"You are currently on a need-to-know basis." She smiles, but there is no warmth there, only a mocking that seeps deep within me, reminding me that I will never be good enough or smart enough to have her full approval.

"Need-to-know basis?" Putting my hands on my hips, I take a deep breath and try to keep the fury from getting the better of me. "This isn't right. We should be brokering peace deals, not dropping bombs."

"As I told you before," she says, her voice low and surprisingly patient. "We have tried that approach, and it didn't work. We are at war, Katelyn. Why do you fail to understand that?"

I shake my head. "But bombs? Isn't that a bit extreme?"

She looks at me with a twisted smile and links her fingers together, putting her hands on top of her files. "That's what war is, fighting until one side gains the upper hand and is able to tip the scales. Don't you think the Resistance would do the same thing if given the chance?"

Dani's words play over in my mind about how we won't survive another civil war. How the people here in the wasteland are tired of fighting. "They're just trying to push us out of their territory. That's all they've ever done."

My mother scoffs and dismisses my comment with a wave. "They claim that the entire nation is their territory. It is not."

"Isn't it? They live here, too. They were here before the NAF even existed. Shouldn't they have a say?" I hate that most of the anger has left my voice.

"Not when what they say would lead to chaos. As it already has." Her tone is sharp. Firm. There is no room for negotiation on the matter.

"They just want to be left alone." It's a weak attempt, especially when I already sound so defeated.

"And that is precisely the problem," my mom snaps. "We need structure! We need one rule!"

"And who's to say *our* rule is the only one that should be followed? Who put us in charge?"

She looks at me as if I asked her the dumbest question imaginable. "Our predecessors."

And that's the problem. I shake my head and sigh. "Yeah, the NAF put the NAF in charge."

"Katelyn." My mother's tone softens, her gaze is soft, almost pitying. I hate that it makes me feel ashamed. "I put you in charge of the area and gave you promotions because you earned them. Because you showed so much potential, even when all my advisors warned me against it."

"What?"

She nods sadly. "There has been some serious skepticism about you leading the aerial unit. That you don't share our vision." She comes close enough to reach out and touch me if she wanted. I'm glad she doesn't. "I promoted you anyway because I know you. I know how strong you are and that you believe in our cause. I know you believe in peace and unity."

"Then why all the secrecy? Why give orders without involving me? Why take my supplies? Captain Daniels seems to know more than I do." She called me a child earlier, and it made me angry. Now, standing here, desperate to know why she doesn't trust me, I feel like one.

"Because I fear there may be some truth to the rumors about your mental state."

I take a step back, shocked and betrayed. After several deep breaths, I will myself not to feel so hurt by the confession.

She still makes no move to reach out. "Sneaking off base? What were you thinking, Katelyn?" I can feel the blood drain from my face, convinced she knows about my meetups with Dani. "It's becoming increasingly clear that you're not ready to make the big decisions or make the tough choices. You're making careless mistakes." She folds her hands in front of her and pins me with a look filled with sympathy. "Have you been seeing the counselor?"

"No, I—"

Finally, she reaches out. She pats my arm three times, then pulls away completely, going back to her chair and her papers. "Focus on getting yourself back to normal. Trust the process. You'll be back on your feet and back to normal in no time. Until then, understand that others will be shouldering some of your responsibilities and taking command of various assignments and redirecting your orders. Any town that fails to commit to the NAF by the end of the month will be forced to do so. No more negotiating."

I want to say something, but instead, I stand there opening and closing my mouth like a fish out of water.

She lifts her head and looks surprised to still see me standing there. "Please tell General Foley I'm ready to continue on your way out. I'm departing tomorrow morning, and I have a lot to oversee before I do."

"You're leaving?" I ask, both relieved and nervous about her sudden departure.

She hums in acknowledgement. "General Foley will stay behind and run things in my stead."

"Where are you going?" I ask, ignoring the part about General Foley.

She glances at me and then back to her papers. "West," is all she says. I stand there a moment longer wondering what means. Where in the west? Why now? What's she doing? She looks at me again, impatiently. "You're dismissed, Lieutenant."

I don't even bother to salute on my way out. Not that it matters. I'm invisible to her anyway.

Out of our entire conversation—doling out my assignments, keeping me in the dark, the general on the move again—the part about my mother knowing I've left base has me the most concerned. How does she know about last night? I left in such a rush that it's entirely possible I attracted unwanted attention. Talib wouldn't have said anything. Maybe it was the guards who let me through the gates. Did she stop by my house and see me gone? But no one knew where I was going. It wasn't logged, and I didn't tell anyone, not even Rodrigues. There was no chatter over the comms or anyone requesting my presence.

Ryan? My stomach twists in knots at the thought. I need to find him, but first, I have a few things to take care of.

Rodrigues is directing the inventory placement inside the flight warehouse, and everyone stops to salute when I approach. "At ease," I tell them and look at Rodrigues. "I'm sorry to interrupt, do you have a moment?"

"Of course." She gives a soldier to her right a few directions and then follows me to the far side of the warehouse where we can speak in semi-private. "I have the files you requested earlier. General Foley was annoyed to pull them together for me."

I take the files containing information on troop placement and gas supplies and tuck them under my arm. At least I'm still privy to that information. "It's not you she has issues with." I glance around the warehouse at the chaotic scene. Everyone is bustling, moving supplies, and assembling pieces of tech on workbenches. If I had more time to look around, I'd check in with them all and watch their progress. Someone carries a small drone past, and I can't help but stare. I haven't seen one this close since my father worked on them. Back when they were a symbol of hope and it was a small team devoted to the cause. Now, the sight rattles me. The addition of aircraft across the country no longer feels hopeful. "Any chance of a flight demonstration?"

Rodrigues looks genuinely upset and shakes her head. "They aren't charged, and we haven't finished removing the blockers in the area."

The blockers were installed by the NAF back when peace was valued above all else, even if that meant crippling their own forces. "Not sure if you can pull this off, but I need a copy of all the maps containing blocker locations for the entire Midwest without Captain Daniels or General Foley knowing."

"I'll do everything I can, ma'am." She stands straighter.

I know it's a risky ask, and I hope like hell that Rodrigues won't sell me out. "In the meantime, I need tomorrow morning's rotation schedule. I'm sure Captain Daniels is on top of it, but since the general is departing in the morning, I'd like another look."

Rodrigues stares at me for a moment, then nods. "Yes, ma'am, I'll get it right away."

"Also," I add before she can leave, "has the general come to you recently?" It seems unlikely, but since my mother is the one who appointed her to assist me, I can't help but wonder if that includes spying and tailing my every move.

She looks at me, her head tilted curiously. "No, I haven't spoken to her at all since I arrived."

I don't elaborate. Instead, I smile and motion to the hustle and bustle of the warehouse. "I won't hold you up any longer. Keep me updated on your progress."

❖

As I shuffle through the mounds of never-ending paperwork, I think more and more about my mother's words and everything that appears to be going on behind my back.

I also think about how my entire mission, the one I've worked on for years, was dismantled and done away with in a matter of days. Is my mother right? Have the peaceful options been exhausted over the years, and do we need someone to make the tough decision to take the remaining part of the country by force? Maybe there really is no chance of a peaceful surrender.

My jacket is draped across my desk, and my gaze lingers on the silver oak leaf pinned to the collar. My stomach churns knowing that no matter what my mother says, I didn't really earn that rank, and there are people who are opposed to it. It makes me wonder if I've ever earned any of my promotions. I once believed my ideals and vision had a huge part in my success and that it wasn't just my leadership skills and excellent marksmanship. Instead, as a harsh blow to the gut, I now know I climbed the ranks because of my mother. With all her grooming, she believed that one day, I'd be just like her.

But being like her was never something I wanted.

Pulling my zip-up cotton jacket higher on my neck, I take a deep, steadying breath. I wish Dad was here. I wish I could talk to him and hear his words of encouragement one more time. I wish I could tell him about my desire to change the course of this war through compromise instead of threats. He would understand. He always understood. Instead, I'm left with a meaningless promotion, no real power to sway either side of this fight, and orders to drop bombs.

Not wanting to wallow in self-pity, I try again to focus on something I *am* able to change: finalizing the plan to get Silva and Miller out of active duty. Staring at the marching orders with my signature at the bottom, I know that if I do this, I not only put Silva and Miller in jeopardy but myself as well. There is no doubt I will have a lot of explaining to do and will only solidify my mental instability as a leader if I am caught. But if it works, I could change both of their lives for the better.

There's a knock on my door, and I quickly shove the orders in a drawer in my desk. "Enter."

Rodrigues pokes her head in, and I motion for her to come in, waving away her salute. "I have those maps and the rotation schedule you requested."

"As always, Rodrigues, you are as speedy as you are efficient." She hands me the files, and I scan the maps first. "How were you able to get this so quickly?"

She smiles slightly. "I was going over locations with Captain Daniels and asked to examine them more closely. Then Talib had an emergency, so Daniels ran off and left the maps with me. I wrote down as many locations as I could."

"Impeccable timing for Talib's emergency," I mumble, noting the blockers still scattered in the area. "This is just what I needed. I appreciate your discretion." She shifts awkwardly on the other side of my desk. When she doesn't move or say anything else, I look at her curiously. "Something on your mind?"

"It's just…" She hesitates and looks behind her at the open door. "Permission to speak freely, ma'am?"

Placing the files on my desk, I give her my full attention. "What's on your mind?"

Quickly, she shuts the door and pulls up the chair opposite me. "Before I left Malmstrom, we were supposed to get a large shipment from Lackland. I spoke with a colleague who said they never received the shipment because they were told to evacuate before it arrived. I was already here, on my new assignment, so I didn't know about any of this." I was expecting her to question my motives. Not give me even more intel I didn't know about.

I lean back in my chair and cross my arms. "Keep going."

"Well…" She shifts nervously. "Back at Malmstrom, we were all given our individual assignments and were warned not to discuss with others. I was more on the engineering and mechanical side, so I never knew the full picture other than General Foley's late request for cameras. I figured we were trying to get the drones in the air to spy, you know, look beyond the gates and canvas more of the land, troop movements and such. There were rumors about explosives but just that. Rumors. Our experiments were with UAVs. Non-combative drones. Then, Supply Specialist Talib got ahold of his cousin who works at Warren, and she said that the shipment meant for us stopped there instead and that it was full of explosives. She also said it was General Foley who called off the movement and told them to hold at Warren. And then"—she sounds almost excited about the next part—"I managed to find this." She hands me a bill of lading with parts highlighted.

"Help me out here. What am I looking at?"

"More sets of gimbals and mounts. At first, I thought they were going to be used for the cameras, but they also could be used to secure a payload. With our missing parts and with the explosives meant for Malmstrom now at Warren, I think they're connected." She sounds enthusiastic now, as if she's on to something big and anxious to tell someone. "I think we were meant to strap the explosives to the drones."

The information dump starts to form a larger picture. "I think we just found out where my mother is headed tomorrow."

"If she's going to Warren, they must be further ahead than we were at Malmstrom." She sounds dejected.

"Do you think they found a way around the blockers?" I ask, my worry increasing.

"Maybe," she says, her expression regretful. "We've been working on an end around. Trying to reflect the signal back toward the blocking towers to essentially make the drones invisible. Maybe they figured that out, too."

At her description, all I can picture are mirrors physically blocking an invisible signal, though I know that's not what she means. There's a reason I went into leadership courses and not engineering and mechanics. "Well, that's…" I let my sentence hang, unable to finish my thought. Rodrigues watches me closely and I take a deep, settling breath. "I can confirm your suspicions about the drones carrying explosives, at least." She looks equal parts pleased and apprehensive. I try to gauge her reaction. "How do you feel about using drones for that purpose?"

She releases a long breath and looks away. "The country is the way it is because of bombs. The destruction is ugly, but I suppose necessary to win the war. Especially if neither side will concede. I knew we were going in that direction eventually. The large UCAVs we worked on—"

"The what?"

"Um, the unmanned combat aerial vehicles?" She looks at me with a regretful expression. Perhaps she didn't want to deliver me more news that I knew nothing about, or maybe she feels bad for not cluing me in sooner.

I dismiss her explanation. I may be clueless but I'm not *that* in the dark. "I know what a UCAV is, my father worked on several at Scott Air Force Base. He had a breakthrough when it came to reactivating them but couldn't find a way around the blockers and didn't get a chance to finish his work. I didn't know they were in Malmstrom or that you got them flying."

"Oh! No, we couldn't figure out how to get them in the air. We had our best engineers working on them. The ones who used to work with your dad. We transferred the two that were left after…" She lets the comment hang in the air and avoids looking at me. I feel a pang in my chest as she clears her throat and tries again. "We needed the parts for the smaller aircraft, so we scrapped them, leaving only the shells behind. I was hoping one day to get them up and running, but they're gone now, too." Her shoulders slump, clearly upset that her work was destroyed.

Two planes cleared of tech.

That's what Dani had said. But they weren't planes, not really. They were the UCAVs. Large ones.

Good information to have as the supposed next leader of the southern aerial unit. "Where are the rest our attack, fighter, and striker aircraft?" I ask.

"I believe they are still at Lackland."

"Great. Still in Texas." I sigh and pinch the bridge of my nose. What an absolute mess. "How many across the country were spared from mass destruction after the war?"

"I'm not sure. It's classified." She cringes when she uses the word, and I do my best not to groan. "But," she continues, "I know Warren has a well-preserved UCAV and are working on it. I was offered an engineering position there but turned it down."

Turned it down to work alongside me. Because of my dad. I ignore the urge to talk about him and question her further about her choice and press on. It hurts too much to think that his life's work is what got him killed. "You could be a top engineer at Warren, but instead, you're here slumming it with me. I think you made the wrong choice, Rodrigues."

She smiles. "No, ma'am. You promised me a promotion."

"That I did," I mumble. "You mentioned something about payload. How much would those large bombers be able to carry?"

"Like the one at Warren?" She waits until I nod. "Approximately 1,700 kg."

I push out a hard breath. "Holy shit."

"The smaller ones can't hold nearly that amount. Not even with the special mounts it seems they put on there but probably enough to do some damage. Depends on how many motors they allocate, really." Rodrigues stops and looks at me with a concerned expression. "Are you okay?"

"They're going to start bombing noncompliant towns," I say before I can stop myself. Rodrigues inhales sharply. "How many complete drones did you say were missing?"

"Two."

"And your best guess, how many explosives can each of them hold?"

"It depends on the missile and their weight but three, maybe four?"

Not wanting to show more remorse about the fate of the Resistance, I hold up the guard schedule and try to appear more casual than I feel. "Thank you for this. I will look over the schedules. In the meantime, nothing we've discussed leaves this room until a formal statement or command is released. Tell Talib to stop digging and to stay out of it for now. The more we get involved, the more attention we bring to ourselves."

Rodrigues stands to leave. She hesitates but decides against whatever it was she was thinking of saying and pulls the door shut behind her on the way out.

Once alone, I rest my face in my hands. 1,700 kg worth of explosives when they get that UCAV in the air. The Resistance doesn't stand a chance.

❖

After leaving my office, I send a secure message to Silva and Miller to meet me at the back gate tomorrow morning no later than 0750 for an undisclosed assignment. I don't give them any more detail than that to help avoid questions or suspicion.

The rest of my evening is spent memorizing the troop locations across the wasteland. They're along all the main trade routes, meant as a deterrent to Resistance sympathizers. I also read the report on taking over the gas supplies in the area. With control over the smaller dealers, it'll be damn near-impossible to get fuel, which is something that worries me greatly as winter is rapidly closing in.

And where the hell is Simon? He was tasked with blowing up Malmstrom and securing the gas lines, but now what is he doing? I toss the papers on the table beside the bed and rub my eyes. Apparently, all of his movements are considered classified, and I'm not privy to those orders. Just something else to add to the ever-growing list of things I don't have access to.

Maybe Dani was right. What am I doing here? How can I attempt to do anything good or stop needless attacks if I don't even know what the hell is going on?

It's risky, but I try to call Dani as I lie awake in bed. If I can just hear her voice and warn her that there's a good chance my mother knows exactly where she is, that their gas lines are cut off, there are troops along their trade routes, and that there's three weeks tops before the drones are in flight, maybe I can stop the anxiety continuing to build inside me. But just like the last time I tried, there's no response on the other end. The silence hurts my heart.

When morning comes, my entire body is tense. I barely slept, and I'm stressed that this plan to help Silva and Miller won't work. Bypassing the general's send-off, I head to the back gates to make sure everything is in place and ready to go.

Finding two fully fueled bikes behind some shrubs and a small bag of supplies, I sigh, relieved that Talib has once again come through.

Next, I relieve the guard on duty, telling her she's been reassigned to the front gates to assist with the general's departure, and I give her the new rotation schedule for the morning. She hesitates only briefly before leaving her post with a quick salute. I listen to the chatter over my headset. Captain Daniels is busy barking orders and seems distracted enough.

It's 0748. I'm getting antsy. In my orders, I told Silva and Miller to be here at 0750. The next guard arrives at 0800. If they don't get here on time...

I look up from my watch and notice Silva and Miller approaching. I take a deep breath, relieved to see them.

"We don't have a lot of time," I tell them as they hurry to the back gate, their uniforms covered by thick coats. "The guards will be here in a few minutes. Are you all set?"

"What exactly is this assignment?" Silva asks. He watches me, his brow furrowed, clearly confused.

"You're not really going on an assignment. I want you to drive to Des Moines." I hand him a sealed envelope before he can ask any questions. "When you get there, give the guards this letter. It will get you into the city. If you are stopped by *anyone*, show them that letter. It contains your marching orders. Once you're in, change into civvies and trade the bike for a horse and some food." I hand him another slip of paper and an old map. "You will then go to these coordinates. Destroy that paper once you have the numbers memorized and don't show anyone. When you get there, look for a woman named Marium. Give her these."

I lead them to the bikes behind the shrubs and hand Miguel a bag with two voltage regulators, a battery charger, and spare batteries. Something I know for certain Marium won't refuse.

He peers inside in the bag. "Trade items?"

Nodding, I continue, "Tell her to be careful, the NAF is close to full-fledged war and to stay close to that radio of theirs. Tell her you're looking for a fresh start, and you'll be useful if there is an attack by helping keep people safe and fortifying their town. If she asks, tell her the stranger in the pickup sent you."

His eyes start to shine as if he may cry. "Lieutenant Colonel…" He sniffles a bit and lets out a deep breath. "I don't know what to say."

"Take one of the bikes. There is more than enough fuel to get you there. Please don't stop any more than you have to. You'll be easy pickings for raiders if you do."

"And the Resistance?" Miguel asks.

"Those coats will hide your uniform. The bike instead of a buggy should help, too. Just try not to stop until you get there." They both stand there, their eyes wide and disbelieving. "All I can do is get you out. I can't help you if you're caught. You'll be deserters. If you're found, you'll both be charged with treason and abandonment. You can't contact me or your families. You'll be on your own." As much as it feels good to give someone a start at a new life, there are major consequences if he or

Miller gets caught. A fresh start is not without risk and will be extremely lonely.

He frowns, his brow furrowed. It's a lot to process and not a lot of time to dwell. "I understand." His voice is a whisper, and I truly hope he does. He clutches the letters a little tighter to his chest. "Thank you."

Miguel's arms come around my neck, and I'm so shocked by the action that I freeze. He doesn't let go, and after a beat, I return his embrace and pat his back, trying not to make this lingering moment awkward.

Knowing we don't have a lot of time, I pull away and pick up the helmets. I hand each of them one as Miguel mounts the bike first. Miller stares at me, and for a moment, I think he's going to hug me too. Instead, he nods once and slips on the bike behind Miguel.

He reaches out, and I grasp his forearm tightly. "Thank you." His voice is so sincere and so grateful that it catches me slightly off guard.

Once his helmet is fastened, I open the back gate. "I hope you both find the peace you're looking for."

"We will never forget your kindness, ma'am," Miguel says and starts the engine.

"Call me Kate," I say with a smile. Over the radio, the first set of guards are being deployed through the front gates ahead of the general. We are officially out of time. "It's time to go, now." I slap Miller's shoulder, and Miguel quickly accelerates away.

"Scouts deploying from rear gates," I say over my headset. Even with switching out the guard rotation and acting as if Miller and Silva are part of the scouting detail for my mother, I still worry they'll be caught before they reach Des Moines.

"Copy that."

There's a long pause as I watch as Miller and Silva disappear into the horizon.

"The Eagle has left the nest. All clear. Secure the gates."

I rip the headset off and take a deep breath. My mother has left, and Miguel and Anthony have safely made it off base. Feeling slightly relieved, I pull the gate shut and secure the latch.

"You know those bikes now have trackers on them." A voice from behind causes me to jump in place and then freeze.

It takes a moment to settle the panic rising in me. How stupid I was to think we were so easily in the clear. Slowly, I turn to face Rodrigues, who's watching me cautiously from several meters away. Straightening my posture, I clasp my hands behind my back. "I am aware." I don't tell her that's why I instructed them to trade the bike for a horse.

"It's just…" she starts hesitantly. Her expression changes, and she appears more confident when she continues. "Did you forget to turn in the new rotation schedule? Or was it done on purpose so that Privates Silva and Miller could slip out the back under the guise of being on a scouting assignment?" I don't answer and continue eye contact. "When they don't return, the bike will be tracked."

I knew Rodrigues was smart and observant, but I clearly underestimated her when it comes to observing *me*. I keep my tone level and my response clipped. "Did you need something, Rodrigues?"

She straightens as if she's been scolded and breaks eye contact. "Yes, ma'am. I've been asked to give you this report, and Chief Matthews is looking for you."

It doesn't take long to read the report, and the entire thing makes me sick to my stomach. I guess I can check "where is Simon" off my list of things to do. Maybe it was best I never asked in the first place.

I shove the paper back into the folder and walk past her without bothering to answer her questions. I'll just have to hope she doesn't report me before I can speak with Ryan.

I find him waiting outside my office. I am an even mix of pissed and distraught. "What the hell is this?" I ask, holding the folder in the air.

He follows me inside, closes the door, and at least has the decency to look upset. "I just found out. I wanted to find you before Captain Daniels sent you the writeup."

"A writeup? A town was just demolished, and people were executed in my territory, and I was going to get a *writeup*? Why wasn't I notified immediately?" I have officially hit my breaking point of putting up with all the secrecy.

Ryan flinches just the slightest. "The report went straight to General Foley, and she didn't seem to think it was urgent."

"Why wasn't it given to *me*?" I ask again. "This is my goddamn base!"

"General Foley outranks you. She instructed all intel come directly to her." He points out the chain of command gently but it just fuels my anger. This is the last straw. There was never any intention of me allowing me to lead. I can't take this anymore.

Trying to get past the anger weighing heavy all around me, I scan the report again. "Why is there no name on this information regarding Deadwood? Why was it left off?"

Ryan shifts somewhat awkwardly. "It's classified."

I give him a look. "I swear, if I hear that word one more time..." He says nothing. I close my eyes and take several deep breaths. We don't have to have a name on the report to know it was Simon who did this. "He strung them up, Ryan. Killed them and put them on display, and the NAF is protecting him by trying to keep it anonymous."

"Plausible deniability."

My laugh holds no humor. "They're using Simon to do their dirty work, and you know he loves it."

"We don't know what the actual orders were. Maybe they went in for a specific reason, and the Resistance stationed there put up a fight," Ryan counters.

"Are you really going with that story?" He deflates, knowing that's not what happened. "And Hot Springs? I checked. We did that, too. The report was given to Captain Daniels while we were out on a diplomatic assignment. They burned Hot Springs to the ground while we were trying to provide aid to Pierre. Someone under *my command* was given alternate orders while I was gone. To burn Hot Springs. Why? Hot Springs was never a threat."

Ryan thinks for a minute as if trying to find any reason why we would do this. "Maybe they refused to comply with NAF demands."

"So we just killed them?" I shake my head. "No. They were a test. We knew they were unable to fight back."

"What are you going to do?" He sighs as if knowing there's no defending what happened in Deadwood or Hot Springs.

"About Simon? About orders being given behind my back?" He nods. "There really isn't anything I can do. My mother seems to have taken him under her wing, along with anyone else willing to do her dirty work. And she's not listening to anything I have to say about it because apparently, I am mentally unstable."

He looks confused. "What? She said that?"

"I'm powerless here." I turn to look out the window and watch as soldiers walk across the campus, away from the mess hall, and to their posts. Taking a deep breath, I try to calm down. "Three towns destroyed. No one will trust our good faith now. Not that it matters. We aren't wasting any more time with peace offers." I stare at two soldiers laughing as they pass. "I feel like everything's changed in just a matter of days. That I've woken up from a haze into an absolute nightmare."

"Maybe there's still time to fix this." His voice is soft but hopeful.

"How? Show up with aid and supplies after we're the ones who caused the destruction? That'll go over really well. Besides, I have orders not to 'waste supplies' on the people here." I turn to face him, feeling tired and defeated. My gaze lingers on the bruise on his jaw. Feeling guilty, I look away. "It wasn't supposed to be like this."

Ryan takes a step closer but stays on the other side of my desk, keeping the barrier between us. "Not everyone in the NAF believes this is the way to go. There are so many people who still want peace and who condemn this type of violence."

"Just not the right people," I say sadly. "If the ones giving the orders want violence, what can we do to stop them?"

"Kate." He shifts uncomfortably. "The general came to me the other night. Looking for you." My breath catches. "She went to your house, your office…she couldn't find you. Then she said the guards at the back gate saw you leave. She said Supply Specialist Talib didn't know where you were going, so she came to me. I covered for you." He pauses again and examines me, probably for some sort of reaction. I refuse to meet his eyes. "Where did you go?"

Steadying myself, I meet his gaze, and don't say a word.

"Dammit, Kate." He takes a step away from me, looking betrayed. "You know, I left your house, and I thought about it. I thought about it all night. How could Danielle Clark have gotten her talons in you like she so clearly has? All night, I wondered how it was possible. And the only thing I could think of was Stockholm Syndrome."

I scoff. "I'm not suffering from Stockholm Syndrome. Don't use that as an excuse to discredit me just because you don't understand."

He sighs, and his shoulders fall. "It's just, how else could the strong-willed, stubborn, focused girl I know fall for Resistance propaganda in a matter of days?"

"Maybe I'm not the same girl you used to know," I snap.

He looks at me for a long time, studying my face. After an eternity of scrutinizing, he nods and rubs his jaw. "You're right. You're definitely not." He sighs. "I just don't want to see you go down a path you can't come back from."

"If I stay here, then I will." My confession slips out in a whisper; staying here is slowly killing me. The moment it's past my lips, I feel lighter.

He looks taken aback. "What are you saying?"

I shake my head, trying to find the words to explain how I'm feeling: betrayed, helpless, sad. "I can't stay here, Ryan. I don't even know the NAF anymore. Blowing up bases? Sacrificing soldiers? Showcasing murders? Threatening and attacking towns unprovoked? There isn't even an option for peace anymore. I can't be a part of it."

He either doesn't hear the defeat in my voice, or he's choosing to ignore it. "So you're just going to give up? Turn your back on your friends and family because it's gotten hard?"

"Ryan," I plead. "It's not like that. Believe me. I never wanted it to come to this."

"But you're doing it anyway."

"I don't have another choice," I yell, wondering why he can't just understand.

"Of course you do. Of course you have a choice." He rushes around my desk and reaches for me, taking my hands, urging me to look at him. "You can stay here and keep fighting. You're not alone in this, Kate."

"I feel alone," I tell him honestly. He drops my hands and takes a step back as if I'd struck him. "I don't feel like I matter here. I don't *feel* like this is my home anymore."

"But you feel like you belong with her? With the Resistance?" He looks so hurt, so betrayed. "You'll be okay with fighting us? With fighting me? Killing me?"

"I could never kill you." The thought of it makes me sick to my stomach.

"You might have to."

"No." I shake my head. I run my fingers down the side of his jaw, angry that I ever hurt him like this. And sad that I'm clearly still hurting him. "I would never."

He leans into my touch and puts his hand over mine. "I can't protect you if you leave."

I think about asking him to come with me. I've never known a life without him. I'm not sure how to navigate the unknown without him by my side. But it would be incredibly selfish of me to ask him to walk away and give up everything just because I'm having a hard time with the direction things are going. I wipe at the tears spilling from my eyes. "I don't need you to protect me. I need you to let me go."

"I don't know how." He looks at me, tears falling from his own eyes and shakes his head.

"Yes, you do," I whisper.

I can see in his expression the exact moment my words cause his heart to shatter. For the first time in our lives, we are on opposite sides. He pulls me into an embrace so tight, I can barely pull in a breath. Yet it doesn't feel constricting. Instead, it's familiar and comforting.

"Know that you have served your land well," he whispers into my hair. I try to swallow a sob.

He pulls away without another word and without looking at me. Watching him leave, I know I'm about to cross a line I can't come back from. Walking away from the NAF and from my mother is hard enough, but walking away from Ryan feels as though I can't breathe.

I take a few gasps and try to collect myself. This is really happening. The sound of a door slamming down the hall startles me into action. I grab a few maps and the files I shoved in my desk drawer, then run as fast as I'm able to my quarters, knowing that it's now or never.

Tossing up the mattress, I grab the radio to call Dani or anyone able to give her a message, hoping that this time, someone is on the receiving end. "This is Songbird for Atomic Anomaly, come in Atomic Anomaly." There is nothing on the other end. No response, no static, nothing. Only then do I realize that the radio is dead. I fell asleep before I could put it back on the charger. "Shit." I look around, frantic and desperate, as if a spare battery will appear out of thin air. My breathing is labored, and it's all I can hear as I spin in circles.

I spot my backpack in the corner chair and rush to throw in spare clothes and the files I grabbed from my office. Tossing in the dead radio and my knives, I zip it shut. Quickly, I dress in my winter coat, hat, scarf, and gloves and rush out, not even bothering to give my house a parting glance.

The second bike from earlier this morning is still where I left it. My contingency plan. I remove the tracking device and push the bike to the gates. No one stops me when I order the doors to open.

Tossing one leg over the side of the bike, I kick it to life. My heart hammers in my chest, and I rev the engine, ready to speed off base. The guards speak into their headsets for a moment, and I wait, ready to fly past them if need be. But thankfully, it doesn't come to that. One of them nods and waves me through. I speed off, away from the only life I've ever known, and yet, I somehow feel lighter.

Chapter Thirteen: The Newcomer

Dani

Lucas and Darby are lying on their stomachs on my bed. As Lucas flips through a comic, Darby tinkers with what I believe to be the engine of a drone. She could be working with a nuke for all I care, as long as she's occupied and quiet.

Mike and Jack are playing a game of cards on the loveseat by the window. They're debating which gun is more deadly, a rifle or a shotgun, but I haven't been keeping track of who's winning in their discussion or their game. Instead, I'm perched on a table near the woodstove listening to Elise and Rhiannon talk about food. My room is warm and filled to the brim with people I love. It's the most normal and happy I've felt since losing White River.

"He made the best pastry I have ever tasted, and that's saying a lot since I make a pretty mean pie," Rhiannon says. She sounds like a bragging mother. It both amuses and annoys me.

"Who do you think taught him to cook?" Elise asks, completely engrossed.

Rhiannon sits up, excited, and waves her hands in front of her. "Oh, he told me his mother did. I haven't met her yet, but she lives on the other side of town. I'll have to pay her visit and tell her what an incredible chef her son has become."

I roll my eyes. "Can we talk about something other than Wyatt Richardson?"

"Why do you hate the kid so much?" Elise asks after she and Rhiannon both scowl in my direction.

"I don't *hate* him." They both give me a look that says otherwise. "I just…he was a bully the last time I saw him. He teased Jess and the other kids and caused a lot of problems around town."

"Yeah, like you didn't cause problems when you were here." Rhiannon's voice holds no malice, so I take no offense. Lucas laughs from the bed, confirming her accusation.

"I wasn't the one going around pulling girls' hair," I point out.

"Weren't you, though?" Elise asks, her voice high and teasing. "Rebecca?"

Jack laughs hard from the other side of the room. I look for something to throw at him but come up empty. Instead, I glare first at Rhiannon for gossiping and then at Elise. "You want to go there? Should we talk about the banging against my wall the other night from your room with Mike? And how I kept hearing you—"

Elise practically dives to cover my mouth. "Okay, okay! Jeez."

There's a small lull in the conversation before Rhiannon's voice breaks through the silence. "What's going to happen to the people of Deadwood?" The question is sobering and instantly brings our dire reality back to the forefront.

"Thatcher sent what she could to help, but there's not much we can do." I hate not being able to provide a better answer. "They're focusing on rebuilding and hoping the NAF doesn't swoop back in to finish them off."

"At least most of the townspeople were able to hide in their bunkers or tunnels or whatever," Jack says.

"But still," Rhiannon sighs. "All those Resistance fighters were killed, and now the people are exposed and vulnerable without protection."

"Prime opportunity for the NAF to come rushing in with aid and acquisition paperwork," Mike supplies.

"What a horrible thing to do," Elise says, shaking her head and sitting back in her chair. "Blow up half the town and then show up acting like the saviors."

"They didn't offer that courtesy to White River or Hot Springs," Jack reminds us all.

"I doubt any aid is coming at this point. Looks like they're trying a new tactic," I say, shaking my head.

"Yeah, Simon." Jack says, his tone laced with hate.

Kate was right. Simon has been let off his leash to do whatever he wants. It was fine when he was coming just for me, but he's crossed a line by hurting innocent people with his rampage.

"But why?" Rhiannon asks. "Three towns demolished and one of their own bases. Is their goal unification by mass destruction?" Roscoe stands and places his chin on her thigh, looking up at her as if he can sense her tension.

"She's attacking cities that harbor Resistance as a warning to the rest of us. And she blew up her own base to prevent us from accessing their research and prototypes," Darby says without looking up.

I look at her, impressed. Her nonchalant attitude doesn't mean she isn't paying attention. Lucas seems to agree because he smiles and pats her on the shoulder as if to say well done. My heart sinks at the sight of him smiling. I didn't tell anyone about the note from Simon.

"She's right," I say. "The general isn't playing around. She isn't patient enough to go the peaceful route. It's faster to take control when you use force. Then watch the chips fall as they may."

"It's still a little weird, right? She didn't do this back east. Like, why does she want the wasteland so bad?" Elise asks.

Half the room looks directly at me. The other half is doing their best to *not* look at me. "Gee, thanks guys." At least Elise has the decency to look apologetic for voicing the question in the first place.

"What about Kate?" Elise asks, changing the subject again. I tense. "Can she help?"

I glance at the silent radio on my nightstand. Since seeing Kate, everything has been an absolute whirlwind. Meeting with Thatcher, the attack on Deadwood, and now the impromptu gathering in my room. I haven't had time to do much of anything, let alone make a private call to Kate. Besides, what could I say that I haven't already said? Apologize, maybe, but I'm not sorry for wanting her here with me.

"I don't think so," I say softly, remembering how quickly she turned me down. Rhiannon gives me a knowing and encouraging look. "She seems to be just as much in the dark as we are."

Roscoe whines, and Rhiannon scratches behind his ears. "I mean, it's clear they aren't going to stop until they've cleared out the entire Resistance and anyone associated with them. So what do we do?"

"William and Thatcher are working on it. I meet with them tomorrow."

Roscoe lets out a bark and sits straight up, eyes on the door. Everyone pauses, startled by the outburst.

A knock on the door follows. "It's probably William," I say, dismissing everyone's worried glances as I jump up to answer.

I pull open the door to find Thatcher. This can't be good. I lean on the door, keeping it only halfway open and blocking her from entering.

She stands straight, with perfect posture, her hands clasped in front of her like she's here to deliver a formal invitation to dinner. "Good evening, Dani."

"Thatch," I say, now highly suspicious of her calm and almost amused tone. "What brings you to my humble, albeit temporary, abode?"

She squints and tilts slightly forward as if telling a secret. "It's rather interesting, really. I was in my office when a call came through about a visitor at the front gate. They knew a codeword to get in. *Your* codeword, to be precise."

It takes a second for my brain to catch up with her words, and when it does, my breath catches in my throat. I've only given one person that code.

"Imagine my surprise when it turned out to be none other than the NAF's Katelyn Turner. The general's daughter."

"Where is she?" I ask, pushing off the door frame.

Thatcher steps aside, and standing awkwardly in the hallway, is Kate. She's in a thick coat with her blue hat in hand. Her hair is a mess, and her cheeks are red and windswept. Honestly, at this moment, she's the most breathtaking sight I've ever laid eyes on.

"Hi," she says, sounding nervous.

"Hi." It comes out as a breathy whisper as I push the door wider and rush to pull her into my arms. "What happened? Are you okay? Why didn't you radio me?" My questions are muffled into her long blond hair.

Her arms link around my waist, holding tight. "I tried, but no one answered. Then the battery on my radio died, and I didn't have time to charge it. I just needed to get out of there, so I left." She buries her face in my neck, and I squeeze her just a little tighter against me, making sure this is real, that *she's* real.

Thatcher clears her throat, interrupting our reunion. "Until I can figure out how I want to handle this, Lieutenant Turner will be kept under guard."

Bristling, I pull away from our embrace and stand in front of Kate protectively. I start to protest the moment I see Thatcher's guard, Bruce, take a step forward with a large rifle across his chest.

"It's for her own safety," Thatcher says.

"I'm not leaving her," I say defensively. There is no way I'm letting them lock Kate up in a cell like a prisoner.

Thatcher sighs. "I figured as much." She nods to Bruce, who seems to stand down for the time being. "Bruce has been appointed to guard our guest. He will remain outside your door tonight. No one will be allowed to enter, and neither of you will be allowed to leave. I expect you both in my office tomorrow morning so we can figure out how we're going to handle this." She gives me a look that says her terms are non-negotiable.

Kate, ever the order follower—and way more polite than I'll ever be—gives a nod. "Yes, ma'am. Understood."

I glance down the hall to the door of William's room. "Does William know? About…" My voice trails off; my eyes flick to Kate.

Thatcher looks from me to Kate, who visibly tenses at the mention of his name. "No. He's occupied elsewhere. But he'll know soon enough."

Ah. That would explain why he's not in the hallway and in the middle of all this.

Thatcher turns to Bruce. "Confiscate all maps and documents. I want the room empty of all Resistance intel." She glances back at me. "And take the weapons as well." I'm about to protest that no one touches my guns but me, but Thatcher holds up a hand, predicting my argument. "Don't make me regret this decision, Danielle."

The tone in which she says my name doesn't go unnoticed. I nod, knowing that fighting her on this will only make things worse. I'm already dreading our conversation tomorrow morning.

Bruce lets himself into the room and begins rummaging. The others jump out of the way but say nothing. Rhiannon looks at me questioningly, but I shake my head. Now's not the time.

Having no regard for my things, he tosses my mattress and pulls the blankets from the bed. "Be careful with my stuff," I instruct. He does not seem fazed by my warning, but when I take a step closer, he holds out a large hand, stopping me.

After thoroughly wrecking my room, and seemingly gathering everything I own into a duffel, Bruce finally steps back out into the hall.

He hands Thatcher the bag, and she gives me one more hard look before slinging it over her shoulder. "I'll see you both in the morning."

I want to fire off a snide remark about if she wanted my stuff, she could've just asked, but I figure I better not push my luck.

"So that's Thatcher Price," Kate says once Thatcher is gone. "She seems nice."

I scoff, nice not being the word I would choose to describe her.

Slowly, Kate follows me inside. She washes her hands, taking her time. Not that I blame her. All eyes are on her. It's enough to make anyone squirm.

"Why is *she* here?" Jack asks, his voice sharp and angry.

Roscoe trots over and nudges Kate's hand for her to pet him. She finishes drying her hands and scratches lightly at his neck, looking a bit relieved for another distraction.

"Because I invited her." I step in front of her, blocking her from the onslaught that appears to be coming. I don't blame them; they still believe she's the reason for the destruction of our home, something I need to address immediately. "Let me just make this clear before anyone says anything else. What happened to White River was *not* Kate's fault."

Jack narrows his eyes. "No, it was her *mother's* fault."

"Back off, Jack." I warn him, not in the mood for this tonight. Not when Kate just walked away from her entire life to be here. Not when she tried to stop the attack on White River from happening and risked everything to get me a message about it.

"I thought it was Simon's?" Darby says, her brows furrowed.

Lucas extends his hand in greeting. "Your presence is most welcome." Hesitantly, Kate grabs his forearm, and he smiles.

"Have you eaten? I can try to find you some dinner," Rhiannon offers, forever using food as an olive branch.

Kate attempts a smile. "No, thank you. I'm not really hungry."

I'm grateful for most of them trying to break the tension, though the air still feels thick with it. Bruce's presence by the door isn't helping. As far as awkward moments go, this is definitely in my top five.

"Well, we should be going," Rhiannon says. "Everybody out." She shoos the gang out of the room. "I'll see you both in the morning," she says, the last to leave and wearily glances at Bruce. "Hopefully."

When everyone has left, Bruce goes to close the door. "No leaving," he warns.

I make a cross over my heart. "No leaving," I repeat. He grunts, and once the door clicks shut, I turn to face Kate, who stands awkwardly in the middle of my room holding her hat and gloves. She looks everywhere but at me.

I can't imagine what she's thinking or feeling, but I can safely assume that she's probably scared out of her mind.

"As far as lock-ups go, this one doesn't seem so bad," I say softly, trying to ease some of the tension. Her eyes are wide, shocked, and glassy, as if she's just barely managing to keep her tears at bay. It only takes another moment before she's in my arms, her face against my shoulder.

I hold her tightly while she cries, content to stay like this for as long as she needs, stroking her hair until her sobs slowly start to subside. She finally pulls away. She still won't look at me, instead wiping her eyes and nose against the back of her hands almost frantically. "I'm a mess," she mumbles.

"How about you take a hot bath, and I'll bring you some clean clothes?" I offer. Slowly, I reach to unzip her coat and slip it off her shoulders. She nods, and once it's off, I take her face in my hands, tilting it up until she looks at me. "Hey," I say softly. "It's gonna be okay."

Her lip quivers, but she doesn't cry. Instead, she nods again. Leaning in, I place a kiss on her forehead and then start the generator and water for her, waiting for it to warm. I hand her one of the lanterns and smile encouragingly. Once the door closes, I plop on the bed, still in shock.

I can honestly say the last thing I expected to happen today was for Katelyn Turner to once again show up on my doorstep. Unlike last time, when she unintentionally ended up in White River, tonight, it was her choice. What Kate sacrificed to be here is not lost on me, and I feel incredibly guilty at the elation coursing through my veins. Even knowing that Bruce is standing guard outside, and that we have to deal with all the ramifications of this in the morning, isn't enough to stop my giddiness.

Grabbing the warmest and most comfortable clothes I have, I crack the door and place them quietly on the sink, along with a fresh towel. I don't linger, wanting to give Kate all the space and privacy she needs, and pull the door closed. While I wait, I clean up the mess that Bruce made while going through my things.

After reheating the water in the kettle and searching for a clean mug and a fresh bag of tea, I sit at the table and try to keep myself occupied. The sounds of bathing and knowing who is on the other side of the door makes it nearly impossible. I wonder what happened to make her leave. I doubt very much it was just because of my heartfelt plea.

It's a grand sight to see when Kate finally steps out of the bathroom. The sweatpants are a little long but otherwise seem to fit. The oversized black sweatshirt hangs off one of her shoulders, and the sleeves fall past her hands. Her hair is darker now that it's wet, and it's pushed back over her shoulders. She looks young and unsure.

"I made you some tea." I hand her the mug, and she takes it gratefully, pulling it toward her chest as if holding it close will warm her up. She sits in one of the chairs and pulls her legs up on the seat, curling into herself. I've never seen her look so vulnerable. "I'm sorry I wasn't at the gates when you got here and that you couldn't get ahold of me."

She attempts a smile. "It's okay. I shouldn't have let my radio battery die. It's in my bag. I guess Thatcher has it now."

"No one was rough with you at the gates, were they?" I pull my chair closer.

She shakes her head. "No, no. They were…pleasant. Once I gave them the code, someone named Isaac whisked me away through a side door and put me in a room. I told him who I was and who I was here to see. He gave me some water and went through my bag while we waited for Thatcher."

"And Thatcher was okay? She didn't harass or threaten you or anything?" My heart pounds wildly in my chest at the thought of anyone mistreating her.

"No, she just wanted to know why I showed up at her town in the middle of the night using your codeword. I told her we've been in touch since White River. She asked if I was your 'important contact.' I told her I was. Then she brought me to you." Kate tries to smile again, but it's easy to tell it's forced. At least they treated her well; the unexpected arrival could've gone a lot worse.

I watch her for a moment and focus on the way she fiddles nervously with the sleeves of the sweatshirt with one hand and grips the mug so tightly with the other that I can see her knuckles turning white. "Are you comfortable telling me what happened? What made you change your mind?"

She stares at a spot on the floor for a long time. So long that I wonder if she heard me. Maybe it was too soon to ask. I should give her more time to process.

"Ever since White River…" Her voice cracks a bit, and she stops. She clears her throat and tries again, still staring at the floor. "Ever since White River, I didn't feel like I belonged anymore. I had assignments, I had a clear path to promotion, and I was doing things. Good things. Or so I thought. Really, I was just going through the motions, I guess." Her eyebrows knit, and she pauses like she's figuring out what to say. I ache to reach out and wipe away the worried wrinkle between her brows. "I thought about what you said before, about the war, and no matter what I did, even as an officer, I wasn't going to change the direction of the NAF. I was supposed to lead. I was supposed to be in charge. And my mother, she just kept doing all these things, these awful things, without telling me. Explosions, attacks, all these drones, bombs…I didn't know about any of it until after the fact, and no matter what I said, no matter how much I *begged* to do it my way, she just wouldn't listen. It was like she was doing it all behind my back. Everything was classified. She was never going to listen to anyone else. Including me."

"Kate," I say and scoot even closer. I gently take her free hand hold it between my own. I give a squeeze until her eyes meet mine. "What you did by leaving—"

"Put a huge target on this place?" she supplies.

I smile and squeeze tighter. "Hate to break it to you, but there was already a huge target on this place."

"Yeah," she says slowly. "I think my mother knows you're here. She and Simon are messing with you, trying to draw you out."

"I know," I tell her with a grimace. "I found the note Simon left on one of the people he killed in Deadwood. It said Lucas was next."

"What?" She places her mug on the table and sits up straight. "He left you a note?"

"Pinned to one of the men he killed." My heart still aches when I think of the sheer size of the funeral pyre we built today. All those townspeople are traumatized and trying to rebuild while constantly looking over their shoulders. I wish I could do more to help them.

Kate stands and pushes her damp hair over her shoulder and starts to pace. "I should have stayed. I should have checked on those people personally and tried to make it right. I should've looked harder for Simon." She stops and looks at me with a horrified expression. "Dani. The drones. She's pushing for the drones to get in the air. She put Rapid City on the top of her list, sent a message to surrender, and now she's at Warren, and they have drones—"

"Hey," I say, gently pulling her closer. "Breathe."

Kate puts her hands on my chest, stopping me. "Dani, didn't you hear me? She knows you're in Rapid City. While she waits for the drones to get in the air, she's trying to distract you with blatant attempts to draw you out."

I scoff. "Yeah, I'm not falling for any more traps."

Kate shakes her head. "No, you don't understand. She wants the drones in the air within a month. And then Rodrigues—"

"Who's Rodrigues?" I interrupt, trying to follow her frantic train of thought.

"My assistant," she answers quickly. "My mother—"

"You have an assistant?" I interject again.

Her eyes meet mine, and they are not at all amused. "Dani, please focus. This is serious. We have to warn Thatcher. We have to get you out of here!"

"Whoa, hang on." I take her arms and attempt to keep her from marching out of my room barefoot and clad in pajamas. "First, you really need to breathe. Second, we already know she's planning an attack. Thatcher and William have been working on that. Third, I doubt Bruce is gonna let you go anywhere." She shakes her head, and I take her face in my hands. "Listen, it's going to be okay."

"Is it?" Her eyes are wide, her voice shaky. "They're shutting down your gas supply. Your trade routes."

"I know."

She looks at me, confused. "How?"

"Thatcher has contacts on the inside, too." I smile and hope it's reassuring. "I was a scavenger for the past seven years. And a damn good one. I've still got some tricks up my sleeves. I don't want you to worry."

"Dani," she says and then sighs. She sounds tired.

"Come on," I tell her and lead her to the bed. "You've had enough excitement for one day. What you need right now is some rest, and we'll figure it all out in the morning." She watches with a frown as I pull back the covers.

"I'm not tired," she says stubbornly.

I roll my eyes. "Well, I am. So you can either sit by the fire and drown in your worry, or you can come lie down with me in the most comfortable bed ever."

Kate looks at the woodstove longingly, as if this is actually a difficult decision. I would've been offended if she didn't sigh and turn back to me, agreeing.

I try to soothe her worry further with a promise. "There's nothing we can do tonight locked in this room. We'll meet with Thatcher in the morning, and we can figure it out from there. Okay?"

She nods and reluctantly slides into the bed.

It's hard to think of anything else with Kate here, in Rapid City, wearing my clothes and settling into my bed. Everything else can wait. Right now, all that matters is Kate.

Once the lanterns are extinguished and I've changed into something I can sleep in, I slip under the covers and settle on her pillow so that my nose is touching hers and place one hand on her hip, pulling her slightly closer.

Leaning in, I brush my lips against hers and smile when she kisses me. "I'm sorry about everything you've gone through but I'm glad you're here," I whisper.

She grips me under the covers. "I'm scared."

I press our foreheads together, slip my leg between hers, and pull her the final little bit so that we're flush together. "Me too." Gently, I stroke her cheek, and she closes her eyes. "But whatever happens, we'll take it on together."

We stay like that for a long time, pressed together, faces close. I can tell she's tired, but she refuses to sleep. I don't want to close my eyes either for fear that this is all somehow a dream, but it's getting harder and harder to keep them open while tucked away in this warm cocoon.

Her breathing calms, and for that brief moment, everything feels right in the world. But just as I'm about to drift off to sleep, Kate's sad voice startles me back awake. "What if the war never ends?"

I consider her words for a moment, debating between telling her what I think she wants to hear and what I feel is true. After considering both, I go with the latter. "I think this country is always going to be divided in one way or another. It's the calm we find in the in-between that we strive for. Those tiny pockets of peace between storms. The war will end," I promise her. "At some point. Even if it's only for a little while, it will end."

"What if we aren't around to see it?" Her voice is small, and when I open my eyes, I see hers are still wide, scared.

Needing to feel more of her, needing to feel her warmth, I move my hand from her hair to under her sweatshirt, with my palm flat on the small of her back. "We will be."

Her nose bumps against mine as her head shifts on the pillow. "Do you believe in an afterlife?"

I lightly rub her back. "Yes. Do you?"

Her eyes fall slightly, and a heaviness takes over them. She swallows back. "I don't know."

"Then I'll take you to mine." I promise. Her eyes finally drift shut, and within seconds, her mouth opens and her breathing evens out.

The next morning, while I'm sitting in an armchair and drinking tea, I watch Kate sleep. She looks at peace, the worry completely gone from her features. It reminds me of a time when Lucas and I were kids and were woken up by soft, slow music coming from the main room. We tiptoed out of our bedroom, hid behind furniture, and watched as our parents slow danced in front of the lit fireplace. They held each other adoringly as they swayed to the music. I remember thinking Mom and Dad looked younger with their eyes closed and soft smiles. They always loved to dance.

I had denied Kate a dance in my house back in White River, and looking at her now, I can't imagine wanting anything more than to dance with her the way my parents did.

Her eyes start to flutter, and she makes a small noise as she stretches her arms above her head. One of her hands reaches to my side of the bed and aimlessly searches, and when she doesn't find me, her eyes finally open and she looks around. "Hi," she says, through a yawn when our gazes meet. "Is it late? Did I sleep too long?"

"No," I tell her and lean forward to push the hair from her face. "It's still early. Bruce is letting Lucas get us some breakfast."

She turns to the window where I've drawn back the curtains, and she squints. "Is it snowing again?"

I glance out the window at the flurries whirling in the wind. "Yes," I tell her with a sigh. I stand and walk to the stove, grabbing the teakettle.

"Does it always snow so early in the season out here?" she asks and sits up, pulling the covers tightly around her, as if just seeing the snow makes her cold.

"Sometimes." Dropping the tea bag in the steaming water, I sit on the edge of the bed and hand it to her. "Snow this early usually makes for a bad winter."

She submerges the bag and lifts it out again with a worried expression. "Dani—"

The knock on the door is hesitant, and I sigh at the interruption. "That didn't take him long."

She places her mug on the nightstand and slips out from the covers. "I'll go get dressed."

She grabs her jeans and a clean shirt and shuts herself in the bathroom before Bruce opens the door and lets my brother and Darby into the room. I suppress a groan. It's too early for Darby. "Surprised to see you awake," I say as she passes.

"Lucas was buzzing around the room like a hyped-up bee and made so much noise, I couldn't block it out. Plus, I have a meeting with some of Thatcher's people. We're going to try to get one of these drones in the air." I notice the large goggles on top of her head, indicating she's in work mode. She places her backpack by the door at Bruce's insistence and looks around while she cleans her hands. "Where's the deserter?"

My body prickles at the nickname. I hope Kate didn't hear it through the door. "Getting dressed. Call her that again, and I'll weld those goggles to your face, got it?"

The tone must've conveyed enough warning because Darby at least has the decency to look scolded. "Got it, jeez, would you relax? Clearly, you didn't get laid last night."

"No more idle chitchat. The fighters must focus," Lucas says, his voice hard, harsher than I've heard in a long time, and he shoots Darby a look. She holds up her hands and makes a show of closing her mouth. Lucas nods once, then holds up a basket. "Rations for the troops."

I refill the kettle while Lucas washes up at the door. As he finishes, Kate emerges from the bathroom. Her hair is combed, and she's pulled the black sweatshirt that she slept in over a clean white T-shirt.

"It's a beautiful day to start a new adventure," Lucas proclaims upon seeing her.

She smiles. "Good morning, Lucas." She looks next to him and nods. "Darby."

"Katelyn," Darby says, a trace of venom in her tone. She looks at me instead of at Kate, as if trying to prove she can play nice and still failing.

Breakfast is quite the experience. Kate is still tense while Lucas is all smiles, as if a long-lost friend has finally returned home. Bruce just stares at us from the doorway. I make the mistake of telling Darby about some tech in my Jeep that I forgot to give her, and after that, she doesn't shut the hell up. She prattles on about drones and blueprints and wishing she had access to more resources, and honestly, I'm already exhausted before even starting my day.

When we're done eating, we slowly put on our boots and jackets, knowing we have a meeting with Thatcher.

"Do I get my guns back?" I ask Bruce who waits by the door. When he doesn't answer, I sigh and turn to Kate. "Ready?"

"Do I have a choice?"

I take her knit hat and pull it over her head. "Keep your head down and you'll be fine."

She nods and shoves her hands in her pants pockets. Her brows knit together, and she stands perfectly still. "You okay?" I ask.

Kate pulls something small from her front pocket and stares at it for a bit before glancing at Lucas and clearing her throat. She steps toward him. "I found this back on base. I thought you might like to have it."

Lucas wipes his hands on his pants and looks at me. I shrug, not knowing what's happening. He takes a couple slow steps forward, looking at Kate's hand as she holds out what appears to be a round black button.

His breath catches, and now I'm curious. Darby cranes her neck, also trying to figure out what Kate is holding. I take another step and see the familiar overlapping M's in the center of the button. It's an old Major Maelstrom pin, and it appears to be in immaculate condition. Something we've never come across before.

Bruce leans in to get a closer look and then stands down. Kate seems nervous. Especially since Lucas is just standing there, staring at her. I know it's because he's overwhelmed with excitement and processing his emotions, but from the outside, it may seem that he's uninterested. Kate shifts her weight from one foot to the other but continues to hold out her hand.

I step around her and stand next to my brother, giving him a slight nudge. "Go on."

Lucas wipes his hands again, his eyes never leaving the button. Slowly, painfully slow, he reaches out with a trembling hand and takes the item carefully, as if it's the most precious thing he's ever seen.

He traces the outline of the circle and flips it to the back to see the pin. One more flip, and his thumb passes over the white logo in the center. I wonder if he's about to cry.

Turning to me, he holds it up, proud. Now I think *I* may cry.

He presses it against the collar of his jacket, testing how it'll look there. "Want me to put it on?" I ask.

He nods, seemingly still unable to voice his excitement. He looks at Kate and holds it out to her.

"Me?" she asks, face shocked. "You want me to put it on you?" He nods, and she glances at me. I smile and motion with my head, encouraging her.

Kate carefully takes the button and fastens it on his collar, exactly where he was holding it before. My eyes get misty, and I quickly swipe at them.

When she's finished, Lucas looks down at his new accessory and puffs out his chest, proud. "My new rank catches the shine from the sun. I stand tall and proud to accept it."

"He means thank you," I interpret, but I'm not sure I needed to.

"You're welcome," Kate says.

"Time to go." Bruce's booming statement makes us all jump, the deep timbre of his voice slicing through the silence.

The moment may be over, but the way Lucas keeps glancing down at his button lets me know that he will never forget this morning as long as he lives. He and Kate share a smile before we follow Bruce out the door. Something inside me shifts and seems to click into place. Maybe Rhiannon was right about love after all.

CHAPTER FOURTEEN: THE STANDOFF

KATE

Despite the chill outside, the small office feels hot. There's a small heater off to the side, red and buzzing, and it does nothing to settle my nerves. Bruce stands outside, giving us the illusion of privacy, but I know he'd storm in here faster than I could blink if called for.

I shove my sleeves to my elbows and push the hair from the back of my neck. I'm not used to wearing it down this much. My mother would have a fit.

"You okay?" Dani asks, a worried expression on her face.

"I'm fine. It's just..." I glance behind me at the closed door. "It's hot in here, don't you think?"

I don't get a chance to hear her response. The door flies open, and Thatcher comes in apologizing. "Wesley is having a terrible time finding the peppermint tea that I like. It's almost like someone is hoarding all the bags in Rapid City." I don't miss the guilty look on Dani's face as she clears her throat. "Are you sure I can't get either of you anything?"

"We're good," Dani says quickly.

"No, thank you," I reply, equally fast.

Thatcher eyes us carefully and sits at her small desk. I would've thought the mayor of a thriving town would've had a larger work surface and accommodations. Something closer in looks to my mother's ornate desk. Thatcher's is worn and chipped. It reminds me of my own desk back in Omaha. Somehow, the familiarity eases just tiniest bit of tension.

"So you're Songbird," she says slowly, with a curious and amused smile. The codename makes me shift in my chair. "Dani told me she had a high-ranking contact in the NAF, but she and Jess were very tight-lipped. My source was only able to confirm the call sign. Imagine my surprise when you end up being the general's daughter."

My skin prickles at the association. Dani must notice because she leans forward a bit in her chair to catch Thatcher's eye. "What's the plan?" Dani asks, shifting focus away from me. "You and William were holed up here all yesterday afternoon. Care to fill me in?"

Thatcher doesn't look happy about the subject change, and I don't miss the skeptical look she gives me. "We've sent a few soldiers and supplies to Deadwood, and William plans to ramp up recruitment. As for here, we received the message that's been circulating. Surrender or else. I'm checking and reinforcing the perimeter and sending everyone outside the gates away for now. We should be well-prepared for a ground attack but—"

"For an air attack?" Dani asks.

Thatcher hesitates and shifts the conversation back to me. "Do you want to tell me why the general's daughter showed up unannounced on my doorstep?"

"I seem to have a tendency for that," I try to joke. Only Dani cracks a smile. "I don't like what the NAF are doing. I thought I could change it, but my mother won't listen. I didn't want to be a part of all the needless violence, and I had nowhere else to go. So…" I hold out my hands and shrug, hoping I don't look as nervous and scared as I feel.

Thatcher stares at me, and it's incredibly unnerving. Dani squeezes my arm. "A lot of people aren't going to be happy you're here."

Dani leans closer to me. "Thatch is having trust issues with some of her people," she whispers dramatically.

Thatcher is far from amused. "Danielle."

Dani winces and leans back. "She's right. We should probably tell Bruce to call off the welcome wagon."

"Can you please be serious?" Thatcher scolds, her gaze intimidating.

"Sorry," Dani grumbles. Their exchange is curious, and I wonder how far back their relationship actually goes.

Seemingly satisfied, Thatcher turns back to me. "Now that you're here, I hope you won't mind if I ask you some questions." Her tone makes it clear that she's going to ask whether I like it or not.

I have no other choice, but as far as interrogations go, this one feels less threatening. It helps having Dani beside me. "Go ahead," I tell her.

She barely pauses. "Do you know when the NAF are getting their drones in the air?"

Any information I give will be selling out my family. And despite breaking with them, it still makes me sick to know I'm betraying not just my mother, but Ryan and so many other good soldiers as well. "We... *they*," I correct myself. It's not *we* now that I've left. I push down the fear that fills my throat with recognition that I'm not part of the NAF anymore. I just have to keep reminding myself that I'm doing the right thing. "*They* have been ordered to have them all in the air within a month."

"That's not a lot of time." Thatcher folds her hands. She's composed, and her posture reads confidence, but the slight furrow of her brow indicates her worry. "I'm not sure we'll be able to mount any kind of aerial defense in that short amount of time."

"Darby will get around the blockers." The conviction in Dani's tone catches me off guard. I didn't get the impression that she even likes Darby, but clearly, she trusts her.

Thatcher sighs. "Let's hope so."

"I..." I trail off and clear my throat as both Dani and Thatcher look at me. "I'm confident that something else is happening. Unfortunately, I'm unsure what that might be."

Thatcher looks at me curiously, head tilting to the side. "Why do you think this?"

My stomach drops. I have a theory, but if I voice it, that will be it. The final nail in the coffin. I will never be able to go back, and I'm starting to feel suffocated with weight of my choice, again.

Dani takes my hand. I look at her, and she smiles softly. My gut tells me to trust her. Trust in the decision I made to help. She squeezes gently, and it gives me the last bit of strength I need.

"The *general*," I emphasize, doing my best to keep familial bonds out of this conversation moving forward, "has always taken critical assignments on herself and oversees them directly, often not bringing more than essential personnel onboard. That's pretty standard here and there, but she's been doing it with everything. Lately, she's become more paranoid than ever, unwilling to listen to any opinions that go against her own. She's surrounded herself with extreme loyalists and is playing everything close to the chest. I feel like she's trying to cause deliberate misdirection by leaving a lot of her officers out of the loop."

"Such as yourself." Thatcher points out gently.

"Such as myself," I confirm, even if it does feel harsh to admit it. "She left for an unknown location yesterday morning. I have a strong suspicion it was to Warren."

As soon as the words pass my lips, I realize I could have possibly signed my mother's death warrant. Instead of feeling lighter with the confession, my chest is noticeably heavier. How did my mother and I get to this point? We never really saw eye to eye, and we always had a distinct push and pull when it came to our relationship, but I never thought I'd so blatantly betray her.

This is apparently news to Thatcher; she sits up straighter and glances at Dani with a questioning look. "I haven't heard anything about the general on the move."

"As I said, she's very keen on misdirection." I keep to myself that her mentality seems to be rapidly declining since the death of my father. That's a line I will not cross. Not with Thatcher, anyway.

"What's at Warren?" Dani asks.

"They acquired some items meant for Malmstrom. Explosives and possibly enough aerial tech to assemble two drones along with four ground pilots," I confess. I feel hot again. I'm unaccustomed to spilling so much intel to someone other than Dani. She must sense my discomfort because she squeezes my hand. I didn't just betray my mother but countless soldiers as well. I wipe the sweat off my forehead.

"That's disconcerting. It sounds like Warren is more active than we anticipated." Thatcher frowns. She reaches for a pen and begins jotting down notes on a piece of paper off to the side. "I'll get in touch with all my contacts and see what I can dig up and get Jess on the radio. Is there anyone within the NAF you still trust?"

I think of Ryan and how he's always been right beside me, my closest confidant and my most trusted advisor. My friend…but not anymore. "No." I swallow thickly. "And I believe the general knows Dani and William are here in Rapid City. That's why she keeps trying to draw them out. She can't get through your walls, so she's trying to keep you occupied and buy herself some time."

Dani scoots to the edge of her chair, looking extremely uncomfortable but doesn't release my hand. "We should probably move out of here sooner rather than later. Draw NAF attention away from Rapid City."

Thatcher considers. "Do you have a plan once you are out?"

"Not yet. I'll talk to William and the others. We'll go off-grid and just keep moving, I guess." She sighs, and I can tell that she isn't thrilled with her own plan.

I consider how desperately the general wants Dani and William. How she assembled an entire team led by Simon just to go after them. With the two of them gone, the spark that ignites the Resistance could very well be extinguished. "She's going to go after any town or city where she thinks Dani or William are hiding. And if they're in a major city…"

"Two birds, one stone," Thatcher says, catching on quickly.

"Okay," Dani agrees slowly. "If William and I split up, we can spread their troops thin. It might be our best chance at fighting back."

Thatcher nods. "I have to agree. I've been discussing going back east with some of my contacts there. This might be a good time to make an internal play."

"What do you mean? You think your leaving right now is a good idea?" Dani asks, glancing at me and then back to Thatcher. "We're going to need you to lead the charge here. Someone has to be the face of the movement."

"There may not be another time to go." Thatcher sounds dejected. "With the general distracted, I may not get another opportunity like this."

I can tell Dani wants to argue, but I agree with Thatcher on this one. "Dani," I say quietly, pulling her attention back to me. "If the NAF comes to Rapid City and you're all here, there will be no survivors."

Her face pales, and she shakes her head again. "If we don't have some sort of leadership here, Rapid City is totally exposed," she counters. "I won't let that happen again."

"My chief of security is perfectly capable of taking charge while I'm gone," Thatcher assures her.

Dani sits back in her seat. "I wasn't in White River, and they killed everyone anyway. There was no option to surrender. All because they were associated with me. And now we're pretty sure the general knows I'm here, and you all have been harboring me. She found White River guilty of treason and had everyone who stayed behind murdered. She'll do the same to the people here."

I flinch at her words. My mother's disdain for the Clarks has gone on longer than Dani and I have been alive. She's right. Mom will stop at nothing to put an end to their family legacy.

"White River was a small town. The NAF is spread thin, like you said," Thatcher reasons. "They don't have the numbers they need to completely take over or survive the winter marching across the wasteland without a place to bunker down. They're going to need a strong foothold like Rapid City and the resources within. I just don't see them burning this entire place to the ground."

I think about all those soldiers she sacrificed to salvage her drones. And all the people she allowed Simon to kill just to prove a point. All those needless deaths that I couldn't prevent. How she wants to make Rapid City an example.

"So we'll go," Dani says after a beat. "And hope that the NAF comes after us instead." She doesn't sound convinced that this will work. And I'm not sure it will either. We can only hope that Thatcher is right, and once the NAF realizes Dani and William are gone, they'll spare the city and put in one of their own to take charge.

"As for you," Thatcher says, turning to me. "I went through your things last night." She holds up the folders from my backpack. I had a feeling she would riffle through it when it was confiscated, but I still feel a little violated. "The information you smuggled out is rather significant. Locations of ariel blockers, troop locations, and known gas suppliers. Very impressive."

I'm not sure how to respond to the compliment since it was an action of betrayal on my part.

"You've earned some trust with me today," Thatcher continues, oblivious to my internal struggle of selling out the NAF.

"Enough for Kate to get her weapons back and to call off Bruce?" Dani asks.

Thatcher chuckles and places the folders to the side of her desk. "Bruce will remain close by. As for the weapons, she will not be allowed to carry any within the walls. You, however, may have your pistols back while you're in the town. You will give them to Bruce when you go back to your room. But if you do anything to jeopardize my trust, Bruce will remove them from you permanently and by any means necessary."

Thatcher opens a drawer in her desk and presents Dani's pistols. The threat is clear. Dani seems unfazed, reaches over to accept her weapons, and slides them easily in the empty holsters on her thighs. I wish I was allowed at least my knives. I hate being defenseless. Though, at least this time, I'm not being strapped to a bomb.

"What about the rest of my stuff?" Dani asks.

"I'll give it to William." I bristle at the mention of his name. "And speaking of," Thatcher continues, "you both will be joining him for lunch. As predicted, he knows we're hosting a high value contact that arrived last night. I told him you would explain."

"Thatch…" Dani says, her voice sounding more like a whine.

Thatcher is not deterred. "Danielle, I held him off all last night and again this morning. I'm tired of dodging his questions. You need to handle this."

Dani groans. I have to agree. I would much rather be locked in Dani's room with Bruce at the door than at a lunch with William Russell.

Thatcher stands but doesn't make an effort to walk us out. Dani opens the door and waits for me to exit first with a sympathetic look. "Kate?" I look over my shoulder. Thatcher smiles sincerely. "Welcome to the Resistance."

I swallow hard and give a firm nod. The reality of her words washes over me like a tidal wave. What the hell did I just do?

❖

I stare at the flames as they stretch upward in the elaborate fireplace. Dani sits beside me in her own wingback chair, looking as anxious as I feel.

Finally, after a long stretch of silence, she faces me. "We don't have to do this right now," she says. "We can go right back up to the room, and I can have something brought up."

The offer is incredibly tempting. "Let's just get it over with," I end up saying.

She gives me a sympathetic look. "It doesn't have to be right now is all I'm saying."

"I think it does." I try to offer a convincing smile. "Thatcher seemed fairly adamant."

She drags her chair so close that when she sits back down, her leg slips between mine, and our thighs touch. "I'll be right beside you. I won't let anything happen to you."

"I know."

She squeezes my thighs. "You don't have to say anything to him. You have nothing to prove to anyone. If you decide this isn't something you're ready or willing to do, then we won't do it."

"If I say I don't want to ever meet William Russell, you'd just make that happen? Avoid him for the rest of your life because I can't stomach the idea of ever being around him?" William is a big part of Dani's life, and I can't expect her to just turn her back on him. It's not something I would even ask.

"If that's what you need," she says easily.

I give her a pointed look. "Dani, be realistic." I run my fingers through my hair and take a deep breath. "This is all so hard."

She laces her fingers through mine and waits until I look at her. "I know what it's like to walk away. To *want* to walk away. What you did, leaving and coming here, was the hardest part. But I also know how difficult it is to jump into a new kind of life. Just because you took that first step doesn't mean you're ready to run. It doesn't mean you're able to turn your back on what you're used to."

"This conversation is strangely familiar," I mutter, recalling our fight back in White River, when I found her journals and accused her of still being an active part of the Resistance. I couldn't understand it then, but I sure do now.

"No one will blame you if you aren't ready to fight the NAF right now." She squeezes my hand.

"Right now," I repeat and look away. The implications of *ever* hurting someone I used to fight alongside or turning on my mother is not sitting well with me at all.

"Hey." She gently turns my head until our eyes meet. "You'll get to the place you're looking for, and I won't leave you while you try to find it. Or force you to be a different person."

I want to tell her so many things. That I'm certain I won't ever be ready to kill my mother or my friends. Or that I desperately want to help, but I'm not sure how to I can do that, either. How I feel like I'm stuck in this in-between of not knowing where I belong. How I feel like a traitor and a fraud, but when I'm with her, I think that maybe I can find finally find some peace.

Instead, I lean in and kiss her. It was meant to be soft and chaste, though it's anything but. Dani doesn't seem to mind at all, pushing her fingers through my hair and somehow scooting closer. I hold on to her arms, keeping her there, and trying to push away all of my self-doubt.

"If you two are finished trying to inhale each other's faces," a voice interrupts, "then I'd really like to get some lunch without throwing up first."

Dani sighs against my lips and pulls away, but her hands remain in my hair. When I open my eyes, I see most of the gang standing awkwardly beside her, with Mohawk glaring. Dani slowly untangles us.

"Sorry to interrupt," Rhiannon says, also sporting an apologetic expression and elbowing Mohawk in the side.

I sit back, wiping my mouth with the back of my hand. Somehow, I don't feel as embarrassed I probably should.

"I just saw William finishing up with security at the gates and heading this way," Mike says and glances at the entrance. "Is he coming, too?"

"Unfortunately," Dani says.

Everyone looks uncomfortable, and all their eyes fall on me. I wish I had voiced my desire to hide in Dani's room and avoid this for another day.

She looks at me, and I nod. Ready as I'll ever be, I suppose. She leads the way and glances at Darby, who has a bag slung over one shoulder. "How did the flight go?" Dani asks as we cross into the dining area.

"Not great." Darby sounds frustrated. "We're going to try again later today."

"You'll get there." Dani looks at her sympathetically and holds out a chair for me. "I'll give Lucas the keys to my Jeep. You can go grab those parts I was telling you about. Who knows, they might help."

"We're still going to eat, aren't we?" Mohawk plops at the head of the table and looks around as if food will magically appear. He motions for the woman at the bar. "Whiskey," he yells across the room, and this time, it earns him a light smack to the back of his head.

"Relax, we're going to eat. Stop shouting. It's rude." Rhiannon lectures. She glances at the door and wrings her hands. "Is Elise coming?"

Mike sits. "No, she's helping out at the clinic. Why?"

"No reason." Rhiannon's gaze shifts to Dani beside me, and she reaches for the necklace inside her shirt, fingering whatever is attached to it. It doesn't take an expert to know she thinks this may get rough. I hate that I agree.

Lucas sits on my other side and gently pats my hand and smiles. "All is well."

I doubt that. But instead of disagreeing, I try to return his smile.

The bartender brings over several glasses and a bottle of whiskey. She glares at Mohawk, who mutters a thank you and starts to pour generous portions for everyone. He slides one to Dani and then to Mike, who looks at it wearily. Darby makes a disgusted face, but Rhiannon takes a glass without hesitation.

"It's showtime, folks," Lucas says, straightening in his seat and nodding toward the door. My stomach drops at his words. I thought I'd have a little more time to get my emotions in check. Or at the very least, a decent amount of alcohol in my system.

William strolls in, flanked by two younger men, one noticeably larger than the other. But I can't take my eyes off him. He's shorter and thinner than I imagined. There are wrinkles around his eyes, and his hair is graying. He looks older than the images that circulate within the NAF. He looks…human in a way I wasn't expecting and not at all like an untouchable myth.

Dani squeezes my thigh as he scans the room and finally lands on us at the table. Dani stands, followed by Mohawk and Lucas.

"Here we go," I mumble, and knock back a sip of Dani's shot before standing.

Dani puts a hand on the small of my back, her touch comforting despite the anxiousness of meeting one of the most hated men in the NAF. I glance at the guns strapped to every single person in this room. My hand twitches at my side, and again, I wish I had my knife.

Though the other two men have yet to approach, they both tense when they see me, clearly ready to move in swiftly. It neither surprises nor offends me because I'd do the same. The big guy rests his hand on the butt of his pistol and stares. He rivals Mohawk in size, and by the look of it, he's not very fond of anyone in this room, least of all me.

Bruce stands off to the side, watching but not moving. I wonder if he truly would step in to protect me.

William pulls out the vacant chair across from me and sits, his eyes never leaving mine.

Rhiannon drops her necklace, tucking it inside her shirt, and stands. "Why doesn't everyone sit, and Darby and I will go see about getting some lunch."

"Why is everything about food with you?" Darby asks, not making a move to get up.

Rhiannon glances at Dani, who has yet to take her eyes off William, who in turn, still stares at me. "It's my go-to when I'm nervous or anxious, and right now, I'm both, so get up."

"Why do I have to help?" Darby whines. "I want to see what happens."

Rhiannon grabs her arm, whispers something harshly in her ear, and forces her out of her chair and then the room. With two new chairs vacant, William's cronies sit across the table from the rest of us. The room feels incredibly crowded, even with Rhiannon and Darby outside.

Dani remains to my right, Lucas on my left. Mohawk and Mike are at the ends of the table with William between his two men. The scrawny one stares at me, brows furrowed as if confused.

"Anyone want a drink?" Mohawk offers as he pours more whiskey. Mike gives him a look. "I don't think that's such a good idea."

"We heard there was a visitor last night," William says. "Thatcher wouldn't tell me who it was." William tilts his head, probably trying to place why I look familiar. Does he see my mother in my features? Perhaps my father?

Dani's right hand falls to the handle of her pistol strap, and she flicks open the clasp of the holster.

When who I am finally seems to register, William stands so quickly that his chair topples, and Mohawk's glass of whiskey spills across the wooden table. William's pistol is in his hand before I can blink, and he aims directly between my eyes.

She leaps out of her chair, her gun pointed at William's head.

It only takes two beats before his men are standing with their own pistols drawn and now aimed at me.

Another second ticks past. Mohawk, Mike, and Lucas are on their feet, their guns on the men across from me. I'm the only one still sitting, though Bruce looks mighty comfortable watching the whole ordeal with his arms crossed. Some bodyguard.

Slowly, I raise both hands, palms up, above my shoulders to indicate I'm not a threat. But my eyes never leave William. Less than a full minute into our meeting and we're already all in the middle of a standoff.

The rest of the dining area is silent, and everyone is staring. So much for being discreet.

Dani and Lucas keep their guns on William. His gun is still on me. Mike has his on the skinny guy, who turns his pistol back on Mike. Mohawk has his casually on the big guy, who looks overjoyed to now be pointing his gun right back at Mohawk.

I dry swallow and hope that nobody has an itchy trigger finger, or we'll all be dead.

"You wanna do something, Bruce?" Dani calls, her eyes never leaving William.

Bruce grunts but uncrosses his arm and starts ushering the handful of diners out of the room. Not sure that's what Dani had in mind, but at least if bullets start flying, there won't be any chance of collateral damage.

"Why is she here?" William asks, still staring at me. He looks both pissed and panicked.

"I suggest you point your gun someplace else," Dani tells him evenly.

His eyes flick to Dani and then to Lucas, as if just noticing the two pistols aimed directly at his face. His double take is almost amusing. "Dani." It comes across as a half warning, half plea.

She answers by pulling back the slide.

"You can't be serious," he says. When she still doesn't answer, he looks to me and then to everyone else around the table.

The gravity of the situation seems to sink in. This town is on edge, and this little showdown isn't helping. Slowly, he lowers his gun and holsters it. He raises his hands in surrender, giving Dani another look of disbelief. "Put your guns away."

Reluctantly, his two men do as he says.

Dani also holsters her pistol with Mohawk, Mike, and Lucas following suit. Slowly, everyone sits. Bruce, having done nothing to deescalate, stands guard at the door, preventing anyone from coming in.

"The general's daughter?" William says angrily. "What were you thinking? Have you lost your mind?"

Dani reaches for the whiskey I stole from her. "You know, I'm getting really tired of people asking me that." She finishes it in one long gulp.

"We're going to talk about this. Right now. Privately." His tone leaves no room for negotiation, but it doesn't seem to faze Dani in the least.

I really hope she doesn't leave me with William's two men. The scrawny one looks freaked out, but the big one is just chomping at the bit to get to me. And clearly, Bruce has no desire to step in.

Thankfully, Dani seems to be thinking the same. "You want to talk? Talk." William looks as though he wants to protest, but Dani doesn't let him. "Say whatever it is you want to say. We're all friends here."

He looks taken aback, but Dani doesn't budge. After a long moment, he finally settles his gaze on me. I wish he would stop looking at me. It's almost like he wants nothing more than to execute me himself. I'm not my mother, but I'm not sure he cares. "This is Katelyn Turner. Daughter of General Judith Turner and major in the NAF."

"Lieutenant colonel, actually," I easily interject.

I didn't think it was possible for him to look more pissed. Clearly, I was wrong. If I wasn't so on edge, I would probably find it funny.

"The same Katelyn Turner that *you* held prisoner not that long ago, who caused this nice little chain of events." William continues his recap as if Dani and I didn't live it.

"I know who she is," Dani says casually.

"Intimately," Mohawk scoffs. Despite the added comment being inappropriate, I feel more proud than embarrassed.

William looks at Dani in disbelief. "We need to get her out of here right now." He stands and walks to the other side of the table. For a split second, I wish he would grab me because it would give me a nice excuse to break his nose.

Dani seizes his wrist before he can touch me and gives it a twist, bending his arm in an unnatural position. She puts herself between us, her grip tightening. William's eyes go wide, and he winces.

"Don't touch her." Dani's voice is hard, serious, and laced with warning. "You want to talk? Fine. But touch her and I'll break your fucking hand. Got it?"

He yanks his arm back, freeing himself. He looks so utterly betrayed. Dani waits for him to make up his mind. Finally, he nods at the doorway. "Not here. Let's go to my room."

Dani's jaw tightens, and our eyes meet. It's probably for the best that any further conversation happens someplace private, so I nod. "Get her to the room. Don't leave her. Not even for a second," she tells Lucas. "If anyone tries anything, you come get me."

Lucas salutes and scoots his chair closer. I'm grateful for his calming presence and that Dani cares so deeply about me, but if I could just have my knife, then I wouldn't need to be treated like some damsel in distress.

"Lead the way," she tells William.

Once he and his men are gone, her expression softens. "I'm okay," I assure her.

"I promise, I'll be back soon. Stay with Lucas." She waits until I nod and kisses my forehead. She stops to say something to Bruce. I can't hear what she's saying, but he uncrosses his arms and looks a little chastised.

Taking a deep breath, I try to settle my adrenaline. That could've gone better. It could've gone a lot worse, too.

Lucas pats my shoulder and gives me an encouraging smile. "The battle is done, but it's only the first of many."

"Issue five," Darby says, appearing with Rhiannon right behind her. She drops a plate of bread and some cheese in the center of the table and eyes the empty chairs. "Oh, come on. Did we miss it? We weren't even gone that long! Was there punching? Please tell me there was punching."

"Bread and cheese? That's it?" Mohawk complains.

I sink lower in my chair. Being alone with Dani's friends feels weird. I think I prefer the standoff.

"Do you think they're going to kill each other?" Darby asks from Dani's bed. It's unmade, and there are parts and pieces of drones everywhere. She's been taking things apart and putting them back together ever since we came up after lunch. It's clear she's incredibly smart. I wonder how quickly she could get a drone in the air with Rodrigues's help.

The thought of my assistant makes me wonder if she's reported me, Silva, and Miller to the brass or if she sold me out to my mother. Was she working for the general all along? I can only imagine how furious my mother is right now. The entire thing makes me nauseous.

"Bloodshed may be imminent," Lucas says, wincing as he does. It is in no way comforting. He gives me an apologetic look and goes back to the comics he brought in from his room.

Bruce is once again stationed outside the door, and having nothing else to distract myself with—and not wanting to think about either my mother or Dani and William murdering each other—I stand and motion toward the stack in his bag. "Lucas, would it be all right if I looked at one of your comics?"

Darby freezes, and I think I may have just crossed a line, but Lucas perks up and takes one off the top of his pile and hands it to me, rocking back on his heels as I look over the cover.

It's Major Maelstrom punching an NAF general in the face. He's tall and muscular, with black hair, and he sports a deep scowl. To complete the look of a vigilante, he wears black pants, large black boots, and a black, long-sleeve shirt with two white overlapping M's in the middle of what appears to be a storm or a vortex. The logo matches the button I gave Lucas earlier. It's a familiar sight, one I've seen on countless Resistance propaganda pieces, but I've never actually seen the comic the image was pulled from.

I take in the rest of the cover. Issue One, Birth of the Resistance. It's in great condition but clearly loved. The edges are a little frayed, but honestly, the fact that it stayed intact after all this time is quite spectacular.

"Be careful with that," Darby instructs, staring at me with an expression I can't quite place.

I nod and sit, with Lucas continuing to watch as I gently open to the first page. Scanning the pictures first, I read about how the major was an NAF soldier, and with experimental treatments and injections of a mysterious substance meant to give him the power of telepathy, he becomes extra strong, with the ability to summon the wind or water into a swirling vortex instead. It doesn't make any sense, but I keep reading, knowing that Lucas is watching. The military keeps him locked away for observation, and with the help of a rogue doctor, he realizes he is to be used on the front lines against those who oppose the military movement.

The story is familiar, and the narration and dialogue are cheesy, but it's clear that whoever wrote it was trying to spark something within the people who opposed the newly formed National Armed Forces. The first issue ends with Major Maelstrom, real name Major Gary Gilmore, escaping the NAF and sparking an underground movement.

Most of how they depict the NAF is inaccurate, but despite it being quite silly, I'm actually curious to see what happens in issue two.

"Major Maelstrom knew he had to be patient," Lucas says, breaking the silence as I carefully close the comic.

I look at him, not quite sure what he's referencing.

"He wants to know if you liked it," Darby interprets. She's still staring at me with an unreadable expression.

Smiling, I hand the issue back. "It was interesting. Not quite how I was taught the Resistance came to be," I joke. "But I can see why you like Major Maelstrom so much."

Lucas takes the comic with a larger-than-life smile, and it makes me feel warm and welcome by someone other than Dani. He rushes to get the next issue and pulls up a chair beside me. I chuckle a little, getting caught in his excitement and briefly forgetting how nervous I am about Dani and William hashing it out somewhere or that I'm now a traitor to the NAF.

Darby frowns and goes back to her project, but it's easy to tell her heart is no longer in it.

Lucas and I read two more comics when a low knock from the door makes us freeze. I think at first that it may be Bruce, but I know by the gentle tapping that it's not.

Lucas looks through the little peephole. He steps back and unlocks the door, opening it wide to reveal Rhiannon. "A warm welcome," he says, and motions for her to come inside.

Bruce doesn't seem to think she's a threat and lets her pass.

Rhiannon steps in with a large thermos and a bag slung over her shoulder. "Hi, Lucas." She looks at me. "Mind if I have a chat with Kate?" He looks uncertain. "You and Darby are welcome to stay."

"I have to work on another flight test," Darby mutters, shoving her gear into her bag. "And Lucas needs to take me to Dani's Jeep sometime today." Now Lucas looks extremely torn. Go with Darby or stay with me.

Rhiannon laughs a little. "You can go. I promise not to let Kate out of my sight, and Bruce won't let us leave, so…" Lucas still looks skeptical. "I promise, if Dani is upset, I will take full blame."

Lucas looks at me, and I smile. "Go. I'll be fine."

He seems to take my response as final and grabs his jacket so he can join Darby on her next flight test.

"I brought you some hot chocolate," Rhiannon says and holds up the thermos. "I thought you could use something other than the tea Dani's been guzzling."

"Thank you." The gesture is kind. I quickly find and wipe down the mugs Dani and I used earlier in the day. Rhiannon generously pours to the very top, the liquid thick and still steaming. "I haven't had hot chocolate since I was a kid," I tell her, accepting one of the mugs. Being alone in Dani's room with Rhiannon isn't uncomfortable, but I'm still finding it hard to completely relax. She's one of Dani's closest friends, and we didn't exactly get off on the right foot. At least with Lucas, we had Major Maelstrom to break the tension.

We sit at the table in the corner, and I cradle the mug, wondering if I should start a fire to warm the room. "It seemed pretty intense earlier. How are you holding up?" she asks.

I shrug. "Okay, I guess. Considering."

She sighs and rolls her eyes. "They're in William's room. I'm right next door, and they aren't exactly quiet. This place may be luxurious, but their walls are thin."

"What are they saying?" I ask before I can stop myself.

"There's a lot of muffled arguing, and the words 'dangerous' and 'fuck' are used repeatedly." Her expression seems apologetic. After a beat, she looks at the hot chocolate and clears her throat. "I wanted to apologize to you. I wasn't exactly warm and welcoming when you were in White River."

The apology throws me off guard. "Why would you be? NAF soldiers were threatening you and your home."

"Still, Dani saw something in you. I should've trusted her and tried harder."

I can't help but scoff. "Dani saw me as a means to an end. She wanted information. Nothing more."

"Until she realized she'd rather be kissing you than fighting you," Rhiannon teases.

My face warms. "That too." I take a sip of the hot chocolate. It reminds me of the cold winters in Chicago with my dad. "You were very welcoming, all things considered. You allowed us to stay and fed us. In fact, I should be apologizing to you." My heart aches at the look of pain that flashes over her face. Her shoulders tense like she knows what's coming. Even if she does, I need to say this. "Rhiannon, I am so sorry about White River. About your home. I never wanted that to happen. Destroying people's lives—"

"I know," she says gently. "I don't blame you. None of us do." She places her hand over mine. The gesture is startling but oddly comforting.

I look at her hand. "Jack does." Referring to Mohawk by his given name feels weird but is probably a necessary change now that I'm technically an ally to the Resistance.

"Jack needs a place to vent his anger, and unfortunately, it's at you." She pats my hand and pulls away, cradling her mug once more. "We're working on it."

I observe her as she stares at nothing and contently sips her drink. "I really care about her," I say after a stretch of comfortable silence. "I'm not going to betray Dani. Or any of you."

"I didn't think you were," she says easily.

"Not even a little?" I challenge. After all that's happened, I find it hard to believe there wouldn't be some distrust. I know I'm feeling it from all sides.

"Okay, maybe a little." She shrugs. "But Dani trusts you, so I trust you." There's a warmth to her deep brown eyes. Her smile is infectious, and her honesty is oddly refreshing. She is clearly incredibly loyal. Her dark hair is pulled back loosely from her face, and I notice, not for the first time, just how pretty she is.

"You two are really close." I hope the jealousy isn't apparent in my voice. I know they aren't romantic, but there is a bond there that I don't quite understand.

"She's like my sister and best friend rolled into one," Rhiannon says with a smile. "Dani's special."

"Yeah, she is."

"It infuriates me that she blames herself for everything and takes on the weight of the world. She's so loyal, kind, and smart." She reaches out again and this time, takes my hand and squeezes. "I know you see the good in her like I do. Promise that you'll remind her of it from time to time. And that you'll take care of her. That you'll let her be vulnerable and let her lean on you when she needs it, even if she doesn't want to."

There's something about her expression that startles me. It's as if she's been taking care of Dani for the past several years, but now she's handing me the reins and trusting me with Dani's heart. "I promise." It comes out as a whisper, but it's not something I take lightly.

She searches my face. It leaves me feeling exposed. I hold her gaze until she seems to find what she's looking for and gives my hand another firm squeeze. "Good. Now that's settled, Dani asked me to find you some clothes. I had to guess your size, and some of it doesn't really match, but this should get you started."

Her focus shifts to the duffel at our feet. She pulls out various clothing, even a pair of snow boots, and places it all on the table. I reach for a pink sweater, and something nags at me. Something Dani said earlier that I was unable to process, but I may be starting to understand. About becoming a different person, the person I *want* to become.

"Rhiannon?" I nervously run my fingers through the tangled locks resting on my shoulders.

"Hmm?"

"Will you cut my hair?"

Chapter Fifteen: The Alarm

Dani

"What the hell were you thinking?" William paces past me again, and I wonder if he's getting dizzy with all the back and forth. "Do you think by asking me a hundred times that it's going to change my answer?" I stand my ground and glance at the door, thinking it may be a good idea to just leave. We aren't getting anywhere, and I'm tired of being screamed at.

He tosses his hands in the air. "I'm at a complete loss as to why you think this is a good idea."

"Kate chose to leave. I need you to trust me on this." My teeth clench as I watch him wear a path in the hardwood. "You've always trusted me. Why is this any different?"

"Even if she chose to leave, do you think anyone within the Resistance will believe that?"

I look away again. He's right, and I fucking hate it. Convincing everyone that she's not still loyal to the NAF is going to be damn near-impossible. Especially if William still doubts it.

"She is staying with me. And if anyone, including you, even looks at her the wrong way, it won't be the general you'll have to worry about."

There go his hands in the air again. "She's the general's daughter!"

"She's nothing like her mother," I repeat also for the hundredth time and pinch the bridge of my nose.

"You don't know her mother. Not like..." He stops short, and I tilt my head, wondering what he's not saying. "Do you have any idea—"

"*You* don't know Kate. She's not Judith," I say again, my voice raw from the loud exchange that appears to have no end in sight.

William whirls around on the other side of the room and finally stops pacing "She was your prisoner. You strapped a bomb on her. And you expect me to believe she's been helping you ever since? What kind of sane person does that? She's manipulating you."

"It's not like that." He gives me a look that says he believes otherwise. I want to strangle him. "I can't keep talking in circles with you. All you've done is yell and repeat yourself over and over. You aren't *listening*."

He laughs humorlessly. "She could be here to assassinate you, or even me."

"Oh, please. Get over yourself." I stand. "I'm done listening to you trash Kate, a woman who has sacrificed *everything* to be here."

"This is a dangerous game you're playing, Dani. And you have no idea how to play it."

"It's not a game. Not to me." I shake my head, unwilling to listen anymore. "Kate isn't like us. She's better than we are." He starts to respond, but I hold up my hand, stopping him. "We've spent our lives wanting nothing but revenge. Kate spent hers trying to make things better. I've spilled so much blood because I was angry. Because I was grieving. Kate was out there trying to make a difference, channeling her own grief into something positive. She isn't who she is because of her mother. She's the way she is in spite of her. Kate is everything good and decent in this world, and I will be damned if I let anything happen to her."

"You've only known her a couple of weeks," he says gently.

"And you don't know her at all." I inhale deeply and close my eyes in an attempt to calm the storm of emotions swirling inside my chest. "Sometimes, someone can appear suddenly, and you know in an instant that your soul has known them in every lifetime before this one. And sometimes, you can know someone your entire life, and in a single moment, realize you never really knew them at all."

"Dani, it's not that simple." William says, his voice sad, my insult clearly landing.

"Do you really think Kate would've left everything behind, her life, her command, her family and friends to spend more time with *you*, the man who killed her father, just for fun?" I clench my fists at my sides, my anger growing.

"Dani." His tone shifts, but it's his nervous expression that keeps me from continuing my tirade. He hesitates for a moment and shakes his head. "I didn't kill Theodore."

I frown, not expecting that response. "Yes, you did. Everyone knows you did," I argue.

"No, I didn't." He sighs and drops to the worn sofa pressed against the wall and puts his head in his hands.

I watch him for a moment, confused. "What are you talking about? You told us you did."

He doesn't lift his head. "No, I didn't. Everyone just assumed I did. There's a difference."

I'm thrown for a loop and not sure I believe him. I think back to when I was nineteen, and everywhere we went, people slapped him on the back, congratulating him for crippling the NAF and offering him drinks. He accepted it all with a smile.

I feel betrayed, played by his lies. "You better start explaining."

He smiles sadly and shrugs. "There's nothing to explain. I didn't do it."

No, this can't be right. William killed Kate's dad. That's what I remember. "He died in an explosion. One that you set."

"I didn't kill him, Dani." He stares at me, refusing to break eye contact, and my stomach drops. Completely bottoms out and I take a step away from him. "Kate may hate me, but it's not because I killed her father."

In an instant, the rug is pulled out from under me. No wonder Kate never mentioned William killing her father. She knows he didn't do it. Why did I think he had? "Tell me what happened."

"Dani."

"Tell me what happened," I repeat.

William stares at me for a moment and then slowly takes a deep breath. "I was there the night of the explosion. But not to kill Theodore. The explosion in the hanger wasn't supposed to happen." William shakes his head and closes his eyes like he's remembering a painful memory.

"You're saying his death was an accident?"

He looks at me, his expression pleading. "I'm saying I didn't kill him."

My head hurts. His confession feels like a betrayal, and I can't pinpoint why. A million questions swirl in my mind, but I just can't do it anymore. My throat is sore from screaming, and my nerves are fried. I need breathing room to calm down, and I need to get away from him. I just—

I need to see Kate.

He doesn't even try to stop me from leaving.

Bruce holds out his hands for my pistols before he lets me in the room. I don't have the energy to fight him. Once inside, I can hear soft chatter coming from the bathroom, but Lucas is nowhere to be found. "Kate?"

"In the bathroom," Kate calls.

"Is Lucas in there with you?" I ask, still not seeing him. "It's cold in here. Why didn't you start a fire?" I run my hands up and down my arms and quickly wash my hands at the door.

"We were busy," Rhiannon calls out happily.

My anger melts into curiosity at the sound of Rhiannon's voice, and I step into a bathroom illuminated by two lanterns on the counter. My breath catches. Kate's eyes meet mine in the mirror, and I stare, frozen in place. Gone is Kate's long blond hair; it brushes just above her shoulders now. Her expression is apprehensive as she stares back.

"Well?" Rhiannon asks, putting her hands on her hips. "What do you think?"

"Uh," I start, unable to form a single word. It takes all my effort to swallow and try again. What was I feeling before? Kate is all I can focus on now. She looks beautiful. "Wow."

Kate blushes and tucks her shorter hair behind her ears.

"Wow is right." Rhiannon runs her hands through Kate's hair, untucking it from her ears and fluffing it a bit. "Long enough to cover the neck in the winter but short enough to feel lighter. A fresh start."

They share a smile through the mirror, and Kate stands while Rhiannon brushes the last stray hairs off her shoulders. "It looks great, Rhiannon. Thank you."

"Of course." She fluffs Kate's hair one more time and takes a deep breath. "Well, now that Dani and William aren't screaming profanities at each other, I'm going to freshen up before I meet Wyatt and his mother for dinner. You two enjoy your afternoon." She pats my shoulder and leans in. "Don't be upset that Lucas left. I made him."

"Thank you, Rhi."

She smiles warmly. "I love you, you idiot." She turns to Kate. "And I'm taking a liking to this one, too. See you both later."

She steps out the door, leaving Kate and I alone. My stomach twists in knots as if I'm seeing her for the first time.

"Fresh start, right?" Her voice is nervous.

Smiling, I close the distance and push my fingers through her shorter hair, forgetting all the questions I wanted to ask. "Right." I kiss her, unable to do anything else. "You look beautiful."

I can feel her grin against my lips, and she holds on to the front of my shirt, pulling me closer. "Do we have anyone else we're supposed to meet with?"

"No." I kiss her again.

"In that case"—she slips her arms around my neck—"how about starting that fire?"

Kate's deft fingers are pulling through her disheveled hair as if trying to get used to the new length. She's propped on her side on the bed with nothing but a sheet covering her long frame. Finally, she brings her face to rest on the palm of her hand with a sigh. "How did it go with William?"

Hearing his name makes me groan and roll on my back. "About how you'd expect. He doesn't trust you, but he won't throw you to the wolves, either." I stare at the ceiling for a while and then flip back to my side, propping myself on an elbow so I can look at her.

"That's nice to hear, I guess." She reaches for the covers at my waist and pulls them up. The fire is dwindling, and the air is getting colder now that the sky outside has turned dark.

The simple gesture pushes a lump into my throat, and Rhiannon's accusation of love springs to the front of my mind. I swallow hard. "I'm sorry I was gone so long."

"Don't be. I had a fun time reading *Major Maelstrom* with Lucas." She pulls the covers tighter, snuggling down deep. "He was very gentlemanly. Charming runs in the family."

"It comes naturally."

She pulls me closer. I rest my head on her chest while she traces light circles on my back. After releasing a long, low breath, my body melts into her, and my eyes drift shut.

She breaks the silence. "May I ask you something? About Lucas?" Her hand pauses, and I can tell she's nervous about crossing a line.

"You want to know about the way he talks," I mumble, taking a guess.

Kate presses her lips to my forehead and kisses me softly. "Yeah."

I take a deep breath. Lucas is always a sensitive topic, and talking about him isn't something I take lightly. I'm naturally protective, and even with Kate, I hesitate to let her in.

But remembering the button she gave him and her confession about enjoying his comics alongside him, I'm willing to try. "Lucas didn't speak as a child. At least, not for a long time. He has always been compassionate and kind, but back then, he just didn't talk. Our mom was so patient with him. She would say that if he was meant to speak, then he'd speak. One day, William came to our house…" I lift my head to look at her, sidetracked from the story. "It was this amazing two-story on the most beautiful piece of land you've ever seen. The views of the sunrises and sunsets would make you cry."

She tucks a piece of hair behind my ear and smiles.

"Anyway, William brought a few *Major Maelstrom* comics with him. Lucas was about four or five, and he was immediately intrigued. Mom read them to him every single day, over and over. We started looking for them when we went out scavenging with Dad. Lucas would get so excited when we'd find an issue, even if he already had it." I think about his eyes lighting up whenever we come across them. "It was about a year later that he started to repeat lines from the books. He started by saying them aloud with Mom when she read, then he started using it as a way of dialogue. She caught on and was the one who encouraged him to continue. We started reading the comics as a family every night, and soon, we had this special way to communicate with him that we didn't have before."

Her nails make long gentle strokes up and down my back. "It's amazing that he's been so passionate about them for so long."

"I was afraid when Mom died that he'd stop speaking," I reply honestly. "He retreated into himself for a while before we could convince him to keep reading with us." I've never told anyone this before. Not even Rhiannon or Jess. "I think…" I hesitate, trying to figure out what I want to say. "We thought it was helping *him*, keeping this thing going that he loved so much. But eventually, I realized it was Lucas who was helping us heal and grieve by sharing his own connection with Mom with us." The lump in my throat returns. Being this vulnerable is new for me. I bury my face into her shoulder and hope I don't cry.

"From what I know, your brother is absolutely wonderful," she says as her light, gentle movements slow to a stop. She brings her arms around my back and squeezes me into a tight embrace.

"Yeah," My sadness slips away with her offered comfort. "Lucas is pretty amazing. Smart, too. He remembers *everything*."

She laughs lightly. "That's easy to see." She presses her lips to my forehead and whispers against it. "What was your mother's name?" The words come out so quietly that I barely hear her.

"Kaya," I say equally soft.

"Kaya," she repeats. "I bet she was beautiful."

"She really was." I think about her dark eyes and kind smile. "Lucas looks just like her."

"She sounds wonderful." Kate loosens her hold and continues to drag her fingers up and down my back.

"Kate," I start and lick my lips, unable to delay my question any longer. She hums, and I take a deep breath. "What happened to your dad?" Her hands stop, and her entire body tenses. Holding my breath, I want to take the question back.

"You don't know?"

"I thought I did," I answer. Silence fills the room. Shifting slightly, I lift my head to look at her, to apologize, to explain, something, but the faraway look in her eyes stops me.

She swallows and stares past me at the ceiling. Even in the dim light of the lanterns, I can tell she's struggling to answer. "He was working on base. He and his team were in the main hangar when a fire broke out. No one really knows what caused it, but it was dangerously close to a fuel supply. People were running around, some trying to get out, others trying to put out the fire to save their work. My dad ran through the building, forcing people to leave it all and making sure no one was inside. The fire spread so fast…" She swallows roughly. "When the place blew, he was still inside."

I think about William's words, about how Theodore was never supposed to go back in the hangar. "Kate I—"

"He saved a lot of lives." She takes a deep breath and smiles sadly.

I stare at the heartbroken look on her face. Confessing that William was there and may have been a part of it can wait until tomorrow. Putting my head back on her shoulder, I wrap myself tightly around her body and instead try to offer her comfort, the same way she did with me. "I'm sorry," I whisper. I know the pain of losing a parent too soon. "I'm so sorry," I say again, wishing I could go back and prevent her from ever having to feel like this.

❖

The light barely peeks in through the curtains, signaling the start of a new day. I pull on my pants and socks and boots while I wait for Kate to finish in the bathroom. I don't regret locking myself in my room with Kate for a half a day, but it did put us behind schedule. Not that I'm not in a rush to break the news to my friends that we're probably going to be on the run and in hiding for the foreseeable future, but we're running out of time to figure out a plan.

I'd really like to introduce Kate to Jess. Maybe I can radio over and see if she has time to meet us for breakfast. We also need to get the next set of supplies, along with my Jeep, into the storage warehouse outside the gates in case we need to make a fast getaway. As much as I'd love to linger and lock myself away with Kate a little longer, we really need to get a move on it.

Kate emerges and pulls on a pink sweater. Looking at her, I smile. No, I definitely don't regret last night.

She sits on the edge of the bed and slips on her boots. "Why did you want to know about my dad last night?"

I freeze for a moment, then reach for my jacket, deciding that honesty is the best policy. "I always thought William killed him." I say it without meeting her eyes.

"Why would you think that?" she asks, but I can tell my answer startles her.

"Because he was there. When he got back, we all just assumed he had." I look at her and watch a myriad of expressions cross her features.

She turns away and finishes tying her boot. "Is this something that came up last night?" Her voice is steady, but I don't believe for a second that what I just confessed didn't stir some emotions.

I slip on my jacket, wondering if it was a good idea to bring this up now. "I threw it in his face as a reason to back off, but he denied having any part of it. Swore that it wasn't him."

"Do you believe him?" she asks, still not looking at me.

That's the million-dollar question. He isn't high on my list of favorite people right now, and it's clear he's been dishonest, but my gut tells me he's telling the truth. "Yeah, but the whole thing is weird. He said something—"

A deafening alarm blares outside, interrupting our conversation. She looks at me, her eyes wide, and my stomach drops. "Put everything you can find into the bags and get your jacket. We have to go. Right now."

There isn't much around the room, but anything not bolted down, we both frantically grab and shove into duffels.

"What's happening?" Kate asks, slipping her arms through her jacket. I toss her the knit cap and grab the radio by the bed.

"Jess," I call into the radio. "Jess, come in." It's eerily silent. I think about the radios not working before the attack in Deadwood.

Bruce throws open the door. "Let's move it!"

"Is this because of me?" Kate calls over the alarm.

"Doubtful," I yell back. Bruce hands me my pistols, and I holster them both. Swinging both duffels over my shoulders, I lead Kate into the hallway. Lucas and Darby appear, followed quickly by everyone else staying on the floor. "We need to get to the warehouse," I shout to Lucas. He nods, and I look for William. "Have you seen William?"

As if on cue, William steps out, weighed down with several bags over his shoulder. Ericson and Hugo appear, lightening his load by each taking one of his bags to add to their own. "Get to the warehouse," he yells and turns to Bruce. "And you, get to Thatcher. Get her out of here."

Bruce eyes Kate skeptically, clearly debating leaving her. It takes only another second before he takes off down the hall. Catching Jack's eye, I nod to the exit. Rhiannon zips up her dark green jacket, Roscoe hot on her heels.

After grabbing Kate's hand, we rush down the hall and through a door to the staircase. The siren is muffled in here, making it easier to talk. "What's going on?" Jack asks as he descends, shotgun in hand.

"No idea," I confess. "I can't get hold of Jess. The radios are dead." Pulling William close as we reach the next set of steps, I lean in. "EMP?"

He looks at me as if thinking the same. What happened in Deadwood is happening here. He watches as Kate jogs down beside Lucas.

"She's been with me," I tell him.

His gaze meets mine. I've known him long enough to be able to tell what he's thinking: Thatcher was right about a traitor.

"Are we under attack?" Rhiannon asks as we continue down.

There's no sound of gunfire or explosions, but that doesn't mean it isn't imminent. "We will be."

I catch up to Kate as we reach the ground floor. Her face is pale, her expression sickened. Clearly, she thinks this is her fault. The lobby is buzzing with a gamut of emotions from panic to anger. A man behind the main desk screams into a radio receiver but appears unable to get a response.

William stops beside me. All the tension between us from last night has evaporated in the present danger. "I have to get to the gates and figure out what's going on and help them arm the traps," he says loudly.

"We have to find Jess," I yell in a panic. "She's as good as dead if the NAF catches her."

"There isn't any time."

Seeing everyone rushing toward the bunker beneath the building, I know he's right. There isn't time to get to the gate, find Jess, *and* get our friends out.

William puts a hand on my shoulder. "I'll go to the gates. You go get Jess."

"What about the civilians?" I look at Lucas. "Someone needs to get them to the bunkers." He nods and hands his bags to Darby, who starts to protest about the added weight.

Rhiannon steps up to my elbow. "I'll go get Jess," she states loudly next to my ear. Before I can tell her absolutely not, she's handing her bag to Elise. "I know where she is," she continues, close to my face. "One of you needs make sure these people get to safety. Once I find Jess and Wyatt, they can tell me where the warehouse is, and I'll meet you there." I grasp her arm, and she puts a hand over mine. "These people need you."

There is no way I am letting Rhiannon go out there by herself. I'm about to protest again, figure out a way to help direct people *and* find Jess, when another voice chimes in right over my shoulder. "I'll go with her." Jack gives his bag to Mike. I don't like the idea of anyone going anywhere but to the damn warehouse, but as frustrating as it is, Rhiannon is right. No one else knows the city like me, Lucas, and William.

"Dani, we don't have time to argue," Rhiannon says desperately. Unfortunately, she's right.

With a reluctant nod, I point to William. "You and Lucas help direct people to the bunkers. I'll arm the gates, and Jack and Rhiannon will get Jess." Turning to Kate, I motion to my brother. "Stay with Lucas."

"I'm not—"

"Kate, please stay with Lucas," I beg. It's loud and almost pathetic, but we don't have time to hash it out right now. "I need to know you're safe." I know she's scared, and there is no way I'd leave her if I saw any other way. But if the NAF break through the walls and see their lieutenant colonel slumming it with the enemy, it puts us in even more danger.

She looks at William, who is clearly not thrilled with my plan either. Lucas puts a reassuring hand on Kate's shoulder, ever the calm in the storm, and she nods. I grab Lucas's bag and rummage for a weapon. Finding a rifle, I give it to Kate.

"Dani—"

"I promise, I'll see you in a few minutes." Leaning in, I kiss her and then give Lucas a pointed look. "Don't leave her. Get as many as you can out. I'll meet you underground." He nods, understanding.

"Ericson, go with Dani. Hugo and I will meet up with you as soon as we can," William orders.

Ericson and I share a look, and I glance one more time at Kate. She grips the rifle tightly, her eyes still wide. Lucas squeezes her shoulder and guides her away.

We all rush out of the lobby into the streets. "Be careful," I yell to Rhiannon and Jack as they turn in the opposite direction. Rhiannon smiles over her shoulder, Roscoe barking from beside her, and they break into a sprint. I glance to my left and see Lucas leading the rest of the group to the tunnels that will take them out of the city and to the warehouse. William pats my back once and takes off toward the back of town. Ericson and I power straight to the gate.

There are people running everywhere. The guards have taken up positions along the gate and have reinforced the doors. The Resistance fighters are with them, ready to take on whatever is happening beyond the walls.

"Get to the gates, make sure they're equipped with the heaviest weapons this city has," I tell Ericson, and for once, he doesn't fight me. He rushes to the command post as I climb the ladder to the watchtower. My ears find relief as I ascend past the hand-crank sirens below and reach the top. Inside the tower is a Resistance fighter trying to contact someone over the radio, and someone else is standing with Thatcher's chief of security, Isaac.

"What's going on?" I ask.

The pint-sized Resistance fighter extends her hand in greeting. I grab her forearm. "Hensley," she says. She appears to be in her early forties, her long dark hair pulled out of her face and with skin that matches mine.

"Danielle Clark."

She motions to the horizon. "There's a lot of firepower out there. A couple of tanks, an earthmover, minesweeper, a half dozen buggies. They're not messing around."

"Is the howitzer in position?" I ask, a sinking feeling coming over me. With that kind of firepower from the NAF, all the city's defenses can do is slow them down. Maybe give people time to escape. "What about the hedgehogs? Are they all out?" I look past the fence at the crisscrossing metal beams, meant to slow down tanks and other vehicles. There aren't nearly enough scattered around. I should've done more to prepare the town for an attack while I was here.

The look from Isaac tells me he's aware of the same thing. "We're armed and getting in position. The hedgehogs are in place but it's only a matter of time before they find a way around them."

Hensley looks past me at the kid on the radio. "Any word on what the hell is going on?"

"It's dead out there," he says. The pain in the pit of my stomach intensifies. We're all alone here.

"They used an EMP to block radio transmissions," I tell them. "You aren't going to get ahold of anyone. They're taking the war to a new level, killing anyone who fights back and burning towns to the ground." I motion for Isaac to unlock the cabinet to his right and give me access to a detonator for the mines I helped lay underground. "Even if they have a minesweeper, our best bet is to arm the—"

"Holy shit," Isaac says before he does anything. I turn to look. He's staring at the sky.

I get closer to the edge and look up. Dread consumes me as two drones fly for the gate. "Drones," I say. "Ignore the radio, and go do what you can to warn the guards. Arm the mines just in case, and get all your snipers in position."

I slide down the ladder. Once my feet hit dirt, I take off toward the command post. "Aerial assault incoming," I yell, running past one of the crank sirens, and hoping like hell someone can hear me.

I find Ericson and pull him close. "What's going on?" he asks, eyes wide.

"Drones are inbound," I yell, starting to panic.

"What?" He's stunned, and for a second, I think he's going to freeze as he stares at the sky. Instead, he grabs my arm and pulls me away just as a drone flies overhead and releases its first payload just inside the wall.

Pieces of the building fly in all directions, several people along with it. I drop to the ground and cover my head. My ears are ringing, but I can still hear muffled screams and the sound of what's left of the command post crumbling. When the siren falls silent, I lift my head, but a plume of dirt and smoke make visibility almost nonexistent.

Someone hauls me to my feet, and I sway, trying to regain my balance. It's Thatcher. "You have to get out," she yells and moves in close. Bruce lifts Ericson to his feet nearby. "I'm going to take some of my people to create a diversion on their six. It'll buy you some time, but you have to move!"

"We need to get Jess out," I shout back. Another bomb drops near the watchtower, and we all dive for some sort of cover.

"Jess is already through the tunnels."

Every bit of air is ripped violently from my lungs. If Jess is safe, that means... "I have to find Rhiannon and Jack," I yell.

"All you have to do is leave. I'll draw their fire away from the city, give you time to escape once you hit the warehouse," Thatcher says.

I try to protest, but she and Bruce disappear into the crowd. The decision is easy. Bucking orders, I sprint toward Jess's place. I have to find Rhiannon and Jack.

"What are you doing?" Ericson yells as he follows. Hordes of townspeople are making their way to the small back exit, abandoning hope of hiding within the bunkers.

Another bomb drops to my right.

I bring my arm to block any flying debris. People are thrown in the air like dolls. Another siren is silenced along with the screams. A building collapses on top of several people attempting to escape. I don't have time to help. I have to get to Rhiannon and Jack. I will not leave them.

My lungs burn from sprinting through the smoke as another bomb drops somewhere in the distance. Another explosion fills the air with debris and stops me dead in my tracks, but I somehow manage to stay on my feet.

The sound of barking catches my attention. Despite gasping for air, I pick up the pace. I see Jack first, lying on his back and slowly trying to sit up. He appears dazed as he reaches for the back of his head.

"Jack!" I crouch beside him. There's blood on his palm. "What happened?"

"Jess's place is empty. There was an explosion from inside." I check the back of his head. For as much blood as there is, the cut doesn't look too bad. "They hit Jess's. A bomb inside. The blast knocked me off my feet." Ericson runs up behind us. Without a word, he pulls off his bandana and presses it to the back of Jack's head. Jack winces but holds it against the wound.

"Where's Rhiannon?" I ask.

Roscoe's barks break through the noise. He's digging frantically at a large pile of wreckage. My heart stops. Pushing to my feet, I race to Roscoe, Jack stumbling behind me.

No. No.

I pull at the wood and stone piled up within the doorway.

"Rhi," Jack yells, desperate and scared. It does nothing to quell my panic. "Rhiannon!"

We both dig. A sharp edge of something slices across my hand. I'm vaguely aware of it starting to bleed, but I don't feel a thing. Ericson comes to help and tosses a large piece of rubble to the side. I see a dark green sleeve, and the contents of my stomach rise to my throat. Rhiannon's jacket. Quickly, I move another piece, revealing more of her.

"Rhiannon," Jack calls again, this time almost like a sob. Roscoe barks as I lift another stone. Then another. Jack pulls off a final beam, and I fall backward, landing hard on the ground. Rhiannon is motionless, her head turned away, her legs trapped underneath a pile of concrete.

"No!" Jack screams as the remaining alarms finally stop. With a show of strength I've never seen, he throws the concrete from her and falls to the ground. He holds Rhiannon's face in his hands gently, as if she may break. Tenderly, he pushes the hair from her face and turns her head to face him. "Rhi, look at me. Look at me, baby."

I stare, unable to move as he wills her to open her eyes.

Please be breathing. Please be breathing. Please be breathing.

Jack leans in close, pressing his cheek against her face. He closes his eyes and waits. And waits. He gently taps her cheek as if trying to wake her. A sob catches in my throat when he begins to cry. Carefully, he pulls Rhiannon against his chest. "Just open your eyes," he begs. Tears stream down his cheeks as he gently rocks her. "Just open your eyes."

For a moment, everything is silent. Still. The world stops.

Another explosion rings out in the distance, but I can't pinpoint where. It doesn't matter. My teeth clench, and my vision blurs. "No." It comes out wet, shaky. A prayer that I know will go unanswered.

"Please," Jack says, "just open your eyes." He pulls her tighter against him and cries. Another blast echoes behind me. I struggle for breath, feeling helpless and unable to move.

Roscoe paces anxiously, whining. The noise comes whooshing back. It was so loud before, but now everything sounds distant and muffled like it's been submerged. Everything feels slow, and absolutely none of this seems real.

Jack sobs and clutches Rhiannon as if she's the only thing anchoring him to this world.

Please don't stop breathing.

"We have to go," Ericson says. His voice is soft, and it's only then I realize he's crouched beside me, his hand on my shoulder.

I reach to push him away, but instead, I grip the top of his hand like it's my only lifeline, squeezing. He puts his other hand on top of mine and squeezes back, understanding. Then he hauls me to my feet. My legs are mushy and unsteady. Ericson keeps me from falling.

Slowly, I approach Jack. I stare at Rhiannon against him, fresh tears stinging my eyes. "Jack," I manage to choke out. "Jack, we have to go."

He continues to rock back and forth. I wait another moment and then place my hand on his shoulder. His sobs start again, but carefully, he stands, bringing Rhiannon in his arms.

Another building crumbles not too far from us. It topples, leaving nothing but a pile of brick and stone. It kicks up dirt and debris. Jack meets my eyes through the haze; his are glassy with tears that pave a windy path through the dust on his face. The agony in his expression is so overwhelming, it makes it hard to breathe. He gives another nod, ready to move. Ericson points in the direction we need to go, and Jack takes a hesitant step, using his body to shield Rhiannon.

I follow them both, Roscoe trotting beside us, his tail between his legs. When I finally chance a glance forward, I see one of Rhiannon's arms hanging lifeless at Jack's side, and my heart completely shatters.

CHAPTER SIXTEEN: THE EVACUATION

KATE

We reach an old brick building and sprint inside as the sirens continue to wail through the city. Instantly, there's relief for my ears. It's still loud, but at least the sound is muffled. Lucas leads us to a large throw rug, already overturned, next to an open trapdoor. He motions down the stairs, and Elise and Darby descend, carrying as many bags as they can handle.

Before Lucas, Mike, or I can follow, a dozen or so people come rushing through the entrance. "This way. Over here," Mike says. "How many people can this tunnel hold?"

"We're taking on water at an accelerated rate," Lucas says, panic in his voice. I may not be as fine-tuned in translating his quotes, but I know this response means he's concerned about capacity.

The screams from outside grow louder, and several people look over their shoulders as they rush into the building. Something else is happening. I push through the growing crowd and into the streets, Mike close behind. An explosion far away rocks the earth. More screams, drowning out the sirens. As I glance at the sky, dread settles in the pit of my stomach.

My missing drones.

They aren't very large, just big enough to carry the three or four payloads Rodrigues said they could handle. These may not be the rocket blasts my mother wanted, but they're powerful enough to do some serious damage.

A second drone flies overhead, and I duck on instinct before bringing up my rifle and taking a shot. Those with guns fire into the sky, but none of us are used to shooting at this kind of moving target.

Another explosion rattles the town. I can't tell if they're trying to blow the gates or aiming for something else, but it's clear we don't have a lot of time. I'm panicked knowing Dani and Rhiannon are still out there. I start to head out, but Mike grabs my arm.

"We have to get back," he says and pulls me back inside.

When he finally releases me, I see the others near the trapdoor with worried expressions. It's enough to keep me from turning back around. "What's going on?"

Elise leans in close. "Jess, Wyatt, and George are already below."

"Are Rhiannon and Jack with them?" I ask, confused.

Elise shakes her head.

"What? Then how did..." There's another blast in the distance. "But Rhiannon..." I trail off as realization clicks into place. Rhiannon and Jack put themselves in danger for no reason.

"We have to close the tunnel and get to the warehouse," a loud voice over my shoulder yells.

I whip my head around. It's William.

"The bunkers are full." He pushes one of the heavy doors closed to reduce the flow of people.

"We can't close the tunnel," I say. He looks at me, surprised. I'm sure he wasn't expecting someone to argue. "Dani's out there. So are Rhiannon and Jack."

He dismisses my worry with a wave. "There are too many people coming this way. We can't get them all out. We can't risk more leaving the city without getting caught."

"They'll die," Mike says, horrified.

"There's no other choice. We need to lock down the tunnels now, or we'll *all* die." A few Resistance fighters appear and stop beside him, seemingly waiting for orders.

"We're not leaving without Dani," I yell, furious that he would even consider it.

Something flashes in William's eyes, his gaze flicking to my rifle and back to my face. I can't quite place the meaning of his expression, but he softens his tone. "I'll help as many people as I can, but we're already on borrowed time. If the tanks reach the front gate, we will have no other choice but to leave, with or without Dani. She knows that."

"I knew you were ruthless, but this…" I can't even finish my thought. My teeth are clenched, and I'm trying desperately to find a reason not to shoot him here and now.

"Dani can take care of herself," he replies confidently. Almost proudly. "She knows the risks." He turns to the Resistance fighters and starts barking orders.

"But can Rhiannon take care of herself? You'd be leaving her, too," I yell at his back.

He barely gives a glance in my direction. "I'm not arguing about this." William and the Resistance fighters start pushing people back out into the street. It's a gut-wrenching sight; men, women, and children are turned away and told to hide rather than flee.

"Get them out of sight and then help the others at the front and back gates," William instructs his fighters and then closes the last door to the building, securing it with a large wooden beam, locking everyone out. When he turns back to us, I point my rifle at his head. I tighten my jaw and attempt to ignore my own shaking hands.

"I'm not leaving her," I say as steady as I can.

"You're welcome to stay and fight," he says, seeming only mildly surprised to be staring down the barrel of my gun. "I'm going to make sure no one follows us down the tunnels."

Mike and Lucas step up beside me. "We aren't leaving," Mike says, standing tall.

William doesn't falter until he looks at Lucas. He deflates slightly but doesn't seem surprised. "You have until the tanks reach the gates, then I'm collapsing the entrance to the tunnels. It's the only way to make sure we aren't followed." It's a warning I know to take seriously. I can only hope the tanks are a long way out to give Dani and the others more time to get here.

William and his scrawny sidekick head down. It disgusts me that he would leave someone he claims to love like a daughter out here to fend for herself while the city crumbles.

"Now what?" Darby asks.

People continue to bang on the door outside. There's another blast farther away, but I can feel it vibrate beneath my feet. Rushing to the window, I look outside. It's absolute chaos. I raise my gun to break the glass and go find Dani. Before I can, Lucas reaches out and gently lowers my arm.

"We must have faith," he says. I can tell by expression that it pains him to stay here and wait. Another blast rocks the town.

"How long do you think we have?" Darby asks, hovering near Lucas.

I stare in the direction I last saw Dani, a heavy feeling settling over my body. "Not long." Smoke fills the sky from where two bombs have dropped in close proximity. I've lost count of the blasts. Knowing the tanks are next, I make up my mind. I can't just sit here and wait. "I'm going to look for her."

Lucas stops me again. Before I can protest, he points out the window. Squinting, I can barely make out a black and white dog slicing through the crowd, followed by a muscular man pushing people aside. It's William's big guy. Directly behind him, I see Jack and Dani.

"Get the door open and let them through," I yell.

Lucas and Mike push the crowd back, and Mike yells at the guards to let Dani inside. It's devastating not letting anyone else in, that I can so easily choose Dani and the others over everyone. I feel so guilty and unworthy of making such a choice while simultaneously relieved that they made it.

With the help of the guards, Dani and her group manage to get inside the building. My relief at seeing her is short-lived as Jack brushes past. Someone is cradled in his arms, someone much smaller and wearing a green jacket.

Rhiannon.

My stomach twists.

Dani meets my gaze, and I'm almost knocked over by the despair in her eyes. She shakes her head.

My knees loosen, and for a moment, I'm not sure my legs can hold me upright. I watch in absolute horror as the others notice Rhiannon's limp body. Lucas reaches for Darby, who stands frozen in place, her hand over her mouth and her eyes wide in shock. Elise screams, and Mike pulls her into his arms and squeezes his eyes tight, refusing to look. My breath comes in short bursts, and my throat constricts. This can't be happening.

None of us seem able to move. I risk a glance at Jack. His eyes are red, but his expression is stoic as he holds Rhiannon tightly. Roscoe barks anxiously, bringing my attention back to the attack.

It's only then that I notice the sirens have stopped. We shouldn't be standing around like this. It isn't safe. I need to be a voice of reason and get us below ground.

I gently squeeze Dani's forearm. "Jess is in the tunnels," I tell her when she looks at me. "William is going to blow the entrance any minute. We need to go."

She places a hand over mine, and my heart breaks at the unshed tears in her eyes. She blinks once, and her expression shifts from sadness to business as she visibly attempts to compartmentalize. I squeeze her hand, hoping she knows I'm with her.

"We need to move," she tells everyone firmly. "Now."

There's no time for mourning. The silence is filled with a low, distant rumble and people still pounding on the door. There's a different kind of blast. It's distant but rattles the windows. It sounds like a howitzer. That means the tanks have arrived.

Dani motions for us go through the trapdoor first. Jack descends, followed closely by Roscoe, Darby, Elise, Lucas, Mike, and William's guy. I look at Dani, wanting to tell her something, anything, to convey how sorry I am, but when I try, the words get caught in my throat.

She puts a hand on my shoulder and gently pushes me. I go without any other encouragement, hearing her close the doors and latch them from the inside just as the people from the streets break the windows above. We descend the darkened staircase slowly, only one or two lanterns lighting the way. Dani takes one off a hook and hands it to me. When we pass another, she takes that too, leaving total darkness behind us.

"Jess is there with George and Wyatt," Elise says between soft sobs and points in their direction.

Dani hurries in that direction, Lucas and I right behind her. I see an old man and two teenagers. The girl's red hair drapes delicately over one shoulder, and she clutches the arm of a tall boy with shaggy dark hair who seems to be watching everything with panic.

"Get out of here," Dani says without greeting. "We've gotta blow the entrance."

"What's going on?" the old man asks. "What happened?"

"Drones," is all Dani offers. "Jess, are you okay?"

"The radios went dead," Jess says as Dani gently takes her other arm. "Wyatt raced to Thatcher before daybreak when I couldn't get a signal. She was already on her way to the gates. The NAF were lined up along the horizon. She told us to go, that she was going to sound the alarm. When Wyatt came to get me, I tried to come tell you, but—"

"Hey, it's okay," Dani tells her gently. "You did the right thing." She carefully guides Jess to where I'm standing with Lucas.

"What happened with the radios? Was it the same as Deadwood?" Wyatt asks, his eyes wide.

"An EMP," Dani says with a nod.

"What happens now?" the old man, George, asks.

"The tanks are blasting the walls. We need to set the charge and go," William yells from the darkness.

Dani gently takes my arm. "Get them to the end of the tunnel. I'll be right behind you." I want to protest. I want to tell her like hell I'm leaving her again, but the look in her eyes is pleading. Desperate. She already lost one person today. I refuse to let her lose anyone else.

I just nod.

"Jess, Kate and Lucas are going to guide you through the tunnels, okay?" Dani asks. "To the warehouse on the other side. I'll be right behind you."

"Kate?" Jess asks, turning her head in different directions, looking for me. "She's here?"

I take her arm. Only then does Dani release her. "I'm here," I say. This isn't how I envisioned meeting Jess, the girl who I was so curious about only weeks ago. But there will be time for talking later. *If* we make it out in one piece.

"The Songbird." She smiles. There's another blast from far away. Was that from the Resistance or the tanks? Either way, we've run out of time.

"Let's go." With one final look at Dani, I follow Lucas through the dimly lit tunnel, careful of each step as I lead Jess, holding the lantern in front of me. Wyatt stays on her other side, his face devoid of emotion, like he's trying to stay strong. George walks slowly behind us.

"Something else has happened," Jess says after several steps of silence. "Something doesn't feel right. What's going on?"

I hesitate, not sure how I should answer. "Rhiannon," I say, my voice cracking. I clear my throat and try again. "Rhiannon is dead."

"What?" Jess stumbles, and George reaches out from behind to steady her. Wyatt and I tighten our hold.

"No, not Rhiannon," George says. "It can't be." I can hear the pain in his voice.

"How?" Jess asks, a hint of panic in her tone.

"She…" I swallow the jagged shaped lump in my throat. "I'm not sure how," I confess, but I leave out the part where she was looking for Jess when it happened.

"Dani," Jess says almost desperately. "We need to—"

"She's about to blow the entrance," I interrupt and keep moving. "We don't have time to grieve right now." My words seem harsh no matter how soft I try to make them. Jess nods and places her hand on my arm, and we start moving again.

"It'll be daylight soon," Lucas says, and I can only assume that means we're almost at the end.

The tunnel leads to a large, dark room. A few people in the waiting crowd have lanterns but not enough to get a good look at anything besides crates lining the walls. We're all crammed shoulder to shoulder at this seemingly dead end.

A loud explosion rattles the ground. "They've blown the entrance," George says when I steady him.

"Where are the others?" I hold up my lantern.

"There," Wyatt says, pointing into the sea of people.

I follow him to the opposite wall near a closed door. Jack still has Rhiannon, and the others surround him almost protectively. Jack doesn't even look in my direction. Elise and Darby nod despite looking shell-shocked. Elise holds Jack's arm and asks, "Where's Dani?"

"I'm here," she says, appearing behind me and breathing hard. Her hand finds the small of my back. She slings two duffel bags over her shoulder. "Let's move."

"What about all these people?" Elise asks.

"William is going to stay with them until nightfall and try to sneak them out," Dani explains. "But we have to go now while Thatcher creates a diversion."

Roscoe barks. There's another explosion, distant and muffled. Dani moves past me to a pin pad and uses a code to open a well-disguised door in the brick. She motions our group to hurry.

Everyone starts through. Darby hesitates, but Lucas urgers her forward. She adjusts her bags over her shoulders, and disappears into the dark tunnel. I don't blame her for hesitating. All these people are left trying to escape while we get to go? Why do we get to decide who is deserving of a quick escape?

William approaches, flanked by his two men. "Do you have supplies?" he asks Dani.

I stop and wait just inside the door for Lucas and Dani. "We'll be fine," she tells him.

He puts a hand on her shoulder. "Head to the ranch. I'll be in touch."

"William…all these people."

"I have a plan." He smiles, seeming to understand her, and extends his arm. "Be safe out there." She grabs his forearm and nods before Lucas hugs him tightly. William grunts and pats Lucas's back twice. "Okay, Maelstrom. Go."

Lucas salutes before stepping past me. William's gaze meets mine, and we stare at each other for just a split second until Dani grabs my hand and tugs me after Lucas. William closes the door behind us, and the sound kicks my nerves into overdrive.

This tunnel is narrow and claustrophobic and not even tall enough to fully stand. It feels like an afterthought, an add-on, much newer than the one we just left. "What if I surrender?" I ask, unable to stop thoughts of my mother seeping into my mind. Would she have dropped bombs over the city if she knew I was within its walls?

"She's not doing this because of you," Dani answers quickly.

My heart sinks, knowing she's right. My mother wanted Rapid City no matter the cost. I doubt turning myself over would have stopped the assault, but I can't help feeling guilty.

We walk upward in silence, the incline so steep that it burns my legs with each step. I steady myself through another blast while pieces of rock and dirt crumble off the walls. I glance at Dani, who takes a beat to collect herself.

"Almost there," she assures me.

Almost feels like an eternity.

Finally, we make it to the end and a waiting ladder. Lucas scoops up Roscoe, tucking him under one arm. Carefully, he climbs the ladder to a decent-size hole above. Everyone else has already made it into what I can only assume is the warehouse they keep mentioning. Dani steadies me as

I take my turn. George reaches down and takes my bags, then helps me through the opening. Wiping the sweat from my forehead, I wonder how far away we are from the city and if the NAF will close in on us before we can escape.

A few piles of supplies and gas canisters sit off to the side, along with a few large crates covered with drop cloths. Taking up the most space are seven vehicles, all packed tightly together. I nearly fall over when I recognize them.

"Darby, Lucas, grab those rations from the corner and load them in the cars," Dani says, heading straight for the vehicles.

My gaze lingers on the officer's buggy parked in the center. "When did you get those?" I ask, though I already know the answer.

"They were the ones your mother used to lure me out," Dani says easily and tosses the duffels into the back of the closest one.

A sense of dread consumes me, but I ask anyway, "Did you remove the trackers?"

Dani whips around. "What?"

"The trackers," I say again. The rest of the group stops moving to look at me, too, the entire building falling silent. "It's a new policy. Location trackers on all officer's vehicles."

Dani pales, and I have my answer. Another explosion rattles the garage. I should've told her. I should have made sure she knew.

"Can you get them off?" Elise asks, sounding panicked.

I move toward the officer's buggy, but Dani grabs my arm. "That small black, rectangular box was a tracker?" she asks with irritation. "It's in a bag in my Jeep back in Rapid City." She frantically searches for Darby. "Did you take the bag from my Jeep?"

With wide eyes Darby shakes her head. "I didn't get a chance to."

"Then it's still there. Right in the goddamn middle of town." Dani takes a step back and braces herself on the closest car. "I didn't know what it was. I just...took it."

My eyes close. My mother wanted Dani to intercept that convoy. She wanted Dani to take the buggies with the trackers.

"We don't have time for this," Jack says.

I put a hand on Dani's forearm. "I'll check the rest of the cars just in case."

Jack blocks my path. "Someone else can check. You knew about these things and didn't tell anyone. It's your *fault*."

I stumble backward at the sheer volume of his voice. The accusation hits hard.

Dani steps between us. "Back off, Jack. I did this. Not Kate."

"She knew," he says through clenched teeth, his eyes wet with tears. "She knew about the trackers, and she knew about the attack. She led them right to us. Rhiannon is dead because of *her*."

His words make me flinch, but I remain silent; now is not the time to argue. He's right. I should've told Dani about the trackers, and I should've pushed harder to get everyone out sooner. I knew what could've happened.

Dani tenses. Her jaw clenches along with her fists. She takes several deep breaths. "Jack," she finally says. "Get in the truck."

"Where are we even going?" he practically spits, still not taking his eyes off me.

"White River. We're taking Rhiannon home."

His face contorts, the corners of his lips pointing down, and his brow furrowing. His breath seems to catch. I want to tell him I'm sorry. That I never wanted any of this to happen, and that I'd gladly shoulder the blame if it brings him some relief.

"We use a couple of the buggies to throw them off if we're spotted. Check for more trackers," Dani tells me softly. "I'm going to refuel the cars."

Elise gently takes Jack's arm. "Come on. Let's get her ready." He seems confused until Elise reaches for a drop cloth. His sobs start up again, and I have to look away.

Wyatt and Mike open the garage door on the other side, letting the light flood in. I search for more trackers while everyone else loads their gear. No one says a word.

Rhiannon's body is wrapped tightly, and Jack secures a tarp over the bed of the pickup. Roscoe tries to hop in the bed, but Jack stops him, scooping him up and holding him close despite his desperate whines to be near his mom. It's heart-wrenching.

Jack gets in the back seat of the pickup while Mike takes the wheel, and Elise slides in the passenger side. Lucas drives one of the buggies with Darby in the front and George in the back. Wyatt helps Jess into the back of another, and I take the passenger's seat.

Once Dani is settled in the driver's seat, she turns. "Jess, you okay?"

"Yes," she says, but her voice betrays her; she sounds absolutely terrified. Wyatt tries to work the seat belt with shaking hands.

"What about you, Wyatt?" I ask.

He does his best to smile, and Jess puts a hand on his leg. "My mom is still out there," he confesses, his voice cracking.

I exchange a look with Dani. "We can't wait," she says softly. She shifts the car into drive. The tires screech all the way out of the garage and into the wasteland, away from the crumbling city behind us and back toward White River.

The lightness I felt last night has completely dissipated. I wonder why grief has to feel so heavy and if I'll ever feel the weightlessness of happiness again.

CHAPTER SEVENTEEN: THE GOOD-BYE

KATE

The ride to White River is brutal. Our buggy is quiet aside from a few random sniffles from Jess and soft murmurings of reassurance from Wyatt. I imagine all three vehicles have the same ominous feeling.

I'm not sure how Thatcher was able to distract the NAF, but the getaway was easier than I expected. I'm still unclear on William's plan to help the others escape. Dani trusts that he knows what he's doing, so I guess that has to be enough.

Dani hasn't made a sound since we left. She grips the steering wheel so tightly that her knuckles are white. Her brow is furrowed, her lips are in a thin line, and her shoulders are tense as she hunches over the steering wheel, staring at the road through her sunglasses.

I press my head against the cool window. This is all my fault. I'm not sure what happens next or how to proceed. With Rhiannon gone, I worry about Dani handling her grief. When she lost her father, she spiraled out of control and tried to burn the entire world to the ground. I want to reassure her, but I'm not sure how. There are absolutely no words that would make any of this better.

I stare at the side mirror, waiting for a glimpse of the NAF, but all I can see are the pickup and the other buggy. We pass a raider camp, and Dani doesn't even spare a glance in their direction, just presses the accelerator a little more as we easily press by.

Finally, Dani brings us to a halt on top of a ledge and gets out of the car without speaking, closing the door behind her. She walks to the edge and looks out over it as the other two vehicles pull up next to us.

"Are we here?" Jess asks, the first words spoken in hours.

"I'm not sure." I open my door and get out to follow Dani. When I'm by her side and look out, I gasp.

It's White River. Or what used to be White River. This ledge is the perfect vantage point to see the remains of the town. I search the charred buildings for Rhiannon's tavern and find it easily. The front half is blackened and caved in, along with half the roof. The back and most of one of the sides are still somehow upright. A small piece of me is glad she isn't seeing this, but the thought vanishes quickly, and all that follows is immense sadness.

Instinctively, I take Dani's hand.

Slowly, everyone else joins us, looking at their home for the first time since the attack. Lucas puts a hand on Dani's shoulder. Elise speaks first. "I barely recognize it."

Dani puts her other hand over Lucas's. "I think she'd like this spot. Watching over the town," she whispers.

"What's left of it," Jack says, his tone bitter and his hands clenched at his sides.

Dani looks at him, but he avoids her gaze. "We should build a pyre."

"We can use some of the boards in town," Mike suggests, motioning to the dilapidated city. "Maybe try to salvage some from her tavern?"

Dani nods and stares at the ruins. "I think she'd like that."

"I'll go with you," Darby volunteers quietly.

"Jack?" Mike asks. Everyone glances apprehensively in his direction.

He continues to stare at the town, his brows pulled down in a deep scowl. Finally, he sucks in a long breath. "I'm not leaving her."

No one argues.

Dani, Lucas, and Mike take the pickup down the long and winding path, eventually turning into the town.

Wyatt sits with Jess and holds her tightly, whispering words I can't hear.

Elise, George, and I try to make ourselves useful by finding any kind of leaves or branches that will catch fire. The sun shines brightly, warming my face despite the cool breeze that whips through my hair.

Birds chirp happily overhead, a stark contrast to the sorrow that looms heavily here on the ground.

I find a patch of trees and collect as many pinecones as I can, stacking and balancing them in my arms. I'm not sure we even need kindling, not with all the gas Dani brought, but it keeps me busy. If I focus on finding dry grass and pine needles, maybe I can keep from breaking down.

I'm so focused on not dropping the kindling that I don't see the root protruding from the earth until I'm tumbling toward the ground, everything I've collected spilling from my arms. I manage to catch myself, breaking my fall. Slowly, I lower myself to the ground and wipe my hands on my pants, angry and embarrassed. Unable to hold it in any longer, I draw up my knees wrap myself around them, hiding my face against my arms as the tears and the sobs break free.

Everything spills out all at once. I cry for Rhiannon. Despite not knowing her very long, her death feels devastating. I cry for Wyatt having to leave his mother, not knowing if he'll ever see her again. For the people left behind at Rapid City, scared and helpless. And for those killed in Deadwood and Hot Springs who didn't deserve to die. I cry for the life I left behind and for hurting Ryan.

I let it all out until there's nothing left. Lifting my head, I wipe at my eyes and nose, drying my face as best I can with my cold hands and the sleeves of my jacket. Slowly, I begin collecting everything I spilled, once again piling it neatly it my arms.

Carefully, I make my way back to the ledge just as Dani and the others return. She looks at the collection in my arms, and then at me. If she notices my red, puffy eyes, she doesn't mention it.

Nobody says anything as we assemble the small pyre. Jack stays with Rhiannon. Once it's finished, we stand shoulder to shoulder in a half circle and wait. Dani grabs the gas canister from the car, and Roscoe paces back and forth between Jack and the rest of us.

"Dani is soaking the wood with an accelerant," I hear Wyatt softly saying to Jess, and having commentary makes the entire moment that much harder to bear.

I try to meet Dani's eyes as she walks to her spot beside me, but she refuses to look at anyone, even Lucas.

The smell of gas floats through the air, and it makes my stomach churn.

Slowly, Jack returns holding Rhiannon's body. She's been stripped of the drop cloth, her green jacket, and her shoes. Her hair falls around the side of her face as he cradles her securely against his chest.

"Jack is going to present the body," Wyatt whispers.

I watch curiously as Jack readjusts Rhiannon in his arms. Presenting a body is not something I've ever witnessed, but I'm familiar with the tradition. I try to focus on the ceremony and not the way my throat is tightening, and my eyes sting with fresh tears.

Elise leans forward and gently pushes the hair from Rhiannon's face to lightly kiss her forehead. She whispers softly against her skin and then pulls back to wipe at her eyes.

Jack moves down the line. Mike doesn't move. Instead, he closes his eyes tightly and turns away, unable to look at her. George strokes her face. Wyatt bows his head and then guides Jess's hand so she can gently squeeze Rhiannon's fingers.

Jack hesitates when he reaches me, but surprisingly, he stops. Rhiannon looks peaceful, as though she's sleeping. The color and life have completely drained from her face, and she's a ghost of the spirited girl I was just beginning to know. Tears fall down my cheeks when I gently touch her arm. She was kind to me. She was accepting. She loved her people and made me feel like I was one of them. I know for an absolute certainty that the world is a darker place without her in it.

"I'm sorry," I whisper, hoping that if she's out there somewhere, she can hear me. "I'll take care of her." It's a promise I don't make lightly but have every intention of keeping.

Jack stares at me, his jaw clenched. His gaze is hard, but he says nothing and waits until I remove my hand before moving on. Slowly, he steps to Dani. She stares blankly at Rhiannon, though I can see her eyes glistening. Jack waits until she offers a small nod and then moves on.

Lucas weeps quietly and shifts his weight from foot to foot. His hands clench into fists at his sides. His long hair whips in front of his face, but he does nothing to push it out of the way. He takes a deep breath and leans forward, pressing his forehead to Rhiannon's for a long moment, whispers something I can't hear, and then pulls away.

Next to Lucas, Darby stands perfectly still, her lips trembling. She reaches out, then thinks better of it, and her arm drops back to her side.

Once he's passed down the line, Jack gently places Rhiannon on the pyre and turns to the group. Only Dani approaches the body. She pulls out a small knife, cuts a lock of Rhiannon's hair, and holds it in her fist. Leaning down, she presses her forehead to Rhiannon's just as Lucas did. She grabs Rhiannon's shirt tightly and quietly sobs. Jack closes his eyes and turns away but doesn't move, standing stalwart beside the pyre.

I avert my eyes, hating to see Dani hurting so much and feeling as though I'm invading a very personal and intimate moment. Eventually, Dani steps back and puts her hand on Rhiannon's chest. "*Tókša.*"

The word is said quietly, but the sound is carried on the wind. I'm not sure what it means, but the emotion behind it feels powerful and beautiful. She finally looks at Jack and takes a few steps back, wiping at her eyes.

Jack pulls Rhiannon close, pressing her head to his chest, and says something into her hair. He rocks her for a long time and kisses her face. Gently, he lies her back down, carefully removes her necklace, and slips it over his head.

Roscoe barks, and the sound makes me jump. He's still pacing anxiously. Lucas kneels beside him and holds Roscoe tight, petting and attempting to soothe him. I squeeze my eyes shut and try to push down more tears. I take several deep breaths, and when I open them again, Rhiannon has been rewrapped, and the pyre is lit.

"This is where the journey comes to an end. Where the heroes say good-bye to one of their own," Lucas says, his voice trembling.

Someone begins to hum an unfamiliar melody. I can't pinpoint where it starts, but it doesn't take long before the rest of the group joins in.

As the flames reach a peak and engulf Rhiannon, the humming finally fades. I take Dani's hand and squeeze, not knowing how else to comfort her except to let her know I'm here.

No one says anything. It's not a tradition I'm accustomed to, but I don't think a grand speech would be any better than the respectful silence that fills the air. We stay until the flames start to fade, and the morning gives way to the afternoon. Nobody moves very far, all of us scattered around the pyre, sitting and not saying much. Elise brings water from one of the vehicles and offers some rations to eat, but nobody seems interested.

Jack sits as close to the pyre as the heat will allow, his back to the rest of us, and looks at the town below. No one approaches him.

Dani stays beside me with our fingers laced together. Lucas eventually drapes a blanket over our shoulders. We remain like that, sitting close, Dani's head on my shoulder, until a breeze whips through and gently begins to pull Rhiannon's ashes over the ledge and down to the broken town below.

Darby clears her throat. "I hate to be the first to ask, but now what?"

Dani squeezes my hand and lifts her head. She looks at me, and I offer a small, encouraging smile.

We'll figure it out. Together.

About the Authors

Kristin Keppler was born and raised in the DC metro area. A lifelong sci-fi and film nerd with a degree in production technology, she owns a small media production company that endeavors to help other small businesses succeed. Kristin spends the majority of her free time helping her husband wrangle their two young sons and their dogs. Any additional free time is devoted to writing, gaming, and cheering on the Virginia Tech Hokies.

Allisa Bahney grew up in a small town that's buried in the cornfields of Iowa. She works in education and has a master of science degree in effective teaching with minors in creative writing and film studies. Allisa spends her free time coaching middle school volleyball, binge-watching TV shows, writing, playing with her children, and entertaining her wife. She loves to travel and misses her dog literally every minute she's not with her.

Books Available from Bold Strokes Books

A Champion for Tinker Creek by D.C. Robeline. Lyle James has rescued his dad's auto repair business, but when city hall condemns his neighborhood, Lyle learns only trusting will save his life and help him find love. (978-1-63679-213-2)

Closed-Door Policy by Erin Zak. Going back to college is never easy, but Caroline Stevens is prepared to work hard and change her life for the better. What she's not prepared for is Dr. Atlanta Morris, her gorgeous new professor. (978-1-63679-181-4)

Homeworld by Gun Brooke. Headed by Captain Holly Crowe, the spaceship Velocity's crew journeys toward their alien ancestors' homeworld, and what they find is completely unexpected—and they're not safe. (978-1-63679-177-7)

Outland by Kristin Keppler & Allisa Bahney. Danielle Clark and Katelyn Turner can't seem to stay away from one another even as the war for the wastelands tests their loyalty to each other and to their people. (978-1-63679-154-8)

Secret Sanctuary by Nance Sparks. US Deputy Marshal Alex Trenton specializes in protecting those awaiting trial, but when danger threatens the woman she's falling for, Alex is in for the fight of her life. (978-1-63679-148-7)

Stranded Hearts by Kris Bryant, Amanda Radley, Emily Smith. In these novellas from award-winning authors, fate intervenes on behalf of love when characters are unexpectedly stuck together. With too much time and an irresistible attraction, anything could happen. (978-1-63679-182-1)

The Last Lavender Sister by Melissa Brayden. Aster Lavender sells her gourmet doughnuts and keeps a low profile; she never plans on the town's temporary veterinarian swooping in and making her feel like anything but a wallflower. (978-1-63679-130-2)

The Probability of Love by Dena Blake. As Blair and Rachel keep ending up in the same place despite the odds, can a one-night stand turn into forever? Or will the bet Blair never intended to make ruin their happily ever after? (978-1-63679-188-3)

Worth a Fortune by Sam Ledel. After placing a want ad for a personal secretary, a New York heiress is surprised when the woman who got away is the one interested in the position. (978-1-63679-175-3)

A Fox in Shadow by Jane Fletcher. Cassie's mission is to add new territory to the Kavillian empire—murder, betrayal, war, and the clash of cultures ensue. (978-1-63679-142-5)

Embracing the Moon by Jeannie Levig. Just as Gwen and Taylor are exploring the new love they've found, the present and past collide, threatening the future they long to share. (978-1-63555-462-5)

Forever Comes in Threes by D. Jackson Leigh. Efficiency expert Perry Chandler's ordered life is upended when she inherits three busy terriers, and the woman she's referred to for help turns out to be her bitter podcast rival, the very sexy Dr. Ming Lee. (978-1-63679-169-2)

Heckin' Lewd: Trans and Nonbinary Erotica by Mx. Nillin Lore. If you want smutty, fearless, gender-diverse erotica written by affirming own-voices folks who get it, then this is the book you've been looking for! (978-1-63679-240-8)

Missed Conception by Joy Argento. Maggie Walsh wants a relationship with Cassidy, the daughter she's only just discovered she has due to an in vitro mix-up. Heat kindles between Maggie and Cassidy's mother in a way neither expects. (978-1-63679-146-3)

Private Equity by Elle Spencer. Cassidy Bennett spends an unexpected evening at a lesbian nightclub with her notoriously reserved and demanding boss, Julia. After seeing a different side of Julia, Cassidy can't seem to shake her desire to know more. (978-1-63679-180-7)

Racing the Dawn by Sandra Barrett. After narrowly escaping a house fire, vampire Jade Murphy is unexpectedly intrigued by gorgeous firefighter Beth Jenssen, and her undead existence might just be perking up a bit. (978-1-63679-271-2)

Reclaiming Love by Amanda Radley. Sarah's tiny white lie means somehow convincing Pippa to pretend to be her girlfriend. Only the more time they spend faking it, the more real it feels. (978-1-63679-144-9)

Sol Cycle by Kimberly Cooper Griffin. An encounter in a park brings Ang and Krista together, but when Ang's attempts to help Krista go spectacularly wrong, their passion for each other might not be enough. (978-1-63679-137-1)

Trial and Error by Carsen Taite. Attorney Franco Rossi and Judge Nina Aguilar's reunion is fraught with courtroom conflict, undeniable chemistry, and danger. (978-1-63555-863-0)

A Long Way to Fall by Elle Spencer. A ski lodge, two strong-willed women, and a family feud that brings them together, but will it also tear them apart? (978-1-63679-005-3)

Barnabas Bopwright Saves the City by J. Marshall Freeman. When he uncovers a terror plot to destroy the city he loves, 15-year-old Barnabas Bopwright realizes it's up to him to save his home and bring deadly secrets into the light before it's too late. (978-1-63679-152-4)

Forever by Kris Bryant. When Savannah Edwards is invited to be the next bachelorette on the dating show When Sparks Fly, she'll show the world that finding true love on television can happen. (978-1-63679-029-9)

Ice on Wheels by Aurora Rey. All's fair in love and roller derby. That's Riley Fauchet's motto, until a new job lands her at the same company—and on the same team—as her rival Brooke Landry, the frosty jammer for the Big Easy Bruisers. (978-1-63679-179-1)

Inherit the Lightning by Bud Gundy. Darcy O'Brien and his sisters learn they are about to inherit an immense fortune, but a family mystery about to unravel after seventy years threatens to destroy everything. (978-1-63679-199-9)

Perfect Rivalry by Radclyffe. Two women set out to win the same career-making goal, but it's love that may turn out to be the final prize. (978-1-63679-216-3)

Something to Talk About by Ronica Black. Can quiet ranch owner Corey Durand give up her peaceful life and allow her feisty new neighbor into her heart? Or will past loss, present suitors, and town gossip ruin a long-awaited chance at love? (978-1-63679-114-2)

With a Minor in Murder by Karis Walsh. In the world of academia, police officer Clare Sawyer and professor Libby Hart team up to solve a murder. (978-1-63679-186-9)

Writer's Block by Ali Vali. Wyatt and Hayley might be made for each other if only they can get through nosy neighbors, the historic society, at-odds future plans, and all the secrets hidden in Wyatt's walls. (978-1-63679-021-3)

Cold Blood by Genevieve McCluer. Maybe together, Kalila and Dorenia have a chance of taking down the vampires who have eluded them all these years. And maybe, in each other, they can find a love worth living for. (978-1-63679-195-1)

Greener Pastures by Aurora Rey. When city girl and CPA Audrey Adams finds herself tending her aunt's farm, will Rowan Marshall—the charming cider maker next door—turn out to be her saving grace or the bane of her existence? (978-1-63679-116-6)

Grounded by Amanda Radley. For a second chance, Olivia and Emily will need to accept their mistakes, learn to communicate properly, and with a little help from five-year-old Henry, fall madly in love all over again. Sequel to Flight SQA016. (978-1-63679-241-5)

Journey's End by Amanda Radley. In this heartwarming conclusion to the Flight series, Olivia and Emily must finally decide what they want, what they need, and how to follow the dreams of their hearts. (978-1-63679-233-0)

Pursued: Lillian's Story by Felice Picano. Fleeing a disastrous marriage to the Lord Exchequer of England, Lillian of Ravenglass reveals an incident-filled, often bizarre, tale of great wealth and power, perfidy, and betrayal. (978-1-63679-197-5)

Secret Agent by Michelle Larkin. CIA agent Peyton North embarks on a global chase to apprehend rogue agent Zoey Blackwood, but her commitment to the mission is tested as the sparks between them ignite and their sizzling attraction approaches a point of no return. (978-1-63555-753-4)

Something Between Us by Krystina Rivers. A decade after her heart was broken under Don't Ask, Don't Tell, Kirby runs into her first love and has to decide if what's still between them is enough to heal her broken heart. (978-1-63679-135-7)

Sugar Girl by Emma L McGeown. Having traded in traditional romance for the perks of Sugar Dating, Ciara Reilly not only enjoys the no-strings-attached arrangement, she's also a hit with her clients. That is until she meets the beautiful entrepreneur Charlie Keller who makes her want to go sugar-free. (978-1-63679-156-2)

The Business of Pleasure by Ronica Black. Editor in chief Valerie Raffield is quickly becoming smitten by Lennox, the graphic artist she's hired to work remotely. But when Lennox doesn't show for their first face-to-face meeting, Valerie's heart and her business may be in jeopardy. (978-1-63679-134-0)

The Hummingbird Sanctuary by Erin Zak. The Hummingbird Sanctuary, Colorado's hottest resort destination: Come for the mountains, stay for the charm, and enjoy the drama as Olive, Eleanor, and Harriet figure out the meaning of true friendship. (978-1-63679-163-0)

The Witch Queen's Mate by Jennifer Karter. Barra and Silvi must overcome their ingrained hatred and prejudice to use Barra's magic and save both their peoples, not just from slavery, but destruction. (978-1-63679-202-6)

With a Twist by Georgia Beers. Starting over isn't easy for Amelia Martini. When the irritatingly cheerful Kirby Dupress comes into her life will Amelia be brave enough to go after the love she really wants? (978-1-63555-987-3)

Business of the Heart by Claire Forsythe. When a hopeless romantic meets a tough-as-nails cynic, they'll need to overcome the wounds of the past to discover that their hearts are the most important business of all. (978-1-63679-167-8)

Dying for You by Jenny Frame. Can Victorija Dred keep an age-old vow and fight the need to take blood from Daisy Macdougall? (978-1-63679-073-2)

Exclusive by Melissa Brayden. Skylar Ruiz lands the TV reporting job of a lifetime, but is she willing to sacrifice it all for the love of her longtime crush, anchorwoman Carolyn McNamara? (978-1-63679-112-8)

Her Duchess to Desire by Jane Walsh. An up-and-coming interior designer seeks to create a happily ever after with an intriguing duchess, proving that love never goes out of fashion. (978-1-63679-065-7)

Murder on Monte Vista by David S. Pederson. Private Detective Mason Adler's angst at turning fifty is forgotten when his "birthday present," the handsome, young Henry Bowtrickle, turns up dead, and it's up to Mason to figure out who did it, and why. (978-1-63679-124-1)

Take Her Down by Lauren Emily Whalen. Stakes are cutthroat, scheming is creative, and loyalty is ever-changing in this queer, female-driven YA retelling of Shakespeare's Julius Caesar. (978-1-63679-089-3)

The Game by Jan Gayle. Ryan Gibbs is a talented golfer, but her guilt means she may never leave her small town, even if Katherine Reese tempts her with competition and passion. (978-1-63679-126-5)

Whereabouts Unknown by Meredith Doench. While homicide detective Theodora Madsen recovers from a potentially career-ending injury, she scrambles to solve the cases of two missing sixteen-year-old girls from Ohio. (978-1-63555-647-6)